MW01616335

Flee

Haven Series: Book Two
Tracy Myhre

NBD
PRESS

First Edition

Published 2026

Tracy Myhre, author.
NBD Press
Suite 146
3080 - 11666 Steveston Hwy
Richmond, British Columbia
V7A 5J3
Canada

Title: Flee

ISBN: 978-1-7380623-2-4 (Paperback)
ISBN: 978-1-7380623-3-1 (Ebook)

Editing by The Open Book Editor
Cover Design by Dissect Designs
Book Formatting by The Open Book Editor
Book Description by Sheppard Edits

To my family, found or otherwise, for their love and support.
To the one person I wish were here to see this accomplishment: Granny.

CONTENTS

NOTE TO READER

This story takes place in Spokane, Washington and across Idaho. For the sake of the story, I have altered some details of the landscape and taken a few liberties with an actual town. Thank you in advance for understanding an author's creative license.

The Haven series covers a number of topics and themes that some readers may find disturbing. For a full list of the trigger warnings, please see the back of the book or the following page: https://tracymyhre.com/haven-series-trigger-warnings/

Maps

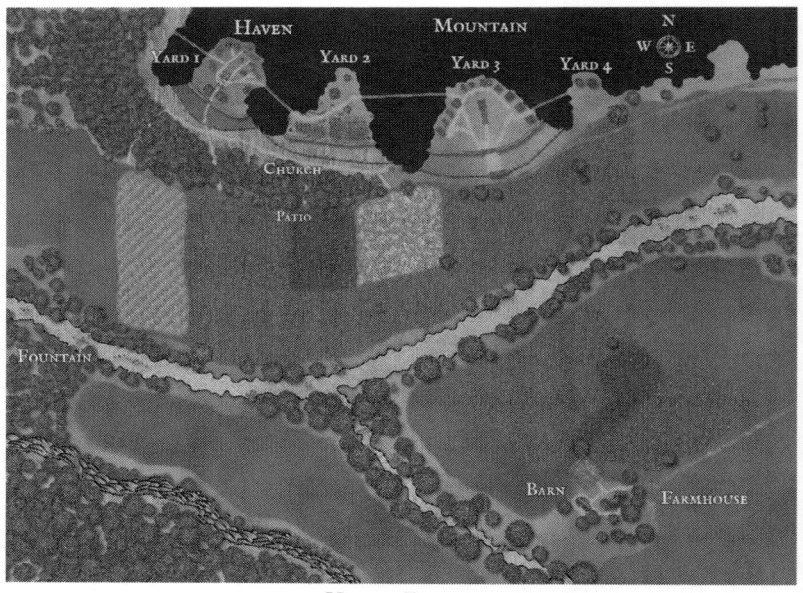

Haven: Exterior

Haven: Yard One

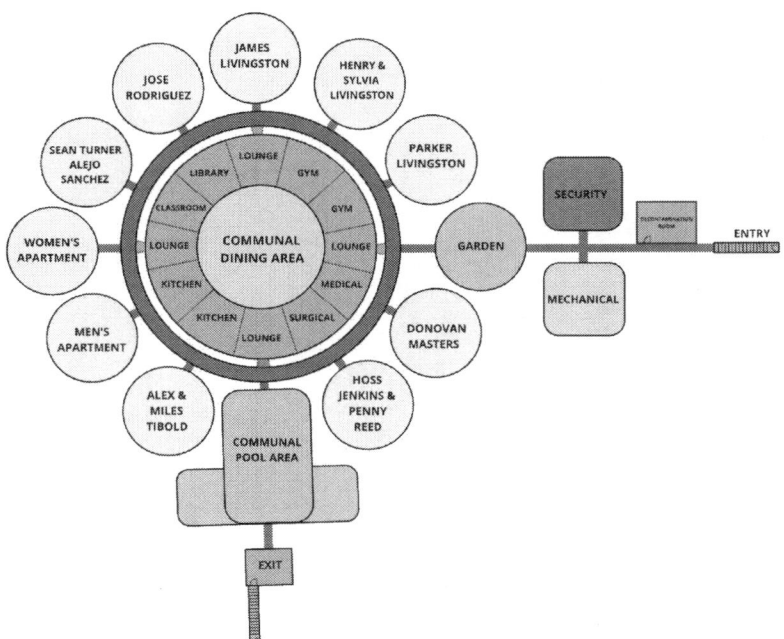

Haven: Interior

FLEE

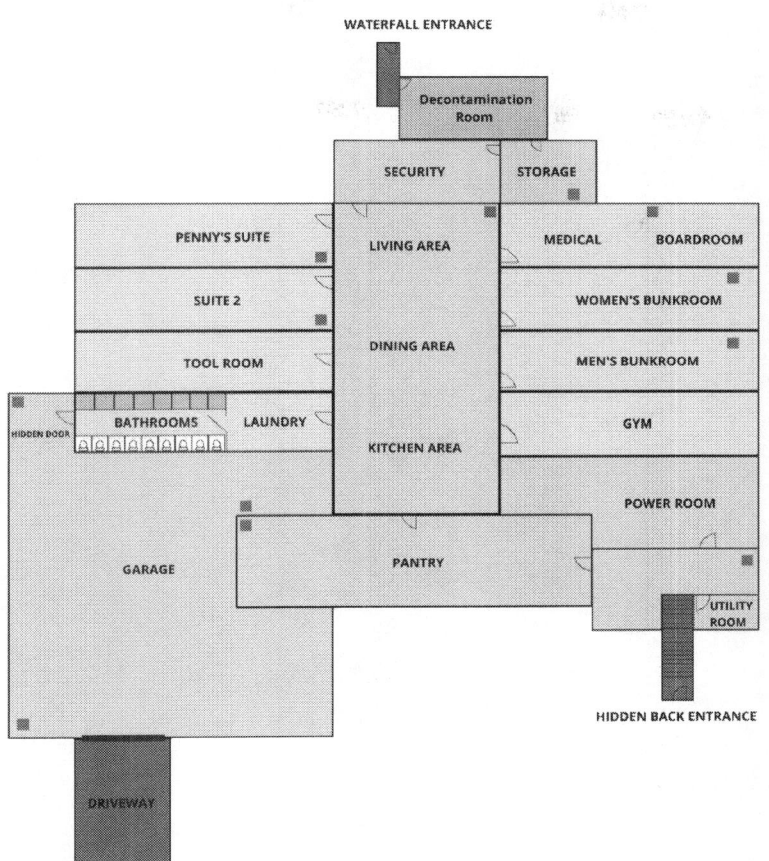

Reed: Interior

FAMILY TREES

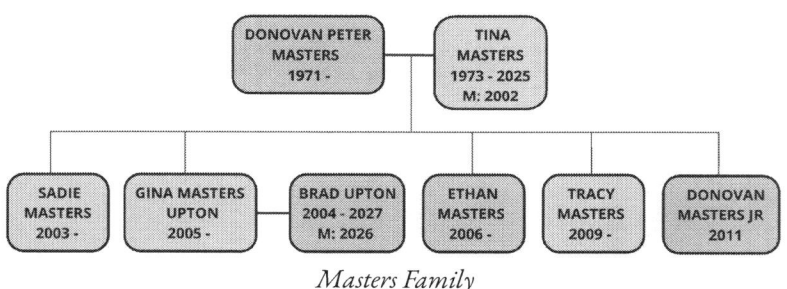

Masters Family

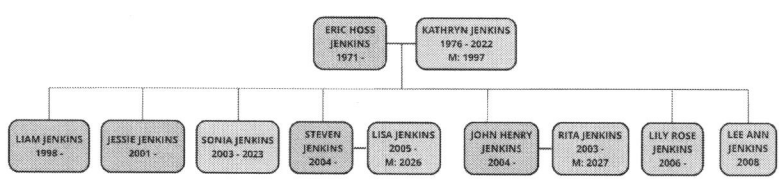

Jenkins Family

FLEE

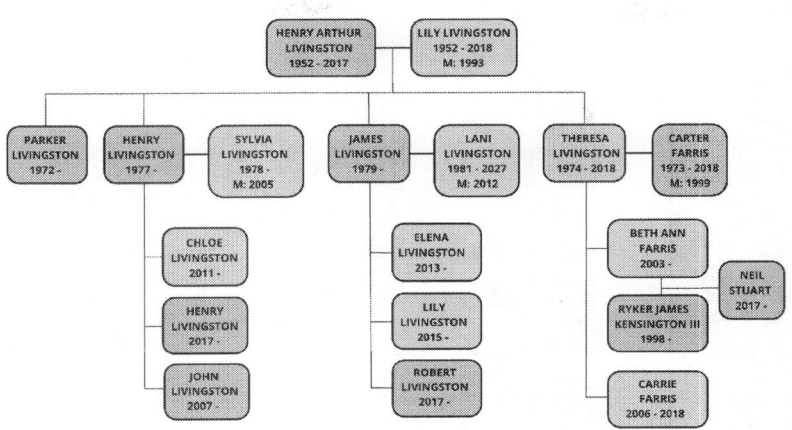

Livingston Family

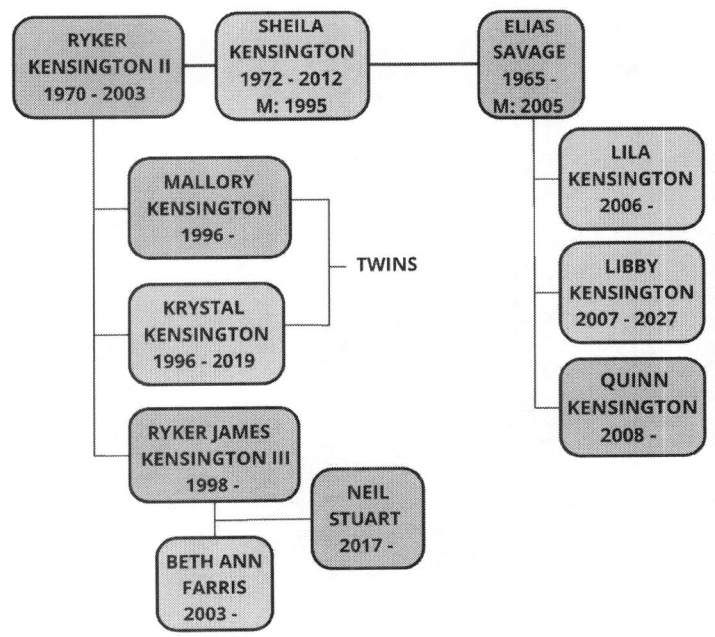

Kensington Family

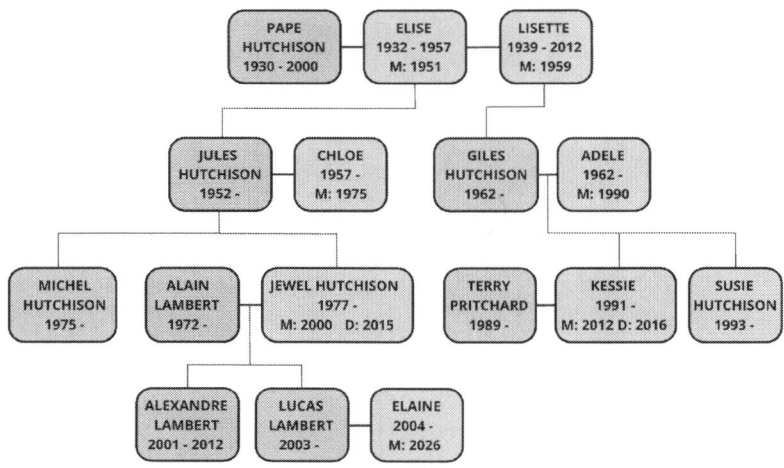

Hutchison Family

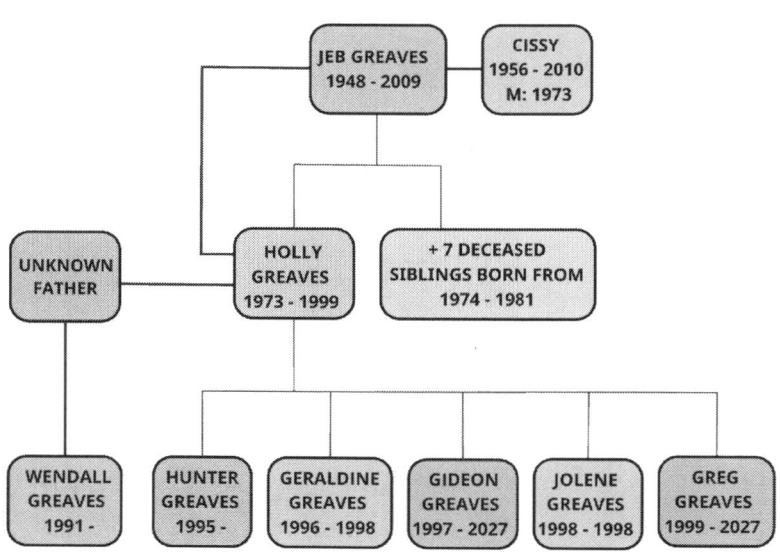

Greaves Family

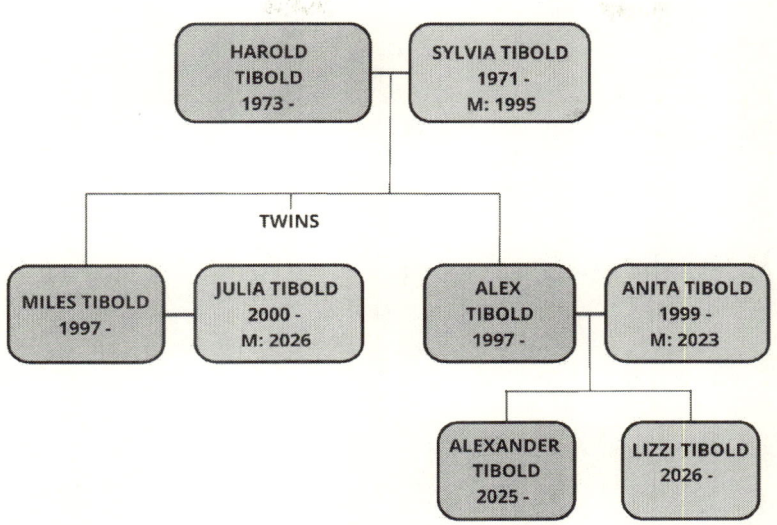

Tibold Family

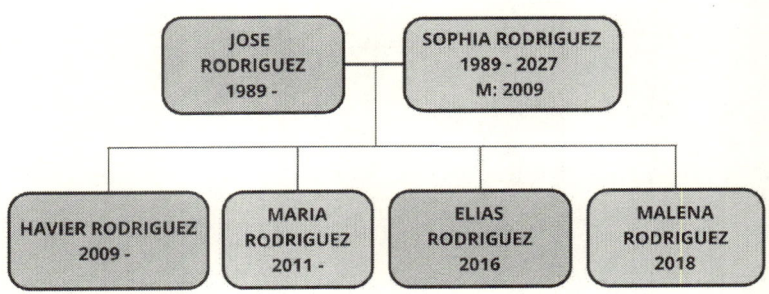

Rodriguez Family

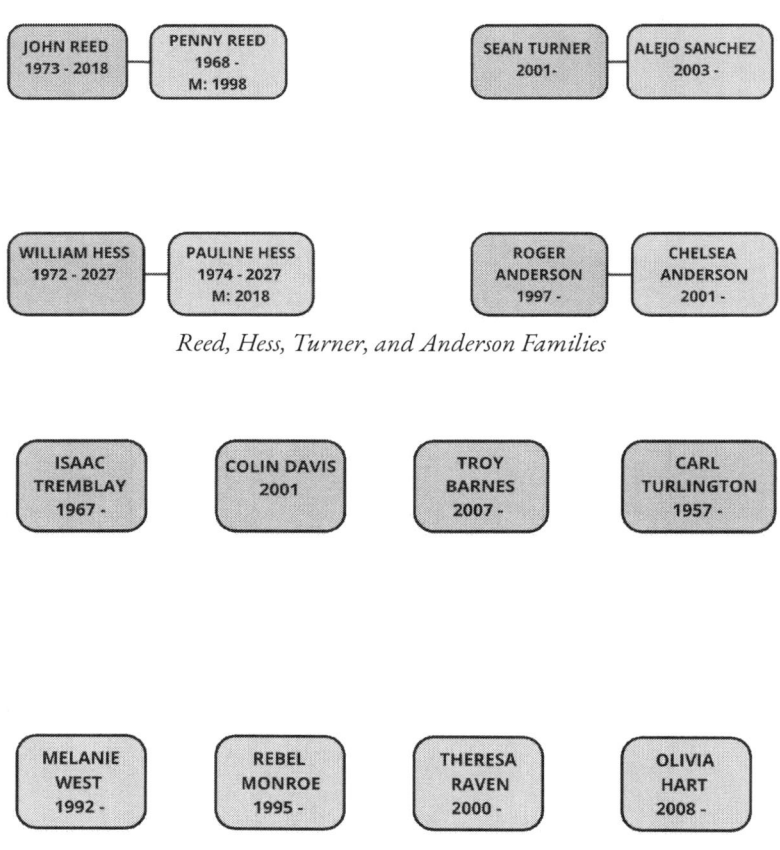

Reed, Hess, Turner, and Anderson Families

Single Men and Women

PROLOGUE
2021

Sadie launches out of the taxi, leaving Liam scrambling over the seats behind her to play catch-up. She hopes he won't follow her because she's done with him.

She hears him say to the driver, "Wait, I'll be back."

Just back to the car, or back to the party after? Probably the latter, because of course he will. He can have a good time, but I can't? She marches up the driveway, fists clenched and fuming mad. She can't believe he ruined her night. Her buzz is wasted. *Actually, no, I'm not done!*

Sadie turns around wildly, swinging her arms and stomping her feet, needing to do something with the anger coursing through her muscles. She stalks back to the end of the driveway, pointing at Liam as a silent warning not to follow to the front door. "You can't stop me from going out."

With his hands plunged deep into his pockets, Liam meets her hard gaze with his own, squaring his shoulders and lifting his chin. "No, but at least I know you're safe tonight."

Safe?! She can handle herself. Sadie's not a wallflower. She was in excellent hands with her new guy and his friends, and Sadie had been looking forward to what adventures the night was going to bring with her new beau. The next thing she knew, Liam had slapped the drink out of her hand and hauled her over his shoulder.

She rushes him and gets up in his face. "You ruined my night...sailor boy!" *In more ways than one.*

His jaw muscle twitches. "Sometimes life doesn't go your way, Auburn." He stares her down with heat in his eyes. "I'm not...a sailor."

Sadie's body vibrates, though she's not entirely sure why. Is it unreleased anger? Desire? Loss? Auburn. She always loved it when he called her that, but the name doesn't mean what it once meant to her. Liam's not hers. He'll never be hers.

Liam's face softens under her stare. Sadie's heart throbs, her ears burn. Something electric surges between them. His eyes dip to her lips; she blinks in confusion, leans in...

He pushes her back ever so slightly, breaking the spell. "Sadie, no."

She averts her eyes but cannot keep the disappointment from her voice. "Right. Because you're—"

"You're just a kid."

Sadie reels. A burning humiliation spreads across her skin, but when the water wells in her eyes, she refuses to give him a single tear, and she twists her face into a grimace. "Fuck you, Liam. Fuck you!" Immediately, she can see the pain in his expression. *Good! It should hurt!*

Liam reaches out. "Sadie."

She sidesteps his attempt to take hold of her, then backs away until she's sure he's out of reach. In one swift movement, she spins around again and storms back up the driveway and toward the front door, not caring if her whole family hears her. Hell, part of her hopes her father is already up and waiting for her inside. For her, it'll be just another fight with Donovan. But when he finds out it's one of his best friends' sons who made her cry, Dad will give Hoss an earful, too, which will make Liam feel even worse.

"I didn't... Sadie!"

She hears the apology in Liam's voice, yet forges ahead, letting her wild movements channel her anger so the tears cannot start. She knows they're going to stain her face as soon as she's inside.

"Don't waste time on losers. You deserve better," he says, his words trailing off behind her.

She bites her lip to stop it from quivering as she unlocks the house, slips inside, and closes the front door as quietly as she can. *I can't have better.*

Chapter 1
May 22, 2027

Sadie exits the Greyhound bus in Pasco, Washington, stepping into the early afternoon sun. It's the last thirty-minute stop before reaching Spokane. Just enough time to fuel up on vending machine food and the lineup for the restroom. She shifts her rucksack, checks her watch, and forces the last bite of her mediocre sandwich down. Sadie chuckles quietly at her nervousness, but doing so does nothing to put her at ease. Yesterday, at the bus stop in Sacramento, she swore she saw someone she'd hoped was in her rearview: Brent Woodard.

She shakes her head as she throws the sandwich wrapper into a nearby bin. *The guy doesn't deserve you thinking about him, Sadie. Cut it out.* But even as she thinks this, she casts her eyes over the faces in the crowd around her, the people standing in the queues for tickets, the passers-by walking in and out of the main entrance. *Relax, Sadie, he's not here. He wasn't on the bus, and he's not here now.* Her self-chastising does nothing to ease her feeling spooked.

After buying a bag of chips and a nut bar from the vending machine and visiting the restroom, Sadie joins the line to get back onto the bus and pulls her phone out of her pocket. There's a series of missed calls and texts she needs to address, but with limited time at this stop, along with her fried nerves, Sadie decides to tackle the messages she feels equipped to handle first.

She dials for her voicemail, and as the first message plays, she smiles at the sound of her sister's voice coming through the phone's speaker: "Hi! We're all packed and ready to go. Can't wait to see you and hear all about your adventure.

We'll be there when you arrive. Oh, by the way, Beth might have a new beau, and it's not Colin!"

Not Colin? Gina is such a tease, sometimes.

Gina and Brad are meeting Sadie at the bus station in Spokane and then driving her up to Haven. It had been a relief when Gina had offered her a ride. Somehow, she suspects that arriving as a group will take some of the pressure off. Her dad will be more likely to spread his questions out over the three of them instead of honing in on her alone. *Should give me some time.*

Sadie checks the missed call list again. Chloe called several times, but left no messages. Sadie met her during Marine Corps recruit training in San Diego, and they forged a strong connection, perhaps partially due to them both being second-generation Marines. But while Chloe is moving on to active service, Sadie is in the reserves. It's only two weeks a year and a weekend per month, but it means she can pursue her career as a librarian, as well.

After several rings, her call to Chloe goes to voicemail. "Hi...um, you called. Guess you're on the plane back to Texas. Let me know when you land." Sadie sends a text saying the same thing, knowing how rarely her friend listens to her messages.

She sighs, thinking about how she only managed to enjoy one day partying with her classmates at the start of their leave before she had to get the bus to Spokane. Everyone had urged Sadie to stay, but she was determined to spend the weekend at Haven. The timing of the end of boot camp and her family reunion was ideal. All the family is heading to the farm, and Sadie is eagerly anticipating finally sharing with her father what she has been up to outside of her studies. She hopes he'll be proud and not disappointed that she went behind his back, but it was the only way she could be sure her father wouldn't interfere, especially once she found out her commanding officer knew Donovan Masters. Thankfully, her CO respected her decision not to tell her family where she was before Sadie was ready.

Sadie climbs up the steps of the bus and lines up in the aisle, waiting for the other passengers to settle in their seats. She notes the wide variety of ages and ethnicities among them and imagines what array of stories has brought such a diverse set of people on this journey. The air is warm and smells faintly of sweat as she continues toward her seat at the back. *Good, no one took it while I was off the bus.* The engine vibrates to life, and cool air ejects from the vents, giving Sadie a boost.

She inhales a shaky breath: part excitement, part nerves. Telling her father that she's enlisted as a Marine in the reserves isn't the whole reason she's so keen to get to the family reunion. Her sister told her Liam would be at Haven. A thrill rushes through her, but reality blankets her high, and she silently chastises herself. Sadie has to remember they're friends and stop thinking otherwise. She hauls her bag up and above her seat, then settles into it, checking the time on her phone. *12:10.*

"Is that seat taken, dear?" A frail woman is standing next to her in the aisle, juggling a cane, a heavy knitting bag, and a friendly smile.

"No, ma'am. Would you like the window or the aisle?"

"I'll take the window. Thanks." After waiting for Sadie to get up, the graying woman slides in and settles in her seat. Sadie follows suit, laying her phone in her lap.

"Delightful picture, dear. Boyfriend?"

Sadie smiles down at her screen. A picture of a shirtless Liam stares back at her with those bedroom eyes she loves so much. She'd taken it the year she'd graduated from high school while Liam was on his leave. Sadie had been swaying in the backyard hammock, watching the Masters and Jenkins families throw the football around at their regular Sunday barbecue. Every time she looks at the tender expression on his face that she managed to capture, she dreams that the look was for her. *Too bad.* "No. Family friend."

"He must be pretty important to be on your phone screen."

He is...or was. Sadie only smiles in response.

The woman holds her hand out. "Name's Tilly."

"Sadie." She clasps Tilly's hand, angling herself so she can better speak to the warm lady, and briefly imagines that if she had a grandmother, this woman would embody that image. A gentle soul, who drags around a knitting bag and says things like dear and other forms of endearment. But Sadie never knew her real grandparents. Her mother's parents died before she was born, and Sadie's dad had long ago cut all ties with his mom and dad.

"Are you visiting or going home, my dear?"

"Both, ma'am. You?" *Is it still home?* she wonders. Spokane is a place she hasn't called home in six years. A lot has happened since then.

"Going up to Spokane to visit my great-grandbaby," Tilly declares, all giddy as she opens her bag to pull out some knitting needles looped through what looks like a nearly completed baby outfit. It is yellow, laced with splashes of blue and green.

"Congratulations."

"Thanks, he's not born yet. My granddaughter's pregnant, poor thing. She'll need some help when the time comes."

Her mom will never see her grandchildren. Sadie's heart cracks. A pang of sorrow, sharp and sudden, brings her father's face to the forefront of her mind. The last two years without her mother have been hard on Donovan. *Has it been that long already?* Sadie graduated with her first degree the year her mom died. "So, she's due any day, then?"

"Nope. Not till February."

How does she know it's a boy, then? The confidence in Tilly's answer puzzles Sadie. "Why are you going up so soon?"

"My second granddaughter needs my help. She's at a crossroads of sorts."

Sadie repositions herself with her back against her seat, but she glances sideways at Tilly. *A crossroads? I know what that's like.* This brings up her mixed feelings about Liam. She knows she loves him, but she also knows he will never love her the same way.

The woman holds her knitting needles with practiced hands and begins *clicking* and *clacking* them together. "Where do you live, dear?"

"I've been in Seattle, at the University of Washington." She could have done online courses, but the thought of living under her father's steadfast need to control everything and everyone told her she was better off on campus. Besides, if she had stayed at home, she'd never have experienced the parties, socializing...and men.

"So, why are you heading home now?"

Sadie hesitates. After growing up under her father's dominance, her desire to get away from him had been strong, but she loved him and missed him. Perhaps now that she is a Marine, like him, she is finally worthy of the respect he has always withheld from her.

"Sorry. I've always been too nosy for my own good."

"Oh, it's not that. I just...well, my family doesn't know where I've been. I'm not sure—"

"No need to explain. Did you have a good time, wherever you came from?"

Boot camp was tough, but it had done much more than give her the self-validation she'd been seeking. Part of the reason she enlisted was so Donovan couldn't hold his training over her anymore—so she could tell him to stop worrying and controlling her because she has proven she can handle herself. But after experiencing a taste of what her father and his military comrades have been through, she understands them in a way she never could have before.

A slow smile spreads across Sadie's face. "I achieved what I set out to do, yes."

"Well, then, that's all that needs saying."

It's not all positive, though. One recruit, Brent, harassed Sadie with crude jokes and unwanted advances. She wasn't the only one, and while she had put the creep in his place with a few choice words, his behavior had continued unchecked with other women. That's when Sadie and Chloe made a formal complaint to their CO. She hadn't seen him again after that. Not until—

"So, what are you studying at school?" Tilly finishes her row and begins a new one.

"I've been finishing my master's to become a librarian. I'll head back for the ceremony in June."

"That's wonderful. So, you're probably going to be scouting out jobs soon?"

"That's the plan." Growing up, Sadie idolized her father and wanted to serve like him. But once she hit her teens, Donovan's forceful nature and their constant fights kept this wish hidden and made her question her desire to be an active-duty Marine.

Tilly looks up from her knitting.

"Have you ever done something with a goal in mind, run with it, and then tripped when something else presented itself?" To escape the stress at home, Sadie spent more and more time at the library, falling in love with books. When she was old enough to enlist, Sadie had mixed feelings because she realized she wanted to be a librarian. And so, she found a way to do both, enlisting in the reserves while completing her master's. She decided the rewarding nature of her reserve duties would complement her civilian life as a librarian.

"Well, that's life, dear. The ride can be smooth or bumpy with a few scary turns, but they say it's about how you handle Plan B."

Chapter 2

A s Jewel Hutchison steps off the plane, a wave of noise confronts her. It is a stark contrast to the quiet of her village south of Paris, a picturesque cluster of stone houses, where the air sings with the twitter of birds and the gentle ringing of distant church bells. Stretching her neck, Jewel feels the strain of the long flight across the Atlantic, followed by the connecting journey to Spokane. A deep ache has settled into her shoulders. She longed for the luxury of first or business class, but the price was beyond her reach.

Dragging along a small carry-on, Jewel pauses in front of a large, colorful screen listing the arriving flights. Her luggage will be on…conveyor ten. Her favorite number. *Things are looking up.*

"Jewel!" Kessie pushes her way between two bystanders.

Jewel opens her arms to accept her younger cousin's embrace. She'd forgotten how much they look alike. They both share the same wavy, blonde hair, but Kessie's eyes are hazel like Oncle Giles's. After kissing both cheeks, they hug again, not wanting to let go just yet, like people who don't see each other often do. Kessie has filled out since their last encounter, and the joy of seeing her so well brought a tear to Jewel's eye. Her cousin had appeared so gaunt before. Thank goodness Kessie's nightmare ex-husband was behind her.

"Ah, Kessie, you never age. Why is that?"

"I was just thinking the same about you."

"It is like we are twins." Jewel laughs softly in Kessie's ear. They part, link arms, and lean their heads together as Jewel leads Kessie to the baggage claim area. "How are my *oncle* and *tante* doing?"

"Mom's been trying to get Dad to slow down, but you know him." Kessie takes Jewel's carry-on from her and starts leading her to a baggage bay.

They stand by the conveyor belt, waiting for it to start up. "*Mon Dieu,* do I ever. *Les chiens ne font pas des chats,*" Jewel says, peering at her cousin with mocking judgment in her eyes. Never one to sit back and let others do the work, Kessie gets right in there like a dirty shirt and gives any project her all, just like her dad.

Kessie laughs. "Indeed. In English, we say, the apple does not fall far from the tree."

"Tell me everything that has happened since we last spoke. How has it been living with your parents again? And how is your fiancée?" Their wedding day nears, and Jewel has come over to see them get married.

"Busy with planting the next crops, but he can't wait to have me all to himself."

"He's good to you?" Jewel studies her cousin's face for a sign of doubt or worry. She's relieved not to see any.

Kessie squeezes her arm. "Yes, he's so kind and patient."

"He wants kids?" This is the reason Kessie's first marriage ended. Her husband's desire for children was why they got married to begin with, yet they remained childless. Jewel had been unaware of the abuse her cousin suffered during their relationship. It was only after the pig locked her out of her own home that the truth started to come out.

The memory fills Jewel with guilt. She went through her own share of heartbreak and undertaken a difficult divorce, but she and her ex-spouse found a way to cooperate for the sake of their child, and a wonderful friendship, full of warmth, trust, and deep connection, blossomed.

"He wants to try right away." As if sensing the panic rising in Jewel, Kessie quickly adds, "Says if it doesn't happen, it doesn't happen."

The lump in Jewel's throat gave way, replaced with relief, and a rush of immense joy washed over her at seeing Kessie so cheerful. "Oh, your man, he is sweet."

"Jewel, you don't have to worry. I mean it. I'm truly happy."

"I'm glad, my bird. You deserve it."

"And I'm so pleased you came all this way to come to the wedding. It's going to be so much fun!"

Jewel feels the corners of her smile twitch slightly. She's thrilled to see her cousin doing so well, but Kessie's happiness casts a spotlight on Jewel's empty love life. She's been happy being single, but to find a man who can tame her wild heart? Be her equal? That would be something.

CHAPTER 3

The soothing rhythm of the bus and the music in Sadie's earbuds lull her into drowsiness. With a gentle tilt of her head toward Tilly's shoulder, Sadie's eyes flutter open. "I'm so sorry." She dislodges a bud.

With her knitting tucked away, Tilly sits with her hands clasped in her lap, apparently taking an interest in the vast and changing landscape—rolling hills to forest—before she directs her warm, kind eyes to Sadie. "It's alright. My kids used to do that. Gives me a fuzzy feeling. I can't wait until I can do that with my new grandchild. Babies smell so good." She mimics squeezing them, adding, "You just want to eat 'em up."

Sadie suppresses laughter and regrets missing out on the grandparent experience after hanging out with this lovely lady. She contemplates Gina's family plans. Sadie would like to be an aunt and learn about baby smells one day.

"You'll find a man and have children, too, my dear." Tilly pats Sadie's hand.

Sadie dismisses the thought of having a son or daughter with Liam. Her heart wants nothing more, but her head says it won't happen. And if she can't have Liam...

Tilly taps her hand again. "Don't fret over it. You're young, and your whole life is before you. You see the hurdles now, but you'll learn to overcome them. We all do."

Now Sadie knows she missed out. Tilly's sage advice has her thinking of her mother lying in her bed, wasting away. She was gone too soon. Sadie covers Tilly's hand and flashes the sweet woman a smile. "Thank you."

"No, thank you, my dear, for the pleasure of sitting next to you. Makes the ride go smoother with good company."

Before Sadie tucks her phone back into her jacket pocket, she checks the screen: *14:28*. She hasn't seen her family since Christmas. Sadie twists her short hair. Even though she has a new appreciation for her father, she's still nervous about how he'll react when he finds out where she's been. It's another reason she's so glad Gina and Brad are giving her a ride to Haven: it will give her a chance to talk things through with her sister first. After all, Gina is the only one who knows Sadie enlisted. She needed an emergency contact, and without any hesitation, she thought of Gina, even if she had to swear her to secrecy.

She gazes down the center of the bus toward the front, past the shoulders of the other passengers, and glimpses trees. They're traveling on US Route 195. *The forest has taken over,* she thinks. *We're close to Spokane.*

Sadie turns back to Tilly. "Is your family picking you up at the station? My sister could give you a lift."

"That's okay. I'm getting off before then."

Sadie's brows come together. "There aren't any more stops till we get to Spokane."

"The driver and I have a deal. Should be any minute now. Before I go, can I give you a piece of advice?" Tilly waits for Sadie to nod. "When you get off, move forward. Don't waste time keeping secrets from the people you love."

Chapter 4

White lines on the highway slice by, each mile bringing them closer to their target. Hunter has already retrieved his stash of weapons, which he'd buried in a nearby wooded area. With the bag between them, Hunter feels calmer than he did before.

Greg vibrates with nervous energy, his leg a blur of restless motion. "There." He points like a child with wild excitement. "Is that the bus?" Four sheriff's cars follow a yellow school bus. Two in front, two behind.

"It's escorted, so yes. Calm down."

"How are we going to stop it?" Greg gazes across the bag at Hunter.

It's not by accident that Hunter hasn't told his brother the plan yet. Greg lacks intelligence and has a tendency to ramble to strangers. But now they are about to execute the rescue, Hunter finally gestures for him to have a look in the bag. "Once we pass them, unroll the spike belt and drop it on the road."

Greg digs through the equipment and pulls out a black roll with glee. "Sweet." He produces more belts. "Why do we need this many?"

"They don't always lie flat. If it doesn't work, then we use the grenades."

"Grenades!" Greg uncovers a cache of various weapons. "Let's skip these and use the grenades."

"No, stick to doing what I tell you. Careful with those, they're live."

"I know."

Hunter bites his lip to keep himself from saying something he shouldn't. His youngest brother has never fully matured in Hunter's eyes, so handing him grenades to lob out the window is madness. But someone needs to hurl things while the other drives, and Hunter's not handing over control of the vehicle. Hunter always knew he and his brothers protected Greg too much, only ever giving him the safe jobs, and it hasn't benefited him.

As they drive alongside the bus, Greg unlatches the straps on a spike roll. "Gideon saw me."

Hunter barely hears him as he plays out the plan in his head one more time. Once the convoy stops, Hunter will disable the guards and extract his brother. He doesn't fear getting shot himself, which bothers him sometimes. Probably something to do with his upbringing, he figures. He'll take a bullet one day, and it'll be the death of him, but not today. Once Gideon is free, the three of them will wait it out in Hunter's hideout in town. *It's stocked with food and closer than the farm. To hell with that farm.*

"What's that?" Greg points to the sky ahead of them. A projectile arcs over the blue expanse, leaving a trail of white behind, and disappears close to the horizon. The engine dies. The sky lights up. Hunter shields his eyes too late. Dots of light burn into his retinas.

Despite Hunter slamming the brake pedal with his foot, the car continues hurtling forward. A deafening crash reverberates through the air as they barrel into the car ahead. Glass cracks, and screeching metal fills Hunter's ears. A searing bolt of agony shoots through Hunter's chest upon impact with the unyielding steering wheel. He wishes his old truck had airbags at this moment.

A nauseating smell of burning rubber permeates the cabin, mingling with the acrid scent of smoke. Hunter's mind is in chaos, struggling to grasp what is happening, when a colossal mushroom-shaped fireball erupts into the sky, killing all doubt.

A warm wind smacks Hunter's face. Pressure knocks him back into the seat. Cars peel off the highway and drift toward them. The truck lifts off the ground and soars into the air. He extends his arms to steady himself. The horizon fades into clouds and merges with the earth below. The sudden impact of the truck's roof hitting the pavement causes his seatbelt to tighten sharply, leaving him dangling in the air. He reaches out, his hand landing on something soft. In a swift motion, Greg grabs his hand, and Hunter feels relief. He digs into his front pocket for his switchblade, cuts his belt, and smashes into the metal ceiling. He groans, cradling himself in a protective fetal position.

Greg's body lands beside him. "What the hell was that?"

Hunter gazes out through the broken front window. With a mix of fear and fascination, he fixates on the mushroom cloud that looms large in the distant sky. *Nuclear?* If it is, the shock wave probably blasted them with radiation upon impact. There's no use dwelling on it. Either they're dead men walking or they're not. Best to presume the latter until they know otherwise.

Screams and breaking glass blend, creating a chaotic symphony. Something explodes. Wind, like a heated flame, strikes Hunter's face, sending his truck and other vehicles scraping down the highway. Chunks of debris and body parts fall from above, crashing loudly into the undercarriage and asphalt. Hunter snaps his attention to Greg. "You good?" He runs his hands over himself, finding nothing but the nagging pain in his chest from where he slammed into the steering wheel.

Small glass fragments tumble out of Greg's hair as he shakes them off, his face littered with tiny red cut marks. "Yeah." He reaches out and swipes the shards off the weapons bag.

Hunter's surprised it's still there but doesn't say anything. He tugs at the door handle to no avail. With a powerful kick, he sends the rest of the front windshield shattering to the ground. He crawls over it on hands and knees, the sound of crunching glass beneath his ragged breathing.

Greg climbs out next, dragging the bag with him. He leans against the side of the upside-down truck and shakes his head. "That was some ride." His face falls as his eyes lock onto the swirling mushroom cloud. "Hunter, is that—?"

"Don't think about it," Hunter says, grabbing the bag and pulling open the zipper. "Focus on what we can control, yeah?" Greg nods, but Hunter notes how pale his brother has become.

As far as Hunter can see, the highway is littered with debris, bodies, and damaged automobiles. People scramble out of their cars or rush to help those trapped nearby. *Time to strike while the fire's hot.* The bus is a little further down the road, lying on its side, the yellow color standing out among the wreckage between them. He plans a route through the labyrinth of twisted metal, broken glass, and flaming puddles of spilled gas, visualizing the twists and turns that will lead him to his goal.

"You take the left side of the highway. I'll take the right." Delving into the bag, Hunter retrieves handguns and passes two to his brother. "We'll meet at the bus."

Greg checks his weapons, tucking one in the back of his pants and the other in front, before eagerly accepting the rifle Hunter offers next. "I hear you. Let's go get him."

"Don't hurt any civilians along the way."

"Why are you worried about them? They don't matter."

Hunter grunts his annoyance. Greg sounds too much like their older brother, Wendall, and that isn't a good thing. "Just do what I tell you. If they show backbone, point the weapon at them, but give them a chance to run."

Hunter steps up onto the truck to get a better look at the bus, the metal creaking under his weight. Guards spill out of the transport's emergency hatch as disheveled-looking police officers close ranks on the road below them, chatting into their radios. Most of them are as distracted as everyone else by the looming mushroom cloud. Hunter counts his targets, then jumps down. "Let's go get Gideon."

Armed in the same fashion as his brother, Hunter motions for Greg to start moving, pointing two fingers in the bus's direction as a guide. With weapons tight to their chests, Greg approaches from the left; Hunter from the right.

People fully involved in rescue attempts leave car doors ajar as they help children and frail adults exit their vehicles, blocking Hunter's path. He avoids the ones that are burning, knowing that occupants might still be trapped inside, but it's not enough to keep the pungent odor of what he suspects is cooking flesh from filling his nostrils.

Before he gets too close, he ducks behind a truck and spies through the spaces where the windows used to be. The guards climb up and out of the bus and scatter off the side to disappear from Hunter's view.

Witnessing the weapon in his grasp, innocent bystanders disperse, creating a wide-open space around him. Despite the commotion, one man stands his ground and reaches into his jacket.

Before the man can withdraw anything, Hunter levels his rifle at him. "You won't be a hero today." His heart is racing, but his voice sounds steady.

The man hesitates, retracts his hand, then starts pumping his legs to move away from Hunter at top speed.

Bullets *zing* past Hunter, pinging off the truck and the surrounding vehicles. He ducks down and turns his attention back to the bus. Gunshots go off to his left. Greg's still breathing.

In quick succession, Hunter takes out three guards before they can take cover. He advances from car to car through a barrage of gunfire. His cheek stings, but Hunter keeps going, not letting his focus falter. Jagged scars already traverse Hunter's face, so what's one more? He gains ground, dropping two other men in his path. As he clears the wreckage on the highway, he scans the area for additional threats. Seeing none, he waits for his brother to back him up.

Greg emerges from the line of abandoned cars, their shattered windshields reflecting the harsh sunlight. They acknowledge each other, and Greg begins a sweep around the bus. Hunter counts to seven while executing headshots to the motionless bodies. No need to cause suffering. Two left.

He doesn't want to do these things, but what choice does he have? His military career is over, and thanks to his brother, he's a criminal in the eyes of the law. His grandmother was right. You can't hide from family. He tried and failed. *Can't put it all on them,* he thinks. *You were young and stupid once. But what about now?* He tosses the thought aside when he spots a guard, in obvious agony, crawling toward a shotgun, smearing blood along the asphalt.

"Gideon, we clear in there?" Hunter is unfazed by the bloody scene before him. In constant vigilance, he peers around the way he came in.

"All clear. Can't feel my fingers. Fucking hurry!" The voice from inside the bus is muffled, but it's definitely his brother.

Bang! Hunter looks at the side of the bus where he saw Greg disappear. He guesses Greg found another guard but waits for confirmation. You can never be too cautious. He looks around and back again as he shadows the man slithering along the ground. Hunter grits his teeth, fighting his instinct to help the guard. *It's us or them at this point.*

Greg reappears. "All clear." He aims his weapon at the man on the ground, but Hunter raises his hand. Greg lowers the rifle. The guard isn't a threat, and perhaps his injuries are survivable. Hunter crouches low as the guard's bloody hand claws the shotgun stock, then shoves his barrel into the man's neck.

The man freezes, his breath caught in his throat. "Please, don't hurt me." Hunter doesn't trust him. If given the chance, this man's plea could just be a ploy, giving him the time and opportunity he needs to call for help.

Hunter jams his knee into the guard's back, inciting a painful howl. He makes sure the man doesn't have another weapon on him, then unlatches some keys from the guard's belt clip and tosses them to his little brother. "Get Gideon out before he loses his shit."

Eager to please, Greg secures his rifle tight against his body and ascends the bus, climbing up to the emergency hatch.

Hunter raises his head. "Gideon, Greg's coming in!"

"How'd you pull this off?" Gideon's distant voice calls out.

"I didn't." Hunter searches the sky. "Everyone in one piece?"

The guard's breathing grows ragged, but still, he reaches for the shotgun. It's just far enough that Hunter knows he won't get hold of it, but the man's tenaciousness is impressive. Impressive and stupid. Hunter crouches lower and whispers into the man's ear. "Pick it up, and it's your funeral. Or don't, your choice. I don't shoot unarmed men if I can help it." The guard retracts his hand, and his body deflates in defeat.

"Looks that way. What do you mean?" Gideon asks.

With his attention back on the sky, Hunter observes the ball of smoke spreading across the horizon. Buildings that should be visible aren't. "You wouldn't believe me if I told you."

"What's the plan?"

Law enforcement won't have the resources to pursue them, and Hunter's precarious hiding place might be compromised. Staying in the city is too dangerous now. *Shit. Then it has to be the farm.* Even though it was their childhood home, they don't own it anymore. His grandfather sold it before he died, with the provision that they could stay, which the owner agreed to. His grandparents have been dead for years, but no one has ever come asking, and Hunter and his brothers haven't said anything. As far as Hunter can tell, there is no downside. Everyone is going to be distracted with whatever the hell has just happened, and without their names on the farm's paperwork, no one should come looking for them there. At least, not anytime soon. Plenty of time to figure out what to do next. They could even use the land to grow their own food in the meantime.

The thought of going back there makes his skin pimple. "Plan's changed." Hearing movement, Hunter gazes up.

"Holy fuck!" Gideon exits through the bus's emergency hatch, his pockmarked face registering the chaotic scene before him. The beard on Gideon surprises Hunter. His brother rubs his wrists as he stares downward, his expression one of utter shock. "We need to get Wendall out."

Hunter's unwavering gaze is severe, he's sure. *No fucking way!* That's the last thing they should do right now. And the last thing he wants to do.

CHAPTER 5

L iam collapses in his bedroom in the Jenkins apartment at Haven. His sheets are tight across the mattress. Two night tables with Swedish lamps stand on either side of the bed. They're switched off. The skylight gives enough light that he doesn't need them right now. It's all so surreal. *Haven was always just the family project. A place for Dad and his friends and their families to enjoy together. We were never supposed to actually* need *it...*

He feels the weight of what is happening out there. Terrible images are coming in. *Though it might not be long before the signals to those TV stations cease,* he thinks. Holes in city landscapes, and estimates of millions dead across the nation. It hasn't settled yet. *Whoever attacked them will invade, if that's their plan. But who is the enemy?*

Liam pulls a bedside drawer open and retrieves a worn photo. He rubs his thumb over Sadie's youthful face. She's cradling her pert breasts in an undone red bikini top on an upper apartment balcony. Sadie is unaware he took that picture, but he can't bring himself to get rid of it. She looks delicious in that skimpy attire. And so, his favorite guilty pleasure will remain a well-kept secret. He places it back in the drawer. *Where are you, Auburn?*

He snatches a few reading materials from his vast collection of books. Liam's shelving units are chock-full of all different genres, and now that the world seems to be ending, he feels vindicated. He dances his fingers along the spines of the books, their textures smooth and worn, until he locates the one he's after.

He's never been one to keep them in any special order or categorize them by color. This way, he has to pay them all equal attention when searching for one.

Liam leaves his bedroom, makes his way down the bare hallway, and returns to the cozy common living room and kitchen he shares with his large family. His two sisters, Lily Rose and Lee Ann, are chatting on the couch. Spotting him, they run over and embrace him. The Jenkinses have always been a close-knit bunch.

"Hey, how come I didn't get the memo?" Hoss comes out of his bedroom, arms open, and encircles the lot of them in a big bear hug. After kissing each of his daughters, he lets them go. "You ready, Liam?"

"As I'll ever be," he says, watching the girls run back into the living room.

"Try not to worry about Sadie. She'll show."

Liam nods. He holds tight to the information Donovan gave them. Sadie wasn't in Spokane at the time the missile hit. And besides, she knows how to handle herself. They all went through the same training on those camping trips with their dads long ago. Liam knows there's no point in worrying and that the best thing he can do is stay hopeful that she'll reach them soon enough, but it nags at him.

Liam's younger brother walks out of the hallway in their direction. "We're all settled in now, Dad." John Henry and his wife arrived just in time, missing the big event back in Spokane. The sheer scale of the disaster unfolding across the United States left them horrified and speechless once they were filled in.

Hoss grabs his younger son's shoulder. "How is Lisa doing?"

They brought up Liam's other brother's new wife so she could feel like part of the family and enjoy the reunion, even with Steven serving overseas. It pains him to know that not all the family is here with them. Steven is John Henry's twin and serves with Liam's brother, Jessie, on mission in Germany.

"Frightened, but at least she's not alone."

Liam doesn't entertain the idea of what she would have gone through if they hadn't planned this trip months ago. Lisa had only visited once before now, so he doubts she could have found her way on her own. The other women in their group have greater mental fortitude than she does. Or so it appears. They've only known Lisa for a little over a year now. Plus, while Sadie and the others have been trained and prepared for such an emergency, Lisa lacks even the most basic survival skills.

Hoss slaps John Henry's shoulders. "I'm glad you made it, son. Hold the fort down while we're away and keep Parker busy."

"Will do, Dad."

CHAPTER 6

Sweat stings Sadie's eyes. Her hair falls over her face. Something is pulling tight across her waist. She feels like she's just lost a fistfight. For a while, she's too disoriented to remember where she is, but when she finally blinks her vision back into focus, cement greets Sadie through the smashed bus window, her seat belt being the only thing keeping her from falling into it. A lone knitting bag sits undisturbed on the seat next to her. *T-Tilly? Where...?*

Sadie unbuckles and falls to the ground with a hard *thud*. Using the seats to steady herself, she rises to her feet, squeezing her eyes shut tight in the wake of the stabbing pain. Touching her head, she recoils, then stares at the blood on her fingers. Spotting her rucksack near her feet, she secures it to her back before grabbing the knitting bag. She looks down the aisle to find passengers helping each other through an emergency window halfway up the bus. One man waves her over. "I'll hoist you up."

"Did you see the woman who was sitting next to me? Older lady."

His frown doesn't fill her with hope. "Everyone who was sitting in the back and survived is outside already."

But then, where's her body? Sadie points to the front of the bus. "Did someone retrieve the first-aid bag up there?"

"Do you want me to get it?"

Sadie holds up her hand. "No, I'll do that." With a great force of effort, and a wince of pain, Sadie hoists herself up over the seat and starts making her way toward the front of the bus.

"Are you sure? I'll wait for you here."

"I can see the windshield is missing, so I'll head out that way." She passes the man, careful not to disturb the few unmoving bodies still buckled in their seats. At the front, she's taken aback. The sagging corpse of the driver has been impaled on a metal sign. The hair on her neck rises. She's never seen or been near this many dead people before. His lips are blue. This odd detail makes her heart race and fills her with a sense of unease. *Focus, get the kit, and get out.* Sadie fixates on the bright red first-aid bag, tempting her from the other side of his body.

With a deep inhale and trembling fingers, she reaches over the driver's shoulder. His body droops forward. Sadie jerks backward, an audible gasp passing through her lips. Pushing aside her discomfort, she stretches her hand past him, careful not to make contact, and snatches the bag.

Sadie looks back the way she came—the kind man is still helping others climb out of the exit while unseen bodies pull them through from the other side—then inspects the gaping hole in the smashed front windshield. It's been so thoroughly destroyed, she climbs out with ease.

When her feet hit the tarmac, she almost wishes she could climb back inside the bus. The highway and its surrounding landscape ahead are in utter disarray. Smashed and burned vehicles litter the roadway, trees are either burning or leaning or both, and to the left of the city, a mushroom cloud rises in the distance. *Nuclear? Wouldn't the damage be worse? But then what did this? Who did this? And do I have a chance in hell of making it to Haven alive?* Voices rise above the wind in her ears, and she turns to see that people have gathered in groups to help the injured and those even less fortunate. Some have already started moving toward the suburbs. Her hope dwindles when she doesn't see Tilly's kind face among them. Sadie climbs atop the bus and scans the surroundings. *So many bodies...*

After jumping back down, Sadie searches the myriad of tousled corpses across the expanse of cold and unforgiving cement. Every step she takes dredges up apprehension, made worse as more and more people gather around the bodies of their friends or family, expressing their grief through tears and moans.

Sadie pauses. With a shaky voice, she murmurs, "Tilly?" while her hand trembles over her mouth. Her heart cries out. Tears threaten as she approaches the still form of her seat partner's contorted body.

Sadie collapses, taking Tilly's hand in her own. She allows the grief to engulf her and prays that the woman's death was quick and painless. Tilly will never see her grandbaby. Sadie strokes the woman's fingers; a numbing sensation envelops her, disconnecting Sadie from her surroundings. *Why her? This can't be happening.*

Do hours go by? Or just the blink of an eye? Whatever the truth of it, once her tears have long since dried up, Sadie rubs the back of her sore neck as she comes out of her trance. The sun has moved across the sky a little. There are slightly fewer groups of survivors around than what felt like a mere moment ago.

Tilly's last words spring to the front of Sadie's mind: "When you get off, don't look back. Move forward."

Sadie's legs are stiff from sitting on the cold, hard ground, but she wills herself to her feet. A nearby group of people sits with the injured, reassuring each other that rescue is on its way. Sadie knows it won't come. This information is deeply rooted in her psyche. If it's this bad here, the city will be far worse.

Swiping at her cheeks with her forearm and breathing out the stress, Sadie climbs back up atop the bus and cracks open a baggage bay door. With so many bags to dig through, it takes time, but she locates her suitcase and yanks it out. Sadie switches her flats for boots, clips a knife to her belt, and transfers essential items into her rucksack. The weight of her Eagle, Globe, and Anchor pin feels substantial in her hand as she pauses, the enamel gleaming, before slipping it into her pocket. She learned a lot growing up—understood that a day like this might arrive and where she'd need to go—but San Diego taught her to hone those skills. She knows exactly what to do and has already begun preparing herself for the likely dangers and obstacles along the way.

Plan A, aborted. Plan B, initiated.

***

Sadie gazes up into the treetops and guesses she's been walking for about an hour. Initially, she stayed on the highway, but as soon as people began showing an interest in her backpack, she couldn't ignore them any longer. Whether alone or in a family group, they all wore the same desperate expression on their faces. And so, Sadie had veered off the road, finding a trail through the trees, hoping to find the next road over. She searches the late afternoon sky for signs of fallout, but no dust or ash has materialized. She doesn't know what kind of bomb dropped back in Spokane or if it even hit the city. *Who would attack Spokane?*

Sadie frowns at the blank screen of her cellphone before stuffing it back in her pocket. It's a brick, but even if it were working, she's not convinced there would be any signal anymore. Either way, she doesn't want to part with it yet. She continues her eastward journey, her footsteps traipsing across the forest floor, when nature calls. She finds a place suitable for her needs and backs up toward some thick bushes while scanning for threats.

Weighing the potential dangers, she made the decision that going back to the city was not a sensible option. The absence of functional vehicles and her dead cell phone indicate that whatever fell possessed EMP capabilities. The knowledge Sadie's father instilled in her during her upbringing is something she is grateful for, even if she won't tell him to his face.

When all she can hear for thirty seconds is the breeze rustling through the leaves, she decides it's safe enough, drops her bag, and goes for her pants button.

The more she thinks about it, the more she knows Reed is the best course to take instead of trying to find her sister. Sadie feels confident in Gina's ability to get to Haven's backup site on her own. She might not have Marine training, but they shared the same upbringing. Plus, Gina is with Brad. And as for the rest of her siblings, they are already at Haven with their father. *No, definitely better to stick to the plan and get to Reed as quickly as possible.* She'll dig up the cache on the outskirts of Freeman, plan her route before nightfall, then head out in the morning. *I just hope there's enough light to make the journey today.*

She pulls her pants up, thankful for the relief she feels now that her bladder is empty. Picking up her bag, Sadie searches for her tiny bottle of antibacterial hand soap.

Snap. "Bitch!"

Sadie recognizes that voice. Brent. Fear crawls all over her, raising her awareness to a new height. She moves her head from side to side, scanning the trees on all sides. She springs open a knife, concealed a moment ago, with sure hands, ready to defend herself.

Brent comes at her from the side, swinging a branch aimed at her head. She ducks. The limb strikes the tree trunk, showering her with bits of bark and a cloud of wood dust. Sadie's muscle memory kicks in, and she scrambles away from him.

He circles, searching for an opening, but she mirrors his actions, denying Brent any chance to get behind her. *Where the hell did he come from?*

She quickly shakes away the shock to assess things intelligently. While already exceeding her in height and weight, Brent also has extra reach with the long tree branch. He always defeated her in hand-to-hand training, but knife trumps stick. He could overpower her, but the victory would come at a steep cost, leaving him wounded.

"Don't do this, Brent. Think." She rotates the knife slightly, enough for the blade to catch the sunlight, which she reflects at him.

But his fierce, unblinking stare tells Sadie that Brent will not be deterred. *Well, I guess if a mushroom cloud isn't going to stop him...* Waiting for his opportunity to strike, Brent swings the tree branch back and forth almost playfully, sending it whistling through the air as he moves forward. Sadie backs up to give herself more room, her breath catching in her throat. The heavy branch, gnarled and menacing, arcs downward, aiming to hurt, its weight promising pain.

Sadie arches her back as the branch whooshes by her, and a low groan escapes her lips. She steps sideways and slashes at the back of Brent's arm on his down-swing.

With a sharp hiss, he squeezes his bleeding wrist. But just as quickly, he seems to ignore the pain and grips the branch even tighter. With an animalistic growl, Brent circles her again, flashing his clenched teeth.

There is no way out of this confrontation, Sadie realizes. She has no choice but to defend herself.

With the branch held high, he rushes toward her.

She backs up, but not fast enough. Sadie raises her forearm while trying to dig her boots into the ground as she braces for impact. She squeezes the worn handle of the blade with all her might, preparing herself for what she's going to have to do the moment he gets in close.

But Brent somehow changes direction, and while staying out of knife range, he swings low, knocking her off balance.

Sadie crashes onto the damp forest floor, and barely a moment later, Brent straddles her, scraping her body on the way down, locking her to the ground.

Feeling the weapon still in her grasp, Sadie jabs her blade into his side, twisting it multiple times, finding resistance, before he wrangles her wrist to the floor. She swings her other hand into his face, forcing her thumb into his eye. His scream echoes out into the forest. The moment he shifts his head out of her reach, warm drops of blood hit her cheeks.

Sadie lifts her legs off the ground, and tries desperately to wrap them around his head and neck, but he leans forward, blocking her from getting her body into position. He weighs too much. She's trapped. Sadie screams, her body bucking underneath him out of frustration, and she spits into his face.

His fist comes down toward her. The pain hits with the force of a physical blow, making her see stars.

CHAPTER 7

J ewel stares at her cell with a slack jaw, still grappling with the fact that her
son was talking to her one moment, and the next, the phone just died. At
least he knows she's landed, but the interruption still bothers her.

"It's probably interference from the mountains. You can call him once we get
to the farm."

This doesn't explain the battery dying. "But it was at full charge."

They exit route I-90, then at the junction, the old Chevy truck, its engine
sputtering, turns left onto the long, windy, dirt road to the farm. The nagging
phone issue tempered Jewel's excitement about arriving, but as they draw closer,
her anticipation soars again. A mixture of nervous energy and exhilaration runs
through her veins as the mountains part, revealing dry peaks and bright green
trees as a single-story farmhouse comes into view down the driveway. It's as
picturesque as the last time Jewel saw it. Farmhands gather around trucks in
front of the building, then disperse in different directions, and as they get
nearer, Jewel sees Giles standing among them. Despite his slight paunch, he
looks rugged and stands with an air of authority about him, his hands on his
hips. A broad, happy smile spreads across Giles's face.

Kessie parks the truck alongside the others. The moment Jewel's door creaks
open, Giles's arms are around her. Memories of the time she spent here as a
young girl return when she smells fresh air with a hint of pine. He could be
knee-deep in mud and still come out smelling like this.

"Thank God, you're alright," Giles says with a twinkle in his eye. Despite immigrating to the United States decades ago, leaving the family farm back in France in the hands of his older half brother, his accent is still thick.

Jewel pulls away. "Why? What's happened?"

The tailgate lets out a squeak as Kessie opens it. "He worries when I go out alone in the truck." She trails the first of Jewel's luggage over to her father and leans in for a hug.

"Of course I do," he says, with no further explanation.

"My phone died while talking to my son. I need to call him back."

"Sure." He relieves Kessie of her burden and beckons them toward the front door. "Let's get your luggage and head inside."

Aunt Adele greets Jewel with hugs and kisses in the entryway. "So glad you're here. How was the plane ride?"

Jewel peers over Adele's shoulder to look inside the house. All the lights are off, and the hallway is dark. "It was long and tiring, but I'm so happy to be here. Is the power out?"

Their humble abode is just that. Humble. Despite how Giles has grown the farm over the years, their house is just as Jewel remembers it being. She loves the simple way they live. Giles isn't flashy, and neither is his wife. Everything has its place and serves a function.

"Yes, but don't worry. The boys are fixing it." Adele ambles into a modest kitchen, inviting Jewel to follow. "How is the family? The farm?"

"My dear, give her time to get over the jet lag before you bombard her with questions." With a sly grin, he leans in and kisses his wife on the cheek.

Jewel can't help but find their love adorable, and for a moment, she can't help but miss her ex-husband. Her heart still belongs to him, she knows, even if she won't tell anyone, and she hates that she couldn't get past what happened. Ten years prior, the death of her oldest son shattered their world, leaving a gaping hole in their lives and hearts. It was a wound that time proved unable to heal.

Giles turns to Jewel and hands her the cordless phone. "Jewel? Call your son." Then he lugs her belongings toward the back of the house.

"Oh, the jet lag, of course. Do you want to sleep, dear? I'll get you some warm milk before you head to your room." Though the inside of the fridge is dark when her aunt opens it, Adele doesn't seem to notice or care. She pours milk into a pan and puts it on the gas stove to warm up.

Jewel recalls her son's number from memory and enters it to call his cell in France. The line is silent. She takes the phone away from her ear, ends the call, and then opens a line. Jewel hears nothing.

"Does the power affect the telephones here?" she asks Giles as he returns to the kitchen.

He raises an eyebrow. "No." He takes the phone, dials out, and looks at the phone as though it's an alien device. "That's odd."

"Mr. Hutchison!" a man outside yells.

"I'll be back, ladies."

Apprehension climbs Jewel's throat as Giles exits through the front door.

Kessie pats her arm. "It'll be fine. Losing power is a way of life here, which is why we have the generators. There's probably something wrong with them." Kessie gestures toward the living room. "If you're not ready to sleep, at least come and rest. You must be exhausted after your trip."

Jewel allows herself to sink into the sofa. She had been determined to stay awake until the evening so the jet lag wouldn't be so bad, but the gentle softness makes her want to fall asleep. She's more tired than she expected. *Maybe I shouldn't have that glass of warm milk, after all.* "When will I see Gary?"

"I told him you'd be tired today, so he's coming for dinner tomorrow night."

The front door opens. Giles walks past them and into the kitchen with a strange look on his face. The way he ambles right by them without looking up causes a surge of adrenaline to shoot through Jewel, and she's suddenly wide awake again. *Something's going on.*

"No!" Adele exclaims.

Jewel leans forward. "What's wrong, Oncle Giles?"

Giles comes around the corner with his arm on Adele's waist. "There's a report of a missile hitting Spokane over the ham radios."

Kessie gasps as Jewel jumps to her feet. *"Mon Dieu!"*

He turns to Kessie. "The neighboring farmhands brought the news over."

Adele gazes at Giles. "They have power?"

"Generators." Giles deposits Adele gently in an armchair. "The boys are getting ours online. Shouldn't be long."

Jewel's mind races. Is her son safe? Without any power, they have no way of knowing what is happening in Spokane. She has to find a way to get through to him. An attack on US soil must be all over the global news already. He will be worried sick.

"What do we do?" Adele asks in a meek voice, beating Jewel to the question.

Someone behind the open front door knocks. "Sir, the boys are ready."

Giles turns to Adele. "I've got to go. Heard the neighbors are meeting down at the hall."

She reaches out to her husband. "Don't leave, Giles."

He glances at the man standing by the door. "Thanks. I'll be out shortly."

Giles kneels beside the armchair and takes Adele's hand. "The girls are here. I have to find out what is happening." He places a gentle kiss on her furrowed brow. "I'll be back as soon as I can."

He looks up at Kessie. "Take care of your mother." Then, without looking back, he heads out the door.

CHAPTER 8

Sadie stares at her mother lying in her parents' bed. A pink scarf covers up where beautiful blonde hair once flourished, and an IV line trails to her arm.

"Mom?" Under a tremendous cloud of apprehension, Sadie surveys the room, bewildered. *This isn't right?* Her mother's dead. Sadie's sure she is on a bus, but where is she? If she's dreaming, why is she questioning herself?

"Sadie!" Tina rips out the IV and casts it away as she stands strong to receive her daughter.

"Whoa!" Sadie holds her palms out. "What're you doing?" *This can't be real?*

"Don't worry. You need me, and I'm here." Tina wraps her loving arms around a stiff, confused Sadie. Her mother lost so much weight in the last year of her life. Sadie encircles her mom's slight form.

Mom...

The tension recedes as Sadie allows herself to relish the moment, and she breathes in her mother's soft scent. Roses translate into "mommy" for Sadie. Her mom's favorite perfume.

Tina whispers in her daughter's ear. "You miss this, don't you?"

Sadie nods against her mother's shoulder. Tina leans back and gazes at her. Blinking away the tears, Sadie takes a breath. Her chest tightens, the weight of loss cutting through her like a sharp blade. She'd pay any price for this to be real. *I miss you so much, Mom.*

"I miss you, too. Life's not turning out how you thought it would be, is it?"

"Something's happened. I'm scared." Sadie glances around as if the bogey-man is about to get her.

"That's good. A path with no obstacles leads nowhere." Tina cups her daughter's chin and gazes upon her with love-struck eyes. "Your dad prides himself on avoiding all obstacles through control. Not this time."

The weight of the person feels real, and she looks and sounds like her mom, but Sadie remembers her advice was usually wise and straightforward. This time, it's cryptic. "What do you mean?"

Tina strokes Sadie's cheek. *"Je t'aime."*

The lilting French words, unfamiliar yet somehow comforting, cause confusion mixed with a blend of surprise. "I love you, too."

"You don't have to choose."

"Choose what?" Sadie clasps her mother's hand. "You're not making sense, Mom."

Her mother's gaunt face softens, and thin lips turn up. "He doesn't know it yet, but he's been waiting for you." Tina narrows her eyes. "Trust him."

"Trust who? Why?"

"Shouldn't need a reason." Her mother fades from view. "I will always be with you."

Sadie stirs in the waning evening light, face down, lying on the ground. It was a dream...

Pain pierces her head. She tries to reach up, but her arms won't move. After fingering the rough bark, her fingers find the duct tape around her wrists, tying her to the base of a small tree trunk. As her memories trickle in, a wave of unease comes over her, intensifying the feeling of dread. *Brent.*

Firewood rests, surrounded by rocks, in the middle of a small clearing among the tall pines, prepped to be ignited. A hunting knife stands erect in a block of wood nearby. He plans on staying. She doesn't like what this means for her. Sadie's rucksack lies open, the contents scattered. Her nerves tingle as sweat forms. The need to flee drives her into action. Swinging her feet under her, Sadie sits up, wriggles her hands, hoping to free them, and rubs the duct tape along the rough bark. The tape rips, tearing away a layer of skin and leaving a burning, stinging sensation. The tree is young, but the angle of her shoulders prevents her from sliding her hands over it.

A sudden crackling and snapping sound comes from the underbrush to her right, startling her. Sadie tries to stand, but the duct tape prevents her from doing so.

Brent, tall and commanding, steps in between the trees. Carrying a new solid branch, he circles leisurely around to her left. A freshly dressed white bandage covers his right hand. Sadie bites her bottom lip in frustration. The rip in his light-colored shirt and the dark bloodstains show her that the knife did some damage, but she thought she'd done more.

He strides into the clearing, his imposing figure casting a shadow over her. The unmistakable rage coming off him causes her to shrink back and shudder. Brent twirls the branch, and Sadie feels her anxiety amp up as he raises it.

Infused with terror, she shies, scrunching her eyes tight, waiting for impact. Solid, rough wood raises her trembling chin instead. She gazes up into a spiteful expression.

"You ruined my life."

Brent hooks the branch around her neck, crouches down, and pulls her toward him. The duct tape tears. Her shoulders pull back. Pain shoots up her arms, and her hands tremble. The way he's moving, the way he's balancing that long, heavy branch in his hand... His injuries to his body might not be as severe as they look. *Damn it!*

"She was easier to find, but you..." Brent releases her and stands. "You took some time." He starts pacing left and right, disturbing the leaves in his wake. "All I had to do was get your bunk buddy drunk to find out when you were leaving. Hell, she even told me what bus you were taking."

Chloe? "What did you do to her?"

His frantic pacing stops. Brent looms over her, his presence filling the space between them with a suffocating intensity. "Time to return the favor...slowly."

She has no time to react as he straightens, winds the branch with both hands, and swings. Under the audible crack of her ribs, excruciating pain signals shoot into her brain as the air is forced from her lungs. The effort to suck it back in again is sharp. Her chest burns. Sadie's vision blurs. Her body wants to curl into a ball, but with her arms still tied behind her, she can only lean forward so far.

Brent lowers over her, close to her ear, and whispers in a venomous tone, "That's for getting me kicked out." The liquor on his breath is stale and pungent. The smell dissipates as he walks away, still brandishing the branch, only to begin his pacing again. "You and that other bitch." He comes to a sudden stop, ponders, and twirls the tree limb. "I gave her what for."

Alarm bells go off in Sadie's head as tendrils of pain snake their way up and down her chest. She finds it hard to concentrate. She leans back against the tree, twisting her legs to keep them close to her body. "What did you...?" She stops mid-sentence and tries to regulate her breathing through her nose.

Brent stares at her. The sharp glint in his devilish eyes betrays the intense loathing and fury he harbors toward her. His lips curl up. He's gone mad.

"Brent, let me go."

"Let you go?" He scoffs at the absurdity of her words. "Never!" The ground vibrates as Brent advances toward her. Fearing he's about to inflict more damage, she recoils and tries to make herself smaller. But just that movement alone is enough to set her cuts and bruises on fire, and she cries out, unable to find any other respite from her injury. She already knows she's close to losing consciousness. *Would that be so bad?*

With a thud, the branch hits the ground, but before she even understands why, Brent's hands are gripping her throat, squeezing. He forces her body down, trapping Sadie under his weight, crushing her ribs. Her piercing scream, which briefly echoes through the trees, comes to an abrupt stop. The more she tries to take a breath and can't, the more Sadie thrashes her legs as fear sends every muscle into panic. Powerless to halt her attacker, she can only bear witness to the malicious hunger in his gaze. He seems fixated on her agony.

This is the end. She'll never see her family again. *Dad!*

Brent releases her.

While gasping for air, she chokes, and the moment her body knows it's going to live, at least for now, the excruciating pain in her ribs returns, only even more severe. Her wrists throb. This can't be happening.

In a raspy voice, Sadie pleads with him. "Nuclear bomb!" She gasps. "Middle...attack."

Towering above, he levels his accusations. "You... Ever since that day, all I wanted was for you and that other cunt to pay for what you did to me."

God, no! "Do you hear..."—Sadie tries to catch her breath—"...yourself?" She falters, unable to hold back tears. "Need shelter. Radiation..."

Brent ignores her. "I didn't just hurt her."

The possibilities of what he's not saying prick her mind with distress. *If he did something bad, the authorities are searching for him, right?* She thinks back to the bomb, the groups of people waiting for help at the side of the road. She is alone. No one is looking for him. No one is coming to help her. No one will hear her screams. "What did you...to Chloe?"

Brent cackles. He grips a fistful of her hair and slams her head back into the ground. Even with the bed of leaves on top, the impact reverberates through her skull. She groans as stars cloud her vision.

"She shrieked through the gag I placed in her fucking mouth." He relives the scene and glares down at Sadie. "I broke things."

A forceful slap makes contact with her face. The resulting whiplash causes a crack to sound from her neck, and excruciating pain erupts. Sadie bellows. Tears fall down her cheeks unchecked.

Brent yanks on her short hair, scraping up dirt and pine needles with it, causing her to wince. Each strand feels as though it's being torn from her scalp. He smirks cruelly. "She didn't last long." Trapped in his vice grip, the gritty texture of the soil invades Sadie's mouth. "This time will be different. You will feel more." He winds up and slams his fist into her face. Liquid spurts out of her nose. Another strike. Another. The ferocity of his assault is impossible to assess, understand, or comprehend. There is no time to think. No time to react. No time to feel anything but pure agony. *Liam...*

CHAPTER 9

The truck's lights flicker up the road amid a pitch-black night, showing Hunter and his brothers through the trees. The chilling air vibrates with heavy breathing and low moans of the men he helped liberate from the prison, the sounds overlaid by the crackling of branches and the soft thuds of their feet on the soil and leaves. Hunter is farther back than his brothers. He can distinguish Gideon ten paces ahead of his older brother, Wendall. He can't believe they were so stupid as to try to break Wendall out. But more than that, he can't believe they managed it. How is it that while so much of Spokane got flattened, the prison was damaged just enough for his brother and his psychopathic band of followers to escape? *The world is a cruel place.*

Wendall and Hunter disagree on most things. As the eldest, Wendall took charge of his three brothers, often mediating their squabbles and keeping them out of trouble. They bonded during childhood out of necessity, but by the time Hunter was in his teens, he saw his family for what they really were. And so, Hunter ran away from the dysfunctional chaos. But Wendall is a black hole: there is no escaping him. And Hunter eventually found himself being pulled back into the fray by his older brother.

With the darkness in the woods so complete, Hunter's other senses awaken. The cold sweat on his skin brings back memories of grueling night drills at boot camp, and he smiles to himself. Hunter felt alive during those weeks he was in the army. Something he hasn't experienced since.

A branch catches his foot. His arms flail out. The rough bark of a tree stops him.

His feeling of freedom was short-lived: like a spark, it ignited and then vanished. Hunter landed in hot water with the authorities, squashing his military career before it even began. He served his time in prison and vacated a few months ago.

Up ahead, Gideon grabs a nearby tree.

"Gideon, keep walking." Wendall's controlling nature is still intact.

Hunter is irritated, but he keeps his composure. He wishes he had put his foot down with Gideon earlier and resisted his plan to break Wendall out more than he did, but now isn't the time to argue with everything going on around them. The journey to the prison was a harrowing one; the sights and sounds of chaos painted a vivid picture of society's breakdown. If the fighting ends quickly and order returns, the isolated farm will be their safest bet. No matter how they proceed, their goal remains unchanged.

Besides, Wendall isn't the only one to have joined them at the prison: his brother has let loose a whole entourage of orange-jumpsuited killers and thieves, promising them freedom in exchange for their help. If Hunter tries to challenge his brother now, who knows how the crazies around him will react?

The silhouette of Gideon up ahead pushes itself off the tree and follows on in silence.

Gunfire trails off behind them, still there but less intense than before. The shooting ahead is a growing concern, however. As they reach the tree line, Hunter hears a crescendo of men's screams and moans. The fighting is coming from the truck. *Their* truck.

Greg!

Hunter steps onto the road to find a mob of fighting orange jumpsuits. The headlights must have attracted other escapees, as well.

The men they've rescued throw themselves into the maelstrom. Bullets zing by. Bodies fall to the ground. A prisoner hops into the driver's seat of the truck. *Where is Greg?*

Gideon approaches the driver's side, aims, shoots, and yanks the body out of the way.

Hunter sprints to the passenger side, hoping to find Greg behind the open door. Empty. Gunfire hits the truck, and clanking metal sounds around him.

Beside the truck is Dugal, another prisoner Hunter rescued from the bus while saving Gideon. The man is crouched down, covering his head with his arms. He's armed, but petrified. *Pussy.* Beyond Dugal, behind the vehicle, a body convulses. *Fuck!* "Greg!"

Without even bothering to take cover, Hunter darts over to his brother and places his hand on Greg's forehead. His brother's eyes follow him. The shaking in his muscles subsides for a moment, but his lips continue to quiver. Blood trails down his brother's cheeks as he coughs. "Gideon!" Hunter screams, his voice cracking.

The frenzied mob retreats as Gideon comes to a stop at the end of the truck. Of all their black hearts, why Greg? They need to find help. Hunter grabs Greg's shoulders. "Lift him!"

Gideon helps Hunter hoist his brother onto the tailgate. Greg has a death grip on Hunter's arm, and his terrified eyes search Gideon out. *Maybe it's not so bad.*

Wendall inserts himself between Hunter and Gideon. "Greg, stay with us. You did good, brother."

His face shows a flash of relief. His lips move, but no sound slips through. More liquid trickles out instead. Too much.

Wendall hikes to the passenger side of the truck. "Drag him into the bed, Gideon. Hunter, you drive!"

Tears prick Hunter into action. He extracts himself from Greg's grip, then bends over and kisses his forehead, not caring what Gideon thinks about that.

Greg, his little brother, the only one of them with a decent bone in his body, is in terrible shape. Hunter needs to make his peace with his baby brother while he still can. He isn't going to make it to the farmhouse.

***

Hunter leans against the Rite Aid in a melancholy mood, monitoring Mal and the other prisoners traveling with him and his brothers. He opted to stay outside while Wendall took some men into the grocery store. That lunatic, Cain, and others investigated the Rite-Aid. Judging by the screams and gunshots, someone is attacking the people inside the building. It pisses Hunter off, but he can't do much to stop them. Self-preservation rules, and they have all the advantages at the moment. It won't last forever, though.

Hunter can't bring himself to look at Gideon, who is sitting in the truck bed, saying nothing. With his back to Hunter, he is still staring at Greg's unmoving body. Hunter mourns the loss. He can't believe Greg died first.

Guilt seeps in. Hunter should have stayed with the vehicles. Hell, they should have left that highway and hightailed it to the farm instead of going back for Wendall. Greg would be alive if they had. He can't help it, but he blames Wendall, adding another reason he hates the brother he used to look up to when he was a young child.

If Hunter had anywhere else to go, he'd take off. With Wendall busy in the store and distracted by his new gang of thugs, and Gideon trying to come to terms with Greg's death, now is as good a time as any. But he doesn't have anywhere else. Or anyone else to go to. He is a killer, like the rest of this bunch, and not fit for being around normal people. It's sick and perverse, but for now, staying with his brothers is his best chance of survival.

Hunter yanks himself out of these thoughts and focuses on the prisoner guarding the trucks. Mal volunteered for the task. Something lurks behind those intense eyes staring back at Hunter. He doesn't trust the guy—Wendall only saved the men he owed somehow—but Mal doesn't seem like the rest of the brutes. He's the silent type. A thinker who gives away nothing unless he wants you to know. But if he's different, then why didn't he leave with the other prisoners who took off in the dark last night? What does he think he's going to get from following Wendall? Or maybe Mal doesn't have anyone to run to either?

"Look what I found!" Sporting new clothes, Cain leaves the Rite Aid with a bag of supplies in one hand and roughly grips a struggling, frightened young woman in the other. Yesterday, as they fought their way out of the prison and back to the truck, Cain was in his element, killing and hurting at will, with no thought for himself or anyone else. He comes across as fierce and confident, but brash. *Now, he's* not *a thinker.*

Upon seeing the other men in the parking lot, the woman's eyes widen, and she doubles her effort to struggle free from Cain's firm hold. "Let go of me! Help!"

Mal tenses, then scans the grocery store. *Is he looking for someone to intervene?* Hunter thinks. He scoffs at the idea that Mal might be waiting for Wendall to tell Cain to stop. It's folly to think Wendall cares for anyone but himself.

The woman throws a punch and a kick, but Cain laughs as he dodges both. "Shut it! There's more inside. I locked the women in the bathroom."

Fuck. Hunter scrambles backward, the sound of crunching gravel echoing in the quiet morning as he searches along the Rite Aid's brick wall. The restrooms should be on the outside. Near the back, he discovers a small window, glances at it, and then attempts to open the solid door. With a gentle creak, it opens, and he steps inside.

At the end of a long, dim hallway, overturned shelves and several bodies lie motionless in dark pools of liquid. In the store's stillness, dust motes float in the light streaming through the windows. Someone forced a short rack under the rattling bathroom handle to keep the door from opening. "Help!"

Hunter pushes the rack aside and opens the door, revealing two terrified women, their faces highlighted in a soft light. They back away. He places a finger to his lips and coaxes them forward.

"Alright, boys, since I found these bitches, I get first crack at 'em at camp." It's Cain, already heading back this way.

Time's up.

Hunter points the way and mouths, Follow me. Without waiting to see if the women have understood him, he leans on the solid door. It creaks open. Light filters in. They dart past him and scamper across the alleyway. He veers toward the parking lot, not looking back as he skirts the brick wall.

"Hunter?" Wendall is in the parking lot, looking for him.

Shit! With a determined set to his jaw, Hunter doubles his pace, his long hair a dark curtain across his scarred face.

"Hunter!" Wendall yells again, sounding closer.

Hunter slows, then fiddles with his zipper as he rounds the corner of the Rite Aid. "Yeah."

Over Wendall's shoulder, Hunter sees heavy bags of groceries have been placed haphazardly on a truck tailgate. Nearby, the terror-stricken woman Cain brought out earlier is in Mal's grip. This disappoints Hunter, but at least he saved the others. Perhaps this is the one way Hunter can help the good and innocent people in this world.

"There you are," Wendall says, turning back toward the store. "Come with me."

As Hunter follows his brother, he glances over at Mal one more time. The quiet prisoner tilts toward the alleyway. *So, he saw the women get away...*

Hunter challenges him with a direct stare, but Mal simply averts his gaze.

CHAPTER 10
May 23

Sadie's body starts to spasm the moment ice-cold water cascades over her. She splutters in shock on the forest floor, unable to shake the liquid from her eyes. Her arms are stiff, and the kink in her neck is painful. The worn strip of duct tape, though less taut than before, still secures her wrists to the base of the sturdy pine.

Something whizzes past Sadie's head, disturbing the air, and a sudden chill touches her stiff feet. He removed her boots.

Brent kicks her shinbone. "Get up!" When she doesn't move, he connects his fist with her face, and she hears a sharp crack. She groans. This fuels his drive, igniting a fire within him to continue. Her cheeks are so numb at this point, she almost can't feel his relentless attack. Blood fills her nostrils and throat, and Sadie chokes. Every so often, she tries to raise her legs, doing something, anything, to protect herself from his aggressive blows. Left exposed and devoid of any protection, Sadie faces his rage with no recourse.

***

In a semi-conscious state and shivering, Sadie lets out a low whine. She's lost track of time. Beneath the birdsong floating above her, she feels a burning ache between her shoulders, and her wrists throb with unbearable strain. She can't open her swollen eyes enough to make out the hour, but by the angle of the sunlight coming through the canopy, she figures it's morning. The sunshine gives her no warmth, and Sadie's fingers tremble as she continues to feel the rough bark of the tree, more out of habit now. The duct tape is no longer tight, but it still holds her captive: she's too weak to break it. The smell of earth and pine grounds her as the pain, ever present, ripples and throbs throughout her stiff limbs, her bones, her face.

Footsteps approach. "Wakey, wakey!" Brent produces a husky noise. She flinches as water droplets are sprayed against her cheek, trailed by stinging sensations. "Not so high and mighty now, are you?"

He spat in my face! She can't find the words to make him stop. Her throat is like sandpaper.

Unforgiving hands cut her thoughts short as Brent attempts to haul her up. The duct tape tears her flesh, but it's not the most agonizing aspect of her torment. Sadie's finally free, but she has no will left to fight back. The excruciating pain in her face and ribs cripples her. A series of moans escapes her numb lips.

A stinging sensation scores through her shirt and up her body. *Knife.*

Sadie feels removed as high-pitched screams tear out of her. The steel edge continues to traverse her body, slashing her skin, splitting her flesh. Warm liquid pours down her body unhindered.

"Nnn—!" she cries through heavy breaths. She knows begging him to stop won't work, but it's all she has left.

And she's right. It doesn't work. The burning sensation starts again. An animalistic cry explodes out of her, and somewhere deep within her, she prepares for the eternal end. Brent's continual slashing is too much.

Bang! A shrill outcry splits the air. It barely even registers as Sadie feels herself plummeting down, down.

"Oh, I'm sorry, did that hurt?"

An unknown man's voice? Confusion reigns in Sadie's mind.

"Don't." Brent laments. *Bang!* Brent screams.

Leaves rustle around Sadie. *Something's happening. What...? Who...?*

"Stop!"

An aggressive voice says, "Where I come from, we don't hurt women."

Sadie's so tired. *Why won't it end?* Is this what happens when you die? Desiring it like this?

"Where you're going, you'll wish you'd treated this young lady far kinder."

Something like dirt—tiny pebbles, perhaps?—strike her cheek, making her flinch. She hears the sound of something heavy being dragged along the ground.

Brent snivels, further away than a moment ago, and pleads, the fear sharp in his voice. "Stop shooting! You're hurting me." He howls.

"Don't care." The mysterious voice sounds unperturbed.

CHAPTER 11

Hunter feels the slap on his shoulder, tearing him away from his night-mare. He wakes to find Sonny above him. "Your turn."

This one is cocky and rubs Hunter the wrong way. Sonny thinks he knows more than everyone else and acts like it, which has caused him to have run-ins with several men in their group. Hunter wishes Wendall would just cut him loose. He's not sure what value Sonny has in his brother's eyes.

Hunter stretches out under the dying crackling firelight and rubs away the cold in his arms. The few men nearby appear mesmerized, their faces cast in orange as they gaze into the flames, lost in private thoughts. Fire-making was a skill he learned as a young boy, on the many nights he escaped into the woods. Those were the happiest times of his childhood. Alone, self-sufficient, and free.

Some men exchange hushed whispers as they voice their frustrations about losing the women while settling down to sleep, and with time, leave Hunter on watch alone. Seeing the men depart the Rite Aid empty-handed has raised Hunter's spirits somewhat. It feels nice, knowing he's done a bit of good for a change. It's not enough to erase his misdeeds—nothing will—but it's something.

He squints, peering past the men, making out the dark silhouette of the truck in the distance. The woman watches them from the truck bed, preferring to suffer the cold of night than to come closer to the men around the fire. It might be futile, but Hunter wants to help her escape, as well. He has to try. From the tailgate, he sees a long rope stretching away from her, ending in his brother

Wendall's sleeping grasp. If she tries to get away any further than she already is, he may feel the rope pull. Wendall was always a light sleeper growing up. *Is he still?*

Tricky.

Mal shifts in his sleep and faces away from the fire, catching Hunter's attention. He needs to be careful. Mal didn't appear to like the woman being held against her will, either, but it didn't mean he wouldn't take advantage of her if given the chance.

Hunter makes his move. He stands, stretches his neck, and rolls his shoulders, acting normal so as not to arouse suspicion. Hunter picks the pot of coffee off the fire and pours the black drink into a plastic cup, taking in the dark aroma that wafts upward, then strolls around the men. A few of them snore thunderous crescendos: something he plans to use to his benefit.

He takes a shot of liquid courage, not liking the bitterness or the grittiness of the grounds not caught by the filter. He has always been a coffee snob, but he knows not to complain: it's all they have. Taking one last look around and deciding no one is paying him any mind, Hunter approaches the truck bed, placing his arm and the cup on the side.

The woman seems unfazed by his approach, instead casting her wide gaze over the sleeping men who surround the truck bed. Earlier, he helped her do the dishes with Mal, so he figures she at least considers him less of a threat than the rest of them. Any trust she has of him certainly isn't to do with his facial scars.

She does not speak. Neither does he. Quietly, keeping his eyes on anything but her, as though he's surveying the trees for threats, he searches his pocket for the blade he keeps there, unlocks it, and serves it toward her. She gazes down at it, then back up at him.

When she doesn't take it, Hunter looks at her, then holds the knife out further, motioning at the rope, then flicks his head toward the darkness, beyond the trucks and heavy machinery they picked up.

She nods, accepts the gift, and once the rope relaxes between her and Wendall for a moment, she starts to cut at her bonds, careful to keep her head and shoulders from moving as much as possible.

Hunter doesn't want to leave her alone yet, so he grabs his now-empty cup with one hand and unzips his pants with the other, feigning like he is about to relieve himself. If anyone were to ask why they can't hear the trickling of his water, he knew he could blame the snoring men nearby.

With a last stroke of the blade, the rope breaks free. A man in the bed turns around, his hand smacking her on the back. Her body tenses with fear, her eyes on Hunter, silently pleading for his help. But Hunter raises a finger and motions for her to breathe slowly, deeply. They stare at each other for what seems like forever, listening to the sounds of the wind and the men breathing.

Hunter glances back at the fire. No movement. He turns back to her. She can't walk to the tailgate without alerting the men sawing logs around her. He's closer and can help her over the side. And so, with outstretched hands, he gestures for her to come to him.

She doesn't move at first, her only twitching muscles being the ones in her hand as she clutches the blade tight. The air crackles with distrust. A silent tension that vibrates between them. *Move, dammit.* He's her sole way out. How can he convey his intentions? He points at the knife. "Keep it."

She gazes over at the tailgate and rises in slow motion. He wills her not to go that way, shaking his head ever so slightly.

Hunter sighs softly with relief when she turns her head toward him again. She folds the knife and shoves it into her jeans. But then she hesitates once more.

"I've got you," he whispers, almost too quietly for even him to hear, then he holds his breath.

She steps across and straddles the man resting below Hunter, trepidation written on her face. Her breath comes in short, rapid gasps, and her obvious fear causes an icy dread to grip his heart. But Hunter keeps his fingers outstretched to her the whole time. A tremor runs through her hands as she connects with his steady ones. He breathes out, grateful for her trust, and silently pats the side of the truck.

She swings her legs over the side. He worries she's going to assume this is all a trick and strike him before he can attack her, but this doesn't happen. Instead, she allows him to lower her to the ground. He moves forward slightly, forcing her to step further out of sight, then leans in and grabs her by the shoulders, searching out her eyes. "Don't look back. Stay near the highway, but not on it. Good luck."

She cups his face in her hands and gazes into his eyes in thanks before letting go. He hadn't expected that, but as he watches her follow his instructions with careful purpose, the warm feeling in his belly grows.

Hunter grabs the empty cup off the truck and saunters back toward the fire. Tomorrow, they'll get to the farm. He scans the bodies around the camp, counting too many men. Their meager stockpile of supplies won't last long. Wendall says he has a plan to keep everyone fed and happy, but he hasn't divulged it yet. Hunter guesses it involves growing crops while continuing to steal whatever else they need in the meantime. He prays that it won't include more humans.

CHAPTER 12
May 26

Water trickles from above and passes Sadie's parched lips, drawing out gargled, painful moans. A wet rag tenderly dabs her face. In her delirium, words sound like distant whispers that Sadie can't decipher. Pain has spread so thoroughly throughout her body that she's not sure any part of her is whole and healed, and the slightest touch, anywhere, is unbearable. Time doesn't exist as it used to. A second feels like a minute, and the sun moves around the sky so much, Sadie assumes she must be falling in and out of consciousness. The world is strange, her body is strange, and so, Sadie retreats inwards. Did her mother visit her, or was it a figment of Sadie's imagination? What was she trying to tell her?

And then, after feeling like she was on the brink of a never-ending darkness for so long, Sadie awakens again, only this time, she is able to focus on a ceiling of branches tied in rows. Shelter. It feels jarring to come out of sleep when she was so sure she was conscious just a moment ago, so she takes her time. The stinging and burning are still there, searing through her chest, face, and wrists, but less omnipresent than it was before. The agony ebbs and flows in its intensity, testing her will to remain silent, but she endures it to the best of her ability out of fear. If Brent learns she is alert, the torture will begin once more.

"Don't move, darlin'. You'll ruin my handiwork."

Not Brent. The exertion of moving her head almost causes her to black out as razor-sharp pain slices through her face. Sadie thinks she felt his hand on her, but she's not sure.

"It's alright. You're safe." The man's voice has a sadness to it. Under normal circumstances, Sadie would back away from it as quickly as possible, not trusting it until she could get a better sense of who its owner is and what he wants with her, but this is not a luxury she has.

Through her hazy vision, she spies a man with a gray crewcut looking down at her with kind, warm eyes. He looks like Clint Eastwood in his seventies.

"Where...?" Her voice sounds dry, broken, barely audible.

"My Gertie here took offense." He holds up what looks like a pistol, ignoring her question. "Saw someone who deserved to leave this world much sooner than perhaps nature intended."

Could it be true? No more torture. "Dead?"

"As a doornail, my dear."

A sob escapes. Tears roll down her cheeks, irritating her more than they should, and trickle into her hairline. *What did Brent do to me?* She feels pressure on her shoulders, but she doesn't feel trapped. It comforts her, and staying still is less painful than moving.

"He was a very intense individual until he saw my barrel between his eyes."

Sadie hears determined conviction mixed with disgust. Tentatively, she raises her hand toward her rib cage. *Ouch!* She jerks her arm down and takes a sharp breath. Sadie's wrists throb with the phantom pain of the duct tape, a dull ache that feels like fire against her skin.

"No movin' now." He points to her chest. "You've broke somethin' important there." He swings his finger up to her head. "You've got some bumps on your pretty little noggin, too."

With tender hands and a keen eye, he inspects her forehead. "I sutured you up in places I'd rather not mention. Hope you don't mind." He points to her cheek. "Hopefully, these heal well."

She's not sure what he's referring to, but she can guess by the sharp sting in her chest and face. "How long...out?"

"'Bout two days." He vanishes from her sight.

"Need...get to...family." The effort of so many words sucks the energy from her.

He reappears, protecting a spoon that he brings to her lips. She tastes beef in the cold fluid. Swallowing hurts, but the liquid coats her dry mouth, and she welcomes the relief.

"Gettin' ahead of yourself, girl. Your peepers are all swollen." More broth flows down her throat. "I'll take care of ya like I did for my late wife. You got a name? Mine's Carl."

"Sadie."

The spoon and Carl disappear again. "Expect you're sufferin', so I'll scrounge up meds for ya."

"Where?"

Silence greets her.

***

May 29

Morning light seeps through cracks in the walls of the cramped shelter. Sadie lies in the same place, in the same upward-facing position, her head cradled by a soft pillow. The inflammation in her face has subsided: enough, at least, for her to open her eyes and see a little better.

Carl has proved himself to be very crafty and resourceful. He built the stretcher she is lying on so he can move her in and out of the shelter on a whim and with relative ease. Although Sadie's lost track of the days, he has cared for her the entire time, even washing and brushing her hair every day, like her mom used to. When he finishes, he tucks her back in the shelter and surrounds her in a rough blanket with his experienced yet gentle hands.

Carl shimmies in with an armload of food and pill bottles. He plunks his booty down on a rough stump beside her.

"Where do you"—her stitches pull—"find this stuff?"

He shakes pills out of a bottle, cups her neck, and helps her swallow them down with a spoonful of the same beef water he gave her before. "Assisted livin' place I lived in. Had to hide Gertie, but a decent residence otherwise. If you sift through enough crap, you can find useful things."

Even though she can see a little better now, her puffy face is still unbearable to touch. She wants to know what Brent did to her, but it would take too much out of her to sit up, plus she doubts anyone has a mirror to hand. But more than that, Sadie itches to find her family, and knowing her body needs to heal before she can resume her journey fills her with frustration. "Sift? What happened?"

"I was outside, tendin' our garden." He holds his hand skyward. "There was a bright light, then I found myself in the shed. How'd you end up in the forest?"

The mushroom cloud. Sadie had forgotten about that with everything that's transpired. She's been in and out of consciousness for untold days. Her only constant: Carl. He tends her wounds with trained hands, keeps her on painkillers, and feeds her what she's determined is broth. She feels minimal pain most of the time, so he has been true to his word about looking after her. He seems far too spry to have been in an assisted living place, though.

"Bus crash. Wanted to get to Spokane, so I hiked it."

He turns curious eyes to her. "Your family in town?"

"They won't be there now. I'll have to follow them to a place in Idaho."

He opens a Swiss knife, cuts off a piece of apple, and slides it into his mouth. "How far is that, 'cause the city's in shambles?"

She raises her head. "What?" Her skull throbs.

He puts the knife somewhere she can't see, lays a hand on her shoulder, and applies soft pressure to encourage her to lie back down. "All the power is out, so the nights are pitch black. Some of the city was flattened by the explosion, though there are still a few buildings standin'. The valley fared better."

Not a nuke, then. Sadie breathes a sigh of relief. At least she doesn't have to add radiation poisoning to her list of maladies.

"I suspect we must have been attacked." Carl retrieves the blade and carves out a handful of slices. "The good ol' US of A has a lot more holes in the ground, I expect. Hope we retaliated."

"Why do you think that?"

"Spokane wouldn't be high on the list of cities to take out. Now the base, that's a different story."

Gina... "My sister!" Her apartment is just a few minutes away from Spokane's military site.

He reaches out to stop her from rising again. "Hey, there's nothin' you can do 'bout it except get better. Old Carl will take care of you in the meantime."

Sadie knows he's right, but he's still a stranger, and trusting a stranger doesn't come easily. Her father's words from her childhood come back to her: "Trust no one when SHTF."

She observes Carl's relaxed demeanor as he chews the apple. Suspicion lifts its ugly head. For someone who seems to understand that the world as they know it has just ended, he is showing no fear, and his survival skills are impressive to say the least. "Why are you helping me?"

He swallows the apple down and ponders this question, then looks straight into her eyes. "'Cause that's what decent men do." He wiggles his way out of the shelter. "Be back soon."

A little while later, Carl crawls back into the shade of the shelter, bringing with him a variety of supplies in a box. He settles at his stump and opens the Swiss knife again.

"Carl?" Sadie asks, her voice husky.

"Hmm?" he mumbles as he picks through the box.

"You mentioned your wife before. Did she...? You know, in the attack."

He pauses, and his eyes seem to focus on something beyond the box—beyond the shelter even—as he appears to conjure up a memory. "She was a hell of a woman, if you don't mind my swearin'?" He directs the question at her. Sadie grunts no. "She took me by surprise at first glance. Wore a bright blue dress, the color of your eyes." He closes his eyes and smiles, and Sadie suspects he is seeing his wife before him right now, the way she was. "Lace at the neck. Sensible shoes. Prettiest sight I ever saw." Carl cuts an orange open and deposits a small piece into her mouth. "Ya ever been in love?" he asks gruffly.

She eats the slice as slowly as possible. Partly to savor the fruit as her stitches pull tight, radiating soreness from her face, down into her neck, and partly to avoid answering the question.

His lips curve up. "What's his name?"

She swallows. "I didn't say I was ever in love."

"You don't get this old and not understand what quiet means in a woman." Carl drops another tiny piece into her mouth.

She eyes him as she chews. "How do you know you're in love?"

"Let's see if I can remember." Carl shuts his eyes and smiles again. "I felt all the air leave my lungs." He edges toward Sadie and props an eye open. "I forgot to breathe, you see." Then he closes it again as he leans back. "She got me with that beautiful smile. Thought my heart would beat right out of my chest. I was a goner."

She's amazed at the detail, the tenderness with which he recounts the moment he met his love. *Wish someone would see me that way...*

Sadie had misinterpreted Carl's intentions toward her. He's been nothing but helpful. Hell, he even saved her from certain death.

"Liam."

"Liam, eh? When it's the right one, there's nothin' like it."

"That's the thing. He isn't the right one. But I wish he was."

***

June 4

Outside, among the trees, Carl tends an unstable pot over the flames of a smokeless fire. Sitting against a tree trunk, Sadie watches the steam rise from the pot. It's been a hard two weeks since the "incident." She's not ready to call it anything else and tries not to think about what happened to her.

It was tricky getting out of the shelter. Carl wanted her to stay on the stretcher, but she insisted on standing up on her own steam. She traces one of the monstrous scars above her belly button with her fingers. The color is an angry red, a shade so intense, it seems to vibrate with rage. In contrast to the one curving around her hip, this one is shallower, shorter, and sits higher on her body.

Sadie's facial skin pulls when she moves her mouth to drink or eat, calling attention to how hideous her face must be. Carl undertook the painstaking task of removing Sadie's stitches a few days ago. He felt embarrassed when she had to undress so he could access the delicate places, as he referred to them. She's not sure how he stitched her up to begin with, but his hands were steady enough, and he said her wounds were healing well. She wonders if he's just flattering to deceive, but then again, she hasn't had an infection all this time. Sadie supposes it's because Carl has been so meticulous about slathering antibiotic cream on her face and body every day.

She stops tracing the scar. Sadie will never look the way she did before.

Closing her eyes and tilting her face toward the sun, Sadie lets the warmth seep in as she breathes deep, the scent of pine on the crisp morning breeze. It's almost calming and brings back memories of past camping trips. She expects her dad to walk out of the bushes any minute with a toilet paper roll in hand. This vision pains her, so she looks for a distraction. "What did you do before you retired?"

"Plumbin'. Weldin'." Carl doesn't look up from his task of guarding the pot. "Stuff like that."

"You know a lot about rough camping and finding food." Once she was able to stomach something more than broth, Carl started fishing from a nearby river to get her some solid food. She wonders if he has any children or grandchildren. Like her father, he doesn't offer much about himself unless asked.

"Oh, that?" He stirs the pot with a spatula. "I lived a different life before Sophie."

He talks about his wife with reverence. Sadie believes he's still in love with Sophie, even though she's gone from his life. His face lights up whenever he mentions her name. *No one will love me like that. Especially not now.*

"A different life?"

Carl hesitates, then grabs a small branch and stokes the fire. She waits him out, curious about what he'll say.

"Ranger."

Her forehead skin pinches as her eyebrows rise. "Really? My dad's a Marine."

He perks up, just as surprised as she is. "Hmm... Well, now his preppin' doesn't seem so crazy. We military types always have a Plan B." He gazes across the fire, smirking at her. "And a Plan C, D, and E." His mention of Plan B reminds her of Tilly's last words, and a wave of sadness follows.

"Dad and his Marine buddies have been working on Haven since before I was born. It was for their eventual retirement." Her dad had been planning to move there along with Penny and Parker once Sadie's brother graduated. *He wouldn't graduate now.*

Carl corrals a cloth to protect his hands and pours soup from the off-kilter pot into a chipped mug. "Like father, like daughter."

"What do you mean?"

"You told me you were studyin' to be a librarian, but I emptied your pockets, remember? You had a Plan B, too."

Sadie brushes her fingers against the cool, bumpy metal of the EGA pin in her jeans.

His eyes drop in shame. "Hope you don't think badly o' me?"

Sadie won't be a librarian if it's as bad as Carl says it is out there, and she won't be able to do Plan B, either. What good is she if she couldn't even defend herself against Brent? "No. It means nothing anymore." She releases the pin, leaving it in her pocket. "Not after the mess I got myself into."

"Have nothing to be embarrassed about. Shit happens to the best of us. 'Scuse the language."

She acknowledges his efforts to make her feel better, but the red on her belly draws her eye again. Her scars will never fully heal, and she'll always be reminded that she failed, that she's not good enough.

"You'll make mistakes, but that"—he points at her pocket—"wasn't one of 'em." He bends and passes over the chipped mug. "He's the one to blame. No man should ever treat a woman that way. As I said, an animal that needed to be put down." Carl yanks a spoon from his coat. "Be proud of your accomplishment, Sadie. No one can take that away from you."

He picks up the pot without ceremony and blows on the contents before scooping some out to test its temperature. "So, you knit? Seems a strange hobby for one so young as yourself to be takin' up. Sophie loved to knit."

She smiles, thinking of Tilly. "I want to learn."

Chapter 13

From the barn, Hunter approaches the house, a pitchfork in hand, its rough wood irritating his new sores that haven't yet hardened into calluses. He leans it against the porch railing, brushes the sweat from his forehead, and surveys the field with pride. They've seeded the first and have already started work on the second one.

Wendall talks to Gideon in the field. Measuring his expression, Hunter figures they're arguing. Nothing new. Wendall says something, then walks toward the house, cutting off his brother's reply. He places his foot on a stair and steadies himself with the railing. "How's the barn coming, Hunter?"

With only a handful of beds, the men have spent the last couple of weeks, sleeping in any available space in the house. It isn't ideal, and Wendall's prison escapees are grumpy and tired, but what choice do they have with the bears coming out of hibernation, not to mention the mountain lions on the prowl for deer? They have been clearing out the barn for the purpose of setting up a place to sleep inside, but it's proven both time-consuming and taxing to do it by hand. "Rotting inside out. It's disgusting and still not ready to live in."

Wendall stares in contemplation at the ground, tapping his fingers on the banister. It's a pattern Hunter knows well: thumb to pinkie and then the reverse, from pinkie to thumb. It's what Wendall does when he needs to say something but can't quite figure out how to say it.

Hunter doesn't want to know what his brother is thinking, so he speaks again before his brother can finish his thought. "We'll need to insulate the walls and doors if you want the men to sleep out there."

Ten yards away, Sonny steps out of the field to a barrel and slurps water from the ladle.

Cain follows, then veers toward them. "We going soon, boss?"

Almost from the moment they arrived weeks ago at the farm, Wendall had wanted to dispatch men to search for more labor, but he miscalculated the work that needed doing and couldn't send them out until the first field was established. Knowing that they were likely to cause trouble, Hunter had consistently pressed how high the workload was around the place and that it made it impossible to spare any men. But now the first field is done...

"I'm leaving today."

Today? Hunter searches out the sun approaching the height of the sky. *A little late to be leaving now.*

"I've decided who will come with me and who will search. Gather the men."

Hunter's not sure where this is leading. He wants to challenge his brother, but rather than the prisoners losing faith in Wendall over time, like Hunter had hoped might happen, the escapees seem to revere his leadership more and more with each passing day. He knows it would be dangerous to question his brother openly, and so, he bites his tongue.

Cain salutes and withdraws, not acknowledging Hunter. If he were easily offended, Hunter would find it insulting.

An hour later, Hunter is driving down a long logging road, jostling through the ruts in the rough terrain, with Wendall beside him. Besides a few fallen trees, they've had no setbacks so far.

They left Gideon in charge of the farm. Letting his younger brother off his leash doesn't sit well with Hunter. Gideon is as impulsive and ambitious as their elder brother, but he lacks Wendall's cold intelligence. *He'll fuck it up somehow.*

Before they mounted the trucks and left, Wendall made a point of telling the men he sent out into the wilderness that if they found any women, they were to bring them back to the farm but not to touch them until he got back. Hunter had scoffed at that. There was no way Gideon would follow that order. But he should have kept quiet. Instead, Hunter made the mistake of opening his mouth and saying he should stay with Gideon. Wendall didn't like him assigning himself his own orders in front of the men, which landed him a ride to the city instead.

Wendall hasn't spoken since they left. Hunter is fine with that because he has nothing worth saying. He checks the rearview. All the vehicles are still following, bumping through the ruts back there.

Hunter slows down as they approach the highway. No one would be on the road now, but the ingrained habit remains in Hunter to look both ways first.

"Stop here."

Hunter complies.

Wendall's door creaks as he opens it. "You take half the men and find supplies for the farm. Anything's better than nothing."

Hunter slides his arm across the back of the bench seat and leans forward. "Where are you going?"

"Labor." Wendall slams the door in Hunter's face before he can ask for an explanation.

CHAPTER 14
June 15

Hunter drives down the highway, the rumble of the engine the only thing filling the silence between him and the two men beside him. He's lost track of the days and weeks since they left the farm. It had taken them far longer than he'd wanted to gather what they needed. It wasn't just finding the things: with the world ended and descended into chaos, they had to survive doing it. The world has gone crazy since the missile dropped weeks ago. Most people have cleared out their properties and taken to God knows where, but those who have stayed defend their homes with a shoot-first-and-ask-questions-later approach. Hunter and his men found less resistance at the seed and hardware stores, but any store they passed that sold food was either impenetrable or empty. The biggest delay, however, came when thieves stole their transportation, forcing them to find new vehicles that would run. They tried several trucks, but they all suffered breakdowns at one point or another. At last, they were heading back to the farm, exhausted from the trip's turmoil, and Hunter is praying their latest wheels can handle the journey.

As Hunter turns off the highway, he realizes this is the spot where he last saw his brother. *Labor.* It left a sour taste in Hunter's mouth. His brother is deceiving him somehow, he's certain. *But why?*

Hunter follows behind the only combine they stole that started. Not having farmed since he was a teenager, he found himself at a loss in identifying the different machines or determining which ones were worth stealing. However, the man in the truck next to him proved helpful. He said everything they manufactured for farms nowadays has a solar model. Super advanced or something, and the combine they have stolen is solar powered. Pilfering diesel proved to be too dangerous—they lost two men attempting that—so they instead returned to where they stole the vehicles to appropriate the equipment necessary to keep the machines charged.

The deaths brought up the loss of his younger brother, Greg. The pain of it lingers. With all their preparations for the farm and the trip into town, Hunter has had little time to dwell on his brother's death. Or grieve for him. His family has never tolerated anyone expressing any emotion besides anger, so Greg's burial was a silent affair, without fanfare, carried out by Gideon and himself. Wendall didn't show.

Behind him is the constant roar of tractor engines and giant tires churning up the dirt. More finds, along with other various solar-powered farm vehicles and solar equipment, to keep the farm running.

One thing is for sure: they are going to be stuck on the farm for a long time. The thought saddens Hunter. It's a place full of painful memories, but having seen what the rest of the world is like out there, he knows it's the safest place for him. The one place he never wanted to see again is his salvation in this upside-down world they are now living in.

They approach the turn to the farm. With the new equipment, they will be able to remove the hay and set up a proper place for the men to sleep in the barn. His truck is filled to the brim with building materials and tools for fortifying the buildings. The other vehicles they poached carried even more.

Hunter flashes the headlights.

The combine turns down a dirt road, and Hunter follows. To maintain an unobstructed view, Hunter slows his vehicle and lingers behind while the harvester kicks up dust on the logging road to their new home. He glances in the rearview mirror to make sure the other vehicles in the convoy are still tailing him. They all turn without incident.

A few miles later, the combine slows down to a crawl, then stops altogether. Sonny emerges from the cab and indicates the direction ahead.

Hunter steps halfway out of the truck. "What's up?"

"Wendall."

That's all Hunter needs to know. He shuts the engine off, turns to the vehicles behind him, and makes the sign of cutting his throat. As Hunter walks past the harvester, the soft solar noise abruptly falls silent, and at last he can hear the sounds of crunching dirt and snapping branches from under his boots. Car doors slam shut as the men behind exit their vehicles for a stretch. Hunter expects to find men changing tires or repairing engines up ahead, but all he hears is people conversing, and then his heart sinks.

Under guard, terrified men and women, tightly bound with ropes, are speaking to each other and their captors from the back of a truck. And among them, he recognizes Giles Hutchison. Like a storm suddenly appearing to destroy everything in its wake, Hunter feels his anger is about to get the better of him. *Labor?*

Giles's accusatory stare tracks him as he walks by. The shame of what his brother has done to someone who was so good to Hunter is too much, and he averts his gaze. Hunter passes two more truckloads of terrified people and a truck hauling a horse trailer. He hears chickens clucking inside one of the vehicles before finally encountering men working on a giant fallen tree blocking the road.

If his brother has kidnapped Hunter's old boss, then Kessie can't be far. She'll be a woman now. Possibly a mother and—

"Hunter!"

Hunter snaps his head toward the sound of her voice and finds Kessie in the back seat of the first truck in the convoy, her hands bound. A striking older woman with captivating green eyes is sitting with her. *What the fuck?* He leans against the window. "Kessie. Are you alright?"

"He's gone crazy. Help us, please."

"You made it!" On his knees, grappling with a harness, Wendall grins. He jumps to his feet and advances toward Hunter with open arms. He seems genuinely happy to see his brother, which takes Hunter aback a little. "Was the trip fruitful?" Hunter's ill temper must be apparent as Wendall's smile fades.

"Labor?! You said labor. You let these—"

Wendall seizes Hunter by the back of the neck and drags him a safe distance into the forest, away from prying eyes and listening ears. His grip is too tight. "What's wrong with you?"

Hunter wriggles out of his brother's grasp and faces him. "What's wrong with *me*? You can't kidnap Kessie's family! Let them go."

Wendall pauses for a moment, staring at the ground. "I went to see if Kessie was alright."

"How did you know where she was?"

"I had her followed long ago. It wasn't hard, brother."

The disbelief overwhelms Hunter as he grapples with his brother's despicable actions. Then again, should he even be surprised? "Why?"

Wendall hesitates again, then takes an emotional breath. When his eyes come up, Hunter sees the distress in them. "Because I love her."

The audacity! "Love?" Hunter points back the way they came. "That's not love."

Wendall's face twists into an ugly grimace. This is the side of his brother he knows all too well. "Yeah? How would you know?" Wendall doesn't ask questions unless he knows the answers. He's using it against him.

Hunter doesn't reply out of spite.

"What's done is done. There's no going back."

"You can't do this."

Wendall exhales his anger out through his nose. "I had to. We need them, and now they need us. Someone has to protect them."

He is crazy. "They didn't need protecting."

"The farm was burning when we arrived! We saved them from their attackers."

Saved them? Hunter suspects no attackers existed. It would be just like his brother to make himself look like the hero. *Does he think I'm that stupid?* "I don't believe you."

The shrill sound of a saw sends a piercing screech through the forest, sending animals scurrying and fluttering in all directions.

Wendall narrows his eyes. "You don't?" Without another word, he turns and walks back out of the trees.

Shit. Wendall's departure is too quick for Hunter's liking, but he follows. When someone pushes his brother, he does rash things. *Can I keep him under control?*

Wendall walks straight to the truck where the women sit, ducks down, and gazes through the window. "Kessie, was your farm burning when we arrived?"

Kessie hesitates, but with downcast eyes, she answers with a nod.

"Did you want to come with us?"

She mouths, No, decisively and without hesitation.

"Would you have survived without crops?"

She bites her lip to keep it from quivering. "No, but—"

Wendall turns around and faces Hunter with crossed arms. "You believe me now?"

Hunter's intuition tells him something is off, but as he considers his answer, he spies Cain and some of the other prisoners scowling in his direction. Finally, he nods in agreement, and the action is enough to make his stomach turn.

Wendall brings him in for a hug. "Stop looking for problems and help me solve them."

He lets go, but Hunter's grip remains strong. "Can you at least untie them?"

Wendall slaps Hunter's back in a friendly gesture. "I'll release them once they relax and acknowledge that we're their sole chance for salvation."

So, when hell freezes over, then.

Chapter 15

With the fallen tree sliced up and removed from the road, the convoy resumes the final leg of its journey to the farm. As Hunter drives in silence once more, following his brother's truckfuls of captives—including people he knows and cares about—his anger festers. To make things worse, Kessie's father, Giles, is at the back of the truck ahead of him, and his unwavering gaze fills Hunter with a cold sense of guilt and shame. *How the hell am I going to get them out of this?*

They emerge from under the canopy of trees. Beams of sunlight break through the clouds, illuminating the fields that stretch out before them. Rows of earth are dark and damp, a clear sign that a recent rainstorm passed through shortly before their arrival.

Against the backdrop of a dull, grayish sky to the west, the farmhouse catches the eye with its faded yellow appearance. The truck rattles and jerks as they navigate the rough, overgrown driveway on their way to the house.

Wendall parks his vehicle and drags an unwilling Kessie out by her hand from the passenger side. The other woman follows. Hunter is pleased to see they're untied at least. Wendall directs the farm vehicles toward the barn, along with the trucks carrying the captives.

The moment Hunter stops his truck in front of Wendall's, everyone piles out, the doors slamming shut in unison. His hair dances in the breeze, brushing against his scarred face. Wendall's stance causes him to pause, and as his brother surveys the surrounding area, Hunter does the same.

The second field's half done, but no guards are working it or lazing around on the farmhouse porch. Where are the men they left behind? If Gideon is here, why hasn't he heard them and come outside by now? Hell, with the noise the new farm vehicles are making, he would have heard them from a mile away.

The cacophony of noise rumbles to a stop after the men piloting leave them in the fenced-in field. Stepping out of the combine, Sonny joins some others and, together, they make their way back toward the main house. The male captives, still bound with ropes, are being led to the barn door, which Hunter notes is still swinging on rusty hinges. Meanwhile, another set of Wendall's prison escapees lines the women up along the back of the trucks, tying each captive to the next as the women cringe in fear.

Wendall glances in Hunter's direction. "Something's not right." He barks orders at the approaching prisoners: "Sonny, Junior, with Hunter. Take the back door." He points to some other men. "You two, front door. Sweep the h ouse."

Hunter leads the four men to the farmhouse where, as instructed, the groups split up. Moving with deliberate caution, two escapees slowly make their way toward the front of the building, weapons at the ready. Hunter leads the other two around the corner of the house, his gun out in front, to the back door, constantly scanning for any signs of movement. His skin prickles the moment he sees dried blood leading from the back door to the nearby bushes. The end of the trail reveals a large patch of dark grass. "Someone bled out here," he says, more to himself than the men standing behind him, "but where's the body?"

Hunter returns to the back door of the house to find it ajar, but not smashed in. He's apprehensive about entering the kitchen. More than any other room in the building, it's the one that brings back the worst memories. He motions for Sonny and Junior to lead the way, taking the extra seconds to muster his courage so he can bring himself to step in behind them. At six feet, Hunter is usually the tallest in any given space, and even with the two men in front of him, he has a clear view of the room.

There's nothing out of place in the kitchen. A man enters from the living room, shaking his head. Sonny opens the cupboards for all to see. The food appears untouched, and someone has arranged the mismatched dishes and placed them on the counter. Gideon is nowhere near a neat freak. Someone else did this.

Hunter gestures for Junior to follow him down the hallway and up the stairs. *One more floor.* Each step creaks even more loudly than Hunter can remember as he ascends. The musty smell still lingers, mixed with the earthy scent of the fields. He recalls that whenever he needed a break, Hunter would retreat to his favorite spot: the roof. Growing up with his grandparents, it was the only safe place in the house.

He and Junior make quick work of searching the empty rooms. They find no threats, though there are plenty of unsettling clues.

Junior calls down. "No one's up here."

Relaxing the grip on his weapon, Hunter leans into the door frame of what was once his grandparents' bedroom. He takes in what he's seeing and does not like it one bit. Blood: lots of it. There's a large dark stain in the middle of the room, and splashes all over the bare mattress, the patterned walls, and even the ceiling. The space carries the aura of a ritual sacrifice. *It's just missing the pentagram and candles.*

Junior waits at the top of the stairs, clutching his stomach. Hunter pushes away from the wall. The scene back there only heightens Hunter's sense of danger. It appears like everyone just up and left, but the bloodstains say otherwise.

From the first floor, a man's voice carries up. "Clear, boss."

"Separate the rest of the women and bring them up to the house," Wendall commands. As Hunter descends the steps again, he sees his brother standing outside on the porch.

"Let me go," Kessie says, her voice strained.

Wendall raises his arm, and Hunter hears the audible sound of a slap before his brother says, "Shut it!"

"Enculé!"

That wasn't Kessie, Hunter thinks. *Must be the green-eyed blonde.*

"Be nice, Kessie," Wendall says, "or I'll make it worse for your family."

She mutters something to him through gritted teeth that Hunter can't hear, but he feels some pride in knowing that Kessie has a backbone. Someone has to when it comes to dealing with Wendall.

Wendall comes inside the house with a flustered Kessie in tow, her red cheek stirring up Hunter's emotions. Wendall glances at him, then continues into the living room.

One of Wendall's lackies shoves the blonde inside and against the wall. She yelps and fights to free herself, to no avail.

The roughness irritates Hunter. He moves up behind the man, scanning the room on his approach. The old couches are as he remembers them, with their faded floral print hidden beneath, torn in places where some curious animal had taken the stuffing, bleached by the sunlight coming through the cracked window panes.

The blonde wrestles her arm out of the man's grasp. *"Sac à merde!"*

This one has spunk. Hunter smiles at her insult, then he taps the man on the shoulder. "Let her go."

He hasn't spoken rudimentary French in so long, but he tries to speak it, anyway, knowing he's butchering the language. *"Calme-toi, mademoiselle."*

Her anger transfers from the other man to Hunter. Her mouth opens—

Hunter steps into her sphere and clasps her hands together, startling her. *"Chut, mademoiselle. S'il vous plaît..."* Forgetting the word for sit, he motions toward the nearest sofa. "Sit."

Her eyelid twitches, and he can see she's still angry, but speaking French did the trick and disarmed her enough to follow his direction.

With Kessie still in his grasp, Wendall observes their exchange. Hunter relishes the surprise etched on his face.

"I didn't know you spoke French, brother?"

Hunter glares back at him. "I learned a little while I was living with the Hutchisons, Wendall. And look at how we're repaying them for their kindness."

When Wendall doesn't respond, Hunter averts his eyes, instantly regretting it when they land on the dining table. He can't help but remember the day when their grandfather slammed his eldest brother's face into it.

Wendall's surprise turns to irritation, and Hunter is certain his brother knows what he's thinking. To Wendall, that moment was his weakest, not only because he was overpowered, but also because their grandmother forced the other three boys to witness the humiliating scene. Wendall's terrified screams had reverberated through the dreary room as the blood sprayed from his nose on impact. It was an image Hunter could never forget.

Wendall shoves Kessie into a beat-up, threadbare armchair, his attention drawn to the substantial bloodstain that mars the weathered but freshly swept floor. Whoever fell there, died there. Wendall casts his eyes back onto Kessie. For a moment, she's sitting on the edge of her seat, looking like she's ready to bolt. But under his hard stare, she shrinks from him. Blood oozes from her lip.

Hunter distracts Wendall and says, "The bedroom upstairs is covered in blood, and there's a pile of ropes on the floor in another." The rope, coarse and worn, is a mystery to Hunter, but its placement suggests that Gideon and his men may have been restraining people with it. The silence presses in on him, amplifying the unsettling feeling in his belly. Gideon enjoyed women, but he wouldn't have taken off with them and killed his own men.

One of the men shuffles in behind Hunter. "There's blood all over the downstairs bathroom as well."

Sighing heavily, Wendall's troubled gaze moves to the dining room wall. Hunter follows his brother's eyes to see the series of bullet holes that zig-zag across the old, discolored paper.

"Time to beef up security," Wendall says to Hunter without looking at him. "Take a gander and see what the neighbors are up to."

"Why? What have they done?"

"They did this."

"You can't jump to conclusions without proof. Assuming this wasn't one of your crazed followers, who let's not forget, are convicted felons, it might have been anyone. Any group could have come by and attacked."

"Wendall?" Sonny calls him from the door. "One of the men found something."

Wendall hauls Kessie up and out of the chair. She resists, but the moment Wendall exerts pressure on Kessie's arm, she gives in with a quiet moan of surrender.

The blonde rises to intervene, but Hunter holds her back. Instead, she redirects her fury onto him, slapping and scratching at his arms and face. *Go ahead. You can't make my face any worse.*

"Miss, please stay here," he says to her in French. Once she's sitting down again, Hunter passes the man at the door. "Watch her, but with care, or you will answer to me."

Sonny leads them outside, to the tiny graveyard at the back of the property with its wrought-iron fence. Large trees shade the weathered cement graves that are no longer readable. Time has made sure of that.

Hunter has only ever been inside the fencing twice before in his life. He and his brothers buried their grandmother long ago in an unmarked grave next to their grandfather's, which they had dug the year before hers. He doesn't want to remember them, though his nightmares ensure he will never forget.

Hunter's eyes move to the spot where he buried Greg. The third and most recent time he was here, wasn't horrifying. Just sad.

"What am I looking at?" Wendall asks. "It's just the graveyard."

The only grave still recognizable is his mother's. At first, his grandfather had merely fashioned a simple cross to show where she had been laid to rest. He'd never shell out money for a pointless grave marker, but one day, a massive stone showed up with her name engraved on it: *Holly Greaves*. On some level, the bastard loved her, in his twisted way.

"There's a recent burial." Sonny extends his fingers toward the other side of the rusted iron fence. "And it's not tiny."

Hunter spots the immense pile of fresh dirt as they turn the corner of the family graveyard. Anger mixed with dread punches through his bittersweet nostalgia.

"Ow! You're hurting me!" Kessie yanks hard as she tries to free herself from Wendall's grip.

This time, he releases her. "Sonny, dig up the bodies. I want a head count... And find my brother." There's a hint of emotion in his voice. Sadness. Regret. It's subtle, but Hunter's sure it's there. For the first time. Maybe the only time.

Sonny nods and scurries off to do Wendall's bidding.

"Hunter!"

"Yes."

"This"—Wendall points at the mass grave—"is why we are going to investigate those people. They came across and murdered our family...our brother."

Hunter wants to refute Wendall's words, but he can't. Someone came over, killed them, and then went through the trouble of burying the bodies. A psychotic prison escapee wouldn't do that, nor would a random group passing by looking for supplies.

Hunter has questions, too, though. *What did Gideon do to provoke them to do this?*

Wendall steps close to Hunter. "This is why you have to listen to me. If those people are hostile, we need to protect ourselves from this threat."

As much as it pains him to admit it, his brother is right. Hunter sure as hell didn't want to end up dead. "What's the plan?"

Chapter 16
June 16, Haven Compound

Liam sits among a large group in the center of the buried Haven compound. The room is a dome and a massive space curated to accommodate the many who now dwell here. Liam guesses the communal area alone is ten thousand square feet. The natural light from the recessed skylights lands on the tables and chairs of the dining area, where many of the lucky souls to inhabit Haven now sit. Beyond them, the space splits into twelve more or less evenly sized rooms, including the kitchen, library, gym, and classroom. The entire central hub, or atrium, is surrounded by an outer ring hallway. It is from this circular corridor that people can access their various private apartments, the garden, pool, security, and mechanical areas, plus the two entry/exit points.

Liam considers the numbers. There are five bedrooms in each of the ten apartments, most with bunk beds that can convert to queen beds. In all, Haven can sleep one hundred lucky souls.

Plenty of space still for some survivors to join us, he thinks. *And Sadie will be one of them.*

Not everyone is sitting. Their leader, Parker, and a few of the council are standing on one side of the room. A soft din of quiet chatter and bodies shifting moves through the crowd assembled as Parker addresses them with animated hands, minus a pinkie finger. Although Haven was built to survive the apocalypse, no one ever actually expected it to happen, and Parker is doing his best to keep everyone calm.

As he relays the rules and answers questions, Liam skims the faces of men behind Parker.

Parker's younger brother and their resident doctor, Henry, adjusts his glasses while keeping his eyes on his brother's back. The man projects assurance like few others.

Standing alongside Henry is Ryker. As a newcomer, Ryker has impressed everyone with his upright and dependable nature. Not only does he fit right in with the men and women running Haven because of his skills, intelligence, and will to survive, but he has also helped Beth to find her confidence again. Liam's honorary cousin has found a life partner in Ryker, and the entire community is delighted for them.

A memory of Sadie walking away from Liam at her mom's funeral two years ago comes unbidden. It's the last time he saw her. She'd retired for the night, and he couldn't blame her. It had been an exhausting day for all of them.

He shifts his attention back to Ryker, whose dedication to Beth mirrors that of Liam's father to his own mother. Ryker has stepped in as head of security while Donovan recovers from the injuries he sustained during their recent rescue mission on the neighboring farm. Donovan was told to rest, but he never does, and he's standing next to Ryker with a grim expression, one hand on his hip and his arm in a sling.

Liam doesn't blame him. Gina's recovery from that band of psychos next door has been bittersweet. While Liam is delighted she survived, he can't shake the sadness that overcomes him when he thinks about her husband, Brad. He had liked the guy, and Brad didn't deserve to go the way he did. And the whole episode is a constant reminder of how terrible things are outside of Haven. With Sadie still missing, Donovan and the Masters family are far from feeling at ease yet. Neither are Liam and his relatives.

Dressed for security detail, Liam sits with his best friend, Alex, and his twin brother. They are both recovering from injuries, as well. One while liberating the people from the farmhouse across the river, and the other while protecting children as they moved from Reed, the backup site, to Haven.

Parker says, "If you need spiritual guidance, our chaplain arrived safe and sound." He extends his hand and entices someone in the crowd, curling his fingers. "Stand up, Father."

Isaac stands with a stole around his neck and waves at everyone. Liam's known Frenchie his whole life, and he's amazed the man, in his sixties, still has a head of brown hair. His old age is showing in his graying beard, though. Isaac's clenched fist flies up to catch a dry cough.

Jose supports him with gentle hands. "You need to lay off the cigs, Father."

Liam's glad Jose is in better spirits following the death of his wife in the missile strike. Losing Sophia is recent, and the pain is still raw. He doesn't know how he'd deal if... Liam pushes the thought of Sadie dying back into a dark corner of his mind: the place where he dumps all his trauma. *Focus.*

Parker continues: "Father Isaac's service is here on Sundays. Thanks, Father."

Movement catches Liam's eye, and he swivels his head to the side to see Alejo and Sean sneaking in nearby to crouch beside Beth, who is sitting with her young charge, Neil. Liam feels for the kid: losing both parents within a week is brutal. At least he has Beth and Ryker.

Sean asks, "What did we miss?"

"Uncle Parker just finished talking about the council. Donovan and Ryker are running security." Beth turns to Alejo. "And you're getting self-defense lessons!"

Alejo jumps with enthusiasm and hugs her. "Oh, goodie!" He throws a playful smile Liam's way, then focuses on Parker.

Liam doesn't know Sean yet, but he's envious of Alejo's recent engagement to him. His dad raves about Alejo's heavenly foxtrot coffee. Up at Reed, Alejo only made some for his father, so until Liam gets a sample, he'll be skeptical about it. *No coffee's that good.*

"We've been raising crops close to the mountains." Parker gazes at Donovan. "Now that the boys are all here, we're planting larger harvests in the fields next."

Up front, someone snickers. Ryker zeros in on the sound in the crowd.

So does Parker. "There will be a learning process, and everyone will need to contribute." He points at the first row. "You too, Colin."

Ryker smirks at Colin's expense. Liam's not sure what's up with those two. When Ryker and Colin turned up at Reed, there was tension between them. They were both competing for Beth's heart. But it looks like they have resolved their differences.

"Some of you'll be doing double duty. We'll figure out the schedule and post it."

Hoss beelines for Liam across the expanse of the communal area in a black shirt with white lettering that reads *Reach out and touch someone* with a picture of a sniper rifle. Liam chuckles. *Dad wouldn't be Dad without a funny shirt.*

"For those of you without a job, we'll figure out your skill sets and work you in. Henry?" Parker turns to his brother.

Henry steps forward, sliding his glasses up his nose. "For those of you who are new, I'm the resident doctor. My brother, James, is our dentist."

Liam hasn't seen James since the rescue, but who could blame him? James lost his wife to grievous injuries. They saved him and his oldest daughter from their kidnappers, and so, like Gina, they've been using the time since to process and recover.

Henry glances at the back of the room and nods. The women they rescued line the back wall. They've shut themselves inside the women's apartment, afraid to be seen. Liam understands why but hopes they will become active members of the community one day. So far, he's only met the lady named Melanie. She's adjusted more quickly than the rest and has been helping Henry in medical.

A tall, lean African American man, Roger, enters from the tunnel, horsing around with his wife on his back. Liam invited his high school friend to join him on that fateful weekend back in May, and he is sure glad he did. They showed two days ago, and Roger's been learning communications for them. They call him Crunch on the comms.

"Roger, over here"—Henry extends his hand—"is our chiropractor if you need him."

The sudden shift in the crowd as everyone turns to look at his friend makes Liam stifle a snicker. Apparently, he is a wanted man.

Roger lets his wife down and waves with a cheerful grin as she covers a burst of laughter. Shy to a fault, she hides behind him. Liam welcomes her laugh into his heart. He needed that more than he thought he did.

"We don't have a psychologist or therapist, so either I or Father Isaac will be available for counseling." Henry points at the room labeled medical. "James, Roger, and I can be found right here. Parker?"

"Can you explain what happened out there?" someone from the crowd asks.

Parker takes a deep breath. "We know the attackers targeted more than just Spokane. The nation's bigger cities also suffered from similar strikes."

"Why?"

"I don't have the answer to that. What I know is that it can't have been a common enemy. The attack was too sophisticated and widespread. And what's more confusing is that, according to the reporter we heard from, we also bombed our own people."

The noise of the crowd rises. Parker lifts his hands, urging for calm. "I know this is distressing to hear, but we need to focus on what we can control, and that's surviving. Community is necessary, and it starts with getting those crops in the ground." Parker's shoulders ease, and he waves everyone away. "Enjoy the day off. Tomorrow, the shifts start."

As the gathering separates into smaller groups, some staying at their tables, others dispersing into side rooms and the outer hallway, Liam ponders how Parker left out one piece of information. It isn't just the major cities the missiles took out. Spokane wasn't the target: its military base, emergency services, and utility hubs were. Whoever did this wanted to bring about total societal collapse. And from what he's seen and heard, they succeeded.

A knot of anxiety tightens in Liam's stomach. The stress of being cooped up down here will take time to get used to, but as long as Sadie remains outside, he knows he won't find relief. Every day, he hopes she'll show, and every day, so far, has been a disappointment.

He's not the only one unhappy. Ryker's brother, Mal, watches from the shadows of the tunnel. Liam loves the bad-boy types. He'd love to scratch that itch, but he thinks Mal's as straight as they come. *Too bad.*

People bustle around, arranging tables and chairs for the lunch hour, their chatter adding to the busy atmosphere. As Parker and Henry step into the crowd, Roger approaches them. "Parker, the compound door alarm isn't working again."

Donovan walks in behind them. "The door code still works, right?"

"Yes, but I can't hear anyone approaching down the stairs now."

With a gentle slap to Roger's back, Parker says, "Leave it with me. I'll tinker with the door."

"Okay."

As the men disperse, Henry holds his finger up. "Oh, before I forget, does anyone have a plunger I can use? My youngest plugged the toilet again."

Parker pauses. "We didn't get enough of those, did we?!"

CHAPTER 17

"A ren't you going to join in?" Gina asks.

On the fringe of the communal room, inside a tunnel to the outer ring, Mal observes the activity within, looking like an outcast who wants to belong. He sensed Gina behind him during the speech, smelled her shampoo drifting around him here and there. Hates it but misses it. He's attuned to her like no one else, and it disturbs him somewhat. Mal shouldn't be missing her. Has no right. She's not his. "Probably about as much as you are."

She steps up beside him. "Touché."

Mal tilts his head to her, keeping his eyes on the crowd. "How have you been?" He hasn't seen her in days. Gina was getting too attached, so he needed some space, but her arm brushes against him, and Mal feels a sudden urge to close any distance still between them. He takes a chance and peeks over at her. Gina shrugs in her oversized sweater.

"That good, huh?"

Those stunning brown eyes gaze up. "You finding your place here?"

Damn, so beautiful. He gazes back out to where it's safe. "Sometimes it feels like I traded one prison for another."

"You were in prison?"

Idiot. He rubs his face with a hand. "Yeah. Wrong place, wrong time." He prays she'll let it go. Mal doesn't want to explain why to her or anyone else.

"So, you feel cooped up?"

"Yep."

"Me, too."

Gina's still struggling after the rescue at the farmhouse over a week ago. She lost her husband tragically, and Mal knows there's no way Gideon left her untouched. Still, he had hoped that Gina being with her family would have started to turn her around by now, even if just a little. His mother never recovered from Elias's abuse, but she was in deeper than Gina. "You have your family here to support you."

"So do you."

God, she's sharp. "Touché."

"I'm going back to the apartment. You want to hang with me?"

Gina makes it sound so easy, but it's not for him. "Nah, I'm good."

"So, you're afraid of my old man, too?"

I'm afraid of myself. "Afraid? Me?" He scoffs. "I don't think so."

"Well, then?"

So, that's how she'll suck him in. He's going to follow, too, like a moth to the flame.

***

As she enters the apartment, Gina glances up at the American flag hanging behind her dad. It's surrounded by disorganized yet colorful picture frames. One, larger than the rest, shows the guys geared up, gathering for the shot, standing on a runway in Afghanistan. Sadness closes in when she thinks about William not being in their lives anymore. A black ribbon has been draped over the frame, casting a somber shadow on him, and Gina silently curses the criminals who kidnapped her and killed the people she loved. *They took so much.*

Mal steps in behind her and closes the door.

With a slight drawl, Donovan says, "Oh, here comes trouble."

Gina grins. "That's no way to talk about your daughter."

"Who says I was talking about you?"

Concern clouds Gina's thoughts. Sadie's absence has aged her father. He appears haggard, and Gina's never seen a beard on him before. She keeps the faith, believing her sister will show, but as each day passes, Gina's hope dwindles.

Mal parks himself and his grin at the table. "Whatever, old man."

Neither of them trusts easily, so it took a while for the two men to find common ground, but they managed it in the end. Their banter calms her and makes things seem...normal. Almost.

Gina slides a picture frame out of her father's grasp and returns it to a shelf. It houses a family photo of her parents, her, and her four siblings in happier times. He's been doing this too much since he got injured—staring at pictures and sitting in the dark, alone—and it's making her worry.

"To what do I owe this pleasure?" Donovan asks Mal. "It was nice not seeing your ugly face hovering for a few days."

Donovan noticed Mal's absence, then, which interests Gina. It's funny, really. The way her dad speaks to Mal echoes the detached dynamic of his past relationship with Brad.

She spots a picture of her and Brad smiling on the shelf. It was the same smile he had on his face the moment she lost everything. Even though they'd forced him to his knees, he'd kept his eyes on her, his love for her obvious, unmistakable. "I love you," he'd whispered, his voice choking with emotion. A second later, he was dead, and those words, in a cruel twist of fate, were the ones that ultimately destroyed her. *They'll haunt me for the rest of my life.*

"So, you missed me?" Mal asks, teasing her father.

Donovan closes his eyes before opening them to look at an amused Mal.

"How about a game of cards?" she asks the two men by way of a truce.

CHAPTER 18

Wendall stands among a throng of men near the barn. "We need more workers, so let's expand the search. Send men south to Swindon and east." With Gideon and so many others dead, work on the farm has ground almost to a halt, and Wendall's not been shy about hiding his ire.

Leaning on the tractor, Hunter grows more disillusioned about his brother's plans. *More "labor," then? When will it be enough?* "How are we going to feed all these captives?"

No one responds.

The sky is cloudless, the wind...warm. He looks over at the men in the fields and recognizes some of them. They took him under their wings when he arrived looking for work at the Hutchison farm long ago. Guilt prevents him from acknowledging them.

"Send a couple of men across the river tonight before the sun goes down. I want to know who these people are who we saw in the fields today." Wendall fixates on Sonny. "They live past the crops, and we've all seen the damage they can do, so be careful. Find out what defenses they have, but don't approach them yet. Just observe."

Hunter's all for protecting what little they have left. It's wise to take a look. But the feeling of danger remains. He knows his family is messed up, and Gideon likely invited the trouble that came his way. Hell, Hunter is living with a gang of escaped convicts who kidnap people and force them to work! Whether their neighbors on the other side of the river are dangerous or not, whether they are responsible for Gideon's death, he knows he and his brother are far from the good guys in this fight.

"Sure thing, boss."

One man asks, "When do we get a go at the women?"

Hunter's hackles rise. It pains him that he hasn't been able to help anyone escape so far.

"You volunteer, and I'll personally pick one for you," Wendall says with a touch of humor. "Sonny, do the honors."

The men crowd around Sonny, rubbing their hands in anticipation before eagerly raising them to be picked for the job.

It makes Hunter sick to his stomach. "They're not animals for you to simply abuse." Wendall shoots him a scowl, though he says nothing as he departs in silence, stirring Hunter's anger even more. "Don't walk away from me!"

Wendall quicksteps toward the farmhouse, outpacing his brother, though Hunter tracks close on the heels of his target. It's only when Wendall storms into the kitchen, through the back door, that he spins around with fury in his face. "Why do you defy me?"

The sudden stop forces Hunter to check his surroundings. Realizing he's in the kitchen pacifies Hunter's rage. The other men in the room, taking note of Wendall's temperament, remember his unpredictable behavior and alert the others in the dining room with silent eyebrow movements and head nods. Quickly but quietly, they all exit through the front door.

Wendall points at Hunter. "You think you're better than me?"

Hunter swallows as he finds his courage. "No... I just don't see why we need to kidnap more people. It'll be months before we can feed them, and we already have enough manpower to work the land. If the men we sprung from prison would just—"

"What?" Wendall snapped. "Work harder? How do you think that's going to go, Hunter? I promised them something better than what they had in prison. Do you think I'll be in charge for much longer if I keep pushing them?"

"It's bad enough that you took Kessie's family, but hurting more people...it's lunacy. You'll make an enemy of every group in the area—"

"And thanks to those prisoners you keep going on about, we'll be able to defend ourselves. You got anything else you wanna whine about?" Wendall starts tapping his thumb over each of his fingers.

Hunter takes another step into the kitchen. The scars on his face tingle and itch. "You can't use the women this way."

Wendall scoffs. "Women are for using, and it was part of the deal for the prisoners coming with us. That's not changing."

"It's not right!"

"Just screw one and get it over with. It's not like they'll enjoy you with your face all fucked up, anyway."

The fire in Hunter's belly erupts into an explosion, and he clenches his fists. "Fuck you, Wendall."

The force of Wendall's punch reverberates through Hunter's body, causing him to crumple to the ground, clutching his stomach in excruciating pain. As if to complete the humiliation, Wendall steps over his brother to tower above him. "I'm the one who takes care of your scarred ass, so have some respect!"

An unwanted memory resurfaces, poking its way into Hunter's consciousness like a sharp thorn. Despite the agony, his fear is greater, and he uses the adrenaline to rise onto his knees and scurry away from the cold tile floor.

At fifteen, Hunter howled in pain, held tight by his grandmother. With a look of stunned horror from the back door, Wendall plowed Cissy over, dislodging her hold. Knocked to the tiles in fear, Hunter pushed away from his grandmother on his hands and knees to the far wall of the kitchen, slipping in his own blood.

Hunter shakes away the haunting vision and hoists himself up. He reaches out, finds the cool wall, and steadies against it. His heart pounds in his chest as he moves closer to the safety of the back doorway.

Wendall steps through the image of their past, anchors a startled Hunter by the neck, and subdues him with words. "Brother, have I ever not taken care of you? We're blood, we stick together, yeah?"

Hunter struggles to inhale deeply to calm down, his stomach cramping. He forces himself to focus on Wendall, but the feeling of helplessness and defeat lingers. "Yeah."

"So shut your fucking mouth and let me do what I need to. Clear?"

Hunter wants to challenge him, but he knows how far his brother can go. Wendall might not admit it, but he learned how to handle people who defy him from their grandparents.

And so, Hunter looks down at his feet, and then he nods.

***

In the field, working alongside the workers, seventy-five-year-old Giles falters. Hunter's hardly surprised. The day is a hot one. He pulls a ladle from a nearby water bucket and travels surefooted with it across the uneven ground. "Here. Don't want you keeling over, Mr. Hutchison."

"You held so much promise. What happened to you, Hunter?" Giles's question tugs at Hunter's heart.

Hunter ran away at sixteen and tried to get work, but his scars left people with the impression he was a rotten apple. *In the end, they were right.* Mr. Hutchison saw something different, though, and hired him as a field worker. They trusted him once.

"Life doesn't turn out well for everyone. Need more?"

Hunter thrived at the Hutchison farm. But any hope of a normal life and future ended when he and Mr. Hutchison went to pick up Kessie at the grocery store one night and found Wendall restraining her. *Of all the people, why did Wendall have to take a liking to her?*

Hunter didn't want to go back with Wendall, but his brother gave him no choice. Hunter traded his stable life with the Hutchinsons' for the chaotic life of his family to stop the spread of Wendall's contamination. Or so he thought.

Giles bites his bottom lip. "Is she alright?"

The truth is, Hunter doesn't really know. Wendall keeps her upstairs, behind closed doors. The other ladies are up there, too, but in different rooms. He wants Kessie just for himself…

"Kessie's alive. Keep your head down and don't get in his way."

"Is that what you do, son?" Giles hands over the ladle and focuses back on his work.

Deep in thought, Hunter makes his way back to the water bucket, the yawning gap between who he is and who he wants to be weighing down on his shoulders. But it's hopeless. It doesn't matter how much he wants to escape; fate always drags him back to this place. It's his fault. Hunter should have let his brother rot in prison after the missile changed their lives. He laid Greg's death at Wendall's feet. Could he do the same with Gideon? Is Hunter next in line to die because of Wendall? With everything his brother is doing—everything Hunter is helping him do—he'd deserve it.

He gazes at the mountains and longs to scale their peaks, come down the other side, and keep walking. He misses nature. Misses the freedom it promises. When Hunter was young, he would disappear for days with food he'd hoard for the trip. *To get away from them, far away from this place.*

Hunter shakes his head. *A pipe dream.*

***

With the sunset imminent, Hoss lounges at the desk in security, hot drink in one hand, a cookie in the other. He's thankful to Alejo and Penny at this moment. *Damn fine coffee.* He takes a sip and catches movement on a monitor. "Camera Nine."

Chair wheels scrape across the floor as Alex shifts over to have a look, coming shoulder to shoulder with Hoss. He's not sure what Alex is bitching about. He's injured, but Hoss believes Alex's wound isn't that bad. The bullet didn't hit any bone or major arteries: it just took a lot of skin. It's more of a deep graze than anything else. *These young-ins.*

Hoss recognizes the three armed men walking on the monitor. They live at the farmhouse. Their clothes are dry, so Hoss figures they must have some kind of craft to get across the water.

Alex keys the mic. "Haven to Pinkie. Three incoming, armed. West of God."

God is the codename for the old stone church they have on the property. He and the boys fortified it a couple of years ago. It's more of a fortress now, with barred blackout windows, a thick inset steel door, and a bomb shelter in the basement. They even reinforced and cleaned the brass bell in the tower.

"Copy," Parker confirms from the patio they built up in the trees near the fields and covered in camouflage netting.

Miles and Colin man the guard trees at the gate. Miles can't run yet, so that's all he can do. His injury is no laughing matter, though. The bullet grazed the top of his thigh, narrowly missing a major artery. He gazes at Alex. *At least Miles doesn't whine about it.*

From the angle the strangers are approaching the palisade fence, Hoss tracks them with two different cameras. Hoss clicks the mic. "Easy does it, Twinkle. Let them look. To them, you look like a tree, not a threat."

He glances sideways at Alex. "Bet he's crapping his pants right now."

"What do you want to bet he's cool as a cucumber?"

Hoss loves a bet, especially when it's in his favor. He's been training Colin and knows all his strengths and weaknesses. *No way Colin's cool. Too green.*

"How about time at Reed? Whoever wins gets Reed on the next run." Hoss extends his hand toward Alex, who shakes it.

"Deal, but how are we going to know? He won't tell us."

"We'll ask Miles."

They turn their attention back to the screens. The men shift left and right, scrutinizing Haven's defenses: those they can see, anyway. From Hoss's camera angle, he can see past the two trees and well inside Haven's yard, over the high cement wall with a steel door in the center. Fifteen or twenty feet in front of that is a line of wired and humming metal palisade fencing, and hidden below the forest floor growth beyond that, a lethal carpet of razor wire awaits. When they built Haven, Hoss and his brothers-in-arms wanted there to be no confusion as to whether the place is open for just anyone to wander into.

Hoss's delight that the men might walk forward is dashed when they slink backward. These men are definitely bad news, so he laments the lost opportunity to test the hidden razor wire.

The intruders move away, swallowed by shadows, or so they think, unaware that they are being monitored by night vision.

Chapter 19
June 18

Sadie protects her ribs as she helps Carl adjust the moss on the roof of their shelter. Her scarred face is no longer swollen and bruised.

"I'm gettin' too old for this stuff." He rubs his sore back.

She waves him off. "You're fitter than I am, Carl."

"Should think of movin' on to your family."

Sadie dreads the day she has to leave this place. How can she face her father? It was her fault that she got caught. How can she face herself? Out here, there's no mirror to remind Sadie of her failure. "I want to see them, but I'm not sure I'm ready to see their disappointment."

"Wrong way to look at it." Carl faces her. "Which is more painful for your family, seein' you alive or not knowin'?"

"But my face is—"

"Your face is. Nothin' you can do 'bout it." He continues to adjust the roof. "Somethin' you need to accept."

Can she, though? Sadie finishes and brushes her hands together, expelling a thin dusting of dirt.

"Family's a solid bunch?"

"Yes."

"Then it won't matter to them. At first, you'll look different, but then they'll be huggin' ya, carryin' on like ya never left." He rubs the dirt from his hands, palms together.

Sadie contemplates his words. She wishes that were so, but her scars... "Will you come with me?"

"Gosh, no. Can't leave Sophie."

He's vague about where she is. Sadie deduces that he buried his wife nearby and wants to remain near the cemetery. This reminds her of her mother. Her dad took her mom's ashes up to Haven and laid her to rest there. *Close.* "I can't leave you here."

Carl pats her hand, a smile touching his eyes. "Thanks for the warmth, darlin'. I feel affection for ya, but my love belongs to another already."

Sadie smirks at his weak attempt to flirt with her. She's happy, knowing she can smile without pain. The itchiness she experienced after the first week was hard to endure, but Carl's antibiotic cream did the trick, keeping her skin both sterilized and moisturized.

"All that's left to do is move forward. Complete the mission, girl."

Mission? He asked what route she was taking to Reed a couple of days ago, and they've been going over it ever since. She's learning Rangers are a different breed from Marines. Think different, do different. *Rangers lead the way.*

"I'll need to get to the cache in Freeman."

"Yes, just be careful. Don't want things goin' south on ya. You're not fully healed yet."

***

Donovan exits the dim staircase of the compound and steps into the light of day. Henry follows him into the farmyard above Haven. They built an animal barn for the goats, planting grass for them to graze on inside the wall, and a chicken coop with no chickens. They were still to be acquired when the missiles fell. They constructed other outbuildings for different purposes: a greenhouse, garden beds, a small barn for horses they don't have, and a butcher shop for processing hunted animals. It saddens Donovan that they couldn't get everything before they needed it. *Not enough time.*

White beehive structures stand out along the wall, and Gina comes to mind. He hoped the bees would draw her back into the world. *She needs to love something again.*

Miles salutes Donovan and Henry as they pass. Taking a page from something the Allied forces did in World War One, they built two fake trees on either side of the steel gate to serve as guard posts, their insides hollowed out to protect the guards on duty. Colin and Miles are manning them today, and Donovan feels a sense of gratitude. Colin's proving to be an asset on the team so far.

Beyond the wall, there's an electrified palisade fence in front of the thick wall they built. The hum of it mixes with the sound of the wind through the trees.

They approach a steel door with a tiny window set in the mountain wall. While Henry punches in the code, Donovan glances back across the farmyard and searches for the other similar steel door that leads to the outside. *Always have an emergency exit.*

The door unlocks with a click. Darkness swallows them. Sounds of the outside world deaden as the door closes behind them, echoing down the shadowy, unlit tunnel before them. Their boots crunch the stones underfoot as they make their way forward, heading toward the light coming from the next door. It creaks as Henry pushes it open. *Needs oil.* The forest sounds return, and the scent of pine welcomes them as they step into Yard Two.

Confined by a doorless high wall, this yard brims with maturing plants sprouting vegetables. The yard is one of four, each one making use of the mountain as a natural protection on the backside. They were going to start small this year, so they only planted enough for the handful of people living at Haven when the bombs dropped. *Who knew we'd need more?* The only reason they had a little more growing was because they had planned on the kids coming up to help them learn to farm. *Lucky...in a way.*

This draws out an image of Sadie. He misses her terribly, and every day is a struggle to fight off creeping negative thoughts and, instead, cling to the hope that she's still alive. He reins in his fear and focuses on Sylvia, Henry's wife, and Donovan's twenty-one-year-old son in the yard ahead of him, teaching the school-aged children about the different plants. Recruit Troy and Ryker stand nearby, armed and alert. From now on, anyone outside has a guard detail, and the cameras are manned twenty-four seven. They'll all take turns learning each occupation from now on. Everyone needs to know how to do everything, in case people become incapacitated.

Henry scoots over quickly and plants a kiss on Sylvia, to the shy looks and laughter of her students, two of whom are Donovan's youngest children. He waves at them, not slowing down, and strides across to the next steel door in the mountainside.

Hoss's two daughters-in-law stand off to the side and watch over their students. Once it became clear they wouldn't be returning to their normal lives, the two women took it upon themselves to set up the schoolroom. Crop production will require the help of everyone to ensure they survive the winter, even Haven's smallest residents.

He enters the code, hears the click, and walks into a tunnel, feeling Henry step in behind him as the door shuts with a *swoosh*. Once again, the sounds from outside are abruptly silenced. The next door opens, minus the creaking noise, as he steps back into the sunshine.

Yard Three is much larger than One and Two, boasting a hoop building and various types of farming equipment under the steel-roofed barns they built to house them. It's also where they buried the garage for all their mechanical needs. Donovan gazes down a steep, wide driveway at two enormous steel doors thrown wide open.

Amid the trucks and farm machinery, he spots Hoss—his ass, to be exact—who is digging around under the hood of his Bronco. If Donovan were more like Hoss and not so serious, he'd grab a pellet gun and use Hoss's rear for target practice. A rare devilish grin graces Donovan's face.

"Hoss, what're you doing?" he asks, sounding deliberately exasperated, like what Hoss is doing is ridiculous. Forgetting about his injury, Donovan tries to cross his arms, but the sudden shock of pain makes him abandon the attempt. It's only been a week since the farmhouse mission, but his wound is taking far longer to heal than expected, causing him considerable frustration.

Hoss's muffled response is unintelligible.

Donovan and Henry turn to gaze up at the new wall they built last year to protect the yard. Thank God they did that, at least. The wall required a much larger gate to facilitate the machinery comings and goings. Unlike Yard One, they still need to install the electric fence Liam hauled up here for Yards Two and Three. The fourth yard is well behind. It doesn't even have the cement wall yet, let alone the electric fence, and it'll need the latter if they want to keep out the animals.

Hoss approaches. "You thinkin' 'bout the electrical fencin'?"

They know each other well enough to read each other's thoughts. Sometimes, Donovan wonders where Hoss goes to find these shirts. Today's says, *My safe space is 1500 yards in all directions.* More than making other people laugh, Donovan knows Hoss wears these shirts for his own sake. Often, it's the people who experience intense emotions that use humor to hide their darkness. "We got enough for the other three yards?"

"Brought up enough for the field, too." Hoss transfers grease from his hands to a gray towel.

Sweet. They'll need to set up security to begin the work. The hungrier people get outside of Haven, the more important it'll be to protect everything they grow here. "We'll build the fencing on Yard Two first."

Henry pipes in. "Sounds good. We could complete all the yards together. We have the labor."

Donovan disagrees. "Priority should be maintaining the crops already in the ground and picking what needs harvesting first."

Henry takes that in with a nod. "True. We'll add it to the list."

Donovan looks back the way they came. Though his kids don't bring up their sister, he knows they're concerned by their avoidance of the subject. Sadie's bus was north of the town of Pasco, Washington, so he knew she was past the Columbia River when the missile struck. He'd checked the schedule before she left the university that morning. Swindon would be her route to Reed. She had a lot of terrain to traverse, but at least there were no major towns to pass. She knew where they buried items, and if Sadie followed her training, she'd have a map and basic survival supplies on her.

"Not knowing is hard," he says to no one in particular, reaching for the rings dangling on his chest, rubbing them through the fabric.

Henry nods, but offers no advice. Hoss slaps him on the back gently. "I feel you."

Where are you, baby girl?

Chapter 20
June 19

S adie awakens to find herself alone. She carefully slides up into a sitting position to spy a note fluttering in the breeze, held in place under a heavy rock. She plucks it out, reads it, already knowing it's from Carl, but it's not his usual note.

Scrawled over old scratched-out messages, it says: *Well, darling, time to mosey. Glad I could do a good deed before I left to find Sophie. Go test out your Plan B. Congrats, well earned. P.S. Tell your dad he owes me.*

Sadie grins, feeling like the bird that flies away from the nest and learns to use its wings again. *Can I do this?* Her fingers trace the cool, smooth surface of the EGA pin in her jeans, sensing its weight. She is not the girl who went to San Diego, but the woman who walked out of there stronger. She tightens her jaw. *Just got to take that first step, Sadie,* she says to herself. One step leads to more.

Sadie crawls out of that shelter with a plan and determination. *I am a Masters woman.*

***

Mal oversees a blindfolded Colin practicing a self-defense move with Troy that Donovan taught them moments ago, but he can't help but feel bored. He finds gawking at the women in their part of the gym much more interesting.

With Alejo's help, Beth is instructing the women. In pink tights and an over-sized button-down shirt, Alejo jumps up with excitement after he completes a move. Beth laughs at his enthusiasm.

So does Mal.

Ryker glances up from the two men fighting for control over each other to look at Mal. He raises his chin, gesturing to the other side of the room. Ryker turns to gaze at his woman, then looks back with a smirk.

If things go wrong topside, every person in Haven needs to know how to defend themselves against threats and make it home safe. Haven might be a fortress, but it's not perfect, and living in this new world will be perilous. Without a doubt, the most dangerous part of existing here will be farming out in the open fields. There's a lot of land they need to cover to keep everyone fed. Good thing Sylvia, Henry's wife, planted seedlings in the atrium greenhouse before all this went down.

Troy gets the upper hand, brings Colin to ground, and twists. Colin taps out.

"Good move, Troy," Mal says. "Let's go through this one again. Alex, replace Troy."

Colin's reaping what he sowed in a bucket of sweat after talking the talk but not walking the walk, saying he could do the move blindfolded.

Alex steps forward. Mal thinks Colin's a glutton for punishment by the way he smiles at his new opponent.

Mal allows his eyes to travel over to the other side of the gym again. Not having a soft woman to entertain is a big drawback. He does not yet feel a sense of belonging within the group. He appreciates his brother being in his life after so many years apart, but Mal's not sure it's enough to keep him here.

The woman named Melanie enters the room, guiding the women with whom she and Beth were held captive until Mal, Ryker, and the others rescued them.

Beth says, "Melanie, ladies, welcome."

The women glance around the gym with obvious apprehension.

Mal averts his eyes, not wanting to disturb the women in any way. They've been through enough, and the last thing they need is a man staring at them.

"They want to contribute," Melanie says. "To the farming. To the community."

That's a daring decision, and he commends them for it. After the arduous things they've experienced, it would be easy for them to keep themselves locked away. But over the last few days, they've started meeting in the pool area during the week to talk things through, and now this. *One step is better than no step.* His mother taught him that.

"Excellent," Beth says.

Mal risks a peek. The ladies already taking part in the self-defense class coax the new arrivals to join them. The newcomers hesitate when they see Alejo, so he saunters over to Beth. "I'll just stay with you until they get used to me, honey."

"Probably best, A." Beth claps and calls out, "Okay, ladies, find a partner for this next move."

Ryker catches her eye. Beth grins back at him.

"You're finally getting it, Colin." Donovan points at the back wall. "Okay, Miles, let's try an unorthodox move. Grab the short staffs."

Colin removes his blindfold. As Miles goes in search of the instruments, Alex offers his hand to Colin on the floor next to him. He accepts, and they help each other to stand.

Elena, Beth's cousin, peeks in at the men from the central dining area. She's wearing a quiver of plastic arrows on her back and shakes a toy bow at Ryker. After blowing a raspberry back at her, Ryker jogs toward Beth. "Hey, gorgeous." He twirls her around and bestows a sweet kiss on her as the ladies giggle at them. "Looks like Elena is ready for more archery lessons. Do I have your permission?"

There's the charmer Mal remembers. It comes out more when he's around his woman. Ryker belongs here, even if he doesn't.

Beth rolls her eyes and shoos Ryker away. "Go on then. Go and corrupt my cousin somewhere else."

He laughs and gestures with his hands on his chest in a not-me look as he backs away, then follows Elena away from the gym. She's become obsessed with the weapon Ryker is training her to use. Mal has watched them practice a few times, and her skill impresses him, especially as she's only using a toy. She'll be even more accurate with the real thing. Today, Ryker said he is going to see how well she does with the recurve bow he's made for her. Mal doesn't think she'll be able to get a grin off her face for a week.

***

In a field, east of Freeman, near a fencepost, Sadie casts a shovel aside. Under the soft glow of a headlamp, she yanks out a long-capped PVC pipe, then recoils, clutching her ribs. She sits back on her knees for a moment and uses her arm to wipe her dirty face. *That was fun...not!* The last few miles have been agony for her.

Once she has her breath, she pulls open the cache and smiles at the treasure trove of items inside.

First, Sadie rips open a bag of beef jerky and dives in for some much-needed nourishment. The sweet and salty flavor assaults her taste buds. She reaches for a can of fruit, peels back the lid, and slurps up the juice.

Carl speaks inside her head: "It'll be more dangerous to travel now. People will be desperate to take what ya have. Keep the gun handy and don't hesitate on the trigger." *No shit.* Sadie's been lucky not to have seen another soul yet. She hopes it stays that way.

Sadie searches inside her backpack, draws out a spoon, and scoops out the last of the fruit.

Once she's finished eating, she organizes the new items into her bag, making sure to keep the map near the top, and straps on a tactical vest. Her icy fingers are shaking, so she cracks hand warmers and sandwiches them inside her gloved hands. After loading and holstering a handgun, she latches a new rifle to her vest.

The sky is dark, and the air is getting cold, but she wants to get a few more miles in before she crashes. The next leg is out in the open, so she'd rather do it at night. It's fortunate that she's practiced at long-distance marches.

CHAPTER 21
June 24

A fter finishing his shift, Mal strolls into the apartment he shares with his brother and his family. Ryker is consoling Beth at the table about something. The distress on her face is clear, but Mal walks through to his bedroom as quickly as possible: he can't cope with anything else right now. With Gina and the extra shifts he's taken on, he's burning both ends to numb what he's feeling. *Trapped.* It's been growing steadily over the last few weeks.

Mal yanks his shirt off, then raises his head to see that Ryker has followed him. *Come on in, why don't you?*

"What's the candle mean?" Ryker is referring to the outline of a tattoo on Mal's right shoulder blade.

His brother's buttering him up for some reason. Mal's not in the mood, so he turns away slightly, exposing a crude black outline of a fox on his upper left arm. Mal ignores the question. Somehow, he knows this has something to do with Gina. "I don't want to know, Ry." Mal opens a dresser drawer. Empty.

Ryker points to Mal's belt. "Is that Krys's?"

Mal looks down at their sister's pink rabbit's foot. "Yeah, I snatched it from her shit-bag boyfriend's place after I beat the crap out of him. He wasn't worthy of Krys's things." *Neither am I...*

Mal hadn't expected it to be on her boyfriend's key chain when he showed up unannounced. Seeing it had been the final straw and set him off.

"She loved the rabbit's foot." *It didn't do her any good.* It was one of the few things she'd had of their dad's after he vanished from their lives forever.

"She did." Ryker sighs. "Gina's refusing to get help."

That's her problem, not mine. Mal bends to the floor, picks up a shirt, and sniffs it before shrugging it on.

"Donovan's worried."

Mal glares at Ryker. "I'll bet."

"She might listen to you." *Why does everyone think Gina listens to me? Krystal didn't.* Mal avoids Gina. Well, he tries, but she makes it so hard. It is torture for him; a double-edged sword. "No, I don't wanna be involved."

"You're the only one she comes out of the apartment for."

He has suppressed his compulsion for more than a week, between isolating himself in his room and working shifts. Mal wants to see her, but he can't. Gina brings up memories he buried long ago. "Not sure why. It's not like we're best buds or anything."

"It's worrying Beth, and I don't like it."

That's a new one, bringing Beth's health into the mix. This puts Mal on edge. They've been keeping it on the down-low, but he's privy to her pregnancy. Mal doesn't want her to worry, either, and sighs with a heavy heart. *Damn it, Ry!*

He longs for the lingering scent of Gina's perfume, a captivating blend of vanilla and lavender, and rubs his neck. *You glutton.* "Okay, I'll try."

Standing at the Masters's door a short time later, Mal sighs. He's mixed about coming here and dreads getting sucked back in, but does he have a choice? He knocks. Gina takes to him, but he doesn't understand why. If the world weren't such a shit show, she'd be seeking a therapist, not him.

The Masters' apartment door swings open, revealing an unhappy Donovan. "To what do I owe the pleasure?" This is the rapport between them, a dance, acting like they don't like each other.

Mal plays along. "Oh, come on, you've missed me. Gina in?"

"Yup, why?" Donovan, the human brick wall, doesn't give when anything comes between him and his daughters. Mal respects that, but it's unnecessary. He won't go down that road. *Not again.*

"Beth sent me." *Should satisfy the old man.*

There's a moment of hesitation. Then resignation. Donovan opens the door wider. "Alright, first door on the right."

Without fanfare, Mal slips inside and strides to where Donovan points, unaware Mal already knows the way after he stayed with Gina that one night. That's the way Mal wants to keep it. *The less the old man knows, the better.*

"Mal?" The troubled look on Donovan's face gives him reason to pause. "Good luck."

Great, what am I walking into here? With clenched hands, he battles to control his nervousness and catches a fleeting glimpse of Gina through the crack of the door. She looks lost.

Mal's mind flashes back to a day in the farmhouse kitchen, where he found his mother wearing the same distant stare. She'd been sitting at the table, a forgotten plate in her hands. "Mom?"

Mal shakes the vision away, takes a deep breath, and pushes the door open, determined not to let the past affect him. "Gina?"

She blinks and gazes up from the chair. Her vulnerability hits Mal, compels him, even, to take Gina in his arms, but he resists the urge, clutching the door frame tight. Gina smiles.

His heart aches because he can't do what he wants. Her dead husband invades his psyche. *She's not yours.* He shifts his gaze to the floor. "Get up. We're going topside."

"Topside?"

Mal regrets the gruff nature of his statement and takes it down a notch, giving his heart time to calm. The need to flee overpowers him. "Just got off shift, and it's nice out."

"I don't want to waste your time. You must be tired."

The strain of seeing Gina hurting and Ryker's manipulation pushes sharp words out of his mouth before he can vet them. "It's my time to do with what

I want, and I want to spend it with you." Mal departs, leaving Gina to decide how to interpret the statement. *Smooth move, Kensington.*

***

In tactical vests, Mal and Gina sit across from each other in silence on a bench in Yard Two under the late afternoon sun. Down in security, he helped her with the vest. As Mal had strapped her in, he'd pulled a little too hard, causing them to collide. The smallness of her waist, the comforting sensation of her soft skin against his rough fingertips... It was a mistake, choosing to be close to her.

Mal pulls at his vest. It's a necessary evil to be protected out here in the open. The wall shields them from view, but there are no guarantees anymore. He glances up at the same time as her. Mal's gaze doesn't waver. He's not sure what to say.

"Aren't we a pair," she says, her lips curving upward.

"Meaning?"

"Two people sitting together with nothing to say."

"I've always been this way." Mal glances away from her.

"Why?"

Life sucked. "Growing up wasn't rosy for Ry and me."

"What was your childhood like?"

Why does Gina have this effect on him? She's like kryptonite, only Mal enjoys being near her. He feels compelled to talk, which is a testament to Gina's power over him. He needs to scale back, but every time Mal looks at her, he starts spewing things he doesn't normally share. "Shitty. Lost Dad. Mom married a hard ass who saw us as farmhands. She died, and he made it worse." No one's ever gotten that much out of him at once. *You've got it bad.*

"How?"

God, does she honestly want to know this shit? Like a sieve, Mal pours out his trauma. "Made Krystal and me quit school and work full time on the farm. She took care of the house and the other kids, and I was his slave."

"Is Krystal younger?"

"My twin."

He expects another round of questions, but Gina pauses and gazes out at the lush vegetable garden surrounding them in contemplation. She's silent for so long that Mal closes his eyes to the beautiful visual in front of him. Her beauty stings.

"I know shitty, too." Gina doesn't clarify further.

What would Gina know about that? He stares into her arresting brown depths. "The old man's tough, but I don't think he made life too bad for you."

Mal sees the struggle, the way sadness envelopes Gina's eyes and makes her mouth pout. "My mom died of cancer."

Okay, shitty.

"It was slow...agonizing. She was so beautiful and brave."

Her statement draws Mal to the conclusion that Gina is like her mother in more than just beauty. He looks at her with concern, noticing her vacant expression once again.

"She never saw me get married."

"Gina?"

Her pained gaze shifts upward as she mutters an apology.

"You need to talk to somebody about this stuff. It'll fester and eat you alive if you're not careful."

"Speaking from personal experience?"

Yeah. Mal keeps the thought to himself. Once he was released from jail yet again, he wasted no time in setting out on a mission to track down Krystal. The harsh reality hit Mal when he realized she had no job, no place to call home, and a dangerous relationship with her dealer. He found his sister in an alleyway, her body trembling as she injected herself.

After the initial shock wore off, Mal observed her baggy, unflattering clothing that revealed the thin body hiding underneath, and her once beautiful hair appeared like someone had cut it with dull scissors. At twenty-three, he lacked the understanding of what Krystal was experiencing and figured she could complete any task by simply applying her mind to it. "Jesus, Krys, you need to leave that asshole boyfriend." Mal walked back and forth in front of his sister, who leaned against a building, appearing drowsy and partially aware because of the drugs. He didn't understand addiction back then.

"I love Lenny. He's sweet on me," she'd said.

Mal was furious with her and himself for ending up in jail. Taking care of her was his responsibility. "No, he supplies you. He ain't sweet."

In the blink of an eye, her demeanor changed from friendly to enraged. "I need it to keep the demons away!"

"What demons?" Mal knew why she had them, but she didn't know that. Krystal never confided in him.

"Nothing." She waved him away.

He saw things, little telltale signs after Mom died: Elias was working his way into his sister's pants. Like the fucking perverted asshole he was. "Krys, tell me. Don't shut me out."

Mal confronted Elias. A showdown witnessed by all his siblings. He was tight-lipped, but Mal never took his eyes off Elias after that. Wherever he went, Mal went, so Elias couldn't be alone with her. Mal did that for three years, waiting for Ryker to reach military age.

"Fucking leave it alone, brother! Leave me, go back to your life." With a cackle, Krystal had danced away. *Life? What life?*

"Mal?" So wrapped up in the past, Mal almost doesn't hear Gina.

Feeling the wind shift, he makes a mental note to gather some supplies later. He turns away, not wanting her to see his torment. Someone's planted marigolds among the vegetables. Needing to change his mood, he asks, "What's your favorite flower?"

After a prolonged silence, she finally breaks it with a soft sigh. "Wildflowers, why?"

He shoots her a glance. "Just curious. Most women say roses or tulips."

"I'm not like most women."

She has that right. "What do you like about wildflowers?"

"They're good for pollinators, like bees."

"Bees, huh?" Mal gestures with his chin to the white box set up near the mountain wall. "There's a colony here."

"I know. I'm an apiarist."

"A what?"

"A beekeeper. I started that colony."

He's impressed.

CHAPTER 22
Swindon, Idaho

In the dwindling twilight, shadows creep over the bodies that lie scattered across the Python Bridge. Sadie's been walking all day, and her feet and ribs are causing her discomfort, but it's too dangerous to rest. Concealed and watchful, she bides her time, searching for a chance to traverse the open expanse and somewhere safe to get to on the far side, all before the full moon makes its appearance.

Two men are already stalking across the bridge. They arrived after her, but she stayed out of sight. *Bang! Bang!* Their bodies drop. The flash of a muzzle in a building beside the road leading up to the bridge reveals the position of a shooter on her side of the river.

The callousness of the execution ignites a surge of disgust in her belly. *How can humans be so cruel?*

But she's grateful she'd had the presence of mind to hang back and watch, thanks in large part to her training as a Marine and the wisdom of an old Ranger replaying over and over in her head: "There'll be a way under the bridge. Do it at night. Look for a way inside."

A short time later, once the sky is dark, Sadie backtracks through a deserted part of town and approaches the bridge from underneath, well out of the sniper's line of sight, even if they have night vision. "Assume they do," Carl had told her.

Under the bridge, Sadie removes a crowbar from her bag and grapples with a stubborn service door, exerting all her strength to pry it open. With each attempt, her ribs remind her of how much her body still needs to heal, but she persists through the discomfort. The river's white noise drowns out the door as it screeches and whines and cracks, but she has to assume that someone—whoever has decided they are the guardians of the bridge—will hear it eventually. *Yes, come on, bitch. Open for me.* She heaves again. The moaning steel grates on her ears as the door separates from the frame, just enough for her to squeeze through. After another glance into the surrounding darkness, she crams her backpack through the space, then forces her body in after it. Sadie leans forward for a moment, trying to get the pain in her chest under control.

A hand claws at her jacket from behind and snatches Sadie back, dragging her halfway out. "No, you don't," a voice hisses.

She gasps, then pulls with all her might. Sadie applies a counterforce against the door, hauling herself back inside. She twists to see the large male arm holding her. The sharp sensation of pain registers, but she remains determined to push through.

The hand loosens, the arm disappears, and a face appears at the gap in the door. "Rick, squeeze in. I'll get her on the other side."

Sadie backs up. *If there's more...*

The man outside pries the door back with his bare hands. *Strong.* She smashes the crowbar over his knuckles. He lets out a deep shout as he retreats, but she knows he'll be back. She runs for the stairs.

The loud current of the river rushes under Sadie's boots as she traverses the metal service pathway to the other side, more by feel than by sight. A breeze kicks up and ruffles her long hair and caresses her face. It feels like she's navigating the darkness for an age, but finally, she finds the cold door with her searching hands, and a handle materializes. She hopes this exit will be easier to open as she listens for any movement behind her. Sadie turns the handle and leans into it. It doesn't budge. *No, no!*

Sadie can't hear anything, and the low light means she doesn't know if anyone is creeping up on her. Panic sets in; her breathing is quick and shallow. Her ribs are sore. *No time to feel.* Sadie applies herself, prepares herself for an explosion of agony, and slams her shoulder into the door. Jarring pain shoots up her arm, as well as into other tender places. "Motherfucker!"

No good. Okay, Sadie, stop and think for a second. She glides her hand over the smooth surface of the door, feeling its solid presence. A deadbolt. Checking behind her once more, Sadie slides it across, filling the air with sound. *Screech!*

In the pitch darkness, heavy footsteps scrape the metal floor, echoing toward her.

Trusting she's faster than the other man running over the bridge, Sadie jerks the door open, jumps out, slams it closed, and crams the crowbar under the handle. The bar rattles as the man on the other side makes contact. *It won't hold for long.*

She scans the area. Trees line the edge of the churning river. She's alone...for now. *At least one more.* The angry shouts of the man trapped behind the door grow louder as he continues his relentless banging. Satisfied he can't break out, Sadie steps away and rests her hand on the rifle. If she uses it, she'll put a target on her back.

Up the road, she sees the faint outline of some buildings. Human shapes move in the darkness there; male voices carry on the night air. Too many to fight her way out. She strains her ears against the noise of the river and hears footsteps on the pavement above her.

Sadie inhales a deep breath, the cold air chilling her lungs, and she runs toward her only escape: along the river's edge. *Hope that sniper doesn't have night vision after all.*

CHAPTER 23

All is quiet in the farmhouse. Hunter has been sleeping on the living room's battered couch since they arrived at the farm, but until tonight, he's spent every night surrounded by snoring, stinking escapees. Now that they have the machinery they acquired, Hunter and the captive men have at last been able to clear the barn of decaying hay, fortify the walls, and put in proper floors in the loft and the ground floor for people to sleep on. Wendall's guards still slumber on the kitchen floor, but the rest sleep in the barn to stay close to the "labor."

Hunter sniffs the caustic odor of the lamp and watches the flame dance behind blackened glass. It's a waste of a precious commodity they won't have for long if the world truly has ended, but he needs something to enjoy in this terrible place.

Small thuds sound from overhead, followed by the familiar creaks in the stairs, and he knows it's Wendall before he sees him. Hunter's brother is the only person with the privacy and luxury of an upstairs bedroom, where he stays with Kessie. Plus, Hunter recognizes Wendall's distinct gait.

Sure enough, Wendall appears at the bottom of the stairs, walks across the room, and settles in the armchair opposite, the orange light illuminating his brother's face. "Kessie's a great piece of ass. Lost time, brother, lost time."

Hunter remains muted, annoyed that Wendall is playing the part of the confiding brother, acting like they're close. They've never been close. And how can he treat Kessie that way? He says he cares for her, but all he does is hurt her.

Hunter hates the way Wendall treats Kessie. He hates the way all the women are being treated.

But of all the armed men on the farm, he's the only one. The other men know it, too. They've seen how Hunter is treated by Wendall, and it's started to rub off on them. He feels more isolated than ever. *Life has no meaning anymore. It ended when the world ended. It ended when Greg died.*

"Our neighbors have quite a setup over there in the trees," Wendall says, filling the silence between them that might as well be a void.

Hunter can't help but feel a little put out. "Oh." He doesn't want to know why his brother feels like parting with his precious intel all of a sudden. Should he feel privileged? It's been a week since the men hiked over there, so why's he only sharing this with him now?

"Lots of surveillance cameras, and they live behind a formidable wall."

A fortress? Impressive. Hearing this convinces him that they must have been the ones who killed the rest of the men while he and Wendall were away. Whoever these people were, then, they meant business. In the mass grave, all the men had been shot. It hadn't been a pleasant experience finding his brother's body: someone had killed Gideon at close range. Kaden and Cain were in there, too, along with a few others Hunter recognized.

Should he hate the neighbors, then? He's not sure what his brother did, but no one does that without being provoked. There were no women in the ground with them. Women who hadn't been on the farm when Hunter had left to acquire the equipment.

"We're going to steal some workers tomorrow."

"Why?" Hunter's voice is soft, distant as he thinks about how he buried Gideon in the graveyard, next to Greg and their other family members. He'd enjoyed Greg's company, even if his baby brother was clueless at times, so he felt that death more than Gideon's. Wendall didn't help bury either of them. And now, Hunter's stuck with the one who ridicules his scars and bullies him like he used to growing up.

"I need to know who my enemy is."

Sounds like his brother's making the same mistake Gideon did. Hunter feels a powerful urge to run, but to where?

"What's up your ass? Been moody lately."

Hunter doesn't want to repeat their last encounter in the kitchen, so he keeps his voice quiet and calm as he continues to gaze into the flame. "Have little to say."

He has run away twice, and both times, he ended up back here. He tried to forge a better way, but in the end... *I'm a rotten apple. Always will be.*

"Lost Greg, now Gideon. We have to be on the same page, brother."

Like their deaths ever mattered to you. Hunter remains silent.

Wendall sighs. "You always enjoyed heading into the woods, didn't you?"

This time, Hunter grunts. Nature is the only place he's ever felt whole. He can pretend to be anyone and disappear from the world. *No rules, no judgment, and no fucking family.*

"Why don't you and Sonny go out and scrounge up some more farmers? Change that mood you got going on." Wendall makes it sound like they'll be going to the corner grocery store to pick some workers off the shelf.

At last, Hunter turns his head and locks his eyes onto his brother. A plan is formulating. He's lived out there before. All he has to do is ditch Sonny, then the apocalypse might just be his ticket away from Wendall.

It nags at Hunter, though. It's not like his brother to worry about Hunter's mood. Why does Wendall want him gone?

Chapter 24
June 25

Sonny and Wendall talk in hushed tones in the farmhouse kitchen. The only place Wendall knows his brother won't venture into voluntarily. He should deal with his trauma like the rest of them. "Let Hunter relax some before you injure him."

Hunter has to be taken down a notch, but not by him. Wendall needs to be the protector Hunter will turn to. Sonny will put him in his place, and then his brother will return with his head screwed on straight.

"You want me to leave him like that?"

Wendall is calling in the debt Sonny owes him for breaking him out of prison. He wants his brother to experience enough misery in the woods—somewhere he'd always run to as a child—to make the farmhouse seem like a haven, a place to crawl back to for comfort.

"Yes," Wendall says, looking Sonny up and down. He is a good choice. Sonny has an inflated ego; he'll make it a point of pride to get the job done. Plus, he doesn't like Hunter much. Of course, his brother will want revenge, but Wendall is prepared to lose Sonny, especially if it means he wins back the trust of his brother. In the end, that's all that matters.

Kessie's cousin, Jewel, is escorted past the men and toward the back door. Her green eyes and blonde hair captivate the men. Not Wendall, though he enjoys the scowl she gives him as she passes. The glint in her eye, the twist of her mouth: Wendall understands these signs of hatred all too well.

Her stare is so intense that Sonny squirms and averts his eyes to the tiled floor.

"Do you like Jewel?" His question is deliberately incredulous. Wendall doubts Sonny can deal with her aggressive side.

Wendall sees and hears his men taunting her and making gestures as she walks by. He smiles to himself, pleased that his plan to keep this one from the men for now is working. Her body is alluring, there's no doubt. But he only has eyes for Kessie, so he's making use of her in other ways. *She's a prize for them to shoot for, and I want her to know it.* And so, she is being escorted outside under Wendall's orders. A scare tactic to show her the wolves she'll be thrown to if she doesn't obey.

Sonny nods, adjusting himself.

"I'll reward you when you get back, then." *You should have something before I allow Hunter to get his revenge on you.*

Jewel isn't just a great motivator for his men, Wendall has realized. Kessie tried to turn the tables on him last night, denying him her body, and got him all riled up. And so, he took his anger out on Jewel. He decided against smacking her face and, instead, choked Jewel, forcing Kessie to watch. In the end, Kessie did what he wanted, and her virginal hesitation pleased him, so he went gentle on her. She didn't fight him for long.

Sonny shows a toothy grin. "I sure do like blondes."

"Done. Have the men crossed the river yet?"

"About to, boss. Saw a bunch of women today. Told the guys to grab them first."

"Excellent! I'm coming with you."

***

Mal scans from left to right at the edge of the cornfield, using all his effort to focus on staying alert, even though the heat of the day is wearing on him. The young plants are thriving, but are not yet high enough to give any shade, there's no wind, and the still air is heavy. Mal unclips his water bottle, the plastic cold against his fingers, and takes a slow sip, savoring the cool liquid.

The mic crackles. Donovan's voice rings through with a grim calm: "Incoming, west of the fields. Get the kids off the playground, Pinkie."

Mal swivels his head to the edge of the western side of the field. "The playground" is their codename for the farm fields; the workers are "the kids."

Parker chimes in. "On it! Move your—"

There's no visible threat, but Mal's not waiting to find out. With a determined stride, he pushes through the rustling corn, his feet sinking into the soft, dark earth, heading straight for Parker.

"Rask, take up the rear." Parker's voice sounds all scratchy through the comms. Before Mal can acknowledge his order, Parker speaks again: "Got a visual, Osmond?"

Donovan answers: "Negative. In the trees. Cover your three."

Mal twists to his three o'clock position, scanning for anything unusual, and continues walking sideways behind the others *Still no visual confirmation.* He rolls his eyes at himself. *God, now I sound like they do.*

"Copy."

Mal feels a spike of adrenaline at the sight of movement in the unseeded part of the lower field. The crack of a gun goes off in the distance. The smell of gunpowder fills the air as Mal returns fire, his heart pounding in his chest.

Parker taps him on the shoulder. "Conserve it. They're out of range. Let's go." Parker turns his back on the field.

Mal follows Parker and the rest of the group, jogging toward the deepening shadows of the forest. He figures he'll have to face the men he escaped the prison with across the way one day. *Won't that be a surprise?*

Ryker's voice comes in crisp and direct: "Slick, with me!"

Their nickname for the new guy, Troy, came about last week when he slipped on oil in the garage. Everyone laughed, and it seems to have stuck.

"Got it!" Troy says.

"Twinkle, you got this?" Ryker relays to Colin through the comms.

Mal's not sure how that name came about, but why judge? The only obvious one is Parker's, or "Pinkie," on account of his missing finger.

"Affirmative!"

"Crunch, there are nine workers in the field. Confirm count once inside."

"Copy that."

"Osmond? We're below. How many?" Ryker asks.

Donovan's codename interests Mal. He asked Hoss about its origin, but the man remained secretive. Mal's never heard Donovan sing, and he doesn't resemble Donnie Osmond, so it remains a mystery.

Roger speaks clearly through the comms. "Kids incoming, Superman! Straight for you. Pinkie and Rask in the rear."

Mal's new nickname is Donovan's doing. Short for rascal. Hearing it makes Mal feel like a young child and brings back memories of watching the *Little Rascals* on Saturday mornings when he was younger. Those were happy times.

First in line, Sean approaches Ryker, then eight workers, with Parker and Mal taking up the rear. Ryker eyes the forest, ready to take everyone the rest of the way to the compound, followed by Troy.

Donovan drops from the patio and unholsters his weapon. "Two armed men. Took cover in the trees when Rask showed them some love."

"Confirm nine kids, Crunch. Pinkie and Rask," Ryker says, then turns to Donovan. "I'll take point."

It took time to understand their coded language. At first, Mal thought it was overkill to use only nicknames over the radio. Boys playing at soldiers.

But that was before he went over with them to rescue Gina and the others, and he saw how dangerous the men he'd traveled with could be.

With determined strides, the group advances toward the entrance leading to Haven's underground complex, their boots crunching on dry twigs and leaves underfoot. In the tree-filtered afternoon sun, the forest is silent, devoid of any birdsong.

"Copy."

In contrast to him, Ryker looks at ease with his role as he runs alongside Sean. *He always was better at following orders.* Mal has never been one to follow in life, so this is strange to him. He feels like a fish out of water.

Troy and Donovan run beside the rest, giving cover from the west. Mal follows Parker's lead, scanning the forest behind them for the enemy.

Roger calls out, "Stop the advance! They're going to cut you off at the gate."

That's another area where they'll need to improve. The sound of rapid gunfire echoes ahead of them. *That sounds bad.*

He turns in time to see Ryker raising his fist, signaling for everyone to freeze. The group obeys. Ryker signals two fingers right. "God, Pinkie"

The group moves again, as one, understanding that danger is present.

"Copy that."

Colin pipes into Mal's ears: "Two down, two headed your way, Superman."

More bodies to bury.

"Copy that, Twinkle."

Built of varied colored granite, a small fortified structure with a steeple appears through the trees. The church looks old and cozy to Mal. Stone steps invite them to a steel door. Donovan enters the number, then everyone except Ryker and Troy files in. *Gotta get that code.*

The sunlight entering behind him cascades over a dusty floor, pushing back the shadows inside, and reveals steps that move in both directions: up and down. Mal doesn't have time to investigate further before Donovan slams the door, shrouding them in profound darkness. *Cool.*

Without sight, his sense of smell takes over: musty, but earthy. He hears the sound of boots shuffling across the stone floor. Their headlamps spring to life, and he glimpses Parker heading up the stairs to the roof.

Donovan points out the steps leading down on his way past. "Mal, get them to the basement. Five-three-oh-nine. I'll tap when it's over." *That sounds familiar.*

"Let me guess. The front door is eight-six-seven?" The song was popular in its prime.

Donovan skips up the stairs, but his voice says into Mal's head, "You're smarter than you look, Rask."

With heightened curiosity, Mal leads the others down a set of rock steps by his headlamp. At the bottom, he's greeted by a steel door. He punches the code in, hears the click, pushes it open, flicks on a light switch inside, and holds the door ajar for the group to file in. As the door closes, the people Mal's just brought to safety fan out behind him in a vast cellar lined with bunk beds and shelves. For a while, the only sound is everyone's heavy breathing as they wait for something to happen.

Donovan whispers in the comms, "We're in position. Kids secured."

Donovan and Parker must be in the bell tower to get a better idea of where the intruders are located. Mal finds a chair by the door and sits.

"Cameras picking anything up this side of Haven, Crunch?" Donovan asks.

Hoss's familiar drawl slides in: "At the east hoop. They're exitin' south of your position. Fire in the hole, boys!"

Muffled shots follow.

***

Amid the trees, along the riverside, Wendall tightens his grip on the binoculars as he listens to the gunfire. He knew some of the men he sent over might not return, but he didn't figure the neighbors are *this* organized. It looks like none of his scouts are going to make it back.

It isn't a complete loss. Wendall knows more than he did before.

They have cameras monitoring the wall within the trees, but none by the river, and there is a peculiar place high in the treetops at the edge of the fields from which he watched a man climb down. *Sniper perch, perhaps?* Wendall has also learned that this group shows no mercy.

How can we breach the wall and still have enough men to secure the place afterward? Wendall has counted eleven people exiting the fields, and five of them are armed, though he suspects there might be others based on the sound of the gunfire. *They are organized, trained. They can crush a small group.*

Wendall has already sent out men to find recruits to bolster their ranks. He just has to hope this group won't attack his farm until they do. Until his people return, Wendall needs to focus on security, as well as planting the field that's left, if he's going to feed everyone. With Hunter gone, at least the rotation of the women will increase. Morale shouldn't be a problem.

The ground vibrates with pounding footsteps. Wendall raises his weapon. Three men crash through the bushes and, faced with the business end of his gun, slide into the dirt.

He smiles. *Good. More intel.*

CHAPTER 25
June 27

Despite the full backpack hanging over his shoulders, Hunter felt a weight lift off the minute he and Sonny left the farm behind. The smell of the forest and serenity of this vast space call to him, like they always do, confirming what he already suspected: he needs to get away from Wendall if he wants to stay sane. His only problem now is Sonny.

"The falls are that way." Hunter points. "It's not that far." He'd rather not go with Sonny, but he doesn't have much of a choice, and Hunter hasn't been to the falls in years. His childhood memories of them are some of the only ones Hunter cherishes. It was a place where he could escape the hell on earth that was growing up with his grandparents. He wasn't religious, but the cascading water had always cleansed Hunter in some way, of both his transgressions and those of others. It was a place where he could confess his sins and find forgiveness.

Sonny stops to face him. "Boss wants us to go to Swindon, and that's where we're going. I don't want to feel his wrath. Do you?" Sonny turns his back to Hunter and walks on. "We can see the falls on the way back."

Hunter doesn't believe him. His intuition tells him something is wrong, but he's not sure what yet. The space between them stretches as Hunter distances himself. Although the farm is behind them now, he is in a miserable mood, and it feels like his emotions are scratching at him from within. Conflict simmers beneath the surface, mingling with the palpable sense of guilt. He doesn't want to go back, but can he leave the Hutchisons to their fate?

Hunter raises his hand and jogs away from Sonny. "Give me a minute. Nature calls."

Sonny sighs, resting his ass on a fallen log.

Hunter forages through the brush and finds a place that suits his needs. He could kill Sonny and not go back to the farm. The damage Wendall is doing to Giles and his family is going to be irreversible, so why bother? What chance does he have against such a large, overwhelming force of men? *Well, there you go. I've lost whatever dregs of a moral compass I had left.* His grandmother said he was a piece of shit and would amount to nothing. *Guess she was right about something after all.*

He surveys the surrounding forest. *Can I slip away without Sonny seeing me?* The number of deaths Hunter's accountable for has risen since he last kneeled at the falls. He feels the weight of all the lives he's taken. There's no forgiveness for him this time.

As Hunter zips up his pants, a camouflaged mound grabs his attention a fair distance away. He approaches with a sense of curiosity. He knows these woods, but it's been a while, and nature changes. *But that looks man-made.*

A glimpse of a woman's sleeping form inside causes him to want to backtrack. He recognizes her tactical gear. *Marine.*

Twigs snap. He braces.

"You done yet?"

Shit!

The woman whips her head up. Scared bright blue eyes entrap Hunter. Then he catches sight of the stitches on her face. *What the hell?*

She jumps to her feet and bolts...right into Sonny's arms.

Hunter hangs his head.

"Well, well, what do we have here?" Sonny says, his voice dripping with smugness.

She stamps her boot onto Sonny's foot and grapples with her weapon. Sonny growls, recovers, and overpowers her. Not relenting, she seizes Sonny's groin.

His hold loosens. Unhanding him, she thrusts her elbow into Sonny's face. He angles his head to the side. With a sharp intake of breath, she cries out, her body recoiling inwards. *She's injured.*

Sonny regains control, crushing her in his arms, and hooks her leg. With a thud, she falls to her knees. A sharp, desperate sob rips from her throat.

Her disturbing howl speaks to Hunter's empathy. *Scars are fresh.* He steps forward, arms out. "Sonny! You're hurting her."

Sonny yanks her away from Hunter's grasp like a kid with a favorite toy he doesn't want to share. "Hey, finders keepers." He locks the woman's arms behind her and forces her face-first into a nearby tree, ignoring her agonizing moans.

Jesus. Not on my watch.

Sonny unlatches her rifle, lays it on the ground, and goes for her pants button. *Think quickly.*

Swallowing back his rage, Hunter waves his hand over the area. "Let's make camp and do it right, eh? We have lots of time." He tries to look calm and collected, hoping this works. Otherwise, he's going to have to take Sonny out.

Sonny's mouth twitches, his eyes untrusting. "Okay, but I get her first." With a grunt, he pulls a rough hemp rope from his backpack and binds her wrists.

Hunter's mood dips even further. He needs a plan because there's no way Sonny's touching her with a ten-foot pole while he's around.

***

The mean one named Sonny callously binds Sadie's hands with rope, making it impossible for her to escape. While he clears out her pockets, Sadie's eyes remain fixed on the man standing at an angle behind him. From underneath his beard, jagged facial scars sprout, reminding Sadie of her own injuries.

After pocketing Sadie's knife, Sonny examines the black pin he finds for a moment before deciding to toss it. *Doesn't know what it means? Or doesn't care...* A fire of indignation burns in Sadie, making her cheeks flush and her fists clench.

The scarred one bends to retrieve it. "I'll watch her. Get some firewood."

He doesn't take his eyes off her as he speaks, and this worries her. *Trust no one.* She deduces that he's the alpha of the two. He's the one she mustn't show any fear to. Sadie hopes the anger she's projecting is masking her terror. When Sonny went for her pants, her mind went blank. She wasn't prepared for that. Has all her training been for naught?

A sudden, sharp pain in her chest feels like a knife twisting, causing her to flinch. One of her wounds has opened, and sweat trickles down the center of her back as she tries to stop herself from shaking. *Something is wrong. I need to get to Reed. To Dad.*

Sonny squares his shoulders in defiance. "I'm not leaving her with you." He is shorter than the other man, but wider, reminding Sadie of Hoss.

"You forget, I'm not that kind of guy."

Sadie doesn't know if that's good or bad for her. *What kind of man is he?*

"Fine." Sonny takes off with her handgun in his waistband.

Sadie blinks back the pain and keeps her eyes set on the scarred man. Given the opportunity to get away, she will grab it with both hands. Her injury hurts, but who knows when she'll have another chance to escape just one of them?

The scarred man crouches close and extends his hand to her face. Sadie rears away, scared of his touch, but she detects sympathy in those brown depths. "Easy, Blue-Eyes. How did you get your scars?"

She remains silent. *Go to hell.*

He lets out a deep sigh. "When I tell you to run, do it."

Sadie's hard expression softens. "Why are you helping me?"

"Shouldn't need a reason."

Her breath catches in surprise. *Those words...I've heard them before. When Brent knocked me out... Mom...*

138

He shoves Sadie's belongings back into her backpack. His eyes slide up to hers, and without another word, he places her EGA pin in her pocket. His arms encircle her with a gentleness she doesn't expect. The scent of wood smoke clings to the man: a comforting aroma that evokes memories of crackling campfires and starry nights. The rough rope loosens around her wrists.

Wood tumbles and crashes onto the ground, and Sadie spins to see Sonny watching them.

"What are you doing?"

Chapter 26

With a sigh of frustration, Hunter gets up, putting himself between Sonny and the blue-eyed woman. "I'm just making sure she's okay." If he mentions Wendall's request of the women, that might keep this brute from touching her. By the look on Sonny's face, though, it may take more than that to deter him.

Sonny waves Hunter away. "You start the fire. I want a pre-dinner snack." He steps around Hunter. The woman cries out as he grabs her and begins forcing her down.

Shit! Hunter searches the ground by the tree for the rifle. *Too far.*

In seconds, Sonny has her face down on the ground, pinning her by the neck, and attempts to rip her pants. She writhes and kicks. Sonny retrieves the weapon from his belt and winds up to hit her over the head with it.

Hunter rushes him.

Sonny redirects the gun, aiming it at Hunter. He comes to an abrupt halt, kicking up the forest floor as he stares down the barrel. *Don't.*

"Thought you'd try to be the hero?"

The woman's breathing scatters the leaves and dirt as she struggles. Intense fear radiates from her.

"Wendall sends his love. He wanted you to know, he's disappointed in you."

What?

Sonny lines up his target. Hunter barrels forward.

P-taff!

He feels a searing pain, but the possibility of death doesn't stop him. "Run!" He plows into Sonny, knocking the weapon out of his hands.

Faster than a jackrabbit, the woman scrambles away and flees into the trees, the rope dragging behind her.

Straddling Sonny, Hunter strikes him once, twice, then reaches for the gun lying nearby. Hunter gasps as Sonny's fist strikes his arm, sending a jolt of pain.

Sonny snatches the weapon, and the urgency of the situation gives Hunter all the wind he needs. Using one hand to keep his opponent from swinging the gun into his face, Hunter uses his other to snake his fingers around Sonny's neck and starts to choke him. He pounds the gun into the dirt over and over. *Let it go, you little shit.*

Sonny continues his assault on Hunter's arm but loses his grip on the gun. He hooks Hunter's leg, and they twist and roll...leaving the weapon behind.

Hunter has the height advantage, but Sonny has bulk. Now on top, Sonny lands an advantageous blow to Hunter's face, then slams his head into the ground. Hunter's skull feels like it has cracked, and his vision starts to spin and swirl. *Body, don't let me down now.*

P-taff!

Sonny's shoulder jerks back.

The woman is standing over Hunter, handgun aimed.

P-taff!

Blood sprays over Hunter's face. Sonny crumples to the ground between his legs in one motion.

The woman falls onto all fours, and the world around Hunter fades away, replaced by an impenetrable blackness.

***

Hunter reaches out and discovers his hands tied tight in his lap. He searches for the sun in the sky. *How long have I been out?* His head feels larger than it is, and his mouth is dry. The sunlight hurts his eyes.

Sonny's body lies where it fell, looking like someone pushed him back on his knees. Hunter, slumped against a nearby tree's rough bark, adjusts his jaw, feeling pain there. He follows the drag marks with his eyes from Sonny's lifeless corpse. Hunter's no slouch, weighing in at over two-ten. *She's strong.* He scans the area for the woman and finds her kneeling at a safe distance, just out of his reach. *Smart.* She's sweating and looks pale as she cradles her ribs. It cost her to move him.

"Thought I told you to run, Blue-Eyes?" His voice is gruff. Hunter needs water to clear his throat and sees a bottle near the woman. Slowly, he leans closer, showing her his bound hands all the way.

"He was going to kill you." She makes no attempt to shift away.

Has she even realized I'm moving? He picks the bottle up, twists the cap, and drains it. "I know."

She looks up at him, her brow pinching with bewilderment. She offers an unwrapped trail bar.

He doesn't move to take it. His attention is fixed on the scars that crisscross her face, mirroring those etched into his own. Broken lines skip from her chin, slashing both cheeks, the bridge of her nose, and one eyebrow. The ugliness doesn't dim her beauty in the slightest; if anything, it accentuates it. "You should have left me."

"I'm not that kind of girl."

She doesn't shy away from his scrutiny. *Her injuries are recent, then. She doesn't remember she has them.* He can't help but smile. It feels unfamiliar to him. Smiling is for cheerful people.

She offers the food again but, this time, doesn't let him decline. He stretches out his arms, accepts the trail bar with both hands, and takes a bite. The taste of nuts and fruit colors his palette, getting his juices flowing. He is hungrier than he thought.

"Who's Wendall?"

Hunter gazes up at her in surprise. "My brother." He attempts to rise, sucks in a painful breath, and rotates his shoulder. *Damn it.*

"Bullet grazed your arm. I dressed it." She says this calmly.

With a wince, he rotates his arms until he can see the blood-encrusted sleeve that has been rolled back. Underneath, he sees a gauze patch. *She knows her stuff.* "Where'd you learn to do that?"

"I'm moving on. Why were you out here with that guy?"

Hunter doesn't want to admit the reason Wendall sent them out. "He was my chance to get away from my brother."

"You were going to kill him, anyway?"

He doesn't like the implication, but sadly, it fits. There is no way to sugarcoat what he is. A killer. "I don't have many options."

He reads her expression of dismissal. "Everyone has choices."

"Mine is this, or go back to him."

Something like understanding blooms on her pale face. "You could die out here."

"I'll take my chances." *Time to turn this around.* "You shouldn't be traveling alone if you're hurt."

"I'll deal."

Hunter can't help but feel impressed as she stands up, and he smirks, but then she falters, very nearly collapsing to the ground again. *She's suffering.* He doesn't want her to leave, but bound, he can't do much. "Where are you heading? The light's dwindling. Stay. Rest. Head out after you've recovered a little."

She produces some bandages and places them nearby. "Here. Extra dressings."

Hunter can see the determination in her vibrant blue eyes to get away. She has a plan, and nothing, especially a loser like him, will deter her from it. Hunter doesn't blame her for wanting to get far from him. There's no real trust between them.

He reaches for the bandages.

"I'd choose life." She coughs. "Good luck."

He recognizes her watery voice. Pneumonia. His grandfather was prone to getting that. "Thanks. I owe you."

"We're even." She raises her rucksack and flinches. "I owed you first. Check your pockets." She hefts it up and heads out without looking back, retrieving her rifle from the base of the tree along the way.

"Hey!"

She twists back to look at him. "What?"

This stimulates a sudden rush. He wants her blue eyes on him, but under different circumstances. Something about her compels him to know her better. He squashes that thought. He's not worth a real woman's time. "You have pneumonia."

Her eyes stray away from his as she heads into the trees and calls out over her shoulder. "I know."

Hunter loves that kind of confidence. *Too bad.*

For a while, he stares at the point in the trees where he lost sight of her. Once he regains his senses, he feels something in his pocket, reaches in, and retrieves his knife. He flips the blade open and slices through the rope around his wrists.

He looks over at Sonny's corpse. Now that he is alone, Hunter can trek back to the highway, find supplies, and live in the forest north of here, well away from Wendall. He tries not to think about Giles.

The waning light signals Hunter to hunker down for the night. His head twists to his right. *Where was that shelter?*

As he crawls under the camouflage, he determines to himself that he must see the falls again before he moves on. He's about to start anew. He'll need a clean conscience.

***

The next day, the thunderous clap of water falling over the rocks drowns out all other sound as Hunter exits the plunge pool wearing nothing. A light breeze skims across his naked flesh, stimulating him. He shakes off the excess drops, feeling the pull of the bandage on his arm. His wound stings.

Hunter had slept far better than he'd expected he would. In the shelter, under the rock inside, he found a stocked cooler with MREs. The military meal wasn't bad, and the candy was a pleasant touch. His headache stayed away today thanks to the medicine he found. The thought that he might have a concussion crossed his mind, but he couldn't do anything about it, even if he did. So, in the end, he allowed himself to drift off to sleep, using a Mylar blanket to stay warm.

Finding a large boulder, Hunter lies down across its smooth surface, crossing his wrists behind his head. He closes his eyes. Hunter spent a lot of his childhood hanging out here in the relative silence. It's good to be back.

He found a journal in that shelter, as well, inside a Ziploc bag to protect it from the elements. It contained a short list of handwritten names, along with notes of encouragement. The last entry had been written in clear, bold letters: *Sadie Masters.*

Is that your name, Blue-Eyes?

Some names were dated weeks ago. He figures there's a safe place somewhere, and hopes she finds it before the fever takes hold of her. The brief contact he's had with her convinces him that she'll fight through it to get there.

Now a little further from the falls, birdsong reaches Hunter's ears, mixed with the wind through the trees, then declines, only to crest again like a song's crescendo. His stress melts into the rock under him as the warmth of the sun evaporates the water off his exposed skin.

He pushes down the thoughts of Giles that linger on the edge of his consciousness, relentlessly threatening to shatter his hard-won peace. Despite the heat of the sun, a chilling coldness envelopes his heart. Hunter needs to look out for himself. This is who he is...and must be to survive.

The sound of retching pricks his ears.

Hunter jolts upright and searches for any sign of danger. The plunge pool is empty, and the surrounding forest seems devoid of animals. A shiver of unease raises the hairs on the back of his neck.

He hears the noise again. To his left. He scrutinizes the water's edge more closely and can't believe his eyes.

The woman named Sadie staggers, falls, and lands on her knees as an outstretched hand contacts the ground, all while clutching her ribs with the other.

He shoots up off the rock. She didn't get far. *How did she survive in the open last night?* If only she'd stayed with him.

She glances up at the falls and struggles to get back up, only to collapse again.

He searches out his clothes, yanks his pants on, not caring that he's still dripping wet, and calls out to her. "Stop moving! You're hurt! I can help."

Apparently unable to hear him over the roaring water, she crawls toward the falls with unwavering determination

CHAPTER 27

Hunter follows the woman's trail from the edge of the waterfall's plunge pool. He can't understand what happened. All signs of her movement stop on the gentler side of the cascading wall of water. She couldn't have vanished...

He's been to the falls many times, and Hunter's never known he could explore under it. He's not sure what's on the other side, but he's a risk taker. *What do I have to lose?* Shielding his head, Hunter walks through the water into a cavernous space. His eyes adjust to the low lighting. *What the...?* A dark metal door with a lit keypad captures his interest.

The woman lies propped against the damp back wall. He approaches slowly, knowing she's armed, but she remains still. He drops and caresses her pink scars. "Hey, Blue-Eyes? You didn't make it far."

Her eyes dart to the door and then return to Hunter with a fevered intensity. She's shivering and wet. He tries to dismiss the distress in her face, but a twinge of disappointment tickles the back of his mind. Her trust means something to him.

"You need antibiotics." Hunter gazes around them. "Is this the place you were searching for?"

"No." She barely whispers the lie, her word sounding like a drowning plea.

She is very sick. Screw his plans to go north. He can't let her do this alone. "If they're in there, I can get you in. What's the code?"

She shakes her head, almost in slow motion.

His frustration builds, but Hunter takes a deep breath before posing the question. "Why?"

"Don't know...you."

Her stubbornness, a trait he is discovering, is unmistakable and resonates loud and clear. *Okay, this is ridiculous.* "You'd rather die out here than give me the code?"

"I'd die to protect..." Her words falter.

Hunter admires her conviction, but he'd never hurt her. How can he convince her? They're at a stalemate, but the longer they're out here, the greater the chance that she'll pass out before he gets that code.

"Why do you...help me?"

Someone hurt her; perhaps the same someone who scarred her. Hunter's anger flares. "Told you, I shouldn't need a reason." She's wasting time.

Her fevered eyes divert away from Hunter.

He quells his emotions and tries a different tactic. "You're hurt. Besides, don't I owe you?" He doesn't, but he needs some way of getting through to her. *Trust me, please.*

She glances back up. "Your scars. Tell me how..."

Hunter averts his eyes. *I am not telling you—*

"Tell me... I'll let...you...in." Her voice is sounding weaker by the second.

Damn it. Hunter's never spoken to anyone about that day and never wanted to. It's fucking painful. He turns it around on her. "If I tell you, you tell me how you got yours."

"No."

Shame? "Then you understand why I'm reluctant. It goes both ways, Blue-Eyes."

He sees the conflict in her, but she nods. "I'll tell...inside."

Hunter will hold her to that. *If she blacks out... Better make it quick.*

He envisions his grandmother standing in the kitchen, angry and crazed. Hunter never understood why she had come back into the house when she did.

"My grandmother... I did something she didn't like." He can still hear the blade sliding out of its resting place. "She grabbed a knife out of the butcher block."

Her lips part. He sees understanding in her gray face. She gets it.

The memory of crawling to the kitchen wall to avoid Cissy's blood still haunts him. It slithered across the floor like a family of red snakes. Hunter closes his eyes to it. "So much blood on the tiles. My screams...the agony." Hunter's head throbs as warmth radiates through him. His anguish appears to subside with every word he speaks to her. Tears gather, and he breathes in to clear them.

The woman's gentle touch pulls him from the nightmare. Sympathetic eyes stare back at him.

He shies from her touch. "Don't." He hates people showing sympathy, like he's weak. A failure. But coming from her, it feels different. She understands. She's living it.

"Seventy-one, forty-three."

Minutes later, with an arm secured around her waist, Hunter rushes the lady called Sadie inside like they're in a three-legged race, through a red-lit hallway, and into a dark room. He needs to find antibiotics, fast. He feels the wall for a smooth, unbroken surface. "Is there a light switch?"

"Master. Other end of the...corridor. Need power." With renewed energy, she struggles to free herself, so Hunter loosens his hold, surrendering some control to allow her to take the lead. Through the darkness, they traverse a maze of interconnected rooms before finally reaching a passage. The floor in this area is lit with luminescent strips that remind him of the ones on airplanes, giving him enough light to drag her to a long table and lower her into a chair.

"Where?"

She points down the corridor. "Room...bottom stairs..."

Hunter follows the strips and jogs past several doors on either side. He slides through a large, robust kitchen and around a center island and into a room full of shelves shrouded in mystery. The lights cast a glow over another door on the left. Hunter finds the stairs and a room where he fumbles in the dark and flips a large-handled switch. The compound hums to life. Hunter raises his hand, wincing underneath the new, piercing light, and heads back to her.

Blown away, he takes in what appears to be a pantry stocked floor to ceiling...with food. There's so much! Hunter enters the kitchen again, rounds the island, and heads down the corridor. Each door reveals a new surprise. A gym, bathrooms, and rooms full of bunk beds.

"How long's this been here? I—"

She lies crumpled face down, unconscious on the floor.

***

The sound of a seal breaks as Hunter opens a can he acquired from the pantry. Keeping his eyes closed, he relishes the taste of a spoonful of peaches. *Fuck me.* Equipment hums around Hunter as he monitors what's going on outside this place. It's a security room of some kind. The bunker fascinates him. Has it always been there, right under his nose every time he came to the falls?

The woman passing out earlier caused him to go into action mode. He found a suite with two rooms and placed her limp body on the first bed he could reach. It is a convenient spot: Hunter can sleep in the nearby bunk beds, so he is close if she needs him. Then, he ran back to the pantry to find something for her to eat. She needs something warm, and considering her inability to feed herself, he figures soup is the optimal solution. He removed everything he needed to heat it up later, once she's awake.

After helping himself to the peaches, Hunter explores the immediate area, where he comes across another suite. Inside, he gazes upon a wall of pictures. The same men appear in them again and again, in and out of uniform, sometimes together, sometimes with various women and kids of different ages, laughing and playing. Lives. Happy ones. He yearns for memories that are worth holding onto, of capturing in photographs, but he knows he has none.

Hunter ducks back into the medical room to look for anything else he can use to help the woman. He can't find the key for the medicine cabinets, but he jimmies another lock to grab the gauze and antibiotic cream inside so he can redress his wound later. *Better check on her.*

Back in the suite, she hasn't moved, but she's breathing a little steadier than before, a little deeper. He climbs across the bed to lie beside the woman, intent on not waking her. Bright blue eyes flutter open at his movement and mark him. He submits and dips his head.

"Liam... Radio...," she whispers hoarsely. Her lips went unnoticed by him until now. Plump, pink, and looking soft, like velvet.

Hunter reaches across her and produces a water glass and pills. "Antibiotics." He props her up so she can swallow the pill, then helps to lay her sweat-drenched body back down. "You're the priority. The radio can wait."

She creases her forehead. "No..."

"Your sassy attitude and fierce eyes will not deter me." He gazes down at her. "Need to get you back on track, Blue-Eyes. I know you'll understand this when you're feeling better, so deal."

"Sadie." She closes her eyes.

The journal was correct. The pleasant sound of her name captivates Hunter, especially when she says it in her delirious state.

"Hunter. Rest now. When you wake up, I'll make you some food." He lies down beside her but stays awake, gazing at the ceiling, feeling like he's in paradise. *I hope I can stay here forever.* Wendall will never find him here.

CHAPTER 28
June 29

Sadie wakes alone in the suite, drenched in sweat, wondering why it's so cold. A rush of panic overwhelms her. *Where is...? What was his name again?* In her delirium, her memory is faulty. Snippets of this strange man helping her to drink water and take medication seem unreal. Is he real? How long has she been here?

The man enters, looking like the guy next door, dressed in a clean Henley and jeans, balancing a tray with a glass of water and what she guesses is food. This is not the same broody man she met in the forest. He sets it down and reaches over to prop her up. The smell of vanilla follows him, which conjures up thoughts of Penny. He showered. There's a hint of lemon, distracting her as he pulls away. *Liam...*

Sadie's eyes are drawn to one scar in particular. It runs from his eyebrow, across his cheek, under his brown eye, and into his beard. The assault left one side of his face a bruised mix of black and purple. It looks like it's painful.

He turns to the tray under her scrutiny. "Made some soup. Hope you like tomato." He picks up a bowl and blows across the surface before running the spoon through it.

"How long?" She's still weak and doesn't have the energy to ask more, even though she wants to. She shivers.

"We came in yesterday. Your fever's down, but not enough."

That's why I'm cold. "Found clothes?"

He examines his attire. "Thought I'd look less scary this way. Now, open wide for me." He offers the spoon.

Sadie sips, but the soup is tasteless. She makes a face, not hungry for more. "Don't look scary."

He smirks. "The drugs must be working. You're either hallucinating or you're going blind. Not sure which."

Sadie flashes a weak grin. She likes a man with humor. Now that he's close up, she notes his stress lines are gone. His facial scar becomes less pronounced when he smiles, but he didn't give her a full smile. *Wonder what it would take to get one?* Sadie feels his nervousness, like he wants to say something, but he's holding it in. "What's wrong?"

He glances at the bowl. "Nothing." He twirls the spoon. "Who are the people in the pictures in the other room?"

The other room... Penny's suite, maybe? "Family."

Saying the word invokes thoughts of her father and siblings, and especially her mother. What was her mother trying to tell her? She said he was waiting for her. Why?

He draws the spoon once more to her reluctant lips. "I saw a girl with your hair coloring. Was that you?"

He said his name is Hunter, she recalls. Did her mother mean this man? Sadie thought she had meant Carl, but it was Hunter who said, "Shouldn't need a reason," not Carl. Sadie sips. Some of the liquid spills. "Yes."

Hunter dabs a paper towel on her chin to catch the soup. "Bet you were a firebrand when you were young."

"Why would you think..." Her voice trails off.

"I like fierce and sassy women. Open." He spoons more into her mouth.

She shies away, refusing more. *I'm not fierce and sassy.*

"Looks like I need to add stubborn to that list." He presents the spoon again. "Open."

***

Later, Sadie studies Hunter while he's relaxing in a chair with a book open between weathered hands, his long dark hair shadowing his eyes from her. Liam has always been clean cut, but Hunter's bad-boy look piques her interest. His lean body differs from Liam's stocky build. Once again, she smells the soap he has used. "You showered."

Hunter looks up, and a slow smile appears through his scar. He snaps the book shut. "It's been a while since I've seen one in such good condition." He runs his hand over his beard. "Found a shaver. I was thinking of getting rid of it, but I think it'll expose too much of my scar."

"Don't. I like the beard." *A lot.*

How long has she been at Reed? Time eludes her. Under the sheets, Sadie feels the soft fabric of her underwear and bra against her skin. A blush warms her cheeks at the thought of Hunter undressing her.

"How do you feel?" He smooths the cover of the book in his lap with his fingers.

He doesn't like talking about his scar. She understands his reluctance. It mirrors her own feelings. "Better. Need to radio my family."

Hunter stares at the floor for a beat. "Where are they?"

She's not sure where this is leading. "They're at the farm. They'll send someone over once I make contact."

"What's this place?" He gestures to the surrounding walls. "Why aren't they here?"

"It's our backup. We call it Reed."

Tension returns to his face. He's afraid. "How long will it take them to get here from the farm?"

With each question, Sadie's wariness grows, wondering if she should fear Hunter and the potential harm he could bring to the people she loves. Did she make a mistake in letting him in? Her mother's words still hold weight, though.

Hunter holds his hand up, palm out. "Don't get me wrong. We'll radio. I just..." His shoulders sag, and he sighs. "It feels like it's been years since I... I just want a day to feel normal."

Years? Where has he been?

She doesn't get to ask before he inquires, "Your family's military?"

"My dad's a Marine." It's strange to think she is one, too, now. She swells with pride and enjoys the feeling. Sadie hasn't felt that since before the missile hit.

"I took that path once, but never got past training. Life tripped me." Hunter throws the book onto the bed and stands to leave. "I'll go get some more soup for you."

Chapter 29
June 30

At the corridor table, Hunter shoves bacon into his mouth, savoring the flavor. Since he started feeding Sadie, he's rediscovered the joy of cooking and all its delightful aromas.

He woke up this morning, having thoughts about what it would be like to be with Sadie. He never found that someone, what with enlisting, then having trouble with the law and dealing with his brothers. Who's he kidding? With his hideous scars, Hunter knows most women only look at him in horror. The ones who tolerated him did so only because he paid for their services.

"If wishes were horses..." A phrase he uses often, but not of late. He holds a fork of scrambled eggs aloft, ready to shovel into his mouth. Hunter's neck tingles. He gazes up at the suite door.

In a robe that barely covers her body, Sadie looks better, but unsteady, breathing heavily and bracing herself against the doorframe for support. "I wanted a shower. Seemed like a good idea, but I'm losing steam."

Hunter feels a twinge in his groin, but dismisses it quickly. He clears his throat. "Let me help you." The fork clangs on the plate as he crosses to her and moves to pick her up.

Sadie raises her hand, her voice firm. "I will not shower with a man I don't know."

Hunter was going to place her back in bed, but she seems determined. He ignores her hand and gently scoops her into his arms. Sadie's robe opens, exposing her legs. "Relax. I got you." Hunter can't help but feast on those beautiful legs.

She's lighter than he thinks she should be. With his cooking, he knows she'll recover some of her lost weight.

"You got me?" She encircles her soft arms around his neck.

"I got you, Blue-Eyes." Hunter carries her into the communal bathroom, walks into a shower stall, and deposits her on a chair he had placed there already. He'd expected this and left all she needed on a nearby stool. Sadie picks up the bar of soap with childish delight. He takes pleasure in the contented smile on her face, following the lines of her scars. *They haven't ruined her smile. Not like mine.*

He turns on the taps. With the water warming up, Hunter grabs the bottle of shampoo he chose, opens it, and squeezes out a curling amount into his hand. The air smells of strawberries. Something Hunter loves the taste of. Especially if they're grown in the wild.

"What are you doing?"

Sadie isn't able to see what Hunter's up to. He smiles, choosing not to say a word as he tips her head back. She looks at him with a frown. Hunter reaches for the handheld shower, not caring that he's getting wet, and lets the stream run along her forehead.

Sadie catches on and closes her eyes. Her lips part. Hunter tries to concentrate on the task, massaging the shampoo into her auburn hair with slow, methodical movements.

She moans.

His body tightens. It's been a while since he's been this close to a woman. What would it be like to bend down and kiss those moaning lips? He curses the jeans he's wearing for suddenly being too tight, but it only gets worse as he sees how close those tempting lips are to his rising bulge. Hunter squeezes his eyes shut for a moment, trying to think about anything besides the gorgeous woman, limp, like putty in his hands, continuing her torturous but provocative moans.

He runs his hands repeatedly through Sadie's auburn hair, loving the silky smoothness of it, letting the hot, soapy water drain over his bare feet. This is a first, he realizes. No woman has ever let him do these things. Things that require such...trust. He finds this attractive, and deeply alien and uncomfortable.

"All done," Hunter says. Sadie stares up, ensnaring him. She's so beautiful. It takes all his willpower to look away. "I put a towel outside the door. Yell, and I'll come get you."

"Thank you, Hunter. That was amazing."

It would be more amazing if I yanked you out of that chair and slammed you up against the shower stall.

Hunter retreats before she can see how sensational he found it. He needs some alone time to cool his heated thoughts and release the tension from...other things.

***

Showered and refreshed, Sadie sits at the corridor table, nibbling on the food Hunter prepared for her. Her favorite part was the scalp massage. It would have been even more satisfying if his hands had ventured further. The showerhead came in handy. Once he left, she took the edge off with thoughts of Hunter doing naughty things to her. A blush crept onto her cheeks.

As she has recovered, her taste buds have made a triumphant return, transforming her enjoyment of Hunter's food. Each meal is now a delightful experience, full of rich flavors and textures. He reminds her of her father and his love of cooking. And how much she misses him.

But Hunter's also reminding Sadie of what she doesn't like about her father.

Hunter hovers in the chair next to her, his arm over the back of hers, his lingering scent distracting.

She shoots him a warning to give her space. "I think I'm okay."

"Well, I'm not taking any chances."

"My father hovers." Sadie gobbles up a piece of bacon.

"It's better than not having one." Hunter's voice is low and melancholic.

Swallowing the bacon, Sadie turns and licks her fingers, excited at the opportunity to get a sense of who Hunter is. "You didn't know your father?"

His eyes dip to her fingers. "I did, but he was also my grandfather."

Incest? She's heard of it, but... Surprised, Sadie blurts out, "Oh, shit! Sorry."

"Don't be. I've come to terms with it." Hunter leans back on his elbow, cupping his chin, but his arm doesn't drop from the back of her chair. "Not like I had a choice in the matter."

The curve of his biceps, the Henley stretching across Hunter's chest, entices her to speculate about how delicious he might look without it.

"My grandmother was psychotic. And I have three brothers. Well, had. Two are dead now. I'm left with the one I don't like."

"Jesus. That's terrible. Have you ever been happy?"

Hunter takes a moment before responding, his eyes darting between her eyes and her lips. Sexy bad-boy is working for her. He struggles to name something he's happy about. *He's seen darkness.*

But then, Hunter's expression turns up. "I'm happy when I'm in nature. What makes you happy?"

It doesn't go unnoticed that he changed the subject, but Sadie lets it go. "Freedom to do as I please, and my family. The first... Harder to achieve with Dad. The reason I went away to university."

"University?" This piques his interest. "What for?"

"Librarian." She chews another piece of bacon with extra aggression, ticked at the world. *Who is going to need a librarian now that the country is in chaos?* "Fat good it's doing me." All those books, lost under the collapse of civilization.

"Do you know what happened out there? I was on a highway, past Spokane, when a missile crossed the sky."

"Saw the mushroom cloud." Sadie twirls a strand of her hair. "I haven't lost my hair yet, and there's no fallout, so it wasn't nuclear." She doesn't have enough information, but she's content, knowing that the book archives will still be intact. "But why Spokane?"

Hunter shrugs, not caring. "The missile took out the base and airport."

"How do you know that?"

A slow and sensual smile plays across his lips. "Sexy librarian."

Sadie is surprised. Other men have brought up the sexy librarian trope, and she's always rolled her eyes. But not this time. In fact, his words send her into overdrive, bringing on thoughts of what she would do to Hunter if he took his shirt off right now. "I think that went out the window a month ago. Don't you?"

His eyes dip to her lips. This time, they stay there. "Uh, no."

Sadie looks for the joke, but his sensual smile stays for her to admire. *He thinks I'm sexy? Even with these scars?* She swallows. "I think you're either hallucinating or blind, but I'm not sure which yet," she says, trying to alleviate the sexual tension between them.

His face lights up, captivating her as he tips his head back and unleashes a low, rumbling laugh.

After dinner, Hunter cocoons Sadie in a blanket and places her in a single leather chair before falling carefree into the other one across from her. She could get used to this attention. Sadie knows she has to call Haven soon, but she's not sure what to say to her dad. She broods over her scars, a reminder of her failure to defend herself. To use the skills she thought she'd mastered.

Carl's words interrupt her thought. "Somethin' you need to accept."

"You okay?" Hunter's look of concern is noticeable in the way he frowns. It's astonishing how quickly and effortlessly Hunter detects and understands her moods.

"I'm scared."

"You? Scared of what?"

Afraid of how they will react to me. Sadie fears her father's outrage and her siblings' difficulty looking at her. Even though Liam will never be hers, she's nervous about him seeing her. They'll pity her. Can she bear that? Being pitied. "I'm...I'm not me anymore."

"I can't speak for your family, but my brother takes every opportunity to tease me about my scars."

"That's awful."

He shrugs. "To me, that's family."

"They don't deserve you, then."

The warm smile Hunter graces her with colors her face. Silence creeps in. Sadie hasn't even seen herself since it happened. Out in the wilderness, there was nothing with a strong enough reflective surface. This morning, she passed the mirror in the bathroom but refused to look, too afraid. Far better to keep up the illusion that the scars don't exist.

"Who's Liam?"

Hearing his name on Hunter's lips seems foreign. *How does he know that name?* "Someone I've known my whole life."

"You kept repeating his name in your sleep last night."

"Did I?" She has thought little of him since Hunter's been around. "I fell for Liam when I was fifteen. He's five years older than me and...not for me."

"Didn't hook up then?"

She feels the pain of that, knowing she never even got one kiss from him. Liam avoided touching her on purpose. *If I disgusted him back then, then now...*

"No." She steers the conversation. "You ever have a wife or kids?"

"I'm lucky if a woman even looks at me, much less have kids."

That saddens Sadie and doesn't bode well for her. She might as well get used to being single. "No one will want me now."

"You're beautiful."

She keeps her eyes on her lap for a while, unsure if he's mocking her or not. When she glances at him, she does so with a forced smirk. "Verdicts in, you're blind."

Hunter leans in with smoldering intensity and conviction, locking eyes with her. "I'm not."

Sadie feels her body temperature rise as her ears start to burn. *Could he be any sexier?*

"A word of advice?"

"Yeah, what's that?" With her gaze fixed downward, she toys with her blanket.

"Give people a moment when they first see you. Let them get past it, and then you'll see who's a keeper and who isn't."

CHAPTER 30
July 1

Liam stands in one of the guard trees overlooking the outside area past the wall and gazes across to the other tree. He can't see Alex, but Liam knows his friend is with him on duty.

Liam retrieves his favorite photograph of Sadie from his vest pocket. He wants to keep the memory of that day alive. It had been one of particularly heightened sexual energy between them. It doesn't help to make her feel any closer to him, though. *Where are you, Auburn?*

Every time Liam's up in the guard tree, he hopes to see Sadie walking out of the forest and toward them. It's been three long weeks since they rescued Beth and Gina, but as crippling as it has been, he keeps up the faith that she's going to show. When she does, he's going to worship the fucking ground she walks on.

Liam's kicking himself for the time he wasted. It's his fault. He should have made his case and fought for her. He was such an ass.

Someone climbs up the tree behind him. "Is it quiet?"

Colin's a good guy. He and Liam have got into the habit of hanging around the gun range in the back of the buried garage when they're not on their security or farming shifts. Colin can't shoot for shit right now, but he excels at hand-to-hand combat, and Liam has no qualms that Colin will improve.

With a nod, Liam and Colin switch positions. "Yes." Liam would rather be in the fields, out in the open, than in this tree. Too much time up here to think of all the horrible things that are delaying Sadie from being in his arms.

"Cool."

Roger's voice rings in Liam's helmet. "Haven to Golden Boy."

"Yeppers." Liam cringes at himself. He sounds too much like his dad sometimes.

"Need you stat."

"Coming down." Liam hustles across the yard, past a half-buried slab of steel they installed to protect the front door of the compound if the walls are ever breached. He hits the keypad code. The lock clicks, and he yanks on the door and descends a flight of stairs to a short landing. The lack of a beep concerns Liam as he steps past the decontamination room. After adjusting to the low light, he goes down more stairs to another small landing, then turns into security.

Racks of weapons of varying kinds and colors cover the walls. One entire wall, floor to ceiling, houses just ammunition. The acrid scent of gunpowder, thick and metallic, hangs heavy in the air. It's a smell Liam has never gotten used to.

Roger and Ryker are standing by a desk covered with monitors as Liam hangs his weapons. He pauses. They never stand when he comes in. Liam's radar heightens. "What's up?"

Roger says, "Sadie's on the radio at Reed."

Holy fuck! Liam's heart jump-starts as he rushes toward the desk. He doesn't even register that Ryker is offering his seat, or that Roger is holding out the mic. Liam clicks it with force. "Auburn? Baby, you there?"

"Yes."

Hearing the tears in her voice, a rush of adrenaline courses through Liam, and water wells up in his eyes. She's alone and scared. Not daring to look up, Liam asks Ryker, "Donovan?"

Ryker pats his shoulder by way of support. "He's coming."

Liam blows out a stressed breath, clutching the mic with shaky hands, knowing what he wants to say, but also knowing he needs to take a moment to realize she's finally here. It's about fucking time.

***

As Sadie's tears flow, Hunter rubs her back from the chair next to her. He knew she was under pressure, but didn't truly recognize why until now. Sadie's in love with Liam, and Hunter can hear the same sentiment in Liam's voice on the other end. He even has a nickname for her. Jealousy rises, but Hunter quells it. *You fool,* of course *she loves someone else.*

"Before I get into it, I gotta say, I've fuckin' missed your smartass voice." Liam's voice echoes through the security room, making it sound like he's in a tunnel. Hunter smirks, agreeing with his assessment of Sadie.

She chuckles and sniffs back happy tears. "Miss you, too, sailor boy."

Hm, there's a lot of history here. Why did she say Liam isn't for her when she clearly loves him and vice versa? Maybe she doesn't see it? Could she be blind to him somehow?

***

Liam rolls his eyes and lets the comment go with a happy breath. "We've been wondering what held you back. What happened to you? Are you okay?" He needs reassurance that she's safe and healthy. It's been too long. If nothing is wrong, why didn't she arrive at Haven weeks ago?

"I have pneumonia. Took some antibiotics."

Her partial evasion of his question makes him feel a little uneasy. *What's she hiding?* He takes a different approach. "Are you hurt?"

"Broken ribs."

That explains the timing, but how did she make it there with broken ribs? The pneumonia must have been a complication. She's skirting the actual answer. *Damn it.* "How long since you broke them?"

Silence.

"Auburn?"

"The day everything went down." She is quiet for a moment. "I don't know what day it is anymore."

Liam reaches up and rubs his face. "It's been..."—he glances at the wall calendar—"six weeks. Are you seeing improvement?"

"Yes."

Thank God. His need to get to her is overwhelming: a desperate urgency claws at him to leave at once. "I'm coming to get you, Auburn."

The sound of the door opening behind Liam makes him turn in his seat. With a worried expression, Donovan walks toward him, followed by Liam's father, Hoss.

"Sadie?" Donovan asks.

"I'm not alone." Her statement rings clear as a bell in the room, unsettling the men.

A sudden chill runs through Liam's veins, causing his body to snap to attention, his heightened senses on high alert. "Say that again."

"I'm not alone. Hunter's with me."

Hunter? A man from school, maybe? Liam hopes he's just a friend.

Donovan snatches the mic away from Liam. "No names! Who is he?"

"Dad!"

***

Hunter guesses who the angry voice must belong to before Sadie confirms it's her father. The news of her being with an unfamiliar person has clearly upset him. He looks around the security at all the equipment: the cameras, the mics, the radio. He remembers the photographs he found of the men dressed in military gear and thinks about all they've built to protect their families. *These people don't like surprises, and I'm a surprise.*

"Hey, baby girl. Who's with you?" Her dad is using a gentler tone, but Hunter notices the repetition of the question.

Sadie's eyes slide back to the mic, but she doesn't respond. She appears unsure of how to proceed.

"What's wrong?" Hunter touches her back again and loves that she lets him.

"I forgot how my father can be. He's going to wanna know who you are."

With her meaning clear to him, Hunter gently takes the mic from her hands. "I'll introduce myself." It won't matter two days from now, anyway. Once he realized she was going to call for rescue, Hunter knew he'd have to leave. Hunter can't be with these people. He'll only bring disaster down on them, like he did to the Hutchison family.

He pulls the mic to his mouth. "I met her in the forest, sir."

Sadie covers his hand with hers and brings the mic to her lips. "More like saved my ass."

Good save, even if it isn't true. He realizes that she's trying to put a good light on what happened to her out there with Sonny. *If it weren't for me finding her, she'd have been with her family already. But I wouldn't have met her.*

"Language, honey."

Ah, so he's that kind of father. Controlling, like Wendall. This irks Hunter somehow.

Ignoring her father's statement, she adds. "He was wounded. He'll need a proper look."

It's better to let Sadie think he's going with her. He'll leave while she sleeps.

"Where is he from?"

Time to fudge the truth. Sadie doesn't know, after all, and she'll have forgotten about him in a few days from now. "Coeur d'Alene, sir."

"What do you do for a living?"

Rob banks, kill people, help criminals escape on any given day. He'll never be boyfriend material. This line of questioning verifies his decision to leave is sound, so he lies again. "Just finished boot camp, sir. Army." This won't impress her father if he's a Marine, but it might put him at ease until they arrive to collect her.

***

Donovan exchanges a dissatisfied look with Hoss. His baby is home, but this guy is a snag he didn't see coming. Donovan doesn't trust him, whoever he is. He could be lying, or worse, coercing her to say she's fine when she's not.

Hoss shrugs, taking Donovan's hesitation as animosity. "Not everyone can be a Marine."

He did call me sir, at least, Donovan thinks as he holds the mic steady. "Baby, we're coming for you. Sit tight."

"Love you. Got you," she says, using the words they used to say to each other before bedtime or when he was deployed. His sweet baby girl. She seems fine.

"I got you, too, honey. A word of warning to your friend. I don't know who you are, but if you mess with her, I will hunt you down. Do I make myself clear?" Donovan hopes that will scare the guy into toeing the line. No way he's going near Sadie without his approval.

"Crystal, sir."

Good answer. "Out."

***

"Out," Sadie says, stifling a chuckle as she swipes away the tears on her cheeks.

"Wow, he's scary." Hunter pushes away from the desk, more resolute than ever that he must leave. He's played his part. The hard part will be letting her go, but at least he got to meet her. To save her.

Sadie stands with him. "My best friend calls Dad a pussycat."

"I don't think she knows what a pussycat is."

Chapter 31

Hoss stops just inside the doorway of Liam's bedroom and watches his son stuffing things into his backpack. Liam thinks, then pats his pockets, mumbling to himself. He snatches a shirt out of a drawer. *Gonna have to slow him down some.* "Son?"

Liam covers his head with a moisture-wicking shirt and talks from underneath it. "Sadie's at Reed." His face pops out of the top. "Which means, I'm going to Reed."

Hoss walks a few steps forward, holding his palms out to Liam. "Yeah, I know. I also know you've been itching to go find her."

Liam confronts his father with eager conviction. "No way in hell anyone's gonna stop me, so fuck yeah!"

It's like holding down a rabid dog. Hoss squeezes Liam's shoulders and holds him fast. "Son! The council decides who goes."

Panic appears in Liam's eyes. "No—"

"Hey...let me work my magic. Stay here till I get back."

A short time later, Hoss strides into Parker's apartment with his arm around Penny. The council greets them with smiles, already seated at the round kitchen table. Donovan walks in with Father Isaac, and they seat themselves.

Hoss admires the picture above the couch in the living room. Beth and her long-deceased sister, when they were little, are giggling over a butterfly held in Beth's sister's tiny hand. A precious moment caught in time.

Parker stands by the coffee machine as it percolates. "So, who's going to get Sadie? I assume Liam. One more?"

"I agree." Hoss perks up. "If Sadie is sick and injured, Liam has the medical experience. Alex should go with him." Liam will need a calm head when he finally sees Sadie. Besides, Hoss lost the bet with Alex over Colin, so it's fitting that he gets his wish to go with Liam.

"No," Donovan says. "I'm going, not Liam."

Hoss narrows his eyes. Normally, he goes with whatever Donovan says, but this time, he's digging his heels in. "What do you have against Liam? You think he's not capable of rescuing Sadie?"

"No, I'm sure he's more than capable." Donovan fires back dryly.

What's that supposed to mean?

Before Hoss can retort, Parker says, "Donovan, I know she's your daughter, but right now, we've got a potential threat at our front door, and we need you here. Let Liam go."

Exactly. Hoss leans back in his chair, crossing his arms.

Donovan is silent for a few seconds, then he concedes with a reluctant nod. "She'll be in excellent hands."

Hoss doesn't need more than an eyebrow raise from Donovan to know he's holding his tongue. *What is his problem?*

"Excuse my ignorance," Father Isaac says, raising his fingers slightly, "but isn't Alex injured?"

Hoss shakes his head. "It's just a graze, and it's been weeks. He'll be fine. A trip outside might be what the kid needs to end his whining."

"Then, I second that. Hoss? Any more activity?" Henry asks, moving the meeting forward.

Thank Christ! Hoss relaxes his arms. "Two more sightings of armed men sniffin' around."

Henry looks Hoss in the eye. "I don't like that. You still love recon?"

With the uptick in mood, Hoss flashes his usual laid-back smile. "Ain't got no problem with it if you want a better look. I can get the boys over and scope it out, 'scuse the pun, on the other side."

Parker shoots his hand into the air. "All those in favor of Liam and Alex going to Reed and Hoss doing recon of the neighbors?"

Hands go up. Donovan's is slow to rise, much to Hoss's chagrin, but it gets there.

Parker slaps the table. "Hoss, do the honors. Let's talk about the timing for this palisade fencing we're putting up next."

Isaac interjects. "Before we start that discussion, there's a leak in the garden shed topside we have to fix. I'll need help to bring the gardening tools down to the atrium and find a way to patch the roof."

"Okay, let's find victims." Henry coughs. "I mean volunteers to help you with that."

***

With both he and Alex all geared up, Liam watches his dad, dressed in a ghillie suit, as he removes his rifle, Candy, from her cradle with reverence. *Just like Jessie.* They're like two peas. He prays his brothers are safe over in Ibiza and then tucks that thought away. *Keep your focus on Sadie for now.* Liam becomes aware he's tapping his foot and stops. He's wanted this moment for so long; he just wants to get to Sadie. No more wasted time.

In front of the monitors, Roger clicks the mic. "How's the playground today, Superman?"

Ryker's voice resonates through the space: "Kids are fine."

"Golden, Pretty Boy, and Hoss are coming your way momentarily."

"Copy."

Donovan walks in, not looking pleased. He pulls Liam aside by his forearm. "Go in with weapons raised till you're comfortable with this guy. And take care of my girl like she was your sister."

Liam glances down at Donovan's hand on his arm and nods. He wants to tell Donovan what he really thinks about that statement, but he respects him too much. When Liam sees Sadie, he won't be treating her like a sister.

***

Bullets hit the tree near Liam's head. He ducks out of habit, then leans against the rough bark, searching for a way to avoid getting tagged. "Did you see that guy?"

"Like a fuckin' tank!" Alex takes cover not far away, behind another tree. "Good shot, too."

They crossed the river with no problems, but then they stumbled upon two armed men in the forest. Two they can handle, but the noise will attract more attention than they want. Gotta keep moving.

Liam clicks his radio. "Two tangos, section one."

Roger responds from Haven. "Copy. Manageable?"

"So far." Liam pops his magazine out, checks his supply, then clicks it back into position. "Hoss, you got a line out there?"

His father's voice spills into his ear. "You'll know when I do. One comin' up on your left."

Bullets whack the trunk, and splinters fly. Liam rounds the tree and takes out a skinny guy with two shots. *One down.* "Let's move."

They open fire and withdraw through the trees.

Bullets make contact. Alex takes a dive. Liam skids, gets behind cover, and looks back. "Pretty Boy!"

Alex catches his breath and pats himself down. "I'm still fuckin' here."

A powerful shot explodes. The sound of his father's sniper rifle. Liam scans the forest for movement while waiting for an update.

Hoss's voice pipes into Liam's ear. "I tagged Tank, but he's still active."

Alex moves toward Liam on his hands and knees, seeking cover.

"Stop, Pretty Boy," Hoss commands. "Tank's movin'. Golden, I can't get the shot. Comin' on your left."

From the ground, Alex tracks Tank's leg and pulls his sidearm. Aims.

P-taff!

Tank slams onto the ground, screaming. Liam rounds the tree, fires twice, and takes the guy out.

Alex scrambles up and joins Liam at the tree. "That was close."

Liam approaches the hulk of a man they just dispatched. The corpse is bald and full of tattoos. Liam divests the man of his handgun and holds it out in Alex's direction.

"Status?" Hoss asks.

Alex takes the weapon, checks the safety, and tucks it into his vest. "We're good. What about the other guy?"

"Don't worry, I'll check the other man for guns and ammo. You go!"

Liam pats the body down, finding ammunition and what looks like a modified toothbrush. It's a prison shiv. Liam gazes at Alex and pauses. "We're gone."

"Right-oh, boys. Haven, present has launched. Takin' Candy to my bunk."

"Affirmative," Roger says.

***

After the morning's incident with the two boys, Parker asked the council to meet again. It seems their neighbors haven't gotten the message after Donovan and co.'s last trip across the river, with too many people continuing to take an interest in Haven.

Henry is the first to speak. "We should send a message or deal with them."

Next to him, Parker's sister-in-law, Sylvia, sighs. "We can't keep interrupting the work we have to do and running inside. I have seedlings to put in the ground."

These people across the way are getting bolder by the day, first scoping out their fortifications, and now sending out raiding parties. Parker doesn't like it.

Henry squeezes her hand. "You're too valuable to be out there, besides being my wife." He kisses her. "You'll have to send out someone else."

Henry's right. They can't afford to lose their botanist. Parker's sister-in-law won't be seeing the outside world until this threat is neutralized.

Donovan strolls in with Mal and Father Isaac.

"Hoss back yet?" Parker asks Donovan.

"Still reporting intel. Need to neutralize this situation before we do more planting."

Parker finds it comforting that they have like minds. It would make his job a whole lot harder if he and Donovan butted heads.

Sylvia sits forward, sliding her arms onto the tabletop. "I know you all want to protect us, but we can't afford to stop planting. If we don't make the most of the warm weather, we won't have enough food to see us through winter."

Parker covers her hand and squeezes. "Can't afford to lose people, either." He turns back to Donovan. "How many jailers, and how many captives?"

Ever the diplomat, Father Isaac pipes in. "Could we not do this peacefully? I could deliver a message."

"They'd probably kill you or enslave you, Father."

Father Isaac deflates under Henry's sympathetic pat on his shoulder.

"Hoss counted fifteen guns," Donovan says, answering Parker's earlier question, "and somewhere in the teens for the captives so far. He can't get a head count on the women. They've sent more raiding parties out."

"Firepower?" Parker asks.

"Hoss says mostly handguns, rifles. Their leader walks around with a detail carrying higher-grade hardware."

Parker's eyes drift over to Mal. Before Mal joined his brother here at Haven, he was with those people on the other side of the river. He hasn't asked Mal why—instead, taking Ryker at his word that Mal will play nice—and he's been too busy over the last month to get to know the guy properly. Parker suspects Mal's not as respectable as his brother is, but he's proven to be exceptional at guard duty and knows his way around a weapon. *But is he trustworthy?* "We should have talked about this before. Mal, what do you know about this group?"

All heads turn. Mal steps away from the wall. Parker notes a slight apprehension and wariness in Mal as he answers. "The Greaves boys rob banks. There were four of them. Greg died en route. Wendall's the worst one, followed by Gideon." Mal looks at Donovan. "He's the one who had Gina at the table the night of the rescue."

He returns to Parker. "And then, there's Hunter. He's a bit of a mystery."

Mystery? Why?

This news agitates Donovan. "Did you say Hunter?"

"Yeah."

"Shit, he's at Reed with Sadie!" Donovan jumps to his feet and makes for the door.

Tensions thicken as the mood in the room swings to anger. This intel doesn't make Parker happy. There's too much up there to tempt someone like Hunter. "Donovan, hang on. Sit down. Mal, he's the fourth brother?"

"Hunter, yeah."

Parker comes to stand next to Mal. "You said Hunter's a mystery. Why?"

"He busted Gideon out of a prison transport the day the missile dropped, so I can't imagine he's a good guy. But while he wanted to hide out somewhere in town, they ended up using the distraction of the chaos to break Wendall out of prison. Apparently, it was Gideon's idea, and Hunter was against it. From what I saw of the guy, it makes sense. He didn't seem to like anything Wendall said or d id."

"Why?" Parker asks, liking that there's at least dissension in the ranks among their neighbors. It could be an advantage for them to use later.

"I don't know. I suspect it's because Wendall was in for first-degree murder."

That jolts Donovan. "That's all I need to hear. Parker, we need to send a team to Reed. Liam and Alex aren't enough."

Parker opens his mouth to calm Donovan, but Mal holds up his hand. "Hold on. Like I said, I got a distinct impression from Hunter. He's not like his brothers."

"Based on what? This is my daughter we're talking about. His other brothers were animals. Why should he be any different?"

Instead of addressing Donovan directly, Mal addresses Parker. "Back in the city, the men trapped some women in a backroom of the Rite Aid. Hunter released them, undetected, before the men could go back in and retrieve them."

Donovan scoffs. "He might not be like that, but he's not a good guy, either. He must have coerced Sadie to let him in. If he hurts her…"

Parker frowns. It's just like his friend to judge people in the blink of an eye, but how to calm him without making him—?

Mal approaches Donovan. "You're jumping, old man."

Ouch! Watch who you call old man, son. Still, Parker's impressed. Mal has been here long enough to know what Donovan is like, yet he's still not cowering before him. He'll make for a fine son-in-law if he ends up with Gina. Parker's seen the way Mal reacts to her. Hell, all of Haven has.

Mal holds his hands out in front of himself but is careful not to touch Donovan. "If his aim is to hurt her, he wouldn't have let her call us."

"Maybe not," Henry says. "But even if he's not after her, he'll still be interested in what's at Reed. Or using Sadie to get his people behind our defensive walls here."

"Look, if I can suggest something," Mal says, interjecting. "We already have a team going to Reed. Let's warn Liam. If Hunter is the only other person there, they can handle him."

Parker nods. "Let's radio Sadie and get a read of the situation."

CHAPTER 32

From the kitchen table, the pungent aroma of garlic fills Sadie's nostrils as she watches Hunter cooking. Her mouth waters. She likes the way his jeans hug him when he moves. He's tall, trim, delicious in the right places, and more attractive to her with each coming day. "Where did you learn to cook?"

Hunter circles a wooden spatula in a sizzling frying pan. "A good friend invited me to come home with him. His mom asked me one day if I wanted to learn." He gazes up at the stove hood fan for a span before continuing. "Haven't thought of him in a while. I spent a fair amount of time with his family." Hunter adds some salt to the pan and mixes it in with the spatula. "It was normal."

The word normal tightens her heart, impressing upon her the reason he wanted to wait to call Haven. He misses it. "All I've ever known is my father's cooking. Barbecues, too. House was full every Sunday."

His smile shines upon her. "Your family's that big?"

His scar cuts through lips she's dreamed of kissing lately. Would he come to Haven if she asked him? "You don't know the half of it. I have eleven honorary cousins."

He whistles. "Wow. What's that like?"

Sadie laughs as images of her and the others running rampant in the neighborhood on bikes, roller blades, and scooters parade through her mind. Before she decided she liked Liam, she'd had such a crush on his younger brother. So did Beth. Sadie's thoughts turn to her group of musketeers, as they referred to themselves, hoping no more are lost. Knowing Beth's anxiety troubles, Sadie hopes her fellow musketeer arrived at Haven unscathed. And her sister, Gina.

Liam... Hunter... Sadie is well aware she's feeling a powerful attraction to Hunter. She's also distinctly aware that she's never felt this with any other man, except Liam. What will it be like when Liam arrives? Will sleeping with Hunter help her move on from Liam? Could it help them smooth over their history and finally be friends again?

"You okay? You have some serious thought going on." Hunter tables a plate of what looks like beef stroganoff and holds up a fork in front of her.

Sadie reaches for the utensil, grazing his fingers with hers. He holds onto it, and the concern in his eyes is unmistakable. So is the desire. *Sexy time?* The tingle returns as a rush of blood heats her cheeks.

"Haven to Reed." It's her father's voice, sounding through the radio in the other room.

Hunter lets go of the fork.

"Haven to Reed!" Donovan demands in an urgent voice.

Where's the fire? Sadie enters the security room and picks up the microphone. Hunter follows, but doesn't enter, instead choosing to lean against the door frame.

"Reed. What's up..."—Sadie almost said Dad, but reroutes—"...Osmond?" She's always known his call sign but thinks this is probably the first time she's ever used it.

"I want to talk to you alone." He says this like she's done something wrong, which makes her feel like a child. She exchanges a look with Hunter. He shrugs and exits, closing the door behind him.

Sadie takes a deep breath. She's sure she isn't going to like anything her father says after that ominous statement. Even through the radio, he sounds controlling. "We're alone. What's wrong?"

"Are you being held against your will?"

"No!" Sadie stares at the mic in disbelief.

"Is it just the two of you?"

Trepidation inches its way into her mind. "Yeah, what's going on?"

"Listen to me carefully. You're in danger. Lock the door. There's food in there to last for days. The boys have been instructed to detain him."

Detain him? Hunter? Her mind goes into overdrive. "You're not making any sense."

"Focus on my words. He's the enemy, baby." Sadie sits back as her father continues. "This man does not care about you. He's there to infiltrate the place."

No fucking way! Hunter could have left her and taken what he wanted while she was delirious. He stayed and took care of her. Why would he do that? None of it made sense.

Her mother's words nag at her: "Trust him."

Chapter 33

H unter sits at the corridor table, his laced fingers clasping its rough surface. The plate of beef stroganoff, cold for a while now, shows him that Sadie has been in there too long. He stares at the closed door as a sense of uneasiness and apprehension gnaws at him.

The door clicks open. Sadie walks into the room. The intensity of her accusing gaze triggers his fight-or-flight response. A prickling sensation runs across Hunter's skin. His muscles tense up, ready for anything. Something happened, and he needs to prepare for either confrontation or escape. "What's wrong?" He doesn't know if he wants to hear the answer.

She levels her eyes at him and leans on the wall: the furthest place from him. "Your farmhouse is yellow?"

That's a strange question. "Used to be."

"Near a river?"

He pulls his eyebrows together. "How do you know that?"

"Haven's on the other side of the river."

The moment she drops the bomb, clarity rushes through him like a lightbulb illuminating a dark room. His past catches up with him once more. *Those are her people? Shit.* Hunter closes his eyes to her beauty in defeat. "How do they know who I am?"

"I don't know." Her muted tone hints at a deeper, unspoken emotion.

Hunter feels a sudden suffocating pressure as the noose tightens around his neck. She's not armed, at least. They'll be here sooner now, though. He's a threat. "What'd your dad tell you to do?"

"Lock myself in and wait for Liam."

She didn't. He straightens. "I didn't know, Sadie. You should have obeyed your father."

"No, I want answers."

Answers? His life has no magic fairy-tale ending. Never did. Just the pain and strife that he forces onto those around him. "I'm not an honorable man, Sadie. I've done things... Terrible things."

"What kind of man are you?"

He'll be gone soon enough. What's the harm in confessing? Hunter looks her dead in the eye, his gaze unwavering. "The kind who'd take this from you."

Sadie's expression goes from suspicious to wary while his words linger in the air between them. Her look cuts him, but it has to be done. She needs to go back into that room and lock the door.

"My brothers and I robbed banks when I was young." The weight of his guilt brings out a heavy sigh. "I didn't aspire to be this man. I enlisted to get away from my family. The military was exactly what I was missing. Brothers who had my back. Respect, dignity, honor." Joy crosses his features, then nosedives into the gloom. "Everything my family isn't. They sucked me back in."

"How?"

He leans back. "When I visited after basic." He clears his throat. "Gideon robbed a bank and got caught. I was outside in the car, unaware of what he was doing."

Hunter rises to his feet and starts pacing up and down. "They convicted me, killing my military career and anything good I had left."

Sadie's body stiffens.

He doesn't like that and sighs. "With everything going on now, I have no choice but to leave or die here."

"Liam won't kill you."

He dismisses her comment with a shake of his head. "He has no choice, Sadie." Hunter's a threat to Liam's woman. *They'll dispatch me just like they did Gideon.* "They won't accept me. I'm tainted."

"I accepted you."

Their eyes meet for a beat, converging into a mixture of confusion and stubbornness. *Sassy.*

"I've seen the man who would steal this place from me." She approaches, ensnaring him with her unblinking stare. "And he saved me. There's still good in you."

"I wish that were true." *God, I wish you were mine.* "I saw the good here with you, but I can never truly be me out there." He wills her to go into the security room. "Let me go. There's no place in your world for a man like me." The closer she gets to him, the more he longs to touch her. He needs her. Life is so cruel sometimes. She's so close, Hunter breathes in strawberries.

"Where will you go?"

Her acceptance of his choice to leave brings no comfort. "North, far away from my brother. Don't worry about me, I'll deal." Hunter burns to reach out, but turns to collect what little he has and goes. He feels the cool press of her hand against his forearm, a gentle contrast to his own warm skin. He glances b ack.

Her hand drops. "Dad couldn't say it in so many words, but your brother hurt my sister somehow."

This news tortures him as he weaves his hands behind his head. The way they found the house when they arrived makes so much more sense now. "Ah, Sadie, I'm so sorry."

Sadie moves to wrap an arm around him. *Don't.*

He holds out a hand, forcing her to step back. "Don't touch me, Blue-Eyes. I'm toxic."

"I don't believe that."

Sadie embraces Hunter again, giving him no choice but to embrace her back. Her scent weaves around him, tempting his resolve to leave her. Instead of confronting reality, he squeezes his eyes shut to hide from it. The harm Hunter's family inflicts on those who are undeserving never stops. "Tell me she's alive." Though his voice cracks, he needs to know.

To his relief, she nods into his chest.

"You need to go to her. Go with Liam."

"I'm not leaving without you."

He wonders if she heard him at all. "You won't have a choice, Blue-Eyes."

Sadie grabs his face and squashes any further talk with her lips. She continues her assault down his neck.

The pent-up desire he's harbored for her is about to explode out of him, but doubt enters his consciousness. "Sadie, we have to stop."

"No."

The softness of her lips drives him to want more. "I'm not yours."

"Yes, you are."

Sadie's words punch through his last shred of willpower. Hunter crushes her against him. Craving envelops him, and control crumbles as the floodgates of passion take over. His want supersedes the abstinence, and Hunter takes her mouth like a starving man. Their tongues intertwine and dance. The sweet taste of her spurs him on to take more. *I'll be gone soon enough.*

In one fluid movement, he sweeps his arm across the table, sending objects flying. *Why not indulge?* He lifts her up and places her where their food was a moment earlier, loving the new rush of desire he feels. *We won't see each other again.*

Sadie's strawberry aroma intoxicates Hunter, drawing him in. She gathers him close, securing her legs around his waist. Pushing her body back, he savors the hunger on her imperfect but perfect face, as if she were made for him. "So fucking beautiful."

Sadie lifts Hunter's shirt off and strokes his chest with greedy fingers, igniting a craving he's never felt for any woman. Hunter allows himself to feel the burning desire, the deep longing for her. To dream she's his.

Her unwavering determination fuels Hunter to where he can't concentrate. To avoid losing ground, he pushes her further back, seizing control of the situation. She protests until Hunter places his finger against her pillowy soft lips and encourages her to lie down on the table. After she complies, he says, "Good girl."

Hunter slowly lifts the hem of her shirt, grateful that she allows him to slide his fingers over her scarred skin. The curtain rises on his personal peep show.

Her belly shrinks from his touch. Overcome with a rush of anger, he sobers, gazing upon her scars, wishing he knew who did this. Three separate lines run from left to right, marring her abdomen and breasts, and another scar climbs between them. *The pain she must have endured...* He recalls his own.

Sadie rises from the table, caressing his neck with her gentle hands, lightly pressing her fingers into his skin, as she whispers, "Don't stop." Her flawless lips, soft as velvet, brush against his own scars. An invitation. A tender caress. He claims her mouth once more.

He lowers her onto the tabletop. "I'm going to fuck you hard."

Her lips part, and her voice hitches, catching in her throat.

"Do you like it when I talk dirty?" He eagerly removes her shirt. Thrilled to discover she's not wearing a bra, he takes a breast in each palm and caresses her erect nipples. He licks his lips, a slight tremor in his hand betraying his anticipation.

"Yes," is the throaty reply he receives.

Her honesty encourages him. "Are you sure, Sadie, because once I start... It's been too long."

In response, she reaches for her jeans.

He claims her wrists. She wriggles, but Sadie's no match for his strength. Leaning over her, he inches her hands up past her head and greedily takes her mouth. He pulls back, then ravishes one nipple with his tongue while teasing the other with his fingertip. She recoils, but then moans. Hunter loves learning what makes her tick, but every new discovery is marred by the disappointment that he won't be in her life to learn more.

He tugs her pants off, one leg at a time. He growls, biting down to curb his compulsion, but it's a losing battle. The sight of Sadie's firm breasts, her budding nipples, and the dark hair of her sex assaults Hunter's senses beyond the brink of sanity. Sadie isn't wearing any underwear. *Hot as... Goddamn!* He fumbles to unfasten his jeans. The roughness of his pants skims over sensitive thighs as he pulls out his aching cock.

Sadie licks her lips and spreads her legs without instruction.

Oh, yeah, that hit him. Hunter doesn't believe he can be any harder than he is now.

Positioning himself, he rests a hand on the table near her head. She grasps his forearm. He slides his manhood against her soft folds and slips through her wetness, one slow inch at a time, savoring her tightness. "God, Sadie."

"Hunter," she whimpers while caressing his chest with such blatant adoration. A look no woman has ever given him. A look that cuts him sharper than any blade ever could.

All he wants is to claim her as his own. Nothing else matters.

Without ceremony, he thrusts in all the way and freezes. Her grip on him is incredible. He gazes down with such gratitude for the gift this woman doesn't realize she is giving him.

She wraps her legs around his waist, urging him deeper as she reaches down between them.

Hunter seizes her wrist. "No, Blue-Eyes, this is mine." While buried deep within her, Hunter takes control, sliding his thumb into her folds. "So wet." He circles her bud, enjoying her moans and the excitement of being the cause of her bliss. This is a first for him. A learning curve he is on board with.

She squirms under his touch. He draws back and forth with slow, enticing strokes into her tightness. A grunt escapes his lips, the smell of sweat thick in the air, as he struggles to control himself before she comes.

Hunter takes it up a notch and rubs his thumb furiously as he clamps his other hand around her throat. Her pussy tightens around him, and he senses Sadie may appreciate everything he's doing. Her tits bounce magnificently. The visual is transcendent.

"Oh!" Sadie's body arches.

He changes his angle and pumps faster.

"Oh!" Sadie clutches the sides of the table, her knuckles turning white. "Hunter!" Her delicious cunt squeezes him. *Fuck, this is amazing.*

Her eyes hunt for his. "I'm going to—" Her head flies back, her lips part, but no sound escapes as she arches again and soars below him in suspension.

Hunter's balls grow heavy under his labored breaths. He concentrates on the feel of her clenching muscles around his hardness, ready for his own climax, and gazes down at the woman who will take him there. *It's a mistake.* The trust he receives in her sated eyes cripples him. Everything he's ever wanted reflects back at him. How can Hunter leave this beautiful woman? *I have to.*

He removes his hand from her throat, curls it around the back of her neck, and draws her body up to him. It hurts to see the trust he doesn't deserve. "Hold on."

Sadie wraps tight arms around him. Their lips lock. He squeezes her ass, securing her to the table, while he drives into her sweetness with savage strokes.

"Oh!" Her nails dig. "Fuck me harder!"

Hunter loses the warmth and wetness of her lips as she makes her demands. He complies with wild abandon, loving the buildup, cherishing every stroke.

"Oh!" Sadie spasms around his shaft. She gazes up with hooded eyes and screams her release. "Fuck, yeah!"

He jacks into her with such a powerful, uncontrollable force, each stroke getting him closer and closer to the promised land.

The damp heat of his skin meets Sadie's hands as they slide up his back, a shiver of awareness between them. With every touch, she intensifies his cravings, twisting his lust into an almost unbearable frenzy. Her climaxes are so wanton and provocative. Unapologetic. Her confidence turns him on.

Sadie's tender eyes rest upon him, brimming with desire, and something else. There's that adoration again. "I see you, Hunter."

His heart melts. *I can't.*

Hunter buries his head deep in her hair to escape those loving eyes. Her neck beckons. He sinks his teeth into her flesh. She flinches. He can't believe the savagery she's brought out of him and tries to scale it back, but he's past civility. His entire universe narrows down to the feeling of driving into her. He rears up

Sadie takes his thumb into her wet, warm mouth, sending shivers down his spine. Hunter gives in as his body trembles with the intensity of the most awe-inspiring orgasm. With a shudder, he roars: "Sadie!"

Hunter trembles between the quick mini strokes he propels into her and comes down from the high, suddenly aware of his heavy breathing. He's afraid to look into those ravishing eyes, but he does.

Maybe Sadie can see right through him. Feel his vulnerability or his conflict. Whatever it is, it encourages her to hold him tight and bury her head in his chest. It's another feeling he's never experienced much of: being appreciated.

Hunter can't leave her. How could he contemplate abandoning someone who finally valued him? He has to pay her back for the trust she's given him. Hunter owes Sadie, and he knows what he has to do.

Not wanting to end their contact, Hunter draws the hair away from her neck, witnessing his possession of her. He smiles, loving that for one night, she was his. Hunter takes her in his arms and lifts her off the table.

Her head bobs up, her arched brow asking an unspoken question.

"Time for the shower I really wanted to give you the first time."

Sadie's gentle laugh brings that unfamiliar smile back to him. This night will be for him. Tomorrow will be for her.

***

In the bedroom, Hunter snuggles deeper into the sheets, pulling Sadie's body close. She inhales deeply, loving the smell of strawberries on his skin. Their time in the bathroom was pure bliss. After taking care of her with his tongue, Hunter held her while he fucked her against the shower wall. After the table fun, she didn't think it could get any hotter, but he proved her wrong.

Sadie enjoys the heat of his body against hers and traces his facial scar. She hopes to persuade him tonight. *He has to stay.*

He closes his eyes at her touch. "I can see why your dad contains you. Your charms are dangerous."

She props herself up on one elbow. "He's never contained me. We're like oil and water. Two peas in a very crowded pod."

Hunter opens his eyes. "He loves you, though."

"He does, but his love chokes me. I need to make my own decisions."

Hunter glides his fingers along her thigh, over a jagged scar at her waist. She shivers as he follows the line between her soft breasts, up her neck, and across her face. His eyes never drift from hers as he traces her failure, his longing and desire ever present. *Perhaps this is a good time?* "Maybe this is your chance to change. Be the man you aspired to be."

His hand drops. "How do you figure that?"

Sadie feels the loss of Hunter's touch too much. "Your brother thinks you're dead. My family will accept you when they see what I see. Think about it."

He cups her face with his warm, rough hand. "I can't think with those beautiful blue eyes so close."

The energy between them becomes palpable, creating a magnetic pull. Sadie fuses their lips and reignites a powerful need.

Hunter breaks their bond and teases. "Dangerous."

Sadie yearns for those lips, but she keeps her eyes on his. *I have to get through to him.* "Hunter."

He touches his forehead to hers. "We can't be." Sadie pulls away, but he keeps her close. "You deserve better than me. I'm not like Liam."

The sting of his words hurt. "Liam told me I deserved better too. Can't anyone let me decide what I deserve?"

"I'm broken. You can't fix me."

His nearness urges her to use her mouth to tempt him as she whispers into his lips, "I don't want to fix you."

"I'm going to hell. There may be some good in me, but I've suppressed it for too long."

He's pulling away. Driven by an intense fury, she inches her face closer to his. "I dug the goodness up...and I'll keep digging...till it's all you see!"

With an abundance of empathy, his eyes sparkle. "So fucking goddamned sassy."

Sadie lets her body melt into Hunter's as he pulls her in for an intense, mind-blowing kiss, overwhelming her senses with desire.

CHAPTER 34
July 2

"Hunter!" Sadie yells in the distance.

She's in the corridor. Her voice brings a sense of relief to Liam's ears. In perfect harmony, he and Alex move down the dim back stairs, their weapons poised and ready, their bond as military brothers evident in their seamless coordination.

The sun hasn't risen yet, and the compound is dark. Liam signals Alex to approach the pantry as he clears the battery room with a flick of the light switch. On. Off. Darkness returns.

He lets his eyes adjust before approaching Alex, tapping his shoulder. They advance through the shadows in the pantry. A faint illumination coming from the corridor lights up the kitchen doorframe.

"Hunter! Don't do this to me."

She's closer.

Upon reaching the door to the open corridor, the boys greet her with guns raised.

Sadie stops mid-step. "Liam, I can't find—"

Liam drags her behind him, resisting the urge to check her over; his first duty needs to be neutralizing the threat. Alex silences her with a finger to his lips and signals her to remain in place as he passes them both. Liam follows his friend as they do a silent room-by-room sweep.

He calls out when he hits the last room. "Clear!"

"Clear!" Alex repeats.

Liam scans the living quarters all the way down the corridor. Under the dim illumination in the kitchen, Sadie stands at the pantry doorway, wringing her hands. The floor light strip highlights her bare, slender legs and feet.

His heart soars. Sadie's finally within his grasp.

He flicks the corridor light on, and Sadie flinches, raising her hands to protect her eyes from the sudden brightness.

Determined to be with her now and forever, no matter what, Liam closes the distance. He picks up additional details that previously escaped his notice. In a man's shirt that swallows her up, Sadie appears gaunt and undernourished.

Liam sees her face. "Oh my God, Sadie!" Even with her hands in front of her nose and mouth, the scars stand out vividly, their pink hues contrasting sharply against her otherwise flawless complexion. *That bastard.*

She drops her hands, and a moment later, her eyes, too. Liam recovers enough to encircle Sadie tightly and cups her head against his chest. "Sadie, what did he do to you?"

She disentangles herself and runs into the suite.

"I'll take your stuff," Alex says. "Go help her."

Liam unlatches his rifle, lays it down, and yanks his vest over his head and into Alex's arms, then follows Sadie. He finds her on the edge of the bed in a sad state, shoulders slumped, her face tilted away from him, staring at the floor. Liam's anger bubbles under the surface, but he takes a gentle approach. "Tell me who did this to you."

"It wasn't Hunter."

"Who then?" He doesn't like that she evaded his question.

She just stares straight ahead, to his disappointment. *God, she can be so stubborn.*

"The coward ran."

She glares at him. "He ran because he thought you were going to kill him."

Under the bedroom lights, Sadie's disfigurement is more pronounced, which only intensifies his anger. "If he had touched a hair on your head, I would have."

192

Her piercing gaze compels Liam to speak. "It shouldn't surprise you that I'm protective of you."

"Of course, 'cause we're friends."

He wants to say, because I want you to be mine, but Sadie's bitter tone doesn't go unnoticed, and he knows it's not the right time. And as much as Liam wants to change her opinion, he can't disrespect Donovan. He ambles closer and deliberately softens his voice. "Would it be alright if I checked your injuries?"

Lifting the Henley shirt, Liam sees bruising across Sadie's ribs, as well as one long scar and three smaller ones crossing it. Under different circumstances, Liam would find the shirt on her appealing, but the scars fill him with outrage. He channels his anger into a focused, medic mindset, setting aside his emotions for a moment.

He sits, and their thighs touch. *Am I dreaming?* He's waited so long for this. Along with their small connection, her strawberry scent captures him. Liam longs to caress her hair, stroke her skin, and embrace her warmth.

Sadie curls her fingers around a piece of paper she grabs off the nightstand. It bears her name, hastily scrawled across the surface. He resumes examining her bruised flesh with a gentle touch.

She flinches.

"Does it hurt?"

"No, your hands are...cold."

He resumes, tilting her head up to inspect her neck scar. Liam's heart collapses in on itself. The angry red hickey is impossible to miss, a visible indicator of heated passion. *She slept with him?*

Liam didn't expect Sadie to be a virgin. Too much time has lapsed for that. He isn't a saint, either, but Liam doesn't want to admit that her brief tryst is anything like what they could have together.

He swallows down the bile to focus on the task at hand. "Stitching's superb." Someone else did them. There's no way Sadie could have reached some of these areas. "Who did them?"

Sadie's face lights up at some memory only she can see. "A sweet man named Carl."

"Carl?" Why isn't this man with Sadie?

The small smile on her lips speaks volumes. This Carl means a lot to her. "The man who found me. If it weren't for him, I'd be dead."

Liam feels a tingling sensation on the back of his neck and sobers up. He continues his ministrations, feeling her forehead. No fever. Sadie appears to be in good health and on the mend. He checks her pulse and finds it satisfactory. "You're taking the antibiotics?"

"Hunter made sure I took them like clockwork. Made sure I ate, too."

Even though Liam's angry, he has to concede that the man did a fine job with what he had. Sadie is safe and on the mend, and that's all that matters in this moment. There's plenty that bothers him still, but he is glad this Hunter has fled and is gone from her life.

"We done?"

"Sure." He lets her wrist go, but doesn't move to leave.

She scoots her shirt down. Liam's at a loss for words. The shock of seeing Sadie's face is still fresh, and he's angry that someone scarred the woman he loves. Liam's known the true extent of his feelings for some time now. He even arrived at Haven back in May with the intention to give her a ring. It was a whimsical dream he'd hoped she'd be on board with. But the world is different now, and he realizes they need to start over somehow before that can be a reality. He has to know if Sadie loves him, even if it means facing the possibility that she might no t.

The overwhelming urge to connect compels Liam to shift closer and cradle her head in his arms. To his surprise, she lets him. He dares to hope. "Auburn, I'm so glad you're finally home."

Sadie doesn't fully embrace him. "Me, too."

At the mere thought that she is being sincere, his heart fills with a temporary sense of elation.

"Can I have a moment, Liam?"

Liam wants to deny that request. Now that he's finally with her, he never wants to let her out of his sight again. But he relents. Perhaps a timeout in medical will clear his mind. He kisses the top of her head and releases her before walking away. Upon reaching the door, Liam glances back.

Sadie unfolds the paper with a long sigh, smoothing it out on her legs.

Liam's certain it's from him.

***

Sadie glimpses Liam's longing gaze, tinged with concern for her. "I'm okay. Be out in a minute."

An obviously conflicted Liam nods before departing, leaving her alone.

Sadie looks down at the letter in her lap and reads. *I wish I was a good man, Sadie. I wish for many things that involve you, but I'll always be the man standing in front of those pictures, seeing everyone else's happiness, never standing in them.*

He's mistaken.

I'm past redemption. These last days... Happiness is not in the cards for me, but I can give it to you. I'm going to make this right.

Sadie raises a hand to her mouth. *Oh, no. What's he going to do?*

CHAPTER 35

O n the patio and looking through a scope, Donovan observes a wet, blonde woman trudging out of the tree line. She's alone and unarmed as far as he can see, but he errs on the side of caution and keys his mic. "Superman?"

"Yep."

With a full view of the workers below, Donovan counts five of them and two security personnel. "Take the kids back to the bunker. Potential threat at the tree line behind you."

"Copy." Ryker turns for a look, then calls out to the workers.

They rise. Some shield their eyes and scan the surrounding area, while others gather gardening implements and begin the trek back to the compound. Ryker takes point, leading them into the forest, bound for home.

"Haven, do we have a clear path?" Ryker asks as Mal, taking up the rear, disappears below Donovan.

He returns to the scope to investigate. The blonde stumbles a few times across the open expanse of the field, then careens to the ground. The woman looks to be in great shape, but her steps are unstable, and she looks exhausted. *Did she cross the river on her own?* It would have been a struggle to do so unassisted.

"You're clear," Colin answers.

"Osmond, you need backup?" Mal asks.

Donovan enjoys the gesture. "No." He directs his next comment to Colin: "Twinkle, keep your eyes peeled for other threats while I tackle this one."

"Copy."

And so, Donovan keeps his scope on the blonde as she stumbles and staggers her way in his direction, occasionally falling or stopping to take a breath as she glances this way and that, more wary of where she's come than what she might be walking toward. He checks his watch as the woman finally passes underneath him. In his haste to scale down the tree, his injured arm causes him to flinch. Slowing his descent, he lands softly, the earth yielding beneath his feet as he raises his rifle.

Did she hear him? She doesn't show any concern about what's happening around her, appearing to be set on looking for something. From behind, she's curvier than most of the women he knows. Shorter, too. Her rumpled clothes have seen better days and look drab and tired. At least they're dry after all that fumbling under the day's hot sunshine.

Donovan pauses. If she escaped from the farmhouse, it's possible that she endured mistreatment there. He lets her walk out of earshot ahead of him. "Twinkle, still no threats?"

"Negative. Just her."

The woman stops, gasping for breath as she leans against a sturdy tree. The Haven wall looms before her. It's a sight that leaves most people in awe when they see it for the first time. She persists onward, the razor wire carpet unknown to her.

Donovan raises his weapon. "I wouldn't go that way."

The blonde snaps her head around, her uncombed hair swirling as she comes to stare down the barrel of his rifle. Her legs buckle beneath her, sending her crashing to the ground in a heap, giving Donovan an unobstructed view. Her beautiful, emerald-green eyes captivate him. Between heavy breaths, she utters in an accent, "Please, do not hurt me!"

***

A short time later, Donovan leans against the wall in medical, trying to appear indifferent, though he is anything but. Henry examines the woman while Melanie offers the woman comforting strokes of her arm, helping her to know that the men here aren't like those on the other side of the river. The blonde glances over at Donovan every few seconds. He's not sure if she sees him as a threat or is simply assessing which way to run. He can't really blame her for wanting to get away. Before entering the compound, he placed a blindfold on her, which agitated the woman, and Henry's probing is almost certainly increasing her anxiety.

"You seem to be in good shape. You could use a meal and a hot shower." Henry gazes over at Donovan. "Make sure that happens."

"Sure thing." Donovan shoots her an awkward smile, but she responds by looking away.

She shied away from him at first, but Donovan was gentle, and she eventually allowed him to guide her as they moved through Haven. The bruise circling her neck enraged him.

Melanie clasps the woman's trembling hand. "My name is Melanie. What's yours?"

"Jewel."

Donovan sees why her family chose it, given her striking eye color.

"I hear the accent. Where are you from?"

"France. I was visiting when things went wrong."

Well, that's a nice way to put it. For all the horror of what's happened, at least Donovan has friends around him, in a place he knows. He struggles to imagine how much more terrifying everything must be for someone not in their native country. In the blink of an eye, Jewel's world shrank. She's stuck on this side of the pond, and if the damage is as bad as they think, Donovan is doubtful she'll ever see her family again. He knows the feeling. Others in his own family haven't shown, and Donovan can't bear the thought that they might have perished. His only option is to hold on to hope. After all, he held out hope for Sadie, and she has turned up at Reed.

Melanie bends slightly to look Jewel in the eye. "The people here are trustworthy. I was held captive with other women, like you, and they took us in." She turns to Donovan. "Will she be staying with me and the others? We understand what she's been through."

"Yes," he says, quicker than he should have. Jewel's predicament plays on his sympathies. Their protocol dictates keeping outsiders locked in the garage until they've been interrogated, but fearing this woman has been through hell, Parker wants her in the women's apartment as soon as possible. Donovan still plans on questioning her, but after the day's work, and in a more welcoming setting. He knows how hard it's been for Gina to recover so far. At the same time, it's his duty as head of security to be cautious, and the woman fascinates him.

Chapter 36

L iam steps into medical, places his hands on a nearby counter, and leans into his arms as he works to pull himself together. He breathes in...out. He can't get over the fact that someone hurt Sadie...scarred her like that. The urge to kill this person out of revenge burns, but without knowing who did it, he doesn't know what to do with his anger or where to direct it.

"How is she?" Alex asks, pulling Liam out of his tortured mind.

He keeps his eyes downcast; he can't face his friend. "Pneumonia's almost gone. The antibiotics are doing their job. The scars..." His muscles twitch, his voice shakes. "There's more underneath. What the fuck?" He smacks the counter hard.

Alex tugs on his shoulder. "Hey, she's breathing, man. Focus on the positives, fix the negatives. She'll be alright now that you're here."

Liam chances a look at his friend. Alex's expression is both sympathetic and hopeful. Liam takes it into his heart. "What do I tell Donovan? He'll want a report."

Alex's face shows uncertainty.

"I'll give it to him," Sadie whispers from the doorway, startling them.

Liam straightens, afraid of how much she heard. This is the confident Sadie he knows well, who wants to set the world on fire.

She turns and backs out of the room.

"Sadie. Wait!"

***

Wearing his ghillie suit, Hoss swaggers into the security room and lifts Candy out of her cradle while shooting a casual salute at Donovan and Roger at the security monitors. He glances back in the direction he entered, piecing together the unfolding situation. In the room across the hall, the bed is a chaotic mess, with the sheets twisted and crumpled, and the pillows scattered. Hoss is unsurprised. *If my daughter were involved...*

The painful memory resurfaces. She turned twenty the year she died. It marked the last birthday they would celebrate together, and the last time Hoss would embrace her. He works hard to remember her in happier times, as imagining what her final moments must have been like in the apartment fire is too difficult.

"We going to finish the fencing soon?" Roger asks, prompting Hoss to look up.

"Meeting about it today," Donovan replies, shifting his neck from side to side, then turns to Hoss. "Where are you hunting?"

He didn't sleep well, either, it seems. "Gonna take a stroll through section six. Check the back door, then head to section one." As Hoss lists off bullet points, he senses mischief in the air and forms a satisfied smile. "I feel the urge to disrupt today."

"Well, have fun, then."

Hoss wiggles his eyebrows. "I always do." He straps his rifle to his back and fetches loaded magazines from the ammo box on a nearby table.

The radio springs to life, and Liam's clear voice comes through. "Reed to Haven."

Roger picks up the mic. "Haven." Hoss is impressed with the man's reactions: he answered before even Donovan could. Hoss is glad Roger is proving himself to be such an asset, especially in the security room. Hoss and his brothers-in-arms prefer to be outside, in the action, but they're all aware of how vital it is to have someone monitoring the cameras and managing comms. And so, since William died, Roger has been a welcome addition to the group.

Donovan gestures for the microphone, and Roger complies. "Give it to me, Golden."

Hoss parks himself against a table, careful of his rifle, curious to see if Donovan will be a bit more respectful of his son this time. He knows his friend's frustration stems from Sadie's unexpected delay, but he'd still like to see Donovan show some gratitude. He should be happy Liam's there, not angry.

"He ran."

Guess he means the brother? Things are looking up.

"How is she?"

"I'm safe, Osmond." The sound of Sadie's voice brings palpable relief to the room.

No smile graces Donovan's face. "I'm glad you are."

What's up with him?

"We're coming home."

"That's a no," Donovan says, shaking his head. "It's too dangerous right now. Put Golden on."

Hoss looks up as he bites his lip in frustration. *Everyone who knows you knows you're blunt, Donovan, more so since your wife passed, but seriously, you've just got your daughter back. Take the edge off a little.*

It's been two years since his wife's death, and his friend still hasn't recovered. Hoss knows firsthand the emotional rollercoaster and the time it takes to get over the death of a spouse. Never.

"I wasn't asking for your permission."

Donovan sits back, looking astounded, then looks at Hoss, who shrugs. Time has not softened his Sadie girl. *Do they have a backbone class for librarians?* Still, Hoss has never heard Sadie take control quite like that before, and he likes it. Now that Liam and she are finally together, Hoss hopes she and Liam can find common ground to build a strong relationship. It'll be easier for both of them if Donovan learns not to interfere.

"When?"

There's a pause. "We're leaving today."

So, tomorrow, Hoss thinks, assuming she's following their protocol of using code. She remembered to use the codenames, after all. *Good. They'll have time to talk...be alone.*

Sadie's announcement doesn't seem to improve Donovan's demeanor much. "Alright, but be careful."

Hoss raises his eyebrows. *He accepted her decision? Just like that.* He chuckles to himself quietly. *Like he had a choice.*

***

Liam holsters his weapon, then reaches for some trail bars. The three of them are in Reed's tool room, but it holds much more than tools. In the back room, they store weapons and gear securely in locked cabinets. Both walls are lined with various tools needed for odd jobs around the compound and maintenance of the stored weapons. A rectangular folding table stands at the center of the space. On it, Alex has lined up all that they need for the journey home, and they're each grabbing at the various items as they prepare themselves.

Liam secures the snacks in his pockets while monitoring Sadie out of the corner of his eye. She loads up her own vest with practiced precision. Donovan must have taught her these things at one time, but this is the first time he's seen her handle military equipment. He thinks it's rather sexy.

Sadie checks the rifle she insisted on carrying. When Alex didn't ready one for Sadie, she shot him an evil glare before producing the one she said she'd carried on her journey to Reed. Donovan would have given her weapons training, but Liam is still shocked that the rifle is her weapon of choice.

She has difficulty holstering her secondary. Her ribs must be giving her trouble.

"Here, let me help." Liam approaches her.

Sadie smacks him away. "I got it."

He steps back, holding his hands up. *Someone has been grumpy ever since our last call to Haven.*

An alarm blares through the compound. Boots smack the floor. Alex jogs past Sadie, with Liam on his heels.

In the security room, Alex lands in a chair, rolls to the desk, and touches a keyboard. He flicks a switch and slides toward the screen for a better look.

Liam approaches the monitor, crouching close behind his friend. "Jessie and Steven?" he asks, hoping to see his brothers.

On the monitor, beneath the glare of the white lights, an old man in a Boonie hat with an urn under his arm smooths himself like he wants to make an impression on a first date. When he's done, he adjusts the rifle slung on his back.

Alex asks, "Who's that?"

Sadie walks in, her eyes wide with surprise. "Oh my God, Carl!"

Liam twists his head to her. "The guy that saved you?"

"Sadie home?" Carl asks, his voice sounding tinny as it comes through the speakers. He is staring straight into the camera, looking like he hasn't a care in the world.

Liam straightens. "Can we trust him?" He stares into those beautiful, bright blue eyes he loves.

Sadie wedges between the men and clicks the mic. "Carl, come on in. Use the shower and grab some fresh clothes. We'll see you on the other side."

Alex flips a switch, releasing the locking mechanism so the man can come into the bunker. Carl two-finger salutes the camera. "Righty, then, if there's a shower, I might be a while. Don't let me keep you."

Sadie's giggle pulls Liam's eyes back to her, and he can't help but smile. "I've missed you."

He reaches out, pulls Sadie in, and runs his fingers through her auburn hair. Without reservation, Liam tilts her head back and kisses her. *Donovan be damned...* She melts into him and kisses him back in wild abandon.

"Liam?" Sadie tugs on his arm, snapping him out of his daydream.

"Yeah."

"I've missed you, too. You okay?"

He covers his embarrassment with a forced cough. "Yeah. Now that you're here."

***

"Carl!"

While still scanning his eyes over the room, Carl stretches his arms wide for Sadie to rush into. *Sophisticated operation.* He studies the contrasting stances of the two men, both in tactical gear, one leaning back in relaxed confidence while the other stands rigid, on edge. Carl pulls away and looks her up and down with a critical eye. "You're all fixed, then?"

"Sort of. I'm taking antibiotics for pneumonia."

"Complications?"

Keeping one hand on his shoulder, Sadie turns to introduce the relaxed one first. "This is Alex." Then she turns to the uptight man. "And Liam."

"You didn't tell me he was military."

Liam steps forward, hand extended. "Thank you for saving her. I consider you worthy of my respect, sir."

"I'm just Carl. No need to call me sir." He stretches his hand out. "But I like your attitude just the same, son." Carl raises his eyebrows at Sadie. "All women are worth savin'. If I weren't in love already, I might consider her." He winks at

Sadie and pats his metal container. "But my love's right here in this urn. Plan B o
ut yet?"

Sadie shakes her head.

"Hmm." *Good thing I didn't speak out of turn, then.* "Wanna do it face-to-face,
then?"

She nods.

"You two have spent a lot of time together, it sounds like," Alex says.

Carl cracks a smile his way. "That we have." He turns back to Sadie, bringing
the smile with him. "Was the bridge a problem?"

"No, you were right. Going under it was better, but not easier. Some people
came after me, but I lost them when I hid beneath a dock further along the
river."

Carl doesn't miss the apprehension in young Liam's demeanor. The boy has
it bad for her.

"See, I told you not to worry. Carl knows his stuff. So, what's the plan now?"
He looks between Liam and Sadie. "Comin' or goin'?"

"Going."

Carl suspects her swift response is a preemptive maneuver to get her point
across before the men can say otherwise. The urgency in her voice speaks volumes. So does the look of unease on Liam's face. *Something's afoot here.*

Chapter 37

Parker fills a mug of coffee from a carafe at his kitchen table and passes it to Henry. The other members of the council are sipping their respective drinks already, lost in conversation. Donovan saunters in looking unhappy.

Isaac holds the carafe up and shakes the mug at Donovan.

"Alejo's?"

"Yup." Isaac starts pouring without waiting for an answer. He places the mug in front of Donovan and sits next to James.

The rest of the council is uneasy, as well. The people across the way continue to be of huge concern. What's stranger is how they keep snooping around without mounting any kind of attack.

Donovan lifts the mug to his lips.

"What's their strength now, Donovan?" This is the first time Parker's brother, James, has been out since losing his wife six weeks ago, so he's playing catch-up.

Donovan halts the mug in midair. "More showed up, so we're at eighteen guns." He takes a sip and licks his lips before placing the mug on the table.

"If they're still looking for labor and all the easy pickings have dried up, they're going to do more than just look in our direction soon." A chilling silence follows James's statement.

This draws a frown on Sylvia. She sets her mug down. "We can't handle any more delays. If we don't finish the crops, winter is going to be even harder. Is the fencing up?"

"The fence is up and running. Almost finished planting, too," Donovan says, taking another sip.

"Parker." Sylvia glances over at him. "What do you think?"

Everyone around the table waits. Despite their equal standing in the council, Parker's opinion always carries weight. "Okay, Sylvia, sounds like we focus on the crops we have growing already inside Yard Two next."

She nods her approval.

Henry selects a cookie from the plate set out in front of him. "How's Sadie coming along, Donovan?",

"She'll be here with the boys tomorrow."

"So soon?" Henry mumbles around the bite of cookie in his mouth.

Donovan shoots him a glare.

Ah. That explains his bad mood. Guess that was Sadie's decision and not his, then.

Parker decides to throw his friend a bone by switching topics. "Do we know anything more about the woman you found?"

"Her name is Jewel. She was being held captive across the way. I've got her under watch in the women's apartment, like you wanted." Donovan looks at Parker's other brother. "Henry's examined her already."

Parker nods at Henry. "How is she?" He hopes the answer will be as general as the query. They already know from Henry what many of the women have suffered over there. Hearing it again will only make him even angrier.

"It was a preliminary exam. The bruises and her skittishness made it clear she'd been mistreated recently."

Parker's glad it was easier than he'd expected it to be to talk Donovan into placing her with the women, rather than holding her in the garage. It is their protocol for any strangers brought inside Haven to isolate and question them first, but the environment isn't appropriate for someone who has been enslaved. "And there are more over there, I take it?"

Henry grunts. "That's what she told Melanie."

Parker nods. "If we're going to rescue them, and I assume we will be, we're going to need a plan for these new people." He looks at Sylvia. "Food will be impacted for one."

Sylvia shrugs. "Clothing and a place to sleep for another. Plus, we don't know what condition these people will be in when they're rescued. But we will make room somehow."

James lets go of his mug and leans back. "Once the threat is neutralized, we could build log cabins."

It is a sound idea. Log cabins would give protection from the cold Idaho winters, and while not as secure as being underground, Parker and his team will continue to work around the clock to keep them safe. Plus, with the extra hands and the reading material on survival techniques in the library, they will have the labor, resources, and time to build them.

Hoss saunters in, freshly showered, followed by a slight young man. In his possession, the man holds a crumpled-up envelope. He seems familiar, but Parker can't place where they've met, if ever. "How goes the battle, Hoss?"

Hoss offers the man a seat. "Fluid. This is Dane Sullivan. Rescued him this mornin'."

The man should be in the garage, waiting for interrogation, but Parker waits to hear why they've broken protocol twice in the same day.

Dane glances at everyone seated, then settles on Parker. "Pinkie?"

This unnerves Parker. "How do you know that?"

"This is for you, sir." Dane turns the crumpled, once-white envelope face up, showing the seal of the United States upon its surface.

Parker looks from the seal to Dane. "There're no sirs here, Dane. Who are you?"

Hoss leans back in his chair and crosses his arms. Parker squints at him. He knows more than he's letting on.

"223rd MIB out of California. My father is Garrett Sullivan."

Military intelligence?

"General Sullivan?" Donovan's eyes slide to Hoss. "Stinky?"

A slow smile graces Hoss's face. "Yeppers."

Dane's father is a highly decorated officer they knew well. He'd invested in Haven when Parker went looking for funds to build it. Unlike most of the people who backed the construction, General Sullivan didn't ask for an apartment in return.

"Yes, though I don't think Dad would take kindly to that name, s..." Dane swallows the last word.

Parker accepts the envelope, turns it over in his hands, but doesn't open it. "So, our military's still active?"

"Navy mostly."

Well, that's new. Parker didn't see that coming, but Stinky sending his son here tells him something else is going on. The general wants Dane safe and knows that even though he didn't reserve a space in Haven, Parker would never turn his family away. *What the hell is happening out there?* He wishes he knew, and toys with the idea of opening the letter there and then.

But then he stands, folds the letter along its existing creases, and places it in his back pocket. He has to keep his focus on the immediate threats in his own backyard before worrying about the bigger picture. Everyone is counting on him.

But when the time comes, he's sure that whatever encrypted message he's likely to find in the envelope will provide the answers.

CHAPTER 38

Sadie caresses her mouth, staring into the light of a crackling fire Carl started. After speaking with her father earlier and walking most of the day, she's been in a trance, pondering the possibilities of how Hunter's going to make things right. She needs to find him and stop whatever he's going to do. But how? She'll need her father's help, but will he give it?

"So, hot librarian, huh?" Alex asks under the firelight, across from her.

Sadie wonders what the story behind his eyebrow scar is. "What's men's fascination with librarians being sexy?" Since leaving Reed this morning, they spent most of the day in radio silence and using only hand signals to talk, so she's glad they are speaking again, but why about this of all things?

Next to Alex, Carl lies back, arms crossed, his Boonie hat over his eyes. From experience, she knows he's awake.

Liam pokes the flames next to her. Their thighs touch. He still excites her, even after all this time. The night air is cool, but she's been burning since his first contact. *Too bad.* Sadie has to come to terms with her relationship with Liam. Hunter might have turned her around.

"Well, he wasn't wrong. He said you were hot."

Or not. Her cheeks burn as she turns to Liam. "Why would you say that?"

He doesn't look at her or smile. Sadie wants him to and wishes she could find the courage to reach out and touch his hand, currently resting inches from her own. It's almost like he's tempting her.

211

Alex continues to tease Liam, unwilling to let his embarrassment fade. "The guys thought you were a figment of his imagination, so we let him have his fantasies."

Liam's eyes slide to Alex in a silent challenge.

If Liam is gay, why would he say those things to Alex? He thinks I'm hot? He's never once said anything remotely like that to me. Sadie doesn't know where to begin and feels uncomfortable asking about it in front of anyone else, so she changes the subject. "You're a Marine?"

"Second gen. Assigned Golden to my unit, which includes my twin, Miles. We're identical, but I'm the prettier one."

Sadie chuckles, liking Alex's humor. "Why do you call him Golden?"

Alex's eyes settle on Liam's blond hair. "Other than the obvious?"

Liam gives his friend the stink eye, which only elicits a chuckle from Alex. "He's a cautious guy when shit hits. He doesn't move without a lot of thought. So, Miles and I... We follow. No question."

"Loyalty."

"Trust, actually." His eyes slide to Liam once more. "When he told us about Haven, we didn't question that, either. Bought in. He's golden."

Sadie was six when her father exited the armed forces. She's never been privy to her dad's military life. He doesn't talk about those days, but Sadie understands more now than she did a few months ago, having gone through basic. "Makes sense."

"Hitting the sack." Alex jumps up, dusts himself off, and turns to Carl. "Twirley?" Alex walks past, slapping Liam. "First watch?"

Liam nods.

Carl tips his Boonie up. "Sounds good, Pretty Boy. Night kids."

"You a snorer?" Carl asks Alex.

"My wife thinks so."

They disappear into the shelter, leaving her and Liam alone.

Liam scrutinizes her. She covers herself, feeling self-conscious about her scars. Hunter comes to the forefront of her mind. *Is he going back to the farmhouse to confront his brother? Wendall doesn't sound like someone you reason with.* Will she see Hunter again?

Her attention goes back to Liam. Carl is right about love. When it's the right one, you sure know it. Flames light up Liam's face in hues of orange. His appearance ticks so many boxes. His blond hair has grown out, along with his beard. She's always wondered what he'd look like with a beard.

"Wish you'd talk to me."

Yep. Hot. Sadie holds his gaze. "About?"

"Who did this to you?"

Sadie turns back to the dying flames. *Not this again.* "I'm not ready." She feels the warmth of the campfire, and it reminds her of that terrible night when she felt faint heat on her swollen eyelids, barely able to see past the pain, terrified she wasn't going to see another sunrise. From the shadows, Brent's terrifying stare, seething with intense anger. She closed her eyes, shutting out the world around her, trying to banish him from her life. Then came the sting of the blade's edge. Her screams...

"We need to talk about that night."

Sadie blinks as she tries to understand which night he's referring to. *He must mean the night he brought her home from the party.* The night they fought. The night that changed their relationship. "Why?"

"Because I was an asshole."

Sadie starts to rise. His hand seizes hers, making her stop. "I'm not done, Auburn."

Liam curls his warm fingers around her hand, then slides their hands across to his thigh, sending her heart racing. Liam's hand is manly...strong. He's never taken her hand in such a loving way before. Perhaps it's out of sympathy for what she's been through? It certainly isn't because he loves her. "Liam."

"I regret..." There's remorse in his expression. "I never saw you as a kid, Sadie. You were so much more to me."

Sadie settles back down. *Does he mean being a cousin? A friend?* "More?"

His eyes caress her in the orange glow. A serene gaze replaces the remorse. He opens his mouth to speak, but then he looks back to the cooling embers. She clenches his hand for encouragement.

"Because my heart belongs to you."

His heart? That revelation hits her square in the chest. "What? But I...I saw you."

His confusion is plain.

Cat's out of the bag now, big mouth. She sighs. "You kissed a guy that night."

She'd strolled into the house where the party was in full swing, searching for her friends. Sadie found Liam, instead, with another man, their lips locked as they embraced against a rumbling washing machine.

He searches his memory. "Oh! You thought I was..."

She nods, unwilling to speak while the emotion is so thick in her throat. Her heart was crushed in that hallway, and it never recovered.

He grins, a slow, sly smile that hints at some secret amusement. "Sadie, I'm..." He furrows his brow, and his eyes narrow as he contemplates.

He's going to admit it. She almost wants to stop him, because if he says it out loud, then there's no doubt anymore, no hope, and Sadie's world will crumble again.

"I'm bisexual."

Her mind goes blank, but her face must be showing the confusion she's feeling. His eyes soften further.

"Does your father—?"

"Yes."

"Alex?"

"Yeah. Not everyone. Back then, I was trying to figure myself out. I knew what I felt for you, but..."

Silence reigns for a beat. Sadie's at a loss for words. She read it all wrong. *Bisexual.* Liam just became hotter to her, and some of her physical parts rejoice. Her mind, not so much. *What about Hunter? Do I have feelings for him, too?*

"That night...you were so angry, but I was full of heat," Liam admits. "I just wanted to crush you and kiss the life out of those sexy lips of yours."

Sexy lips? Aroused by his words, she squeezes her legs together, and her mouth goes dry as she visualizes what he's saying. "Why didn't you?"

It's dark, but she thinks his eyes smolder for a moment. He recovers. "Rule number one: don't mess with someone's daughter. I respect your father too much."

Sadie bites the inside of her cheek. She knows how much the men in her life want to do the right thing, the right way. And she knows all too well how controlling her father can be. If she hadn't gone to university, she's certain he would have done whatever it took to keep her a virgin forever.

"That, and I like my limbs and head still attached."

She smiles to humor Liam, but she doesn't laugh. It's true. Her father would have done that if he'd caught them doing anything other than talking.

"I asked your dad for permission the next day."

"You did?" Sadie holds her breath, wondering how her father dealt with that.

"He saw us that night, so he denied me." He lets go of her hand. "Thought I was messing with you. I tried to explain, but you know him."

He's always trying to... Her mother's words tumble forth: "Your dad prides himself on controlling the obstacles." This is her father's doing? Her jaw tightens. "Boy, do I ever." So much wasted energy. So much time lost.

"It hurt, but I had to let you go. We were going in different directions." He stokes the fire with a branch, causing embers to fly upward. "A relationship, even one with permission, would have been hard for both of us."

His honesty draws out Sadie's own truth. "Seeing you with that guy crushed me. I was angry with you, then with myself."

Liam faces her. "I want to know if there's a chance for us."

Sadie's at a loss for what to say. She doesn't want to say no. But Hunter sees past the scars. Does Liam?

He cups her chin, runs his thumb across her scarred cheek. She turns away. "You don't have to hide the hickey from me."

"What?" She instinctively moves her hand to her neck and finds a painful, inflamed lump. *He knows.*

"Isn't that why you're hiding from me?" Liam says with a pained expression. "Didn't think I'd notice his mark on you?"

"No, I thought... My scars... I'm disfigured now."

He scoots close and drapes one leg over both of hers, positioning the other behind her back, and slides both palms along her cheeks and into her auburn hair, forcing her to look into his kind eyes. "Your scars don't change how I feel about you. And frankly, neither does his mark."

The fear of being unlovable because of her scars melts away, leaving only warmth and tenderness in its place. Drawn in by his closeness, Sadie leans in, bringing her lips so close to his. The ache of restored love brings a fiery blush to her cheeks.

Liam's lips part. He tenses up and teeters, not closing the distance, but not drawing away. "I want to kiss you with every fiber of my being, but please, don't make me betray your father's trust."

Sadie has to respect that, but only because it's important to him, so she withdraws.

He holds her fast; their foreheads touch. He asks, his voice a rough, husky whisper, "Will you give us a chance?"

A week ago, she'd have wholeheartedly said yes and jumped for joy. But now...

Liam is the one for her, but Hunter vies for her heart, too. How can she choose? Hunter isn't afraid of her father's wrath, and Liam's confession makes things clearer for her. She should choose sweet and caring Liam, but Hunter's bad-boy attitude makes her pulse race, and there's good in him, even if he refuses to see it.

Her silence upsets Liam. "Why won't you answer me?" He disengages altogether to stare back into the flames.

"I want to."

"But?"

Though she wanted her father to be the first to know, the secret feels like a burning brand on her heart, and it's even more painful knowing she's keeping it from Liam. "Hunter's gone back to the farm, and I need to stop him."

Liam releases her. "There's no way in hell you are going anywhere near that man!" He stands up and starts pacing.

"Liam—"

He stops, points at her. "He told you in that letter. That's why you wanted to leave today."

She hesitates.

"Not because you wanted to go home, but because of him?!" Liam throws his hands up in the air, paces, then stops to stare at her. "You have feelings for him, don't you?"

Her silence delivers a painful blow to both of them. She has to be honest with herself.

"You know he's the enemy, right? His family... They couldn't tell you over the radio."

Sadie stands up. "Tell me what?"

Liam sighs, breathing out his rage. "They hurt Gina."

"I know. My father told me. Is there more?"

He points at the darkness beyond the trees. "That man's brother raped her."

Sadie's hand flies to her mouth, and her body starts to shiver and sweat at once. Tears stream down her cheeks. She wants to throw up.

"Shit, I'm sorry." Liam pulls her back into his arms. "I was there during the rescue. She was a wreck. There were other women, too. Your sister wasn't the only one."

The hell they must have endured. Sonny's assault on Sadie is still fresh, but she keeps that to herself, knowing it'll fuel Liam's hate for Hunter.

"There's more," Liam says into her hair. His arms tighten.

Sadie's not sure she wants more, but she prepares herself.

"They killed Brad."

Not Brad, God, not Brad. Gina will need Sadie now more than ever. But before she can help her, Sadie needs Liam. She's glad he's holding her, because that statement shoots straight through her heart. Sadie leans into him, feeling his solid strength and warmth, drawing comfort to face whatever is next. More hot tears trickle down her cheeks and onto Liam's chest.

"This is why I want you nowhere near this man."

"Hunter's not like that." She swipes at the tears on her face in anger, forcing Liam to drop his arms.

"The evidence says otherwise. He was with them when they arrived on the farm."

"Was he there when the women were?"

"Yes."

This contradicts everything she believes and knows about Hunter; it feels wrong. By his own admission, he would never hurt a woman. It has to be his controlling brother, Wendall. He's the rotten apple decaying the nearby fruit. "Hunter wouldn't—"

"Sadie, don't be so naive. They've kidnapped another group of people."

Naive? Sadie's anger flares. "Hunter wouldn't be a part of that."

With a look of disgust, Liam spits, "Geesh, he really got to you, didn't he? He can do no wrong. The man must be a saint!" He turns his face to the fire. "Don't let the enemy deceive you. He and his brother have already attacked Haven and attempted to kidnap our people out in the fields, and they will try again."

Sadie gets up and moves away. This time, Liam doesn't try to stop her. She knows it's futile to try to convince Liam otherwise anymore. But at the same time, doubt enters her mind. Has she been duped by Hunter? The message he gave her said he's going to make things right. Why would he write that if it is all an elaborate trick? Liam's words don't align with the connection she felt with Hunter.

"We have different perspectives on this," Liam says, his eyes reflecting back the dancing flames, "but I won't give up on you. He doesn't deserve to breathe the same air as you."

CHAPTER 39
July 3

H unter overlooks the creek on the outskirts of the farm. He's close, but he knows the land well. In the shade of the trees here, he's hidden from view. The smell of rich overturned earth is strong. He stretches his neck, enjoying the breeze on his skin.

Hunter lost track of the days sooner than he'd care to admit, so he doesn't know the date, but by the heat, he thinks it could be midsummer. During the spring runoff, the creek is more turbulent and fast flowing, but now, the water is low. It bubbles like a brook; the sound calms his nerves.

He lets out a brief snort. Hunter can't believe he's nervous. It feels foreign. Something he hasn't felt since he was a young child. *Why now?*

She is why. Sadie has inspired him to find a purpose worth fighting for. He realizes she is what he has been missing in his life. Normal. He regrets not having confessed his feelings. He misses her. Painfully so. He didn't expect that.

Perhaps he would have, if only he'd had more moments like this in life. He would have understood why it was so difficult to detach himself from Sadie's cozy body while she was sleeping, and why he'd felt such reluctance with every step he took away from her and the compound under the waterfall. Hunter felt drawn to stay because of the exciting new experiences they were sharing. He wanted to know what it was like to have morning sex, but he couldn't wake her. Hunter had had his fun. It is time to repay the favor. Today is the day he will take that bullet. The bullet he has always known is out there, waiting for him. He never thought he'd be afraid to take it.

The feel of the cool creek water squishing between Hunter's toes doesn't bother him as he crosses. His focus is elsewhere. He has to regroup and hide his new heart from Wendall. Why does he have to have a heart now? The damn thing grieves for losing her light, the shine in her eyes. An experience he will hold on to as he transitions to the afterlife. In order to carry out his upcoming task, Hunter must revert to his former self. He also has to leave all thoughts of Sadie out of his mind. He closes himself off from thinking of her. It's hard, but it has to be done to get through this.

The farm looms up ahead as he clears the tree line and enters the yard between the barn and house. With a sturdy walking stick in hand, Hunter emerges from the shadows and steps into the sun-drenched field. Several men raise their weapons in response to his arrival, but then lower them.

Giles and his family tend the fields under the watch of armed men. Once again, a strong sense of guilt overwhelms Hunter. He must trust that after dealing with Wendall, Giles and his family will be alright. At least he'll give them a chance to get away, which is more than they have at the moment. Hunter is doing this for Sadie, but Giles will benefit from his brother's death, as well.

Wendall is also in the field, surrounded by guards. Even though Hunter's not in the mood, he fakes a smile and waves. "Brother!" He steps between the rows of growing corn, happy that the Hutchisons will have a harvest of food to sustain them once he and his brother are gone.

Wendall's wary eye greets him as Hunter approaches. "If I didn't know any better, I'd say you had a piece of ass with the silly grin on your face."

Hunter worries that if he stops smiling, it will prove his brother's point. *How does he know?* He scoffs. "I wish."

"Was wondering when you'd show." He looks over Hunter's shoulder. "Where's Sonny? No people with you, no equipment?" His voice is laced with impatience, and a couple of the guards step back.

Tread carefully. "Bear attacked us. I played dead, and he didn't." With a grim expression, Hunter raises his arm, displaying a shirt covered in dried blood. "I didn't come out unscathed, though. He kicked me around some." Hunter's glad his old clothes were still in the bin he'd thrown them in. Even though he preferred his new clothes from the compound, he couldn't wear them.

"I can see that. More scars?"

Hunter remains silent. Wendall's always poking. Does he expect a response? *Wait him out, Hunter. Don't give him more than he needs, more than you would give him normally.*

Wendall's foot disturbs the upturned soil under his feet. Though he didn't expect his brother to show him any concern, Hunter feels there is more to this coldness than meets the eye.

Time to change the subject before he starts to find holes in the story. Hunter points his chin in the direction of the river. "What's happening with the people across the way?"

Wendall turns his back on him as he twists his body toward the house. Hunter follows, putting his hands in his pockets so no one can see them shaking. He expected his brother to display some kind of anger at him for coming back empty-handed. Actually, it's worse than that. He's also lost a man. *Something's amiss.* Keeping his emotions in check will be crucial until Hunter can determine what it is.

The shade of the farmhouse cuts into the heat, but walking into the building brings with it the usual trepidation and wall of painful memories. Wendall lounges on the couch in the front room, and despite not saying a word, Hunter knows he's expected to sit in the armchair. A shiver runs down Hunter's spine as the armed men step out of his peripheral vision. He settles back in the chair, stretches his legs out, and crosses his ankles, doing his best to look unperturbed.

"We're attacking their compound tonight."

"Tonight?" Hunter maintains a serious scowl. "Have you found a way in?"

"Yes."

FLEE

Hunter finds it odd to hear his brother answer with a single word. It's like he's closed himself off. "So, what's the plan, then? We splitting and attacking from two sides?"

"Did you lose Sonny before or after Swindon?"

Hunter's surprise is genuine. "Just before Swindon, so I came back. Why?"

Wendall frowns, pinches the bridge of his nose, and unleashes a long, slow sigh. "My men found Sonny."

Hunter's face betrays nothing, but inside, he's swearing bullets. *Shit! How do I turn this around?* "And?"

"And no bear attacked him, so what really happened, brother?" Wendall emphasizes the last word.

Hunter glances back at the two men, the metallic gleam of their weapons catching the light, their expressions hard and unforgiving. Deep down, Hunter knows Wendall won't hurt him. Not by his own hand. But the pain can come from somewhere else. Giles comes to mind.

Don't panic. Think. As long as Wendall has nothing to use against Hunter, things might go his way. He leans forward, resting his forearms on his thighs. "He shoved a gun in my face and tried to kill me. Why would he do that, brother?" Hunter mimics his brother's tone. He enjoys the confusion that crosses his brother's face. It's seldom that Hunter has one over him.

"Did he say anything before that?"

Hunter recalls the words too well: "Wendall sends his love..."

But if I let Wendall know he asked Sonny to hurt me, or kill me, what then? "No."

A brief flick of relief crosses Wendall's expression, and then it's gone again, replaced with a heavy frown. "I'm sorry he did that, Hunter. I asked him to go with you because I knew there was tension between you both. I'd hoped the trip would help you both work together better, and I was wrong."

Hunter tries to shift the focus of the argument away from his brother prying anymore. He knows his brother is lying to him, but he doesn't need any more reasons to know he has to kill him. "Why were those men there? If you knew Sonny and I were heading in that direction, why send more?"

"Idiots got turned around," Wendall says, rushing his words. "They were going east and ended up heading south. It was a miracle they found their way back."

The answer feels rehearsed, and this worries Hunter. Is his brother just covering his tracks, or did those men see more than Wendall is sharing? It doesn't escape Hunter's notice that his brother hasn't shared the plan, either. Hunter thought he had time to set things in motion, but Wendall preparing to move on Sadie's people tonight means he'll have to improvise. Like the rest of his miserable life, things never go his way.

***

"Doctor, I think you need to see her ankle." A young man carries Jewel into medical and deposits her gently on a hospital bed. The doctor sitting at his desk is the same one who saw her when she was first brought inside. She recalls his name is Henry.

Henry pushes his glasses up his nose and wheels his chair away from his desk and toward her. "What do we have here, Jewel?" He reaches out, lifts her ankle.

"It's my fault, Doc," Dane said. "No one had told her that she's not allowed to go wandering around Haven just yet. She came out the door and ran straight into me."

She hisses. "I think I have sprained it." Jewel doesn't enjoy lying, but she has no choice. She looks around the light green room. Other beds are just about visible behind closed curtains.

"We'll ice it." Henry gazes up at the man. "Thanks for bringing her in, Dane."

White-towel-covered trolleys line the walls. There is a stark, clinical feel to the environment. It smells sterile. None of this is surprising, Jewel realizes, yet she'd half expected never to see any kind of hospital setting ever again.

"No problem." Dane turns to her. "I hope your ankle gets better."

His demeanor is pleasant, evoking memories of her son. Jewel smiles in gratitude. "Merci beaucoup. So do I."

Solid wood and glass cabinets occupy the rest of the walls. Henry walks to one of them with a visible bar fridge and extracts a cold pack from it. Jewel breathes a sigh of relief, glad her goal is possible and within reach.

"Doc, I'll be outside to take her back to the apartment when you're done."

Henry nods.

Now she just has to distract Henry, but how?

He probes her ankle with his gentle fingers while monitoring her reaction. "Not much bruising." He wraps the blue bag with a towel and lays it across her bare skin with care. "There. Fifteen minutes, and we'll investigate further." He walks back to the cabinet amid the sound of his rattling keys.

"Doctor, do you have water? I'm thirsty."

He stops short of the cabinet, keys in hand. "Sure." He walks to his desk and searches, finding the bottle there empty. "Will you be okay while I go get you a fresh one from the kitchen?"

"Yes, I don't think I am walking far."

He exits into the common room.

Jewel leaps from the bed, her heart racing, and rushes across the room to the cabinet. She picks through the bottles and syringes, searching for anything with ketamine written on the label. *Come on, come on... There it is.* It's the only drug she knows by name from the farm at home. The veterinarians used it on the animals to get them to drift off into a state of sedation. She snatches up syringes.

"Water coming right up!" Henry calls from outside in a jovial tone.

With swift movement, Jewel tucks the syringes away, feeling the cool plastic against her skin. She runs to the bed, her breath catching in her throat, and scoops up the ankle bag as Henry enters.

He greets her with a grin and a bottle of water in hand. "Hey, no peeking. Let the cold do its job."

She fakes a smile.

He positions the bag over her ankle a second time, noticing her shortness of breath. "Are you feeling okay?" He holds the back of his hand against her forehead. "You're burning."

She feels the plastic under her clothing shift. The syringes are sliding out and onto the bed. "I feel hot."

Henry gazes down, reaching into his breast pocket.

She shoves her contraband back where they were, afraid to take her eyes off him.

"Open for me." He places the thermometer under her tongue. It's cold but soon warms up. Strong fingers touch her wrist as he checks her pulse against his watch. He removes the glass rod after a spell and gazes at it. His brow rises. "Well, no fever. But let's keep you here and see if your internal temperature stabilizes."

"Okay. Water?"

He refocuses on the bottle he brought, uncaps it, and offers it to her. Jewel relaxes against the pillows and gratefully drinks the water.

CHAPTER 40

S adie's been anxious since she awoke this morning. Alex takes point, traveling from tree to tree ahead of her and Liam. They've been in contact with Haven, so they're expected. Today's the moment of truth. Despite everything she achieved to complete boot camp, to become a Marine reservist, there's no hiding that she failed to keep herself safe from Brent, and her father will see it. Sadie bolsters her nerves. "Nothin' you can do 'bout it." Carl's words encourage her to keep moving forward.

Abrupt words burst from the communications headset in Sadie's ear. "Freeze, Pretty Boy!" It's Hoss.

Alex signals by raising his hand above his head in a fist. Liam and Alex lift their rifles. Sadie does the same. Liam raises an eyebrow at her. She realizes they don't know about her training and that she understands Alex's gestures and signs.

Sadie had a feeling she was being watched, so she is glad it turns out to be Hoss. They are close to the farmhouse and Hunter. *It's almost over. I'm home.*

"Five tangos lounging at two o'clock. See the smoke?"

Alex motions that there is an enemy in sight, points right, and their rifles move in that direction. He replies into his mic. "Copy. Heads up. The guy in the Boonie is with us."

"Ranger?"

Carl pipes in: "Call me Twirley."

Alex points at Liam, smacks his chest, and then motions for them to go in the opposite direction. Liam gazes at Sadie. She nods, and once again, he looks confused. They slink left.

"Welcome, Twirley. Hoss."

"You camouflage well."

Hoss's familiar chuckle comes through the comms. "You, too."

She misses his squeezes. Powerful emotions come to the surface, but Sadie quells them. *Plenty of time for that later.* She breathes her jitters out and forges on behind the boys.

It takes them some time to get through the underbrush, but once they reach the riverbed, they hang back by the trees. Sadie searches the opposite shore for any hostiles. The soil has been broken down for planting in one field while a crop grows in another. It looks like corn. She wonders if they'll put her on security or farming?

The butterflies in her stomach amplify as Hoss, in a flowing ghillie suit, barrels down the river, bearing on their position in a Zodiac. And behind him is...

Dad!

Her father appears stoic in the back of the craft. *Is that a beard on him?* Seeing him brings joy to her heart, but also fear. Tears prick her eyes.

Liam encircles her waist, startling her, and whispers into her ear, "It'll all work out. He missed you something fierce." Sadie covers his hand and leans against him.

Alex faces his palm out to Liam. He responds in kind and squeezes her hand to follow him, still assuming she doesn't understand the signal, even though she's proven otherwise. Carl runs alongside the river, his backpack bobbing up and down, to catch up to them as the Zodiac grazes the bank.

Donovan's boots hit the gravel, anchoring the craft for them. She dodges around her father and hops in, facing out. With everyone accounted for, Hoss turns the Zodiac on a dime, and they start back down the river. Shots ring out, and Donovan shoves Sadie low and gives cover fire as bullets whiz by in the blink of an eye.

They hit the opposite bank downriver, out of range, and catapult out. Liam and Alex run the craft to the trees. The others follow on their heels up the muddy side and into the tree line. It isn't a steep climb, but Sadie breaks out in a sweat, excited for the reunion, but dreading how she will inevitably have to explain her scars and Hunter.

The boys hide the Zodiac away in the lockbox buried in the ground. Hoss turns to her first, reacts, but then recovers. She redirects her head on instinct, only to come face-to-face with her father.

Donovan gasps. "Oh, sweetheart!" he exclaims, yanking her into his caring embrace.

Sadie pulls away shyly and glances at Liam. "No time, Dad. Let's fuckin' keep going."

"Language, honey."

He never changes. She's still a child in his eyes. *And the scars are going to make it harder than ever to convince him to give me space.*

Hoss clicks his mic. "Crunch, we're going west, up to section six. We'll enter the tunnel there."

"Copy that."

Sadie feels her father glancing her way as they run. "Sadie? You okay, baby girl?"

Donovan's asking because he thinks she can't run like the men. Isn't he going to be surprised? "A-okay, Dad! By the way, love the beard."

He grins.

A short time later, boots crush gravel in the tunnel's darkness. After jogging through the fields and up past Haven's gate, they entered the secondary exit tunnel they'd carved through the mountain. They walk toward a solid, single steel door. As Hoss enters the inner courtyard, light floods the tunnel, and the rest of them follow inside. Once the door is secure, they stand in a circle in the open yard with the goats, catching their breath from the run. Alex strolls to the guard tree as an identical man drops out of it gingerly. They embrace. He's right, he is the prettier brother.

Hoss yanks Sadie toward him, bringing her in for a proper hug, kissing her forehead with his gentle nature. "So glad you're safe, Sadie girl. Missed ya."

That wasn't so bad. Then again, it's Hoss, and Hoss never pries. With a smile on her face, Sadie relishes the familiar, warm embrace. "I'm glad to be home."

A voice sounds through her headset: "Auburn better come down. Hallway's getting crowded here."

"Is that Roger?" she asks Hoss.

"Yeppers."

Roger used Liam's nickname for me? Her eyes meet Liam's, and Sadie can't help but notice the unmistakable affection he has for her openly displayed.

Donovan crosses between them, pulls Sadie in, and tightens his arms around her. His familiar scent releases pent-up anxiety as she melts into him. "I don't want to face them yet, Dad."

He holds Sadie out at arm's length and gazes straight into her soul. As Donovan's touch grazes her facial scars, she glimpses the fury in his eyes. She senses that a sergeant's speech is imminent. "You're a Masters. We face everything head-on. The good...and the bad."

And that's my dad.

Everyone around them averts their gaze to respect her privacy.

"I will, but smaller groups first."

Donovan lets her go with a squeeze and a small smile. She knows a deeper conversation about her scars is coming, but it means something that he isn't pushing her to explain right away.

Hoss steps forward. "Tall order here, but I'll take ya." He clicks the mic. "Crunch, clear the hall to Osmond's apartment. Auburn isn't ready to face her fans yet."

This is the reason she adores Hoss. He always knows what she needs and steps up to the challenge.

"On it."

Sadie mouths Thank you to Hoss and feeds one arm through his. Liam extends his hand as she passes. Wanting to kiss him, she catches his outstretched fingers and gives them an affectionate squeeze.

***

Donovan frowns during their exchange, but Liam knows he's given no indication that he and Sadie are anything more than two friends supporting each other. Liam stares back with a slow smile growing on his face. He will not give Donovan any reason to say no the next time he asks for permission.

"Liam, Alex, I'll need a report."

Whatever Sadie feels for this guy won't stop Liam from asking Donovan. It's something he needs to do to move forward with Sadie. Sooner or later, Hunter will show his true colors, and Sadie will come to her senses. Liam just has to be patient.

Carl enters their circle with a confident, outstretched hand to Donovan. "Twirley. Or you can call me Carl."

Donovan hesitates. "And you are?"

Liam takes solace in Carl throwing Donovan off balance and answers quickly. "The Ranger who saved Sadie."

Donovan takes Carl in with renewed interest. "A Ranger?" He grasps Carl's hand with equal vigor. "You saved her?"

Carl nods and glances at Liam. "I did. Outside Spokane."

"Tell me what happened to her."

Liam's not sure Donovan's ready to hear what happened from someone else, but Liam's starving for information, so he says nothing.

Carl shakes his head. "You should get her side of things."

The man is smart, dodging the question.

"I want your side first."

Carl sizes Donovan up and down. Liam understands Carl is a man who doesn't do things on a whim. He thinks before he acts, and he never likes to rush. "When she's ready to tell you, you'll know, but not from me."

On some level, Liam's relieved and respects the man more for it.

Donovan seems to agree. While a silent assessment plays across his face, Donovan's posture relaxes slightly. "I owe you, then?"

"If you wanna see it that way. I'd appreciate livin' here until I meet my maker and my wife again."

"Done."

"I'd also appreciate it if you'd let me help ya out. You've got logistic issues that need fixin'."

Liam smirks. *Got a good eye, this one.* Maintaining this place and ensuring everyone's safety requires considerable work.

"We're working on that, but yeah, we could use you for sure."

"Much obliged."

They shake hands.

"Welcome to Haven, Carl."

CHAPTER 41

Sadie clasps Beth's ring finger on the couch as they both share tears of joy. Gina sits nearby, looking distant, empty. Sadie's reunion with her sister was bittersweet. They cried in Gina's room and hung onto each other before Beth showed, neither of them uttering a single word, neither prepared to speak out loud about their traumas. Besides, Sadie already knew Gina's turmoil from Liam, and Gina didn't need to hear anything when Sadie's face spoke volumes.

Sadie feels eyes on her and gazes across the apartment. Her father is standing just inside the open front door, enjoying their laughter. Despite his smile, his eyes betray a sense of concern as his eyes dance between her and Gina. Sadie glances at her sister and reaches out for her to come closer. Gina complies and scoots over to hug Sadie like a child. This worries her, too.

Her other siblings rush around Donovan and toward Sadie in a frenzy of excitement, creating a cacophony of noise. As they shower her with kisses and hugs, Gina retreats back into the corner. Sadie notices, but also permits herself to enjoy seeing her family again, and her insides warm as their love radiates through every interaction.

First in line is her younger brother, Ethan. With the same brown coloring as their father, he stands almost as tall as Donovan. After pulling back from the hug, he sends her with a warm smile, even though she can see the anger behind it. "Hey, sis. Missed you."

With her seventeen-year-old sister's white-blonde hair cascading over them, Tracy leans in for a kiss, her voice filled with excitement. "I've got so much to tell you. I'll be graduating soon, and I'm learning to teach now."

Not to be outdone, Ethan pipes in. "I'm the new animal keeper. I raise the goats."

The last to hug Sadie, Donovan Jr., is grumpy, his coloring a unique blend of his mother's blue eyes and his father's brown hair. He makes a hole between his siblings near Sadie and plops down in defeat. "I wish I had a job. I'm stuck in school."

Sadie grabs his hand. "Don't worry, you'll find your way, Donnie."

"I think I missed you the most." He conveys this with a glum attitude, causing her other siblings to argue loudly.

Donovan laughs over the ruckus, then yells in a commanding voice, "So nice to have all my kids home, but damn, simmer down now!"

The room quickly grows quiet, as if someone pressed a mute button.

A mysterious man with long dark hair tied back strides into the apartment. Donovan greets him, and they whisper to each other. The man pauses before leaving and turns his attention to the couch. Sadie follows his gaze to Gina. *Hmm...an admirer, perhaps?* Her eyes slide back to this man with curiosity, but he's already exited the apartment.

"Sorry to interrupt the reunion, kids," Donovan says. "Sadie, need you to come with us to see the council now."

They have a council? Sadie is apprehensive about seeing everyone, but she kisses each sibling on the way to the doorway and walks out with her father. The mysterious man is waiting for them in the hallway. He seems unfazed by her appearance.

Donovan holds out his upturned palm. "Honey, this is Mal."

Beth told her Ryker had a brother. He's leaner than most of the men here, but he reminds Sadie of Hunter: tall, like her father, and giving off the same bad-boy vibes. "Nice to meet you."

Mal nods but says nothing before walking ahead of them, leading them through the outer ring of the compound. They travel in silence, but Sadie's mind is busy. The council needs something from her. Intel? Information on Hunter, perhaps? Liam updated her on the situation across the river, revealing that people are being abducted and exploited for farm labor. This is one of the "bad things" Hunter had referred to, she realizes.

Moving inside Parker's apartment, the unexpected number of people catches her off guard, and their different reactions to her, some of sympathy, some of rage, serve as a painful reminder of the shame etched across her face.

Carl leans against the back wall alongside Liam, Alex, his brother, and some men she doesn't know. Sadie recognizes the people seated around Parker's round kitchen table. There's no mistaking the military vibe in the room. Donovan seats himself at the table and turns to face her, just like the others.

No one asks Sadie to sit. All eyes are on her. Anxiety courses through her, but Sadie readies herself for battle, standing at attention with her hands clasped behind her. It feels like an inquisition. Feels like boot camp.

"Welcome home, Sadie," Parker says with a warm smile. "Heard you've had quite a journey?"

She nods.

***

Liam notes the way she stands, like she's facing the executioner and ready to hear her punishment. He has a sudden urge to protect her, but he stays put. He hopes this meeting gives him the answers he seeks.

"How did Hunter get you to let him into Reed?" Parker asks calmly, though his voice is laced with authority.

Sadie was tight-lipped about Hunter with Liam. *Will she tell the council?*

"He didn't coerce me, if that's what you think."

"But you let him in. Why?"

"The man he was with captured me and wanted to..." She searches for the words. "Hurt me."

Some people shift, and others look uncomfortable. Liam clenches his jaw in irritation, convinced Sadie's not telling the truth. *Hunter isn't as innocent as she's portraying him to be.*

"Without thought for his own safety, Hunter fought this man so I could escape. I saved him by taking the man out. He was my first kill."

This admission troubles Liam. *First kill?*

"I left Hunter wounded and moved onto Reed alone, but I was already showing symptoms of pneumonia at this point, and my condition worsened. We stumbled upon each other again at the falls. I couldn't reach the keypad, but he could."

The bastard used her.

Looking incensed, Donovan waves his hand in front of his face. "He followed you to the falls, honey, and used your weakness against you."

Liam is of the same mind as Donovan for once.

Sadie's jaw tightens. Growing up, her and Donovan's fights were epic, almost legendary. When their eyes locked and their voices rose, everyone else knew to clear out or be caught in the crossfire. Liam recognizes the same tense feeling that he used to feel when they were younger. He tries to swallow, but his mouth is dry.

"Donovan!" Parker pacifies him with a look of warning before turning back to Sadie. "You trust him, then?"

"Not once did he mistreat me. He didn't make the connection to Haven until I confronted him. Liam told me about what's been going on over the river. You have a plan to rescue the captives, right? When we go, I want him untouched."

We? Liam isn't the only one to notice: eyebrows rise throughout the room.

Parker seems to be the only one not fazed by her demand. "Why?"

"Because he's over there righting a wrong and he feels he doesn't deserve a second chance."

Donovan exhales through his nose loudly. "You think he deserves one? He kidnaps people, and who knows what else. He told you just enough to trust him. We can't trust him."

"Understood."

Liam's eyes slide to Sadie. That was too quick for his taste.

A hint of wariness crosses Donovan's face. "Understood? What does that mean?"

Sadie faces her father square on. "Means if you can't let him be a part of Haven, then so be it. If he goes, I go."

Liam pushes himself off the wall as the people around him descend into a frenzy of whispers.

Donovan raises his arm. "Hold on!" The whispers in the room cease.

"I'm also going with you to rescue him!"

"You're not going!"

"I am!"

Liam's eyes dart between the two of them, taking in the escalating argument and the way their voices grow louder with each statement.

"You're not trained!" Donovan counters.

"Tell them, Sadie!" Carl's deep voice slices between them, cutting their sparring short. All eyes land on Carl.

"Tell us what?" Donovan asks Carl.

Sadie slides her hand into her front pocket and pulls something out. "The reason you're gonna let me go." She approaches the round table doggedly, her fist clenched. Sadie places an object on it and takes a step back.

Liam's lips part in shock. *Holy...*

Marines around the room recognize the black pin of an eagle, globe, and anchor, eliciting grunts and smiles. Liam's stunned. A new respect grows inside him. *Fuck the librarian, she's a sexy Marine!*

It's clear from the way his face has contorted in pain that Donovan has taken a hard hit. *He didn't know,* Liam thinks. *None of them did.* Regardless, Donovan should be proud of her. He knows what it takes to become a Marine.

Hoss fist pumps with glee and yells, "Oorah!"

Every Marine in the room repeats the call. Including Sadie.

Liam's heart swells with pride. *Why didn't she tell anyone? Why keep it a secret?*

Looking down at her father, she musters the courage to speak. "Dad?"

He takes a moment to swallow down whatever he's feeling. When he looks up at her, his expression is soft, tender. "Baby, I'm proud of you." He rises, and she falls into his welcoming arms.

After a few seconds, Hoss wiggles in between them. "A Marine, Sadie girl? I'm so goddamned proud!"

"Reservist," she says, but her face still glows with pride.

As it should, Liam thinks. It doesn't matter. *Reservist or active duty, they all went through the same training.*

"Holy shit!" Hoss high-fives her. "Why didn't you tell us? We'd have gone to your graduation."

Liam remembers his father approaching him with the same pride in his chest. It was the best feeling in the world.

"It was something I needed to do on my own." Sadie glances at her father. "Without interference."

Parker's voice interrupts their little party. "Well deserved, but you're untested. You haven't been briefed on this mission, so I'm grounding you."

Oh, shit.

Sadie winds up. "You can't—"

"Yes, I can. The safety of everyone here rests on the council's shoulders, and I will not have you jeopardizing this mission. Do I make myself clear?"

No one refutes Parker's order.

Liam doesn't like the pause that follows, but she eventually sighs. "Yes." In the next breath, she asks, "What about Hunter?"

"I can't guarantee his safety." Parker hands the pin back to her.

Upon receiving the pin, she raises her voice and speaks to the whole room. "Hunter's dark-haired, with a beard. The same height as my dad, and you won't miss the scar running through his face."

Donovan glances sideways at his daughter and studies her disfigured face.

"Donovan."

Everyone in the room turns to see Dane standing in the apartment doorway. But Liam won't be distracted. For Liam, the last piece of the puzzle has just tumbled into place. He finally understands why she protects that man. *He's disfigured...like her.*

Desiring a connection with Sadie, Liam comes in for a hug, not caring that Donovan sees them together. He mumbles in her hair, "You could have told me."

She seems rigid. Ticked. "Please, Liam, you have to make sure they don't hurt him. You have to bring Hunter back here, okay?" Sadie's fingers intertwine with his belt loops, the gesture a quiet, intimate comfort that warms him.

He holds on, letting out a sigh. "If he's injured, I'll do what I can for him." He could only promise that. He is a medic after all, sworn to save lives, not to take them.

But Liam knows the best thing that can happen is for Hunter to die on this mission. Whatever Sadie thinks of him, the man is a threat, and with no prison at Haven, with no justice system in the country anymore, the only way to be rid of a threat for good is to eliminate it.

CHAPTER 42

J ewel climbs the steep stairs, making her way toward the closed door at the
top.

With the stolen syringes of ketamine safely tucked under her clothes, Dane
had returned her to what they called the women's apartment. The ladies there
had avoided her at first. Melanie explained why they stayed in the apartment,
and a heavy sadness settled over Jewel. She understood and kept to herself,
respecting their need for distance, as well as maintaining some for herself. She
knew she wouldn't be able to stay on task without it.

She had to wait a little to avoid arousing suspicion, so she opted to have one
more amazing shower before she made her attempt. Once she was dry, Jewel
waited by the door in that apartment, listening, hoping Dane would relieve
himself from his guard duty for a moment. Anything to give her an opening.
She had the drugs to do the job. All she needed now was time to figure out how
to escape this maze of rooms and hallways to open that door in the compound wa
ll.

The man named Donovan had brought her down some stairs, so she knew
the place was buried deep underground. He blindfolded her, but she counted
every step on the descent, and the pungent aroma of damp soil along the way
told her there was a garden somewhere. She found it hard to believe anything
would grow without sunlight, though.

When Dane showed no sign of leaving his post, Jewel opted to request food.
Outside the medical office, a large space served as a kitchen where she saw others

eating. Once he was on his way, Jewel summoned her courage and ventured into the hallway, finding it deserted. *Opportunity.*

Her head turns from right to left as the apartment door closes behind her. The hallway bends in both directions like she's in a part of a circle. Across the way, Jewel sees the lounge with couches and tables set up. This was the tunnel Dane and Donovan used to bring her to and from medical twice today. People walk by the opening to the huge communal area carrying trays of food. She ducks right to avoid being spotted and listens for anyone approaching. Not hearing anyone, she continues past another set of apartment doors with an engraved plaque numbered seven and a piece of paper covering it which says Men's apartment. The place she came from is six, and they call it the women's apartment.

Silver lockers line the left side of the wide, sterile hallway as far as the eye can see. Jewel finds it odd, like she's in a spaceship. She passes apartment eight. The plaque says Tibold. The sound of people mingling carries as she draws near to another tunnel toward the communal area. Across from it, on her right, two doors with frosted windows appear. Above the door, the words say: Communal Pool Area. Fancy.

For fear of being caught, she refrains from taking a peek and scurries across the tunnel entrance to continue to the next door she finds. The plaques must bear the names of the people who inhabit them. Number nine says: Jenkins. Two young girls emerge. Jewel's heart jumps. They greet her with smiles, but continue down the corridor to the tunnel without delay. Jewel releases the breath she choked back in terror. She needs to find a way out before too many people spot her.

A large commotion of noise calls her attention as the hallway continues to curve left. As expected, number ten appears with the nameplate saying: Masters. Her favorite number. She wonders who the Masters are.

The pattern of doors and tunnels changes, and the noise becomes louder. It emanates from the next door over and sounds like everyone is in there. The opening on her right looks promising, as a staircase slants up in her favor. This must be the way out.

The door up ahead swings inward, voices spill out into the hallway, and Jewel darts up the staircase, taking them as fast as she can climb.

A wave of warm air and damp earth hits her as she inches a door open, her senses on high alert for any sign of someone being there. The wow factor hits her as she steps into an incredible space. It's clearly a garden. A magnificent glass ceiling, or so it seems, allows sunlight to pour in from above. This vast space, filled with a dizzying array of plant species, hums with the gentle whir of the conveying system, and long, white PVC tubes climb the walls.

Jewel walks through the maze of tubing, marveling at its ingenuity. *The planning that had to have gone into this place is remarkable.* She breathes in. The smell reminds her of the farm. Her family's farm. *Home.* Her parents and son. Ex-husband. Jewel's heart feels heavy; her soul, desolate. *Will I ever see them again?*

Doubt creeps in, but then she remembers why she's doing this. Jewel can't let those pigs hurt Kessie, Oncle Giles, or Tante Adele. She doesn't want these people to come to harm, either, but what choice does she have? Jewel has to pick the known over the unknown.

Kessie will suffer, though, whether they are over there or here. If Jewel has the chance to kill that horrible man, she will take it. She doesn't enjoy hearing his name or speaking it.

A metal door on the opposite wall calls her to get on with it. She squares her shoulders and walks away from her memories. That was her past, this is her future.

With slow deliberation, Jewel slides the door aside. More steep steps. From this vantage point, the end is dark, but a low light illuminates the stairs halfway up. Curious, she ascends, counting again. She's sure the next door will take her outside.

The higher she climbs, the brighter the light gets. This must be where the stairs leveled off when she came down them. A sliver of light streams through an ajar door, falling onto the cement floor before her. It's a room.

A man's voice inside says, "On it."

The light vanishes as the door's lock clicks into place, encasing her in complete blackness. The significance eludes her, yet she presses on upward, relying on her sense of touch and keeping count.

There's another landing, more steps, then a door. The handle is cold, suggesting it's metal, but it doesn't budge. *That's odd. Perhaps there's a keypad, but shouldn't it be lit for people to see it?* She slides her fingers over the cement wall to the right of the door. It's bare.

She returns her hands to the door, feeling the cold metal frame. What feels like a pipe leads her to a tiny box. *A light switch?* Jewel flicks the toggle. Nothing happens. *This is frustrating.*

All of a sudden, she's bathed in red light. She recoils from its illumination, fearing exposure. Feeling the panic rising in her throat, Jewel finds the door has several manual bolt mechanisms to lock the door from the inside. She attempts to slide one bolt. It's unlocked, and so are the others. She puts pressure on a lever. A keypad on her left lights up. *Ah.*

"Going somewhere?"

Startled by the voice behind her, she spins around, her hand flying to her chest. *Where the hell did Donovan come from?*

***

Parker takes a sip of his umpteenth cup of joe, or more correctly, Alejo's coffee. He asked the security team to stay behind after the council meeting, and Ryker is explaining some things to the newbies in the room about tactics and strategy. His gaze drifts to the picture of William on the wall next to Parker's shadow box of medals. He misses his friend's calm demeanor. Even now, the loss hurts, heating Parker's face.

Donovan strolls into the apartment with a striking, terrified woman and slides a chair out for her like a gentleman. With his hand on her shoulder, he forces her into the seat as he introduces her. "This is Jewel Hutchison."

Okay? Parker is aware—it was his idea to allow her to stay in the women's apartment—but why is she under Donovan's guard and looking guilty about it? Her arresting green eyes scan Parker's kitchen, and he can tell she's intimidated by the number of men in the room. She is attractive in fresh jeans and a billowy cream blouse.

Donovan answers Parker's question by placing a clear bag containing syringes labeled ketamine on the table. "I caught her taking a stroll up top. Found these on her."

"Hmm." Parker's day gets more complicated by the hour. They have a mole in their midst and a pretty one at that. The oldest trick in the book. Their enemy works fast, sending a beautiful captive, thinking they wouldn't think twice about protecting her.

Donovan stands in front of her, crossing his arms, and flinches, lowering them back down. He covers up his discomfort by focusing his anger Jewel's way. "So, what do they have on you?"

Jewel's anxious eyes glance around the room again, but somehow, she finds the courage to speak in a melodic accent. "I don't know who you speak of."

Could be French? He takes a sip of coffee. *Hope she doesn't choose the hard path for much longer.* Once they extract the information from her, Parker is afraid it will be much harder to forgive her.

Donovan bends over until he's inches from her face and rests his hands on her chair. "The assholes who sent you to sabotage us."

Losing color, Jewel slinks further back in her chair, shielding herself with her hands. Parker feels for her. Donovan's size usually scares most people into talking when he's in interrogation mode, but this tactic isn't working. She suffered abuse. The fading dark mark circling her neck tells Parker so. Parker looks at Hoss and then tilts his head, indicating the need for a shift in strategy.

"Darlin', we understand blackmail all too well." Hoss crosses the room and takes a knee by her chair as Donovan backs up. "You help us, and we'll help you."

Jewel looks from one man in the room to another once more until those defiant green eyes land on Donovan. "If I help you, I want something in return."

Donovan crosses his arms, forgetting his injury once more, closing himself off to the prospect of negotiation. Parker knows his friend too well and speaks up first. "Well, you tell us what we need to know, and we'll see what we can do for you."

Her distrusting eyes scrutinize him. "*Pourquoi moi?* I just want life to be the way it was before. I hate all this shit!"

Survival mode is taking a toll on her mental state, but Parker hopes she'll see sense. As a Frenchman himself, Isaac will be excited to meet her.

She turns to Hoss. "If I don't go through with it, they will..." She shakes her head. "They will kill my family."

Parker bubbles with anger. They need to move the timeline up. This has to stop.

"What do they want you to do here?" Hoss asks in a gentle tone.

Jewel closes her eyes. "I'm supposed to take out the...guards, and open the gate for them before the sun sets tonight."

"How were you going to do it?"

Her body slumps, and for a while, there is silence, disrupted only by the occasional nervous cough as everyone waits, eyes fixed on her, for the plan to unfold. "Back at our farm, after they captured us, I tried to escape. Two of our people paid for my foolishness. We were no match for these *bêtes*...beasts." She gazes up with a broken look at Donovan. "I didn't want to kill anyone. I stole that"—she points to the syringes—"to knock them out."

"It's not dusk yet. Why were you upstairs?" Donovan asks.

"You blindfolded me. I needed to see what was on the other side of the wall and find a way out. I'd knock your men out, locate a weapon, kill those pigs, and then rescue my family."

It was a bold move, but foolhardy at best.

"Why tonight?" Hoss asks.

"They will kill one person every night until I do, starting with my *oncle*, Giles."

Parker exchanges looks with Donovan and Hoss. *Heartless, this one. All the right elements to get her to do what he needed. A manipulator of the worst kind.*

Donovan relaxes his arms. "Courage. We understand that, too, but you wouldn't have made it to your family in time."

"Why not?"

"If one of our people hadn't shot you? You would have drowned in the river. It's unforgiving in the darkness without light or a safe way to cross."

Jewel startles when Hoss places his hand over hers. "Thank you."

She removes her hand. "You will let me go. I want to kill the man who took us from our home. If you cannot give me a rifle, I will take a knife. I'll make sure he fucking dies, even if it kills me!"

Her admission takes Parker aback. Glancing around the room, he sees he's not only one. Conviction and fearlessness define her. A person with nothing to lose is a scary thing. Unless they're on your side.

The most interesting response comes from Donovan, who raises a hand. "That won't be necessary. You're safe, and when we're done, your family will be, too."

That is quite a promise. Her words affect Donovan like Parker hasn't seen for a while. For a stranger, at least.

"No." Jewel glares at him, her temples pulsing as she clenches and unclenches her jaw again and again. She's not used to being told what to do.

Donovan glares back but is quiet as he contemplates something for a moment. At last, he signals with his chin. "Dane, take Jewel back to the apartment."

But before Dane can lift her out of the chair, Donovan looks her in the eye and says, "I have a job for you, if you're so inclined to help us get your family back?"

This news causes her to rise, and she nods.

"Good, I'll come get you."

CHAPTER 43

Hunter watches the slave labor from the shade of the farmhouse porch. He needs an excuse to walk out there. Wendall has assured him already that there are enough guards in the fields overseeing the workers, so if he goes against his brother's way of doing things, it'll look suspicious.

Hunter voiced his opposition when a man came to collect his share of the women confined upstairs. The injustice of their exploitation fuels his determination to end his brother's reign.

One worker approaches the water bucket and bends to take the ladle. The guard standing nearby says something and laughs. The worker's head jerks toward him, and rising to his full height, he replies. It's a challenge.

Hunter steps off the porch. He doesn't care what is happening, only that it's his chance to get closer to the workers without anyone following him.

The guard raises his gun.

The other man cowers.

Hunter whistles, distracting the guard enough that he doesn't shoot, but he doesn't lower the weapon, either. As he closes in, Hunter hears the indistinct murmur of their voices. "What's going on?"

In the time it takes for Hunter to get near, Giles has come forward to support his man. Although some other captives tried to join in, the men on watch shepherded them back to work.

"Nothing." Hand on his rifle, the sentry dares anyone to say otherwise.

"Guard somewhere else."

The man shoots Hunter a look of simmering resentment, his jaw tight with barely contained anger. Hunter crosses his arms, waiting for the order to be carried out. He's displeased by the hesitation.

The man passes close. "Heard you killed Sonny?"

A chilling threat crackles between them. "Hesitate again, and I will show you precisely what happened."

The man strides to a different spot, all the while glaring over his shoulder.

Hunter proceeds to the old wooden bucket, ignoring the look, his boots sinking into soft dirt. To the distrustful man at the water barrel, he says, "Go ahead, drink."

Hunter scans the other guards, finding them minding their business again. Men relax on the porch up at the house, not caring about what's happening in the field. After taking his share of the water, Giles taps the man's shoulder.

"Didn't think you'd be back." Giles takes the ladle from the man before he returns to the field.

Hunter plunges his hands into his pockets as he stares down at his feet. "I need you to be ready tonight. Can you spread the word?"

"What are you doing?" Giles says before swallowing some water.

"What I should have done a long time ago after he attacked you in that grocery store. I'm going to kill him."

Giles took Hunter that day to fetch Kessie from her shift at the store. The drive gave them time to talk. Hunter had felt included in Giles's discussions back then. He was both seen and heard. Almost part of the family. Then Wendall came back into his life...

"Hunter, be careful. He's not an idiot."

"I'm well aware."

"When?"

"When you hear the gunshots in the house, take the guards out if you can. I'll try to take out as many as I can before they figure out what's happened."

"Who's protecting you?"

After all Giles has been through, he still worries about Hunter's safety. From a man Hunter considers his closest approximation of a real father, it's quite endearing. "No one." He'll miss Giles's fatherly wisdom. "If I can get to the women upstairs, I'll get them to escape over the roof."

Wendall steps out onto the porch, taking an interest in their exchange. His hand goes up, and a man crosses the dirt toward them.

Giles beckons another man to come get some water. "Don't worry about that. I've got it covered."

Hunter gazes up.

Giles's face softens. "You aren't the only one with connections here." He hands the ladle to the next man and walks away, concluding their interaction.

Some of Giles's men traded sides during the battle at the Hutchison farm in exchange for Wendall sparing their lives. Hunter's scar rises under his grin.

"You're summoned," one guard says, relieving Hunter of his position.

Hunter glances across the field of maturing corn stalks to the house. Wendall waits. Approaching from the other side of the farmhouse, armed men are returning from their latest search. They're empty-handed. They start a conversation with his brother as Hunter treks toward the porch.

Their conversation is long. Hunter quickens his pace, arriving in time to hear his brother's last words.

"Did you bury the bodies?"

They nod.

"Okay, clean up and rotate yourselves into the farming."

With no smiles, they glance at Hunter while walking past. *Bad news? One can only hope.*

"What's up?" Hunter climbs the stairs at a snail's pace.

"A group of people arrived this morning and killed two of our men."

Sadie and Liam must have left quickly, if it was her. "Captives?"

"No."

That's a relief. "Hmm. You're thinking it's them from over the river, aren't you? You know, you still haven't told me the plan yet."

Wendall does a cursory scan of the surrounding men on the porch. "Let's go inside."

Two men follow his brother. Wendall doesn't seem to go anywhere without them. It doesn't matter. If Hunter can't get his brother alone, he'll just have to set up a plan to include these two.

Wendall, once again, commandeers the couch, putting his feet up, thus blocking Hunter from sitting beside him. He gestures toward the armchair as his guards take their places behind it.

No thanks. Hunter diverts into the dining room, sits in a chair by the fractured window, and gazes outside. A warm breeze sways the trees on this side of the house, providing shade.

"Why all the way in there?"

Just as Hunter avoids the kitchen, Wendall has his reasons for staying away from the dining room table as much as he can. Hunter rests his arm on the dining hutch, aware of the Mossberg shotgun he placed against the cabinet earlier. It's not the only firearm he has. He'll go out guns blazing if he has to. He deserves it for his part in this mess. "So, the plan?"

Wendall's chin drops, his eyes dipping to his lap in contemplation. "The plan."

But he doesn't add anything further. Instead, Wendall glances up at Hunter with a coldness that he's familiar with. A look that sends shivers up his spine, yet Hunter meets it with equal measure. He's not a scared teenager anymore.

He leans the chair back on two legs, moving his arm to his lap. *You think you're well protected, Wendall? Time to die.*

Hunter goes for his shotgun.

"Which one?" Wendall asks, halting Hunter's reach.

His thoughts race with a whirlwind of anxieties and possibilities. There's a piece of information missing, and Wendall's holding it close. What is it? Hunter withdraws his hand from the weapon and gazes across the dining table and into the living room at his brother.

His brother looks cool and collected from his relaxed sitting position, his stare unwavering. "You two, out."

Their boots echo on the bare floor as they follow the orders and depart through the front door. Hunter would have preferred to take them out, but he'll have to wait for that privilege.

"What to do with you is on my mind more than the plan right now."

"With me?" Hunter lifts the shotgun, carries it over to the armchair, and lays it across his lap. He yanks a cleaning rag off the rickety table next to the chair and rubs the barrel with it.

"You lied to me."

The rag stops halfway down the barrel, then Hunter continues.

"That puzzled me, but now I understand."

Hunter plays along. "Understand what?" He points the weapon toward the window behind Wendall and gazes down the barrel.

He finds his brother's intense stare unsettling. He always has. With a sigh of disbelief, Hunter lowers the weapon. A metallic click rings out, a sharp sound in the otherwise silent room, as the scent of burned gunpowder fills the air when he cracks the barrel open. Where bullets should have been, only a chilling void exists. *Shit!*

Noisy and deliberate footsteps sound behind him. A shove sends Hunter off the chair and stumbling forward, and before he can recover, he feels the heavy pistol slide out of the security of his waistband.

"What the fuck?!" He struggles against his sudden confinement to no avail. Course rope loops around his wrists with efficiency, the rough fibers digging into his skin. Two pairs of hands clamp down on his shoulders and force him back up.

Wendall stands, picks the shotgun off the floor, and sits down again. "Don't start on a road you can't come back from, brother."

Hunter's anger is palpable, the silent rage making it hard for him to speak. He clenches his jaw tight, grinding his teeth.

"You're not curious about who murdered two of my men earlier?" Wendall reaches into his jacket pocket.

"No, should I be?"

Wendall comes up empty-handed. "A woman was with them."

She's safe, then. He shrugs. "So."

Wendall pats his jean pockets as he glances over at Hunter. "You were with that woman when Sonny got shot."

How the fuck...? Hunter finds it hard not to lose the mask he's taken so much care to keep in place. He curses himself for ever thinking he could outsmart Wendall. His brother knows a lot more. *Of course* he does. He set the trap, and Hunter fell into it. "You had me followed?"

"I stopped trusting you the day we brought Kessie's family home." He produces a shotgun shell and examines it.

What a crock of shit! "Brought! You kidnapped them! And this has never been home."

Wendall loads the shell. "What did you do with this woman for a week? I'm curious. Why is she with the enemy now and not with you?"

Enemy. Both sides use this word so freely. Why does there have to be one? Hunter remains silent.

"Where did you go?"

He doesn't know? Good. Even if they followed him to the falls, they must have missed the front door. His and Sadie's sudden disappearance would have jarred his brother's men. Hunter doesn't answer. His silence will drive his brother—

Wendall lines the barrel of the shotgun up with Hunter. "I want answers!"

Hunter has lost count of how many times he's stared down the barrel of random weapons. It has no effect on him anymore. His only regret is that he didn't manage to kill Wendall before he finally took his long-awaited bullet. "Don't start on a road you won't travel, brother."

Wendall sighs deeply and lowers the barrel. "You're the only family I have left."

This is the Wendall he is more familiar with. *He's trying to play on my sympathies.* Well, the manipulation, just like the shotgun, is ineffective against Hunter. He maintains the silence.

"I would never do what you were thinking of doing to me."

Guilt. This approach has yielded results for Wendall in the past. Only by submitting has Hunter previously won back his brother's confidence. *Do I have to pretend to do it again?*

"Once this place across the way is ours, we'll talk more. It's us against them, like when we were younger."

Hunter turns away from Wendall and sighs. "Why do you never attend the funerals of our family?" It is a question intended to confuse Wendall, to throw him off, but Hunter finds he really wants to know why.

"Family?" Disgust colors Wendall's question.

Hunter clarifies. "Greg. Gideon."

"Whoever remains is family. They're dead." No longer useful is what his brother means. "You and I are all that's left. We need to mend fences, brother."

Hunter snarls. "And if I don't want to?"

Wendall shrugs. "Would be a shame if something were to happen to your precious Giles out there in the fields."

CHAPTER 44

Sadie stomps into her room, her fists clenched. *Men...* She digs her nails into her palms, seething with frustration. Their unanimous decision to cut her from the mission is unjust. *Colin has no experience, yet he's going?* She's a Marine, not to mention a Masters... *That's the problem, isn't it? I'm a Masters girl. Not a woman, but a girl.* Heat warms her cheeks.

A sharp rap on the door breaks her concentration.

Wrapped in a sweater, holding herself, Gina steps past the open doorframe.

Swallowing her anger with a gentle smile, Sadie intercepts her sister. "Are you okay?" The sweet fragrance of lavender lingers over them both as she hugs her.

"They're going over there." Gina refrains from saying anything more specific.

"Yes. Everything will be alright."

"Are you going over there, too?"

"No, I'm tired. I think I'll take a nap." She doesn't want to lie, but the fragile state her sister is in necessitates a little dishonesty to keep Gina calm. "You should go back to your room and take a nap, as well."

"Can I sleep here with you?" Gina asks, her breath warm on Sadie's neck, like a small child seeking comfort.

"Why don't we sleep in your bedroom? The bed is bigger." Sadie has to tuck a body pillow under her blankets in her room to appear like she is sleeping.

Gina's happiness shows in a small smile as she leads Sadie out and into her own room. The state of it is disturbing. The floor is strewn with clothes, a chaotic jumble of fabrics and colors, and the room's disarray gives Sadie a powerful urge. She picks up a shirt and reaches for a hanger on the dresser.

"Don't," Gina implores from the bed. "Leave it."

Sadie continues to arrange clothes and hangs them in the closet. "You lie down. I'm not letting you do this to yourself. Besides, you know I can't handle a mess." Sadie may have been a wild child, but growing up, her bedroom was always in tip-top shape. Gina's room used to be, as well.

Gina kicks off her flats, shimmies up the bed, and lays her head on a pillow.

Sadie circles the room, straightening things and putting items where they belong. She picks up a book, slides it into the bookshelf, and notices a pink headscarf. Their mother wore it in her last days before passing. The delicate fabric whispers memories; its color is vibrant against the dark wood. The faint, lingering scent of her mother's rose perfume still clings to it.

"I will always be with you." Those were the last words her mother spoke to Sadie in her dream. A soft, loving murmur, barely audible, lingers in Sadie's memory. She was there when Sadie needed her most. The strange timing of the memory cuts her deep, a sharp, visceral reminder of her loss, bringing with it a wave of grief. *Was she trying to tell me something?* It plays with her mind as Sadie finishes by placing Gina's shoes next to the others. She hoped that her sister would fall asleep while she tidied, but to no avail. In the massive bed, Gina looks tiny, but very much awake.

Sadie sits on the bedside. "Have you taken any of the pills Henry prescribed for you?"

Gina shakes her head.

Knocking Gina out tonight might help. "I'll go get you one."

"No." Gina reaches out. "I just need you."

Sadie feels like it's the wrong move, but she gives in to her sister's request. She understands losing someone, but watching their murder...

The chilling details of her sister's account, each word a sharp, icy shard, haunt Sadie. Gina's assault, coupled with the loss and grief, has devastated her mental health.

"Move over." Sliding in next to Gina, Sadie lies down and faces her. She reaches and closes her hand around Gina's. "Go to sleep."

Gina closes her eyes, believing Sadie will be there when she awakes. She waits, the regret eating at her. She has to leave her sister.

Liam thinks he knows what's best for Sadie. Her father smothers her, thinking she needs protecting. Even Parker is holding her back. Why does she have to prove herself? The EGA pin should have been enough. If she were a man, it would have been.

Sadie needs to take back control, to be on that mission. They won't spare Hunter. Sadie has to save him.

***

Jewel's conviction got to Donovan. He hasn't witnessed such strength in a woman since his wife. Jewel knows what she wants and has the courage to fight for it, even if it means ending her own life. It stirred him. He's not surprised. Donovan's wife inspired the same feelings in him long ago.

"Donovan?"

With his mind in a fog of his thoughts, he missed Ryker's last few statements. They've been hashing out their new plan to tackle this turn of events in security.

Ryker stares at him like he's waiting for his reply.

"Sorry, a lot on my mind. Repeat, please."

Ryker isn't the only man in the room. Hoss, Parker, Carl, Liam, Mal, and the twins are all looking at Donovan with kind, concerned eyes. The rhythmic *click-clack* of magazines snapping into place on their rifles punctuates the tense atmosphere as the new recruits, Colin and Troy, prepare their gear for tonight.

"Parker and Liam will set up behind the steel slab at the front door. The others will use the yard boulders as cover and neutralize any survivors." Ryker gazes over at Colin. "Test the radios in the helmets. It'll be crucial that we stay in contact during the shit show we're creating."

Colin places a helmet on Troy's head. "Will do."

Alex places his arm around Miles's shoulders. "Where you want us?"

"Alex, you take this tree." Ryker stabs the diagram they made of the yard above. "Your brother will be stationed here with Mal."

Jewel's new information has allowed them to speed up the rescue plan. They'll have to improvise somewhat, but it's not their first rodeo. Donovan is hesitant to endanger Jewel, despite her eagerness to take part. It goes against his nature.

Ryker continues: "Since Carl got the short stick, he gets the privilege of surprise in the other tree. Questions?"

"What do you want to do with this Hunter fellow?" The weight of Hoss's query hangs heavy in the air for a moment.

"What do you think?" Donovan turns the question around, needing the advice. *If this man dies, Sadie will never forgive me. That much is certain.*

"Under pressure, he'll show his true colors. If he's armed and pointing in the wrong direction, I won't hesitate. But thinking of Sadie, Donovan, I say don't shoot him unless you have to. Keeps the heat off you and on one of us instead, if it comes to it."

Donovan ponders his friend's points. If things go wrong, as they usually do with plans, they might have to lie to her if Hunter dies.

"She'll need someone to support her if the worst happens," Parker adds. "If not you, then there are plenty of others here to take your place."

Donovan's gaze shifts to Liam. She'll gravitate toward him if Hunter dies. *Am I ready for that?* He's still mad at Liam for messing with Sadie. *Should I let that go for the sake of what might happen tonight?*

His gaze drifts to Hoss. "And if he's not pointing in the wrong direction?"

His friend chews on it as he strokes his rifle in its cradle. "Everyone deserves a second chance."

Does he mean Hunter, or is he talking about Liam?

CHAPTER 45

Regret manifests as a cold chill on Sadie's skin as Gina's bedroom door clicks. She questions whether this is the right move and takes a deep breath. *It is.* If Sadie doesn't go, she's sure Hunter will die, and she can't live with that. And Gina needs more than Sadie to get over what's going on in her head. She mentioned the man named Mal several times, and Sadie has noticed that when Gina speaks about him, she comes alive a little. Once things settle, she will persuade Gina to go to the women's group meetings...and go with her.

Her father isn't in the apartment, of course. He's up in security, where she should be. Sadie tries to clamp down on the anger as she crosses the room to their apartment front door. Sadie draws it open, listening for footsteps or conversation, and hears only silence. She must leave before her father returns, which he will. He always checks up on them. It comforts him, but she knows it's also his way of controlling.

Peeking through the door, Sadie glimpses the entrance to the communal pool two doors down; the usual splashing and laughter are absent. Unable to use Haven's main entrance, Sadie has to use a different way out...and get to it while remaining unseen. But her father and his friends always think about contingencies, so the compound has an alternative escape route. And Sadie knows where it is.

A coolness radiates from the smooth floor as she enters the corridor and turns left. As she makes her way, Sadie wonders what her father was like prior to her arrival. She expects the lack of control he had over everything was driving him nuts, and she can't blame him this time. Sadie once asked her mom how things were when Dad was deployed. Hell was the answer her mom gave her before avoiding the rest of the conversation. It was a sore point. A time her mom didn't want to remember.

Her dad's baritone voice travels down the corridor behind Sadie. *Shit!*

Adrenaline surges. Sadie's heart pounds in a frantic rhythm against her ribs, spurring her to pick up the pace. Unless Sadie reaches the door unseen, her plan will fail.

The stinging smell of chlorine fills her nostrils as she dashes through the door to the pool, quickly shutting it behind her. She doesn't dare risk a glance through the plastic window. Instead, she flees, the sound of her breathing loud in her ears. Low, solar-powered lighting casts a muted amber glow across the room. Sadie focuses on the far side, ignoring the grandeur of the high, carved rock ceilings. Her gaze locks onto the nondescript door at the far end, the pool's dark surface unmoving as she passes.

The coldness of the doorknob shocks her, and the stifling humidity gives way to a refreshing chill. Sadie peers back through the open door. No one is following. She releases her stress with carefully timed ragged gasps, each one offering a sharp release. *That was close.*

She closes the door, plunging the stairs into darkness. Sadie doesn't need the light; she climbed the cement steps she used many times as a teenager. Back then, it was a fun, exciting adventure to sneak around behind her parents' backs. Until someone caught them leaving. It was through such infamous antics that the girls earned their nickname, the Five Musketeers.

After a quick climb, Sadie flicks a switch, illuminating a large room with floor-to-ceiling lockers and benches. The labels on some show family names, while others list the contents.

She enters the code on the Masters's locker. Each family member's bug-out bag sits ready, filled with essentials and survival gear. This exit and the equipment here are intended for a grab-and-go scenario.

Several tactical vests hang on hooks. Sadie slips one over her head and cinches the straps for a snug fit. The back of the locker houses an array of weapons for selection. Sadie selects a rifle and a lightweight handgun, attaching one to a rifle harness and the other to her vest. She loads up on magazines and sheaths a knife.

Sadie reaches into the locker, pulls on the heavy plastic radio headset, and slips it onto her head. She'll use it to communicate once she catches up with them at the river. They'll have no choice but to involve her in the mission at that point: she won't come back voluntarily, and they can't afford to lose a body or two escorting her back. Her father will have to deal with her because they aren't going over there without her.

The rifle feels reassuring in her hand as she double-checks her gear one last time before ascending the final stairs to the heavy blast door. For anyone else, this would be another complication: the alarm will sound once she opens it. But during one of her shenanigans, she found the hidden override.

She grazes the frame with her gloved hands as Sadie locates the switch; a sharp click follows the decisive flick. She slides the three bolts out. A keypad glows to her left. She punches in the code they never change.

The door clicks as it opens, flooding the space with sunlight. Shielding her eyes, Sadie glances at her watch. It's later than she realized. The sun won't be up for much longer, and she needs the light to make out a clear path to the river that will allow her to avoid the cameras.

Bowing her head, Sadie prays to her mother. "Please protect Hunter." The radio crackles to life with a faint, ghostly static. *Guess they don't have much to say as they approach the river.*

***

Gina wakes up alone, worsening her feeling of dread. She suspects Sadie is doing something she shouldn't be; that her sister is up to her old tricks. With Sadie gone from her room now, she can't help but think she's right. It's too much.

The thought of her father going back over to that horrible place again is already vexing her. She watches from the darkness of the hallway as he downs a glass of water. Something bad is going to happen.

Gina shudders at the thought of the farmhouse, with its musty smell and creaking floorboards. Heat climbs the back of her neck as she remembers the feeling of Gideon seizing her, pressing his body into hers. She shivers, scrunches her eyes closed, and wishes these memories would go away. Numbness creeps up on her.

"Hey, baby girl, what's wrong?"

Gina opens her eyes. "I'm scared." *You're going over there.*

"Ah..." Donovan opens his arms. "Don't worry."

Gina dashes over like she's running from something wicked. Someone. It's eating her alive, piece by piece. *Should I tell you that Sadie is up to her old tricks?* Gina's never betrayed Sadie's secrets before.

Donovan strokes her hair with loving hands. "I'll be back before you know it."

With a contented sigh, Gina relishes these stolen moments, the scent of his cologne, the comfortable silence between them. He can't protect her from her demons. She wishes he could reverse time.

A knock. "Time, old man."

Donovan swings with her still in his arms.

At the door, Mal tenses up, then strides toward them. "You okay?"

His concern stirs something warm inside Gina, but he can't protect her, either. It's rare to see Mal with his hair down.

Donovan answers for her: "She's nervous. Where's Sadie?"

She can't bring herself to do it. Gina trusts her sister knows what she's doing. So, like old times, she lies. "She wasn't happy, so she went to stay with Beth. Sadie said to say good luck." She hopes this satisfies her father, and he doesn't go searching for Sadie.

"I'll meet you topside, Mal." Her father kisses her forehead and walks out, leaving them alone.

The numbness returns. Her father doesn't understand the turmoil inside her. No one does. Gina's life will never be better.

Mal holds out his hand. Reluctant at first, she accepts it, slipping her frail fingers into his strong, rough palm. He offers Gina a rare smile. Normally, this helps to calm her, but Mal's leaving, too. To that place.

"When I get back, I'll have a surprise for you." Mal steps closer and grazes her forehead with his lips. A rare, unexpected moment. *Like my Brad would.*

Gina leans into those lips, cherishing the warm sentiment. Tilting her chin, Mal compels Gina to look at him. He's so close, his dark, cascading hair surrounds her face. The sharp scent of his aftershave wafts down to her. His gaze devours her, a poignant intensity in his eyes that speaks of a last look: it's as if he's etching her image into memory. Is she projecting, or is this real?

"Promise me you'll hang with Beth." He strokes her cheek.

Smelling mint on his breath, Gina lowers her eyes to the floor. She nods, knowing it's just to ease his apprehension.

He squeezes her hand, releases it, then yanks a hair tie off his wrist and corals his straight dark mane into a man bun. Upon his exit, the cold seeps back in. Gina shivers in the empty apartment as the demons close in on her.

Chapter 46

Hunter sits against a tree alongside Giles, their hands tied out front, linked by rope, watching Wendall's men come across the river. He doesn't know how they acquired the aluminum boat, its engine drowned out by the river's noisy current. Wendall speaks quietly to four of his men. They nod and head out in pairs in opposite directions along the riverbank. Scouts.

Hidden in the tall grass, Wendall observes the surrounding fields. "This won't take long. They're a small group."

Hunter stares up at his brother's back as the wind whispers secrets through the growing cornstalks. The landscape of trees to the west hides the sun, but the rays climb into the heavens. Everything Hunter tried to prevent is happening. Wendall is forever one step ahead. Hunter's impulsive decisions and lack of foresight are the reasons he always comes up short.

To make matters worse, Wendall never did share the plan, which makes Hunter nervous.

If Reed was any sign, his brother doesn't understand what's beyond that wall he desperately wants to conquer. These people must eliminate him; Hunter is powerless to do so. He tried to talk Wendall out of going, then realized it was futile to try to steer him from this endeavor. Hunter switched to believing that whatever god is watching over them will help Sadie's family to kill Wendall. In the same breath, those same people will likely extinguish Hunter's life. It's okay. He never expected to survive the day. He accepts his fate, as long as his brother leads the way.

Wendall is too confident, and Hunter's not sure which ace his brother thinks he has up his sleeve. Sadie's protected, but will she be safe if things don't go the way Hunter hopes?

A man approaches Wendall. "Everyone's here."

One thing Hunter knows: with four out scouting, there are six ruthless men behind them, armed to kill, and ten others back at the house. Two of those men are from Giles's farm. Regardless of where their loyalty truly lies, taking the farm will be an arduous task for them.

Another thing Wendall underestimates is the abused women with nothing to lose. Even Kessie. If they are strong, they'll exact revenge on their captors. The captives outnumber the armed men back there. The odds are in their favor if they make a move. *They just have to be brave one more time!*

The wind rustles through the trees overhead. With a slight nod, Wendall continues his watch over the fields, then tilts his head. "I sent a spy in, brother. If she achieves what I tasked her with, the place will be ours."

A spy? She? None of those women would... Hunter gazes at Giles next to him. He confirms it with a sad frown. *Who? Kessie?* "And if she doesn't?"

Wendall's frosty stare comes across loud and clear. Giles is a dangling carrot: leverage so this woman toes the line. *You bastard!* Ignoring the burning in his wrists from the rope, Hunter unleashes a guttural growl as he throws himself at his brother. Wendall lunges toward him, a wild glint in his eyes, daring Hunter to act. Hunter's resolve is absolute: he will use any means necessary, fair or foul, to take Wendall down.

The rope suddenly snaps taut, yanking Hunter's arms down and to the right, throwing him off balance. He forgot he is linked to Giles. He hits the ground, and the air rips from his lungs with the sudden, brutal impact.

Wendall's wild punch sails past Hunter's face as he trips over his brother, his knee impacting with the unforgiving ground. Hunter takes advantage and knees Wendall in the groin. He cries out, though the sound is muffled by the impact as he collapses on top of Hunter. Something cold and hard crushes Hunter's hand. He reaches out and closes his fingers around steel. A handgun.

Giles's foot connects with Wendall's shoulder, sending him sprawling off Hunter with a grunt and a thud.

Hunter curls his finger around the trigger. This is his chance. He raises the weapon.

Giles's foot lands on Hunter's chest, stopping him from using the weapon. Giles shakes his head. Hunter turns his back, letting the object fall under his waistband, and covers the gun with his shirt.

Men rush in. Cold metal presses into Hunter's cheek as his brother's groans continue in the dirt behind him. Eventually, Wendall sits up, only to slump over again.

Wendall might manipulate Hunter's emotional weaknesses, but the family dynamic is a double-edged sword. Hunter knows Wendall's vulnerabilities well and targeted his attack to inflict maximum hurt. With his grandparents unable, or unwilling, to pay for health insurance when they were young, Wendall never sought treatment for his groin pain. Hunter chances a glance at his brother, still writhing in agony. It feels liberating to see him squirming around in the dirt like this. Too bad Hunter will have to pay the inevitable price when Wendall finally gets up.

***

Sadie scans the riverbank from the tree line, listening for voices, and not finding any. The radio is still silent, too. Despite flicking through the channels, she hasn't heard a peep. It worries her. There should have been some comms chatter by now . *Where are they?* Doubt crosses her mind, but she remembers her training and finds her strength. She isn't privy to the plan, but she can handle herself, whatever Parker thinks or says.

She gazes at one of the lockboxes, which is still secured. That doesn't mean they haven't crossed already, though. They will leave the Zodiacs under camouflage on the other side, well away from prying eyes, and besides, this isn't the only lockbox. She continues to the next box, finding the lock still in place, as well. *Where are they?*

Sadie tries the channels again, hoping she hasn't missed her ride. She feels vulnerable out here, but it's mixed with something far more interesting. Freedom.

She turns the dial again. Static.

No one to report to. No one to watch her every move.

The dial turns. Static.

She's not safe, but it still feels good.

The dial turns.

A powerful impact, accompanied by a crack, punches into Sadie's back. She propels into the tall grass and scrambles behind a thick clump of bushes. Sadie brings her rifle in front of her, but a white-hot agony rips through her, leaving her gasping for breath. A bullet hit her. It must have hit her plate armor. Hearing the rapid beat of her heart, she tries to regulate her breathing. *In...out...*

Her rigorous training helps her clear her mind. The raw, physical force of the blow brings the reality of the situation into stark focus. She's still green, alone, and in danger.

A lone figure creeps closer from tree to tree, rustling leaves underfoot. Sadie isn't sure if he's friendly. Unless he is, she cannot call out. Into view comes a man with messy hair, visible tattoos, and no tactical vest. *Not friendly.*

Sadie lines up her sight with the man, the metallic tang of gun oil in her nostrils, and waits, holding her breath.

With a sudden burst of energy, the man moves, a blur of motion against the backdrop of the tree line.

She takes a shot.

With a heavy thud, he crashes into the underbrush.

Sadie rises, runs, and smacks her body into the rough bark of the nearest tree. She checks her surroundings. No one...yet. More will emerge after firing her rifle. She needs to get back to Haven. This was a futile attempt to prove herself. Parker was right. She was untested.

She spies the man on the floor, writhing in pain. With a clear shot, she raises her weapon to end him before she heads back to safety. The hairs on her neck rise. Sadie gazes behind her. The impact of a gun butt against her temple sends a sharp jolt through her head.

***

As Wendall's men go to his aid, Hunter readjusts. The gun is heavy and falling into his pants, so he shoves it into his pocket instead, hoping he doesn't end up shooting himself in the leg. He doesn't have the time or space to check if the safety is on.

Blinded by anger, Wendall hurls his men away, their pleas lost in his fury. He's losing control. If Wendall wants to continue with his plan, he'll have to rein it in. *That's it, brother, feel the rage.*

Giles stands up. The men aim their weapons and eyes his way. Hunter struggles to rise, and Giles extends his hand and says, "Two gunshots."

Hunter didn't register them but figures the scouts Wendall sent out must have encountered a threat. *That was quick?*

Wendall recovers a little dignity before raising a hand in the air. A man assists him in standing up. Hatred stares back at Hunter. *Bring it on, brother.* Hunter is ready for anything.

Wendall resists the urge for revenge and dusts himself off instead. Hunter sees through the ruse. It's not a question of if, but when the unexpected will happen. Wendall loves playing dirty.

A smile cuts across Wendall's face, throwing him off.

Footfalls draw Hunter's attention away from his brother. His gut wrenches. Fear takes hold of his senses. *Fuck, no!*

Struggling to break free, Sadie is being half-dragged toward them by one of Wendall's men. When she spies so many hardened criminals, her face drains of color, and she starts to fight even harder to escape. The empty strap on her tactical vest sways in the evening air; her rifle is slung over her captor's shoulder. *How the hell did she end up out here? She was supposed to be safe.*

A new, reddish bruise darkens the side of her face, doing nothing to calm Hunter's rising anxiety. It brings Hunter back to the day he met her in the forest. He doesn't like her being manhandled or hurt.

Her struggle ceases at the sight of Hunter amid the throng. Her gaze travels up and down his body, lingering on the rough rope circling his wrists before meeting his sympathetic eyes. The need to protect her overwhelms him; a fierce rage consumes Hunter as he is powerless to act.

"Well, what do we have here?" Wendall turns on the sweetness, upsetting Hunter further.

Sadie stumbles backward, colliding with her captor, who shoves her forward. Hunter's jaw draws tight.

One man behind Hunter speaks up. "Boss, that's the girl your brother was with."

Wendall moves his eyes to Hunter, then back to Sadie's trembling figure, and Hunter can see the wheels turning in his brother's mind.

"I see why you like this one."

"Fuck you!" Hunter can't stop the words from spilling out of his mouth, and he immediately curses himself. His emotions are taking control. He has to hold them back somehow.

Wendall's guttural laugh travels. "Oh, come now, it's ironic. Poetic, even."

"Why do you always have to mock my scars?"

Wendall pauses. The smile falters. "Because I'm tired of it."

FLEE

"Tired of what?" Hunter's eyes stray to Sadie's. He reads the sympathy in her gaze, a gentle understanding that soothes his worries.

"The guilt." Wendall steps closer to Sadie. With a visible flinch, Sadie shrinks away from him, her eyes wide with a mixture of fear and revulsion.

Hunter tests his bonds, the rough hemp rope itching against his skin. "Of course, because everything is all about you," Hunter spits, the words laced with bitterness and frustration.

Wendall sneers. "You fucked up your life, not me."

"What are you talking about?"

Wendall turns on him. "I had to save you from yourself before you"—he points—"infected the others. I asked Cissy to fetch you that day."

The missing piece falls into place. That day, when he fooled around with his best friend, comes back to haunt him. Hunter never understood why his grandmother walked in on them. She was supposed to be out for the day.

Wendall's betrayal cuts him deep. His older brother was the only person Hunter confided in about his attraction to men. And he told their grandmother? It was beyond manipulation. "I don't fucking believe it! You set me up?"

"I knew what she'd find when she did." Wendall's face twists into a grimace. "She'd see the demon in you. So I invited your gay friend over."

His anger flares in response. "Demon? What you did was demonic." Hunter points to his chin. "Look at my face!"

It's subtle, but Wendall winces. "It went down different than I thought, but I saved you in the end." He takes a few steps and lifts Sadie's chin.

Hunter's anger flares. "Don't you fucking touch her!"

The flick of Wendall's finger sends her chin snapping up as he releases her with a sharp, sudden movement. He clicks his fingers, and an instant later, four hands clamp down on Hunter's upper arms with powerful grips. "You still want to know the plan? Well, the plan's changed. Help me take out this threat, and I won't let anyone touch her. She'll be yours."

Another dangling carrot? After what he's just admitted, how can he possibly think I'll toe the line? "Why should I trust anything you say?"

"You're the one who made the wrong move today. You know why, and I don't need to say it again."

Hunter's gaze shifts to Sadie.

Wendall's strange need to have the family unit intact, despite how he disrespected their brothers after they died, is so against what is happening. *He's mad,* Hunter decides. *There's no other explanation.* But he's mad and powerful, with a gang of thugs at his back.

The weight of Sadie's safety rests on Hunter's shoulders, and he knows he has no choice but to do his brother's bidding.

"Take the rope off."

Wendall stares down at his bonds. "No, I think we'll keep that on for a bit. See how you perform first."

I'm not a trick pony. Hunter stifles his inner rage. He clenches his fists. "I help you, and you let Giles's people go."

"It's a little early to say what I'm going to do. We'll discuss it later."

Like hell they will. Wendall doesn't discuss. He dictates.

"I want to talk to her."

Wendall makes a sweeping motion with his arm, then cringes, stepping back to adjust his pants. Hunter hopes Wendall's groin injury continues to hurt. If he'd known how deep his brother's betrayal went, he'd have kicked harder.

Sadie sidesteps Wendall, her eyes fixed on Hunter. Up close, the bruise forming at her temple enrages him. Something's not right with the way she walks toward him. "Are you hurt?"

Her face scrunches in reply.

He checks her over, not able to see any injury or blood. She doesn't want to say it out loud. He gazes at the scout, realizing there's only one.

She reaches out. The warmth of her familiar touch sends a sudden surge of intense pleasure coursing through him. Hunter shuts the world out as he lays a steady hand over her trembling one. "Will you be alright?"

She nods.

His heart aches with the torrent of emotions he can't express. Feeling the need to connect with her, Hunter caresses her with his thumb: a silent gesture of support. "Stay close to me."

She squeezes him in return.

"After you, my lady." Wendall takes Sadie's arm and gently leads her out of Hunter's range. Doling out the charm is Wendall's signature move before he strikes. Hunter will have to stick close to protect Sadie.

CHAPTER 47

J ewel leans against a tree in the compound yard near the metal door to the outside world. Farm buildings occupy the rear of the area. The air smells of freshly cut wood. It reminds her of home. As a child, she would read nearby as her father chopped logs on cool spring evenings. She inhales, wishing she were back there.

A faint, continuous tingling of a bell fills her ears, yet she cannot see where it's coming from. Benches sprout from a wildflower-sprinkled grassy yard. A row of white beehives stands against the formidable wall that keeps them safe here, trailing away from her on both sides.

The place buzzes with activity as the sunlight fades. A massive slab of thick metal projects from the ground in front of the door. The men congregate there, whispering as they hold some form of meeting, then disperse to complete their tasks. Almost all of them are armed, dressed in military-type vests, helmets, and rifles. The only one without a weapon is Donovan, who instead carries a grim expression.

He approaches her from across the yard. Three men follow. One exits through the metal door, while the other two climb the two trees near her. Jewel wants to know what Donovan's thinking, but feels it's not her place to ask.

The same metal door opens and shuts again, and the man whom everyone calls Hoss walks into the yard, his hands animated as he explains something to a young blond man. Jewel likes Hoss for the compassion he showed her during the interrogation. Earlier, he approached her and said, "Strength in a woman

274

is a beautiful thing. Standing up for others in times of hardship is a powerful trait and deserves praise." Then, he handed over a knife. It was the clearest sign that the men meant what they'd promised her, and a warmth spread through her chest at that moment.

"You ready to do this?" Donovan says, snapping her out of her reverie.

She's still not sure what to make of the huge man. Their first meeting was unpleasant, and ever since, he has scared Jewel, which is rare for her. She intimidates people with her aggressive confidence, not the other way around. Jewel is slowly realizing that her charms might not work on this man.

"Of course." Her nerves ramp up, but more out of anticipation than fear. A frantic buzzing fills Jewel's ears as her palms grow clammy. The moment she finds a way, Jewel will cut Wendall's heart out. After she uttered those vengeful words down below during the interrogation, the chilling possibility of dying alongside him started to sink in, but her conviction remains. The anxiety hasn't subsided with time, but she knows what she has to do.

Donovan shuffles his feet, and Jewel feels slightly more at ease with him. She is used to this kind of man: a man of few words, but whose actions speak volumes. Once again, she hears the faint sound of bells. "What animals do you have here?"

He recoils before uttering, in a voice barely above a whisper, "Goats."

Shortly before the men gathered by the door to have their hushed meeting, Donovan told her not to get in their way. Her part is to get the enemy through the gate, walk them toward the men hidden behind the metal slab, and get out of harm's way. He explained this while strapping her into the uncomfortable vest she is now wearing. For her protection, he said.

Some of the team had argued against Jewel using it, afraid it would give the game away. Donovan won that battle. She refused the helmet, but he insisted on her wearing the cumbersome communication headgear. Jewel shrugs her shoulders, not used to the weight of the vest yet.

"Is it bothering you?" Donovan reaches out and readjusts the vest to give her more breathing room.

With a gentle but firm grip, she covers his hand with hers, halting his movement. "I'm fine." His hands are scarred and strong: indicators of a life fully lived. They slide away as Donovan takes a step back, creating a space between them.

Donovan's closeness affords her a close-up view of his clenched jawline, the stress lines on his forehead, and his knitted, furrowed brow. He carries a heavy burden of responsibility in this place...or is it something else? He is a mystery, enticing her to want to learn more about him.

His ring finger is bare, but two circles dangle from his neck. The necklace carries grief with it. Her own sadness comes from loving a man she can never have again, but at least her ex is still alive.

Jewel's not sure if it's her thoughts of dying or never seeing her ex again, but she motions for Donovan to come closer. He bends to lend her an ear. She snakes her arms around his warm neck. He stiffens, but then curls an arm around her waist. The thrill of the moment excites her, then she whispers in French, "Donnie, with more time, I would've liked to do more than kiss you, but that is life." Boldly, she presses her lips to his. There is silence, heavy with tension, and the woody scent of his cologne fills her senses. And then, to her utter amazement, Donovan's lips devour hers, a fiery kiss that steals her breath and sends shivers through her. *Mon Dieu!*

Hindered by the vest, Donovan pulls her against him, releases her lips, and says in fluent French, "You'll get the time. Follow my instructions and we'll...talk about this later. *Oui?*"

Breathless, all she can utter in reply is *"Oui."*

From above, a man climbs down a tree. "Did she just call you—?"

They step back, surprised. Donovan says, "Shut it, Superman." He guides a flustered Jewel to the open entrance, and his low voice cuts into her headset. "Don't walk out there, even if they call you. Entice them inside." He walks away. "Jewel?"

"Yes?" she says, still catching her breath. When there's no response, she fusses with the communication button and repeats. "Yes?"

"I'll be right behind you."

She turns her head to Donovan. He presents his wrists to the man he called Superman, who wraps a rope around them. It is a ploy to appear captured. This gives her some security, knowing he'll be close. Her nerves, however, stop her from saying anything else. If that is to have been her last kiss, then it was worthy. Could she have found the one who can capture her wild heart? The promise of more serves as an extra boost, but she wonders if it will be enough to keep her alive.

Her head fills with static, then a voice Jewel doesn't recognize says, "Slick to Osmond." *Perhaps the young man who left the compound yard just now?*

"Osmond, go."

Why do they call Donovan Osmond? She wonders if she'll have time to learn the answer.

"Thirteen targets approaching the patio."

She's not sure what this patio is, but it's clearly out there in the forest. With so many men around him, will Wendall be easy to reach? A chill shoots up Jewel's arm as her fingers find the icy steel of the blade's handle.

"How many have weapons?" Donovan asks.

There's a pause. "Ten. Rifles. Handguns. Three captives, two tied with rope."

Three? She pushes the talk button. "What do the three look like?"

"One is an older man, pudgy belly."

Giles.

"Where are they?" Donovan takes control of the conversation away from her.

"Sticking to the edge of the field west of our position."

Jewel needs to know. "What does the second one look like?"

"Avoiding the cameras, or trying to?" Donovan says, interrupting again.

"Osmond, I need to know who is captive," Jewel says, a slight tremor in her voice betraying her frustration. "Slick, second person?"

"Tall, lean man with long hair. Scars on his face."

Hunter? "Are you sure he's tied with rope?" Another pause amplifies the pressure building in her thoughts. *It has to be him, but why is Wendall holding him captive? It doesn't make sense.*

"Yes."

Fear takes hold of her. *Is he faking it to gain sympathy?* "Osmond, that's Hunter. He wouldn't be tied up unless he's in trouble."

"Or fooling us."

"Osmond, we have a problem." Through her headset, Slick's voice rings out, his words frantic, his tone almost childlike.

"What?"

"Auburn's the third captive, and she's out front."

CHAPTER 48

The stalks of corn brush against Sadie's lower legs as she and Wendall skirt the edge of the crops. He grips her arm firmly, the sultry summer air hanging heavy around them. Her father underestimated this man, and now they are over at the farmhouse, oblivious to what is happening. She's confused about why these men are attacking, though. Haven is impervious to this kind of threat. They are on foot and carrying guns, but no grenades or other projectile weapons, as far as she can see, at least. Unless they have ladders hidden in the dense underbrush and can get past the cameras, Sadie is at a loss for what their plan is.

She wants to share her thoughts with Hunter but dares not risk being overheard by Wendall. If he is under the mistaken impression that Haven can be easily conquered, it's not going to end well for him and his men.

Hunter... Sadie can see the anguish in the way he keeps swallowing so hard and gritting his teeth. To be so betrayed by his own brother, let alone the cruel, shocking reprisals his grandmother committed on him, violates her deepest beliefs about the bonds of the family. The truth might as well have hit Hunter like a physical blow, igniting a desperate, aching need in her to race to his side. Her inability to do it is upsetting.

She looks back at Hunter. It's the best she can do under the circumstances to connect with him. He encourages her with a curt nod, but no smile. His fearful demeanor and tight jaw don't elude her notice. The other captive, an older gentleman, seems to be no worse for wear, but sweat covers his brow. She hopes all three of them make it.

Wendall tugs at her, and she faces forward again. The pain in her back isn't getting better, and her head feels like it might explode under her helmet. Her communications headset dangles around her neck. The blow to her temple cracked it, rendering it useless.

They clear the fields and enter the forest. Before the uphill climb to Haven's wall, they stop. Wendall gazes upward. Not acknowledging it, Sadie doesn't move as unseen eyes watch from the platform hidden in the canopy. *How does Wendall know it's there?* She studies him for a moment, noticing the deep-set lines etched on his weary face. Though he and Hunter have the same coloring and high cheekbones, there is little resemblance otherwise; Wendall's eyes are closer together, his build heavier.

What is he waiting for? Whoever is up there on the patio won't fire at them, but it reassures her that they will be identifying her right now and radioing it in. The group attacking the farmhouse will be realizing their mistake now...and that they can't intervene. *Dad will be losing his shit.*

She berates herself as she realizes what Wendall must be planning. She underestimated his intelligence, too. He has been watching, studying, and he picked his time to assault their home with precision. He will use Sadie to get in by assaulting her until they open the door. Panic starts to rise as a cold sweat breaks out all over her body. *Brent... I can't endure that cruelty again! I won't!* This has disaster written all over it, and she is to blame. Sadie walked into a trap that Wendall didn't even know he'd set for her, giving the enemy what they needed to gain access to Haven.

Knowing this angers her, but also humbles her. If Sadie makes it out of this alive, she'll face her father's wrath. There will be no sympathy if someone gets injured or killed because of her stupid mistake. Sadie will never forgive herself.

Wendall continues his ascent into the forest, dragging her along. She thought he'd send someone up the tree, but she realizes why he didn't. Wendall pushes her out front and center, shielding himself. He knows Haven is watching.

***

Carl lounges high in one of Haven's guard trees, armed with a delightful piece of hardware and a rare set of night vision goggles. He loves climbing trees. The view and its range are unparalleled. From his perch, the melodic jingle of goat bells drifts up from the yard below, blending with the rustling of leaves in the wind. The evening air is already crisp and cool. They're losing daylight fast.

His vantage point offers a view of the empty pathways below, leading to the animal buildings. All the players are in position. A massive piece of steel hides the entrance to the buried cement bunker they call home...and Parker and Liam. Donovan and Ryker stand together, their wrists bound out front. Dummy bodies in tactical gear lie spread out on the ground, ten yards in from the open gate, where a lone, brave woman stands in wait.

Turning toward the forest, Carl breathes in the scent of pine. Beyond the fifteen-foot-thick cement wall, a palisade stands tall, with its gate wide open. *One way in, one way out.*

Sadie materializes out of the trees in front of a long line of rough-looking armed men.

Carl sighs. She made a tactical error, but that's what new kids do. Now they need to make sure she survives her mistake.

The man behind Sadie gives her a shove, and she moves forward. Two other captives follow behind them.

"They're here," Alex says in the comms from the other tree.

Carl's energy sparks. His ticker goes bonkers, knowing it's about to get real. He hasn't felt this way since saving Sadie, but he embraces the sensation. His enemy's tactical use of Sadie as a shield shows a surprising level of cunning...and disregard.

***

Sadie approaches the palisade fence, their first line of defense, already basking in the evening twilight. Haven's concrete perimeter wall looms beyond this, tall and covered in a thin layer of young vines. The metal door to the inner yard is...open? *Fuck! Someone has compromised the security room.*

An unidentified woman in a tactical vest with blonde hair stands vigilant inside. *Spy? There must be others like this woman inside.*

"I told you, brother. Knew she'd come through."

They didn't need Sadie after all. How could she have been so stupid? Of course Wendall had a plan in place. And Sadie's mistake means all she has done is make things even worse. By getting caught, she's given Wendall another weapon in his arsenal.

Who is this woman, and what has she done to my family? Did she use the mission to the farmhouse as a distraction to overpower everyone inside? How? That doesn't seem possible. Surely, not everyone has gone over the river.

Sadie halts.

Liam?

Bodies lie still on the ground in the yard beyond the woman.

N-no...it's not possible. She bites her quivering lip.

Nearby, her father stands with his head bowed, a coarse rope binding his wrists. The sight makes her blood run cold. *They didn't even make it across the river.* Sadie's confusion deepens, and panic sets in. *Is anyone at the farmhouse? If they captured Dad, where are the others? Who is on the ground? Tell me Liam isn't among those bodies...*

"Jewel, you've outdone yourself," Wendall says, startling Sadie.

This Jewel woman hardly looks pleased with her work, but she motions for them to come inside and retreats into the yard.

Sadie resists Wendall's push, then cold metal taps her cheek. "Move!"

She shuffles forward slowly. More bodies come into view, and the cold dread grows colder. *So many casualties.* Her father taught her lots of things, but witnessing her family and friends dead wasn't one of them. Sadie enters the area between the fence and the wall and gazes up. *Fuck, is that a...*

A tiny, terrified whimper escapes Sadie's lips as she steps back in terror, afraid to take another step forward.

***

From the safety of the tree behind that solid wall, Carl sees Sadie's hesitation. "Call her in, Osmond!"

"Sadie, come here!"

"Dad?" Sadie quickens her pace, leaving Wendall struggling to keep up. Carl grins at this. The bound men chase after them. The absence of any resistance bolsters their confidence, and the rest of the group enters the palisade through the choke point, two at a time.

No point in being too trigger-happy just yet. Entice the enemy first, like bees to honey. Instinctively, Carl moistens a finger and gauges the wind.

After entering Haven's outer yard, Wendall's men fan out. *Knew they would.*

Carl ducks. "Fire in the hole." The firing device feels cold and hard beneath Carl's clenching fingers as the mechanism gives. A metallic shriek sounds, and seven hundred steel balls set flight in a six-foot-high arc. His tree convulses as the shockwave sends a deafening roar through its branches. In the distance, the goats protest, their sharp bleats mixing with the agonizing screams of dying men *Claymores come in handy sometimes.*

He rises and aims as Alex fires death from the other guard tree at the few uninvited men who still breathe between the cement wall and palisade. They hit the ground hard. There's no time for them to yell out.

Carl peers into Haven's yard mid-fire. Sadie and several men are lying on the ground. Miles and Hoss shoot from their concealed places at two men trying to stumble out of the yard. They never had a chance.

Alex continues to fire, but Carl has already stopped. The contorted corpses are still. It's over in a flash.

Alex announces to the others. "Seven confirmed down in the outer yard."

"Two down in the inner yard," Parker clarifies. "Two targets left."

A short-lived silence settles once more amid the chiming of goat bells. Carl searches out the remaining men and captives in the yard.

***

Before Sadie can get her bearings, a sudden yank pulls her backward. She slams into someone: the impact is jarring. Sadie's balance is off: her ears are still ringing from the explosion. A weapon sweeps outward in a circle, ending up against her temple. "Stay back!"

Wendall.

Sadie looks up to see her father, his bonds gone, and Liam converging on them, their faces grim, their weapons aimed in her direction. She releases a gasp so suddenly that her chest spasms. *Thank God that Liam's alive!* To her side, Hunter is struggling to free himself from the rope around his wrists, as is the older gentleman.

"Get up!" Wendall yells at her.

Sadie wants to comply, but she struggles to use her legs. They feel like jelly, her knees feel weak, and her heart is pounding. But with a strong hand under her arm, they rise as one.

Movement catches her eye, and Sadie sees the blonde woman wielding a knife and heading straight for her. But before she can get any closer, the older captive frees himself from his restraints and intercepts her, whisking her off toward the slab of metal in the yard amid the woman's protests.

Other men assemble, backing up the first three, giving Sadie some comfort. She knows these men. They are family. They are alive.

With his rifle raised to kill, Hoss slowly approaches Hunter from behind.

"Come over here, Hunter." Wendall's voice trembles as much as the gun in his shaky hands.

The palpable fear radiating from him does nothing to ease Sadie's terror. If anyone is capable of killing someone out of spite before they get gunned down themselves, it's this man.

"Let her go!" Hunter demands, desperate to be free of his bonds, unaware of the danger behind him.

Sadie needs to give them a chance to take out Wendall. If she drops, her people might still hurt Hunter.

Wendall pulls Sadie along with him across the yard, closer to the metal door. "I don't think so. She's my ticket out of here."

"You won't make it out of this yard." Her father's prediction, delivered with an unnerving coolness she's never heard before, sends terrifying ripples through Sadie.

Don't test him, Dad. The guy is crazy.

The cold, hard metal of a gun barrel slides under her helmet, pressing against her skull, tilting her head. "I will, or she won't either."

***

Wendall's words harden Hunter's murderous intent, but also awaken a new emotion. Fear. Fear that Sadie will die. He breaks out in a cold sweat as her feet stumble. The panic on her face is painful, yet he's powerless. Hunter wrestles with his bonds, ignoring the sharp, scraping pain that tears at his skin.

Wendall directs her to the front gate, all the while whipping his head from side to side. With predatory focus, her father and a blond man match every step of Sadie's with one of their own, poised to strike.

"We need to stick together, brother. Move your ass!"

Rope hits the ground with a thud, and Hunter fumbles in his pocket before producing a stubby handgun with a short barrel.

Sadie raises her hand. "Hoss, don't!"

A weapon taps the back of Hunter's head, and a man's low voice says, "I'd lay that down before you hurt someone, son."

Son? He's no one's son. Hunter continues to move with the others, neither dropping the weapon nor raising it.

"It wasn't a request. Do as I say."

"Don't you fucking dare!"

Sadie's terror-stricken words cause Hunter to rethink the situation. His eye twitches with doubt. She believes Hoss will kill him. Wendall has to die before Hunter will accept his fate. He makes a calculated decision and gives up some control to her people.

"Wendall, you can't talk yourself out of this. It's over." Slowly, Hunter extends the weapon, holding it out front, stock first.

"I hand her over, and we both die. You good with that?"

"I am." Hunter drops the gun. When the bullet he's been waiting to kill him most of his life doesn't come, Hunter advances again, slowly, keeping himself in line with Sadie to stay alive. "Sadie, are you alright?"

All he gets is a curt nod.

"Talk to me, Sadie." He needs to hear her, to know she'll be okay without him.

Her mouth opens.

"You're a coward," his brother says, almost snarling, cutting her off before she can speak.

"No, I'm tired, Wendall. Tired of running away from you." *How can I signal for Sadie to drop somehow? The man behind me needs a clear shot, but he can't shoot with Sadie in the way.*

"Who were you running from, you idiot? It was us, your brothers, your family."

Family? "I was trying to find a better life for myself. Even found it, too, before you ruined it." For a fraction of a second, his eyes dart to the corner, in the direction he last saw Giles.

Movement in his peripheral vision alerts Hunter to the two other men changing positions. *Good. Make the most of this, then take him out. Shoot through me if you have to.*

"First, it was the wilderness that called to you, then you ran away, and then you enlisted!" Wendall fires back, stepping within reach of the metal door. "We weren't going to let you walk out on us. I told Gideon to rob that bank so you'd get caught."

"Hold on." Hunter holds his palm out toward the two men on his left, signaling them to wait. "You fucking didn't?!" Hunter asks with an air of disbelief. "I was convicted and dishonorably discharged because of you!" A burning rage consumes him, making his muscles tense. He clenches his hands into fists.

"Hunter, don't fall into his trap!" Sadie says.

Wendall seizes her throat. "Shut it, bitch!"

Hunter's done with Wendall. He can't control his anger any longer. He walks toward them at pace.

Wendall drops his hand and turns his attention back to Hunter. "You think Gideon could have planned a heist on his own? No, it was never going to work. It was never supposed to. I just had to keep you away from that gay military shit. They screwed with your head!"

Hunter keeps himself in line with Sadie, not stopping.

"I kept this family together. Without me, you wouldn't have survived childhood. You need me to survive, even now."

"What did I do to deserve you?" Hunter almost pleads. *Wendall's self-importance knows no bounds.*

"You think these people will let you live after I'm dead. You're a murderer. A criminal. You are nothing to them. I'm your flesh and blood. You owe me."

Lies, all lies. Laughter spills out of Hunter. "I'm going to hell, but you're going first." He steps closer, needing to stop Wendall. For good. *Drop, Sadie, drop.*

"Hunter. Stop!" Sadie raises trembling hands.

Hunter freezes. His heart pounds a frantic rhythm against his ribs.

"Did you tell him how I lost to Sonny?"

Lost? Hunter's mind races. A whirlwind of confusion and speculation erupts as he tries to recall. Sonny held her firmly, until she grabbed his...

With a swift motion, Sadie grabs Wendall by the balls. The pain from Hunter's earlier assault causes him to cry out and fold inwards. The moment Wendall loses his grip on Sadie, her elbow makes contact with his face, sending him reeling.

Sadie lunges forward.

"Sadie!" Hunter reaches for her.

With a deafening bang, Wendall fires, the sound echoing. Sadie's head snaps away mid-dive. They tumble to the earth, a tangled mess of limbs, and Hunter throws himself over her.

P-taff! P-taff! A barrage of gunfire surrounds them. Hot shell casings strike Hunter's legs. Then there is silence as the acrid smell of spent gunpowder permeates the yard.

Dismissing a sharp pain and seized by panic, Hunter grabs Sadie's helmet. "Are you hit?" He shakes her head from side to side. The bullet nicked it, but missed her. *Thank God.*

Sadie throws her arms around him. Hunter matches her gesture. He lingers, appreciating her gentle touch and captivating scent. *Sadie. She is safe.*

Hands haul Hunter off and cast him aside.

"Sadie, baby, are you alright?" The tall man scoops Sadie up and into a hug, the way only a father can. He removes her helmet, fearfully combing his hands through her auburn hair and over her body.

Hunter's gaze falls upon his brother's unmoving body. The finality of it all crashes down, a crushing weight on his chest. He has no family left.

"Yes, Dad."

Sadie's words catapult him to the now. The rough nylon of zip ties tightens around Hunter's bound hands as another man grips Hunter's shirt, holding him in place, causing the fabric to stretch taut. *Guess they're not killing me just yet, then. Not in front of her, at least.* A burning sensation pierces his chest. "Mmm."

The world tilts as treetops appear in his vision. His head hurts. He moans.

"Hunter!"

His body thrashes through searing pain. Hunter feels hands. His eyes snap open, meeting Sadie's gaze. Her presence brings some kind of joy. His heart swoons. *One last time, Blue-Eyes.*

"How we doing, Liam?" Sadie's father's voice sounds far off.

As Hunter blinks, he is acutely aware of the rapid thumping of his heart and the harsh, ragged sound of his breathing. Sharp pain. He groans, turning from Sadie, and discovers the blond man on the ground beside him. Without hesitation, he lifts Hunter's shirt. *Liam?*

"It's not looking good." Liam's eyes come up.

Sluggish, Hunter twists his head back to the potent scent of strawberries. *Why am I so hot?* Gentle hands cradle his face. He gazes up, blinking through a haze of agony that seizes him. *She's here.* He reaches for her but fails to touch her. He moans. "Sa...Sad...ie?"

Liam says, "Don't talk."

"Copy." Hunter looks up. A figure looms, clad in tactical gear, talking into a mic. "This area is not secured." *Donovan.*

In a weak voice, Hunter says, "Li...am. Sto...p."

"Crunch, tell him we're coming down."

Hunter stumbles on his words. "I... I..." *What the hell is...? Why can't I...?* He looks down. Liam pours something into his chest. *I've been...*

He gazes at Sadie's worry-stricken face, so he smiles. *Dying. Don't care. I did it. And she's safe.*

"Osmond, time's ticking here. Let's roll!"

Hunter's eyelids droop. *No...* He wants to tell her before... Hunter loses focus under Liam's experienced eyes. *Sadie! I love...*

Chapter 49

I n a hurried shuffle, Liam and the others bring Hunter through the communal area. The enormous space is alive with activity; onlookers crowd around
those keeping a path to medical open for the stretcher to pass through. They
haul their charge into medical and lay Hunter's body on a gurney in the back
room. They fan out and away while Henry rushes in with Melanie by his side.

Donovan caught up with Sadie as they entered the communal area. He
attempts to hold Sadie, but she shakes him off, wanting to hover with her anxiety
alone. He backs off, but lingers close enough to study his daughter's disfigured
features and the bruise taking shape at her temple. His face reddens.

Liam feels his own anger flaring, as well. Sadie attempts to evade him, but he
locks her wrists in his hands. "Let me check you over."

He considers her relaxing arms and lack of objection as permission to proceed. She recoils from his light touch. *They roughed her up real good this time.*
This isn't a punch from a fist, she sustained. Might be a concussion. He draws a
penlight over her eyes, and her pupils react normally. "Follow my finger."

She ignores him.

"Sadie! Follow my finger."

She sighs but complies, passing his test.

Penny peeks her head in, and Liam's happy she's here. He wants Sadie out of
this room. Sadie might need comfort because of the potential emotional impact
of Hunter's death. Liam's eye strays to the flutter of activity around the injured ma
n.

Henry slides a blood pressure cuff on and listens through his stethoscope. Melanie cuts off Hunter's soaked shirt with safety scissors, revealing an ugly mess of red, and Liam's medical assessment is instantaneous: the wound Hunter has sustained might be fatal.

His eyes dart back to Sadie.

Donovan watches them with interest. "Liam, her plate armor took a hit in the back."

Liam's impressed she's still on her feet, but the adrenaline is likely preventing her from feeling any sharp, agonizing pain.

"I need to get her into the other room."

Donovan nods his approval, but Sadie doesn't seem to hear him.

Henry's voice booms throughout the room: "Everyone out!"

With a gentle tug, Liam pulls out a trembling Sadie, who cries out, "No!"

Penny bursts through the door and reaches out to Sadie. She lets Penny gather her into a hug. Emotions tug at Liam as he witnesses hot tears stream down the face of the woman he loves. Sadie buries her head in Penny's arms, and her body racks with sobs. He feels powerless to improve her situation.

***

Liam watches Sadie pace up and down in the communal area. Her constant movement irritates him. He gets up and tries to console her, but she wriggles out of his grasp. He sighs. Seeing her pine for someone else burns, but he has to accept her decision. He has no choice.

To distract himself, he tries to stay professional and finish his assessment of Sadie's health, but she keeps refusing. It hurts. He's lost her trust somehow.

Liam walks into the center of the room and plunks down at a table in a glum state. He runs his middle finger over the smooth surface. Donovan and his dad join him as Penny approaches Sadie.

FLEE

"She's okay," Hoss says, slapping his son gently. "Just let her work through it, son."

It would be easy to follow that advice if Liam didn't have other sources of distress. He wants her, needs her, but can't have her. He fucked that up. It's his own fault.

Henry walks out of medical, wiping his hands on a towel. Everyone stares at him. Sadie flies over, in a state of anxious energy. Henry braces her with both hands and says, "Sadie, I've done all I can. It's up to him now."

She straightens, accepting Henry's words with a strength Liam's never seen before. "I want to see him."

Henry looks at Donovan. The intensity of Henry's gaze catches Sadie's attention, and her eyes immediately lock onto her father.

"One condition," Donovan counters. "You let Henry check you out first."

Liam can't believe Sadie actually considers it before nodding. *She's so stubborn.*

The love of Liam's life dashes past Henry, and his heart breaks.

***

Mal and Ryker walk down the circular hallway, toward the Livingston apartment. The place is busier since the captives back at the farm rescued themselves. Apparently, not all of Wendall's men were as loyal as he'd thought. With the help of Jewel and Haven's security team, they had arrived safely in Haven, and everyone is busy helping them settle into various apartments as a temporary measure. Parker says they are reaching capacity. Mal finds that hard to believe with all the space they seem to have.

Mal caught Jewel escorting the battered women to the single women's apartment. Their desolate looks spooked Mal, forcing up things he didn't want to remember. Their despairing expressions, etched with so many hardships, triggered a flood of unsettling recollections in Mal, obliging him to confront his past. The dark river's current churned, making the ride agonizing.

It goes against his better judgment, but Mal's eager to see Gina. Clutched in his hands, hidden from prying eyes, Mal holds the gift he has for her. Anticipation courses through his veins. It'll be a welcome finale to wrap up his day.

Walking into the room, Mal searches for Gina, but she is nowhere to be seen. Beth is lounging alone on a couch, wrapped in a blanket. He glances at his watch. It's late. Neil must be asleep by now.

"Hey." Ryker stops inside the doorway and waits Beth out. This is their usual ritual greeting. It's cute but really overdone.

"Hey." An exuberant Beth runs into Ryker's open arms, leaving a rush of air in her wake. "You're home safe."

Mal almost wishes for that kind of greeting. Almost.

"Of course. Always," Ryker answers before kissing her.

Mal glances around with nervous energy and asks, "Where's Gina?"

Beth tilts her head toward the bedrooms. "She fell asleep in your room." *Oh, boy. Donovan will have a fit.* "She wanted you to wake her when you arrived."

She did? He relaxes a smidge, but then remembers the state of his room. *Shit.* "Thanks." He enters a darkened space, not sure if he should close the door or turn on the light.

"Mal?"

His palms start to sweat. He feels silly about the gift. *It's a stupid gesture.*

The night table lamp flicks on. Gina blinks under the harsh light and sighs. Mal turns away from her and shoves the gift inside his pocket, crushing it.

"What are you doing?"

Mal turns back. "Nothing." He pauses. For a second, he thinks he's in the wrong room, as the place is tidy. She cleaned it. He'll have to search to figure out where everything is. "You... Wow, you picked up my crap."

Gina gazes around. "I hope you don't mind. I had too much time, and it was begging for help. Sadie tidied my room earlier. Figured I'd pay it forward."

Begging? He opens a drawer, finding no underwear there. *God, she...* Now he's really embarrassed.

She points to the corner of the room. "I put your laundry in the hamper."

His gaze gravitates to a brown wicker basket. *Huh, so that's what that was for.* This seems too domestic, making him feel uneasy. "You fell asleep."

"I did. Sorry." Gina appears unsteady as she swings her legs over the bed. His b ed.

How to turn this around. "Um, we were successful. Everyone is safe."

Gina stands and stretches her arms into the air. Doing so lifts her shirt up, exposing her midriff. Mal can't help but glance at her flawless olive skin, the way the light catches on the smooth surface. It's a place he'd love to learn the feel of.

"Sadie?"

He finds this to be a curious inquiry. "What about her?" He's not sure how much he should say.

"I found the dummy body in her bed." Gina saunters toward Mal.

Her walk is alluring, his gaze constantly drawn to the sway of her hips and the curve of her...

"She used to do that when she snuck out of the house." She stops within reach. "Is she safe?"

He swallows. "She is." He should take her back to Donovan's apartment so he can fill Gina in.

She points at his jeans. "What's in your pocket?"

Damn.

She reaches out. He blocks her, his fingers tightening around her wrist, the softness of her skin a stark contrast to his calloused hand.

With a playful glint, her brown eyes rise, making his heart leap with excitement. "A gift?"

Mal averts his eyes. "It's silly."

Gina closes the distance, not losing the connection with Mal's hand. "Let me decide."

He pulls out the crumpled and bent wildflowers, their stems snapping with a dry, brittle sound, and presents them to her. *I'm an idiot.*

"Ah, Mal." Gina takes them off his hands. Pieces fall to the ground between them. "It's not silly." She smiles.

Mal gazes anywhere but at her.

"Mal."

"Yeah."

"I love them."

He glances at her and forces a smile. "Donovan will be looking for you."

"I suppose. I'm glad you're safe. Will you walk me home?"

Pride creeps in. He loves that she asked. "Always."

Chapter 50
July 5

P enny hands a plate of food to Hoss, winks, and blows a kiss from across the cafeteria serving station while they wait in line for breakfast. Donovan hears his friend's deep, hearty laugh. At least someone's life is going well. She passes a tray of food over the top of the serving station to Donovan. He smirks at the addition of his favorite cookies next to his plate. "Thanks, Pen."

She smiles while raising a tray and her eyebrows at the next person in line.

Parker is engaged in a conversation with Jewel's uncle, Giles, and his wife at a nearby table, their plates now cleared.

Giles says, "We long for our farm, but we realize going back is simply not practical. The fire that took out the crops destroyed the house and outbuildings."

Donovan puts down his tray next to Parker and takes a seat. Hoss follows suit across from him.

Parker asks, "So, you'll stay in the valley, then?"

Haven won't be able to sustain these new guests for an extended period, so Henry's solution of log cabins has been proposed to Giles's group, if they want to stay. A dull throb of melancholy settles over Donovan at the thought of seeing Giles and his people leave. *Jewel will go with them.*

"I talked it over with the others," Giles says, "and we'd like to make a go of it across the river. We'll take the farmhouse down and build those log cabins you proposed, and farm this land together with you."

Donovan feels a surge of optimism, followed by a nervous tremor in his stomach. With all the excitement surrounding his family, he's just remembered he kissed Jewel and that they haven't talked about it like he promised. He needs to remedy that.

"Sounds like a plan."

"I noticed you have a proper chicken coop. We made a temporary shelter for our chickens in the barn across the way to protect them from the predators."

Parker's eyes light up. "Okay, we'll get a group over there to collect them."

Donovan's mind is still on the cabins. Before taking his first bite, he says, "We should figure out how to build a bridge, too. You'll be out in the open."

"In the meantime, we'll house you till it's done," Parker adds.

"Thank you for your generosity.

***

Someone shakes Sadie's slumped shoulder. She raises her head and rubs the kink in her neck. Hunter lies peacefully beside her in medical. She feels like shit, but she knows it'd be futile to try to sleep properly while Hunter is still out. *When he gets better, I'll find my bed.*

Sadie twists her head to see Jose. He's wearing an apron, a hand on his hip, standing over her with a fork. He's brought her food. "I'm not hungry."

"Not going to avoid eating on my watch. I'll sit with you while you fuel up. Go! It's over there," he says, pointing to a TV-tray setup with a steaming plate of pasta.

The problem with her military family is that they know too much about her. Pasta is her favorite dish, and Jose knows she can't resist his version. With a sigh, she drags herself up to appease him. "Jose, you didn't need to do this. I'll eat when he wakes up."

Underneath the apron, Jose wears black, mourning the loss of his wife still. The news hit Sadie hard. Sophia was the real reason Sadie had returned to university. At Sadie's mother's funeral, Donovan asked Sadie to stay home and finish her schooling online. Overhearing that, Sophia and her dad went for a stroll outside in the backyard. Sophia was never one to let the grass grow too long. She didn't take orders; she gave them. It was something Sadie always admired about her.

Acting like Sadie's commanding officer, Jose follows on her heels until she settles in the chair. "Stop yapping and chew."

Hunter hasn't woken up since they brought him in. His wrist is tied to the bedrail, and every time she sees the handcuffs, they anger her. But the delicious aroma of the pasta, a symphony of garlic, herbs, and tomato, envelops her, reminding her that everyone here means well. Her stomach rumbles.

Hoss and Carl stroll in, smile her way, and greet Jose.

"How many of these shirts do you have?" Jose asks Hoss.

Sadie enjoys her first few bites. *So good.*

Hoss draws the attention of everyone in the room. His shirt reads, *The effort I put into NOT being a serial killer really needs to be acknowledged.* He wiggles his eyebrows. "Tons. Love 'em!"

Carl rubs her shoulder. "How you doin'? You look like you're two days past your bedtime. I'll take the next watch."

He says this like she's a child and not a grown woman who knows her own mind. Sadie holds back the first words she thinks of and, instead, says, "Sweet of you, but I'm not leaving him."

"Girl, you always were the most stubborn of the bunch," Hoss pipes in with a grin.

A deep, gravelly voice says, "I agree... Sassy and stubborn..."

The words ignite a fire within her. "Hunter!" Sadie drops the fork and rushes to him as relief rolls off her.

"Blue-Eyes."

She cups his face in both hands, but he recoils, leaving her feeling perplexed and unsure. "You didn't have to leave Reed."

"Wendall wouldn't have stopped until he had...complete control over this place." He remains weak. "My only choice was to take him out."

"Did you not hear me when I said we all have choices?"

The men approach, and Hoss says, "Son, we do things together here."

"I'm not part of your group. I have no illusions about being...a part of it much longer." He hoists his arm, moving his handcuffs until they become taut, and glances around the green room. "You're either going to let me go or kill me. I can guess from this place...it's the former."

Why is he being confrontational? Sadie sits and places her hand on his leg. He slides it over and away. "If you leave, I'm coming with you."

"I'm going alone."

Sadie's exhaustion only fuels her irritability. "We're going together!"

He looks her straight in the eye. "There is no 'we.'"

The sting of Hunter's words hit her heart like arrows on a target. Straight, fast, and solid. "You don't mean that."

"I didn't like him abusing the women. Just wanted to free them. That's all I wanted."

Sadie doesn't believe a word he is saying. "And to free yourself of your brother. You can't fool me. I know you."

"No, you don't!" Hunter stares her down.

Her heart bleeds. "What's wrong with you? We spent time together, confided in each other, and you wrote that letter."

"I told you what you wanted to hear."

"Why are you doing this?"

"Don't worry." He pauses. "Liam still wants you, even if you're not perfect anymore."

Sadie recoils, feeling her heart burn in agony. It's more painful than the slashes were when Brent scored her face. *How could he, of all people?* She would have moved heaven and earth to be with him. Tears spring forth and trickle down her cheeks unbidden. Sadie's anger flares. "How dare you?" She jumps at him, not caring that he's flinching from her assault on his wound. "How fucking dare you?!"

The men burst into action, peeling Sadie away from Hunter before she can do more damage.

"Take her out." Carl steers her into someone's arms. "She needs a breather."

That son of a bitch! They guide her through the bustling communal area, leading her to the tunnel to the outer ring, where they encounter Liam. He walks into her space and cups her chin. "What happened?"

Sadie bristles with unspent anger, pulling away from him.

Hoss says, "She needs some downtime. We're taking her home."

Under Liam's gaze, Sadie remains silent and refuses to meet his eyes. Anger boils red hot through her veins at Hunter's last remark.

"Why is she angry, Dad?"

"Someone's grouchy. Took a shot at her."

"Auburn, I'll be right behind you." Liam strides toward the communal area.

In the apartment, upon seeing Sadie's angry appearance, Donovan moves toward them with questions in his eyes. "What the hell happened?"

***

The sting of Hunter's words hit their intended target. *Had to be done this way.*

While everyone else leaves, the elderly gentleman remains, his face etched with lines of time. With a sigh, he closes the door and turns the lock. *Click.* Hunter guesses he's going to cut him a new asshole for being one.

The man turns a chair around and straddles it, his expression neutral. "Hear you and I are both Sadie's heroes. Carl."

"You saved her?"

"Yep. The same." He pauses. "Why ya pushin' her away, son?"

"You heard me. I used her."

Carl gives him the I-don't-believe-the-bullshit-you're-shoveling look. "That's a great love you got there. Does she know what you're sacrificin'?"

This one's sharp. But Hunter can't back down now after what he just said to the woman he loves. He doesn't respond.

"We all think we aren't worthy of a woman's love, son. Don't you think she deserves a say in her own life?"

If only it were that simple. Hunter wishes he could stay, wishes he could just erase his horrible past to be with her, to be the man she deserves. *If wishes were horses...* "Yes, but it can't be with me."

"Why not?"

With an audible sigh, Hunter washes his face with his hand. *This is futile.* "The taint of my family. I'm not a good man. The things I've done."

"You don't think you're past redemption? All the men here have made hard choices in life, too, son. You're no different."

"Our time together was an illusion. She loves Liam, not me."

"I admire your need to lie down for her, son, but we military are all cut from the same cloth."

Hunter's always wanted this. Support. But it's a little too late for him. "Someone slashed my cloth a long time ago." He doesn't say it, but the pun isn't lost on him. *He's wearing me down.*

"Don't matter. You're still one of us."

And he knows it. "I'm nothing like you. I'll never be one of you."

The metallic rattle of the handle, mixed with the heavy, rhythmic thud of fists against the door, reverberates through the room. "Someone open this motherfucking door!"

Carl tilts his face toward the sound, then his keen eyes come up. "Sounds like Liam's seen Sadie."

"Let him in." *Perhaps it's time Liam and I face off.*

Carl clasps the back of the chair and says, "No can do. I ain't helpin' you with that death wish."

"I'm going to kick your ass for hurting her. You hear me!"

Hunter remains muted. His loss is Liam's gain. He'll know it soon enough.

"Henry, open this door!"

"Son, what the hell?" an unknown voice asks.

Muffled sounds follow mixed angry voices as something or someone slams into the door. "Take your hands off me!"

"Go get some air! Hoss, take him outside." After a long pause, the doctor says, "Let me in. He's gone."

Carl walks with a determined stride across the room and unlocks the door.

CHAPTER 51

S adie's fingers tremble as she adjusts the buttons on her shirt, one by one. Henry wraps up his blood pressure cuff and stores it in his medical bag. Her family summoned him. She's not sure why. He examined her two days ago and gave her a thumbs-up. Well, he did after doing a battery of tests on her.

"I'll check on you later." He places his hand on her shoulder. "Sadie?"

She stops fussing with her buttons. "Yes?"

"You're young and healthy. For now, take it easy."

"I will. Thanks."

As Henry departs, he leaves her bedroom door ajar.

Her father's voice reaches Sadie's ears. "Henry, give it to me." His familiar phrase is comforting, but Sadie tenses up, anxiously awaiting Henry's response.

"Take the girls topside. They're both under too much stress and need some downtime."

The tension in Sadie's shoulders dissipates. Her senses heighten as she moves to the doorway and listens.

"What did he say to set her off?" Donovan asks.

Hunter's insult pushed her over the edge. Even now, just thinking about it causes the anger to build. *How could he?*

"I think it was something about her scars."

"That son of a bitch!"

"Calm down, Donovan. The man's in hostile territory, and I need him to heal first before you rip him to shreds."

A lengthy pause prompts Sadie to peek through the gap in the door. *Did they leave?* The front door didn't open or close.

Her father and Henry are sitting at the kitchen table, facing each other. Henry's back is straight, while her dad slouches forward.

"Carl says he's determined."

"Determined to do what?"

"To erase himself from her life."

Sadie takes in the phrase. His words plant an idea in her head.

***

Donovan slides his finger over the glass surface and the face of his departed wife, Tina, in a gentle caress. Tina was the love of his life. They had twenty-three years of marriage under their belt by the time the cancer took her. He used to refer to her as his blonde bombshell. Even though the disease robbed her of her lush and shiny hair, she was brave and beautiful until the end. *Can I move on?*

Ever since Jewel showed, he's had trouble submitting to his feelings for her, and feels guilty, like he's betraying his wife somehow.

Today is the day Donovan needs his wife the most. He's not sure what to do. This was his wife's field of expertise. Tina was the one who calmed Donovan while dealing with whatever the girls slung her way with ease. They're unraveling before his eyes, and Donovan's lost control somehow and can't find the track to get back on. He needs someone to blame, but deep down, Donovan blames himself. He should have gone looking for them the minute the missiles dropped.

"Dad?"

Donovan straightens in his chair and lays the frame down on the table. Sadie's hand travels across his burdened shoulders. He gazes up into his oldest daughter's once-angelic face. Her scars and bruises remind him of his failure to protect her. *A poor excuse of a father, I am.* "Yes, honey?"

Taking a seat next to him, Sadie asks, "Has the council reached a decision about Hunter?"

"No, we're convening tomorrow." Donovan doesn't want to say anymore on the subject. He understands the connection between his daughter and Hunter, but Donovan can't trust the man. If it were up to him, Hunter would have been released, but Sadie's threat to leave is too risky to ignore.

"Why didn't you tell me Liam asked for your permission?"

Liam told her? Figures. "He told you that, huh? I was waiting on the lawn that night he brought you home." Donovan watches the realization dawn on her face. "We knew you went out at night. I honored your mom's request not to interfere, but there was no way in hell I was going to sleep while you were God knows where." He'd set the rickety lawn chair up and sat with the shotgun in his lap, waiting for his opportunity. When it finally presented itself, though... "I always hoped you'd bring a guy home. When Liam showed it was...disappointing."

"Why didn't you confront us?"

"It took all I had not to. He was into you back then, but he respected me enough not to mess with you. That night, I thought differently." Donovan runs his hand over his head. "I wanted to break his hands for touching you, but again, your mom held me back." *Smart woman.* "You didn't see Liam after that, so I let it lie. But that was when things were normal."

Sadie lays her hand on his forearm. "Dad, Liam never touched me. He escorted me back home from a party he felt I shouldn't have been at."

Crap! I fucked it up again. He doesn't like what he will have to do to make up for this. "I owe you and Liam an apology, then." He forced Brad to wait, and he's interfered in Sadie's happiness. "I'm sorry, honey, for screwing up your life, too."

"Don't do that to yourself. You did the best with what you had, Dad. We didn't make it easy on you, either."

Glancing sideways at her, Donovan covers her hand. "I was afraid before all this went down, but now, I'm terrified most of the time. My worst fears for you girls came true, and I couldn't protect you."

"It's not your fault." Sadie moves to wrap her arms around his shoulders. "I'm sorry for making you worry, Dad."

He recalls the moment Sadie was born. Donovan saw Tina's radiant smile and felt overwhelming panic as the doctor carefully placed a tiny Sadie in his strong, trembling arms. "You're my firstborn. Different from all the rest." He pats her. "The first time I held you, I thought I'd break you."

"Really?" She laughs at his foolishness. "I'm not fragile anymore, Dad."

"No, you're not. But I can't stop being your father, you know. I love you too much." He reaches out to caress her cheek, marvels at the love in her eyes, cherishes the moment, and thanks whoever is looking out for her that he has the chance to love her some more.

"I love you, too. Remember that because I need you to do something for me."

"Why does that sound like I won't like what comes out of your mouth next?" he asks, his regular scowl back in place.

Someone knocks.

Donovan rises. "I'll get that. You go see how your sister is, and we'll talk later."

They part.

Donovan opens the door to see Liam. He turns to make sure Sadie is gone before saying, "What's up?"

Chapter 52
July 7

S adie walks into medical. At his desk, Henry focuses on completing paperwork while Melanie examines Colin's stitches on a nearby bed. She hasn't
had a chance to speak to Colin, but she knows of him. He's the man who loves
Beth, even though she's with Ryker now. She sympathizes with him.

After neutralizing Haven's newest threat, someone pointed out that the next
day was Independence Day. Parker called a meeting the following morning, and
after a closed-door discussion, the council decided to have a low-key affair for the
families. The school had prepared a celebration for the kids, and disappointing
the children is against their goal to keep life as normal as possible for them.
Haven gathered in the communal area to share a meal and watch light-hearted
movies.

But that wasn't the case in the entire compound. Whispers spoke of a raucous
gathering—a heady mix of men and drinking—in the garage, although the exact
details remain tightly guarded secrets. Perhaps it's best she remains unaware of
what unfolded out there.

The council held the debate on whether to let Hunter stay or shun him, but
he has allies among Giles's released captives. They gave testimony on his behalf,
and Parker has decided to leave it up to Hunter if he stays or goes.

As Sadie gets closer to Hunter's room, a wave of unease washes over her,
intensifying her anxiety. He's had time to think about his decision. She hopes
this works.

Sadie enters and begins pacing up and down the room, hoping she's pulling off a pissed expression. The deep chest wound has left Hunter weak and immobile. It will take days, maybe even weeks, before he can muster the strength to sit up on his own. He has no choice but to sit there and watch her.

Sure enough, Hunter's eyes track her as she walks around in circles, ruminating on how she's going to come at him. An idea pokes at her. *What do I have to lose?*

Sadie draws an old cell out of her pocket. The EMP didn't affect the electronics at Haven. They kept their old phones in Faraday cages here for this purpose, knowing they'd lose the ones they had in town during this type of event. She points the phone in his direction. "Say cheese."

Hunter remains neutral as she snaps a photo of him. She peers at her handiwork. "No, it'll be better with both of us." She climbs onto the bed on her knees and gazes down upon him and waits.

Hunter doesn't budge.

"Move over."

Hunter scowls as he makes room for her to lie beside him.

Sadie cuddles up to him, careful of his wound, and lays her head on his shoulder. Both of them stare back at her from the screen. He isn't smiling. "Smile, or I'll poke your wound."

Irritated by her audaciousness, he complies, and she snaps a happy photo. The moment Sadie captures the photo, she swiftly exits the bed, allowing herself space to muster the determination for her next action, hoping it will yield the outcome she wants. "I never upheld my part of the bargain."

"What bargain?"

He's curious. Good. "Remember when I promised to reveal the story behind my scars?" When he says nothing, Sadie continues. "When I was sure I was going to die, I had one thought. I regretted not telling Liam I loved him."

A flicker of jealousy appears in Hunter's eyes. *Just as I thought. He does care about me.*

"When you thought you were dying, what was the last thing that came to you?"

Hunter turns from her, afraid to show her she's right.

"You're afraid of being happy here. Afraid of yourself."

Hunter stays silent.

"Wendall made sure you never saw past the scars. You fought him for a while, but along the way, you let Wendall win. If you leave Haven, he wins."

Hunter says nothing.

"You told me once, give them time, and they'll see past the scars. Hunter, you need to give Haven the same consideration."

His face sours. *Time for the big guns.*

"Your little show hasn't deterred me from convincing you to stay. Remember, I told you I would dig up the good in you until you could see it?"

At last, Hunter gazes back at her. The pain in his eyes is clear. *This is hard for him.*

"I'm offering you something you want more than anything else in this world."

"What?" Hunter says flatly.

Sadie moves to sit with him, hoping this will tip the odds in her favor. Hunter is mistaken: Sadie does know him. She leans forward, arms on her thighs, and gazes into those handsome, scared eyes. "Normal. You want normal."

Hunter's shield falls, and his emotions burst through. Tears spring forth as he shakes his head in denial.

"No more being on the outside looking in." Sadie turns the phone so Hunter can see their smiling faces captured in the image. "You're going to be on that wall of pictures with me."

Amid the fear he's wrestling with, Hunter's love comes through as he takes her hand in his.

"I'll tell you about my scars if you tell me you'll stay. Trust goes both ways, Brown-Eyes," she teases, feeling that they have turned a corner.

A small chuckle puffs from Hunter's lips. "My final thought was of you." He grabs her neck, tugs her forehead to his, and says, "I didn't mean what I said the last time we talked. Please forgive me."

She rejoices, not hesitating to say, "I forgive you." Sadie's lips meet his.

Hunter returns Sadie's kiss with equal fervor, his soft lips sending heat through her. "I love you, Blue-Eyes."

Sadie's heart skips a beat. "I love you, Hunter."

***

Sadie stands in front of the assembled group, gripping trembling hands. Hunter's not fully recovered, so everyone has gathered in his medical room. She's not sure she can go through with this, but it's the right thing to do.

The women's group met yesterday, and Sadie mustered the confidence to attend. It was a start. She couldn't convince her sister to go with her, but today, Gina has come out to support her.

The worn wooden chair creaks under Gina as she rubs her anxious hands together. Beth is sitting next to her, her calming hands over Gina's as she encourages Sadie with a smile. Sadie wouldn't trade her friends and family for anything. Their unwavering support, like a warm hug, bolsters her confidence.

Ryker stands behind Beth, caressing her shoulder. His loyalty to her reminds her of Liam. Sadie's gaze drifts to him. Of everyone, Liam is the most anxious and the farthest from Sadie. A knot of icy nervousness tightens in her stomach: a sickening feeling that makes her palms sweat.

Hoss enters last with Penny. He helps her find a chair near Hunter's bed, then crosses the room to Sadie. With his powers of perception, Sadie expects his usual greeting, but instead, he cradles her face in his hands. "You got this."

Sadie's heart might burst. She gathers her thoughts as he crosses back to stand behind Penny. Sadie avoids looking at her father, but she's aware he's fidgeting against the wall, waiting along with her siblings. He's tense, she knows, partly because he has no idea what she's about to share. Letting out a long breath, she knows she has to do this for herself, despite the guilt it will bring him.

"I made a promise to Hunter, but I want all of you to hear it," Sadie says to the floor, afraid she won't be able to speak if she looks up. "To prove something to myself, I completed boot camp in San Diego and graduated as a Marine Reservist. I didn't want anyone to know. If I failed, it wouldn't matter, and I could continue with my career as a librarian."

Standing next to her, Carl covers Sadie's hand with his in solidarity.

She swallows, knowing the next part will be difficult. "During training, this guy, Brent..." Saying his name brings up the last time Sadie uttered it and other things. The flash of a knife...eyes full of rage...screaming. She breathes out, her fingers trembling in Carl's hand. There's an awful taste in Sadie's mouth as she struggles to continue. "He harassed the women. Tried it on me, but I wouldn't stand for it." *Dad trained me well.*

Sadie looks up. Her dad's facial muscles tighten. Her eyes tilt back to the floor. *Breathe...* "Unfortunately, he took that as his personal mission to undercut me. I reported him. Nothing happened. Just a slap." Sadie shifts and taps her foot in agitation. "But he made a big mistake and messed with another cadet who was...um...connected. High-up connected." Sadie refrains from telling them what happened to the poor woman and prays Chloe has found peace after what Brent did to her, wherever she is.

Hoss growls in anger.

Come on, face them. You're a Marine. She forces herself to gaze up, choosing to focus on Hunter and Liam. Sadie reads anger in both of them, but sympathy, as well. "They removed him from the recruit depot, and he threatened anyone within hearing. He didn't finish training or graduate with us."

Hunter frowns, but a satisfied grin springs up on Liam's face at this news.

"During the missile strike, I was knocked unconscious on the bus. What I didn't know was that..." She blinks, teetering on the edge. All she can hear is the sound of her heartbeat in her ears. "Brent followed me."

Liam's smile drops. "He was stalking you?"

Carl squeezes her hand. Letting go, she hears the words elude her lips, propelled by an unstoppable force, and feels the urgency to keep going. "I decided not to wait for rescue and hiked toward town. He ambushed me."

Sadie wrings her hands in agitation and tries to stay calm. Memories bombard her. Firelight...pain...hatred. She can't keep it together and shakes her head, but she has to voice what she sees. Tears threaten to show. "He was fucking full of rage. He, uh, broke my ribs with a tree branch...beat me till I lost track of time." *What a failure I am.*

Sadie looks up at her father. In a moment of vulnerability, tears well up in Donovan's eyes and trickle down his cheeks. He opens his arms. Unable to resist the offer, she sprints toward him, her heart pounding in her chest.

No one moves, lost in their thoughts, taking in what Sadie has said. The only sound is her muffled cries into her father's chest.

Carl takes his cue. "That's when I stumbled upon them."

Sadie recalls the moment with such clarity that it feels like it just happened. The images play on repeat in her head, impossible to escape.

"Sorry for sayin' this in front of the women, but he was cuttin' her shirt off and slicin' what she couldn't protect 'cause he had her tied to a skinny-ass tree," Carl says with a sniff. "I took offense. Shot him in both kneecaps first... Sorry again, ladies. Kept him alive long enough to show him where he was going after I was finished with him."

The part of the story she wasn't privy to coaxes her away from her father's chest.

Donovan acknowledges Carl with a tip of his head. "Thanks. We're indebted to you." Then, he pulls back to cup Sadie's chin. "Baby, your bravery... I'm in awe. I'm so sorry that you had to endure that. I should have come looking for you."

"Dad, Mom was with me."

"What?" he asks, puzzled at her strange admission.

"I blacked out, and she came to me. Mom said something strange about you." Sadie swipes at her nose.

"It was just a dream, hon."

"No, it wasn't." Sadie dries her tears. "Mom said you pride yourself on controlling things. She said, 'Not this time.' Then she said I love you in French."

Sadie witnesses the moment his confusion gives way to a dawning realization. Hoss hides a growing smirk. *Interesting.* She is looking forward to forcing the story from them later.

"Did she say anything else?"

"Yes." She turns to Hunter. "'He doesn't know it yet, but he's been waiting for you. Trust him.'"

Liam hangs his head in sadness.

"She meant Liam, not me," Hunter says with a shake of his head.

"I asked." Sadie readies herself to drop the next statement. "Mom said, 'Shouldn't need a reason.'"

Hunter's eyes expand in surprise. "I said that."

"I know. Twice."

Donovan turns to Hunter. "That's high praise if that came from my wife."

Liam's eyes, heavy with discontent, linger on the rumpled bedsheets. Sadie feels bad for Liam. He loved her mom like his own.

Gina moves toward Hunter. He hangs his head. "I can't fix what he did to you." Hunter is unaware of the full extent of Gideon's mistreatment of her sister, but he knows enough for the guilt to be consuming.

"Why should you?"

"If I hadn't—"

"Hunter, can you predict the future?" Gina's question hangs in the air for a moment.

"No."

"Then stop thinking you can. He made his choices, not you."

314

With a gentle grip, Gina takes hold of his hand. "Sometimes life tests you, and the only way to get through it is to come out in one piece. You won't be perfect when you come out the other side, but who is? If you need my forgiveness to do that, then I'll gladly give it, but Hunter, you need to forgive yourself."

"I'm not used to all this support."

"Hunter's never had sisters," Sadie says by way of an explanation.

A rare smile appears on Gina. "Prepare for a rude awakening, then. This family can be a stubborn lot."

Hunter turns from Gina to Sadie. "I'm getting that vibe."

CHAPTER 53

L iam walks into the Jenkins apartment, heading for his bedroom. His two younger sisters play *Embolus*, the first-person shooter game, in the living room, seemingly oblivious to his arrival. He is okay with them being preoccupied as he isn't in the mood to talk.

Having Sadie's ordeal relayed to him plays over and over in his mind. *What kind of person has that much rage to hurt a woman, much less a fellow human being?* The brutality of her captivity breaks his heart. The strength she had to find fills him with an overwhelming love for her. Against all odds, her fierce independence and defiance of expectations fueled her survival.

But Sadie's mom's words from the grave are disconcerting...and they sting. Liam's not sure where he fits in anymore.

The apartment door opens. His father enters, and his concern is evident.

"Ah, come on!" one of his sisters shouts.

"We need to talk." Hoss gestures toward his bedroom. "In there. It's quieter."

Liam plunks into an armchair in the room's corner as Hoss closes the door. Penny moved in when they arrived from Reed. The light furniture she brought with her stands out against his father's dark walls. It has an air of a man cave about it. If they had any paint, Liam's sure Penny would lighten the place if given a chance.

"You okay, son?" Hoss sits on the bed, leaning back on his hands.

"Not really." Liam rakes his fingers over the fabric of the chair. "The strength Sadie had in the face of such cruelty..."

Sadie's story angers Liam, but knowing he hadn't been able to rescue her from her causes him even more torment.

"That was a lot for anyone to experience. You okay with what she said about Tina?"

Of course, his father picked up on that. Tina was always Team Liam, rooting for him to ask Sadie out.

"If it was a dream, it was a pretty convincing one."

"You don't believe in such things?"

"In the supernatural?" He shakes his head. "No."

"But it still bothers you?"

Liam doesn't answer. Tina mentioning Hunter instead of Liam is upsetting. She knew Donovan had turned Liam down when he asked for permission to date Sadie many years ago. Tina even consoled Liam after their heated argument, telling him not to give up on her daughter.

"You goin' to fight for Sadie?"

"I don't have a choice." Sadie made that pretty clear on the way home from Reed. Liam regrets their argument. *Is that the moment I lost her?*

"I thought the same a long time ago. Bit me in the butt, and I never recovered. Lost everythin'."

"You talking about your first marriage?" Liam leans on his thighs. His dad usually avoids discussing that relationship, yet Liam knows at least part of his father is grateful for it. After all, Hoss has a tattoo on his chest that displays the names of his ten children. Liam's never met the first three.

After his father stays silent, Liam continues: "I asked Donovan for permission again." He went to him after Hunter said his hurtful words to Sadie. He thought the odds were in his favor then, but her story today cut that short-lived hope to pieces.

"And?"

"He gave it this time. Too late, it seems."

Hoss sits up, crosses his ankles, and nestles his hands between his legs. "If you don't fight for her, you'll regret it."

"How do I do that? She's focused on him and dealing with her trauma. I think I've missed the window to win her over, Dad." It hurts to hear, but Liam needs a dose of reality.

"That might be true, but if you aren't on her mind, you won't have a chance."

"What are you suggesting?"

Hoss raises his hands into fists. "Fightin' for her doesn't have to involve throwing punches." He points at Liam. "You have advantages over Hunter. He's stuck in medical, and you aren't."

"How's that an advantage?"

"Talk to her and show her you aren't goin' anywhere. Be the man she wants by bein' her friend and see where it leads."

Liam enjoys the fact that Hunter might get jealous about that. "Won't he try to undercut me if I do that?"

"He can't, or he looks like the villain."

Liam can't help but think Hunter already looks like the villain with his scars, but he loves his father's suggestion all the same. He's an evil man sometimes. "Very conniving, Dad."

"You're talkin' to a man who knows how to disrupt, son."

"Sounds like a skill you could have used long ago."

"Yeah. But I wouldn't have had you and your siblings if things had ended up differently, so I can't complain, can I?"

Liam agrees with that. It's amazing how one decision can change everything. Each one sets us off on a new path, twisting and turning and full of surprises.

"You and I run hot under the collar, son. Don't let your anger get the best of you and you might turn things around in your favor."

Liam chances the topic a second time: "Is that what happened between you and your first wife?"

Hoss sighs deeply. "It is better to have the courage to fight and lose than to give up without even trying."

***

Sadie exits the compound and steps out into the night. *It's nice to be outside after the sun sets,* she thinks. Since their immediate threat is gone, the council has relaxed the restrictions a little.

Hoss found her in the communal area and told her Liam wanted to see her topside. She is curious about why. Their latest interactions have been a mixed bag of anger and sadness. In security, Alex showed Liam on the screen, waiting on the bench on the other side of the metal slab in front of the compound door. The yard is dark, as the sky is moonless. Alex made sure she had some night vision goggles on her helmet to help her find her way, but she didn't want to use them, preferring the darkness.

"Liam?"

"I'm right in front of you."

Upon hearing the screech of the metal door, he must have moved to intercept her. She thinks about his words. *He's always been in front of me, hasn't he?*

"Reach out."

Liam's firm hand connects with hers, and she steps forward. He curls his arm around her waist. The light brush of his fingers ramps up her heart rate as he walks her to the bench. The familiar feeling of being safe spreads through her chest. She doesn't know what to say to him. So much has happened to her, to Hunter, and for sure to Liam. She picked Hunter, but she feels the loss of Liam. *How can we be friends?*

"It's so dark out."

He clears his throat. "Look up, Auburn."

A gasp escapes Sadie's lips as she looks skyward. The Milky Way blazes above, a river of light against the inky blackness, a sight that fills her with awe. To enjoy the stars without stress at last takes her breath away. "There are so many."

"It's amazing, isn't it?"

She expects that he has something he wants to discuss. His fingers crawl across the divide between them and cover her hand. It is simple, relaxing: the gentle breeze is calming, and the sounds of nature soothing. She smiles at the sky. This is what she needed.

"I know you've chosen." He gives her hand a warm squeeze. "But I want you to know, I'm here for you and I'm not going anywhere."

Chapter 54
July 8

S adie approaches Parker's apartment. Dane stands guard, tall and thin. She hasn't met him formally. His eyes, devoid of warmth, track her as she leans against the opposite wall, her body angled to meet his gaze. All she's been told is that he was in the military. He opens the door quietly and, with a subtle nod, beckons her inside.

Through the opening, she sees Liam and Carl leaning against the kitchen counter and acknowledging her with soft smiles. The air is heavy with unspoken tension. Parker lounges on a wraparound couch with her father and Hoss, while others sit at the table or stand with their backs to the walls, waiting. She is the only woman in the apartment.

Parker gestures for her to come inside and sit in the lone chair in front of them. This time, at least, they will let her sit. She doubts it will put her at ease. Sadie's hands are shaking, so she conceals them in her lap. She faces Parker, Hoss, and her father, her head held high, and takes a measured breath. Sadie knew there would be consequences for defying her orders, but she didn't think her punishment would be decided so swiftly.

"I'd like to start off by saying you are on trial." Parker sweeps his hand around the room. "These are your security brothers, and they are here to witness what transpires to prevent rumors. I know you don't expect special treatment, but I must state for everyone present, Sadie will not receive any because of her father's position."

Sadie shifts under the scrutiny. These three men before her are not the same men she grew up with. These are her military superiors. She keeps her eyes on Parker.

"Your conduct constitutes an act of insubordination. You willfully disobeyed a direct order to remain in the compound, out of harm's way. Instead, you embarked on a personal mission to join an operation in progress without a proper briefing. You could have compromised that very mission and endangered the lives of every person involved."

Sadie swallows.

"Your subsequent capture alerted the enemy to a potential threat that could have jeopardized the actual subterfuge mission we were engaged in and did, in fact, create an unnecessary hostage situation. Fortunately, we were able to extract you from it without casualties."

They didn't extract her, but she knows it isn't appropriate to refute his words. The gravity of what she did sinks in. She clenches her jaw to keep her lips from trembling. Guilt weighs her down.

"A true Marine is a piece of a larger whole, the tip of the spear, but a spear nonetheless."

Way to go, Sadie. Only you could get dishonorably discharged after the world has come to an end.

"However, we recognize you have yet to be officially recognized as a Marine in this community. In the eyes of this council, you were acting as a private citizen, newly arrived and yet to be properly caught up in a rapidly dissolving, unprecedented chain of events that you have been struggling to survive in. Most importantly, we are all grateful that you made it to Haven alive, especially in light of the challenges you faced out there."

She looks away to hide her face a little, understanding why Hunter often does the same thing. It's to avoid seeing the sympathy in the eyes of the people staring.

322

"While we condemn your actions, we admire and respect your tenacity to survive, and the determination you showed to fight for what you believe is right, even while putting yourself at risk."

Behind her, someone coughs.

"Do you understand the severity of what you did?"

"Yes." Sadie's eyes lift to see Parker.

"We may not wear uniforms anymore, but the collective wisdom and experience we bring to ensuring everyone's safety here demands respect. Your misconduct created a rift between you and your brothers, a profound breach of trust that has left them feeling betrayed."

The silence stretches, thick and suffocating, and she feels the weight of countless stares pressing down on her. She fights the urge to look at the carpet. She lifts her ankles an inch off the floor.

"Sadie, we cannot blame you entirely. We should have expected you would disobey the order, based on your past with your father."

She stares deeply into Parker's eyes, not daring to look in her dad's direction.

"We demonstrated poor judgment because of your father's influence, preventing you from the promotion you rightfully earned during basic training."

She revisits the moment in front of the Marine Corps memorial as her drill instructor deposited the well-earned pin in her dirty palms and called her a Marine for the first time. Tears well, but she sucks them back with renewed conviction.

"Before I proceed with disciplinary action, is there anything you wish to say in your defense?"

The sharp, controlled tone of Parker's original order five days ago initially felt like domination, yet she now sees it was a protective measure. Although her father had done the same thing during her teenage years, she perceived it solely as an attempt to exert control. Her actions were wrong.

"I acknowledge my error in judgment and should have heeded your advice. I saw it as the council trying to assert control instead of offering me its protection. You were right. I am untested."

Parker nods, but his expression remains neutral. "Your training down in San Diego was a beginning and not an ending. You won't be on security detail until we see an improvement in your conduct. You will continue to train with your brothers, though, when you aren't helping with the farming chores."

She takes an inward sigh of relief. They are giving her a way to earn her spot on the security detail. It's fair, but she knows they won't make it easy. It'll be an uphill battle to win back their respect. Her mother's words echo in her head: "A path with no obstacles leads nowhere."

"Sadie."

She turns toward the sound of her father's stern voice. *Here it comes.* She needs to pull herself together. *I'm a Masters and a Marine.*

"You've been running since the missile dropped. I know it's been longer than that, but I'm here to tell you, you don't have to flee anymore. You are home." Donovan's lips curve up.

Home. The tension eases from her muscles. Her happiness reflects his, even as she feels the pull of her facial wounds.

Parker addresses the room. "Welcome your new sister-in-arms, gentlemen."

The Marines call out, "Oorah!"

Sadie replies in kind.

Chapter 55
July 9

"Camera's up. See anythin' yet?" Carl asks, perched in a tree high above the ground, waving into the little camouflaged black box. "Do you want me to change the direction?"

Colin's voice comes through across the comms: "To the left." Carl tweaks the camouflaged box. "Ya, that's it. Perfect, Twirley."

Carl looks out over the river and the riverbed below and reflects on how good it feels to be alive. He hasn't had many days like this since the missiles dropped.

Funny thing, Sadie's mom visiting her like that. Carl kept silent through that part of Sadie's retelling of her ordeal. He isn't a superstitious man, but that story prickled him some.

He shimmies down the tree, getting a glimpse of a small camp of men across the river working on rough logs with saws. Half a log house stands near the farmhouse among sheltering pine trees. Giles and his family are staying. Carl reflects on how he'd feel, leaving all he worked for back at the farm, and wonders if Giles will miss it. It's quite an adventure, life is. You never know where you will end up.

For years, Carl believed he would be alone. Then, as if pulled by an invisible force, he found himself completely entangled in Sophie's orbit. *You were my sun after that, my dear.*

He steps out onto the field after collecting his weapon, overseeing his new community as it tends to the maturing crops. On security detail, Ryker waves. *Upstandin' fellow, nice family.* Carl returns the gesture. The learning curve of farming has been greatly reduced with Giles and Ryker around. Carl's happy he found his way to these people. It was the right choice.

Armed men patrol the edges of the field as workers pick smaller crops closer to the compound. Sadie's auburn hair makes her noticeable among the farmers. She and Hunter are making a go of it. Carl's glad they found each other, but he knew they would. Something else his wife told him would happen. He's not sure about Hoss's son, Liam. The boy is like a fish fighting a strong upstream current, taking the toughest of paths, but not necessarily heading in the wrong direction.

Only time, with its slow, deliberate pace, will reveal if the other whispered predictions from his wife hold any truth. In the forest, months ago, when Sadie had asked him why he was helping her, Carl had paused. What could he say that wouldn't make him look like a loony? Carl was told where he'd find Sadie and where to look for her. He had his wife to thank for that. Sadie's mom wasn't the only guardian angel the day the missiles dropped. *Sophie, dear. You were right.*

***

Showered and fresh after her first farming shift, Sadie peers into a book set on the kitchen table, then glances at the knitting in her hands. She checks her stitches. *Did I miss one?* She looks back at the book, counts, then goes back to her work. She is teaching herself to knit, wanting to finish the baby sweater Tilly started. It's been a frustrating battle, but she's determined to figure it out.

She'll do a few more lines, then go visit Hunter in medical. His recovery will take over a month. Long enough for Sadie to prepare her room for him to live with her.

Donovan walks into the apartment. They smile at each other. Her gaze drifts to the analog clock hanging above cherished family portraits, its second hand circling behind the clear plastic front. A brand-new face is on the wall, with her, in a new frame.

The black ribbon draped over William's photo catches her eye. Sadie reminisces about past barbecues when William would play games with her. He kept to himself in those days, single and still grappling with his demons, but still made time for the kids. She will miss him. He was the one who told her to keep her heart open and that Liam would wake up one day and ask for it. Little did he know how things would turn out.

The potent scent of cedar-infused aftershave causes Sadie to gaze upward. Her father's beard is gone.

"You shaved."

Peering over her shoulder, Donovan assesses her work. "Where did you get that?"

She straightens, finding her nose out of joint. "Is it unrealistic to think I can learn a new skill?"

Her father laughs. "No. I just don't recall stocking yarn and knitting needles for the end of the world."

"I met a woman on the bus. She didn't make it when we crashed."

Donovan's eyes, full of sympathy, find hers as he squeezes her shoulder. "I'm sorry. That must have been hard."

"It was. She was really lovely." Sadie scrutinizes her father's sharp outfit. "Are you dressed to go out?"

"No." Donovan walks toward the apartment door and yells over his shoulder. "You missed a stitch."

She gazes down and counts, then realizes the ruse. *That's a clever dodge, Dad.*

A pang of sadness hits Sadie as she reflects on Tilly's wise words: "Well, that's life, dear. The ride can be bumpy or smooth with a few scary turns, but they say life is about how you handle Plan B."

EPILOGUE

J ose slaps Isaac's shoulder as the council breaks up for the day at Parker's kitchen table. "I'm glad the shed's fixed. Did you need help putting the tools back, Father?"

Parker stands at the counter, placing mugs in the sink for washing later. "Sure."

Donovan waits until everyone leaves before asking Parker, "What's the letter say? The one Dane brought you."

Parker's gaze rests upon his friend seated at the table. "It's not good."

"Does it say anything about what's happened?"

The military's cryptic style characterized all its correspondence, but having served so long with Dane's father, Parker could decipher his message.

"It says what we all know. US cities and bases were targeted. But it's worse. The president is dead."

Donovan sits straighter in his chair. "What? How? Shouldn't he be in a bunker, or did the plane go down?"

Parker reacted this way when he read it. The letter's message was one of dread. The deep-seated issues plaguing the US won't vanish overnight, and anyone attempting to make things better will have to deal with others like Wendall and his gang of escaped convicts. Fixing the downed electrical grid alone is no simple task. That might take decades to bring back up. "The missile, the Auntie, in Washington hit the White House. It doesn't exist anymore."

With a mumbled exclamation of surprise, Donovan lets out his breath. "Don't we have defenses to shoot those things out of the sky?"

Parker gives his friend credit. He expected profanity. "I know we do, but can't tell you. The letter didn't elaborate on details like that."

The forecast is dire indeed. "General Sullivan is handling those left behind and securing a new president from the line."

"Isn't that someone else's job? Who is taking President Huxley's place?"

"It doesn't say, but he claims that non-nuclear missiles destroyed all military bases and major cities worldwide on the other side of the pond the next day." Parker lets that sit.

Donovan voices the unsaid. "Hoss's sons."

That's all that needed saying. They are stationed at Ramstein in Germany, but as far as Parker knows, they are off-base in Ibiza. The delay in time between attacks means they may have reached safety before the attack, but he can't be certain. "I haven't told Hoss yet."

"Told me what?" Hoss swaggers into the room.

His timing is always impeccable. Parker and Donovan exchange glances, then Parker speaks to his friend. "You might want to sit for this."

"I'll stand."

Parker waits in silence. Hoss changes his mind and crosses the room in one fluid motion. He slides a chair out.

Parker takes a deep breath. "An Auntie hit Ramstein."

"The call Liam got, to head back to base?" Hoss rests his elbow on the table. "My boys would have received the same message." He runs his hand down his beard several times.

The beard stroking is a coping mechanism Hoss uses when he's stressed. Parker rarely witnesses such a habit. The last time he saw him do it was when he lost his daughter. Overwhelmed by sorrow, grief consumed his friend back then. *Can he cope again? Hoss and his family might have to come to terms with never knowing what happened to the boys.*

"John Henry has felt nothing bad from his twin," Hoss says with confidence. He shakes his head. "No. Steven is still with us."

Parker doesn't refute his words or point out that John Henry can't feel if Jessie is still alive. Instead, he lets him have hope. "That's a good sign, then."

"Until we hear otherwise, we'll keep the faith that they're still alive," Hoss says, perhaps more to himself than anyone else.

PREVIEW OF BOOK THREE OF THE HAVEN SERIES: TREK
23 May 2027, Ibiza, Spain, 0730 hours

In the early morning, most of the guys have gathered on a U-shaped couch on the Beach House restaurant's patio that overlooks the ocean. The polished square table gleams under the soft light as they each succumb to their own thoughts.

Last night was rough. Steven's heart aches with worry for his wife. He was easing Lisa into the crazy part of his family when their phone call was interrupted and the line went dead. *Their prepping doesn't seem so crazy now.*

Half-eaten breakfast lies scattered across the table's surface. No one is hungry. They stare at a muted television broadcasting BBC News on a stand in front of them. The ticker tape scrolls across the bottom, and the captions are on, but the pictures don't need explaining. The aerial footage paints a grim picture of cities across the US. Images of burning buildings and dark, gaping holes where structures once stood.

None of the phones they've tried can connect with the US, and Steven hasn't been able to get through to any of his family. He's grateful that John Henry is with Lisa and that they were almost at Haven when the missiles hit. He has to trust that his father and brothers will take care of her. It kills Steven that he can't go to her right now, but he knows he still has a duty to perform. He'll go to Ramstein, but he's vowed that last night's conversation with her won't be their last. Next to Steven, Phil shifts on the couch, pulls his phone out of his pocket, and glances at the screen. "Carter and Roy are slow as all hell. Doesn't take that long to pack, man." He gazes over at Jessie. "No earlier flights?"

Jessie is their travel agent when they need one, and a navigator when maps are involved on missions. They are all itching to get back to base ASAP, and tensions are growing with every passing minute they spend on the island.

Sean runs his hands over his face, hops to his feet, and ambles into the restaurant while shaking out his arms. His camera bag sits on the table. He has no stomach to take further pictures of the guys after last night's horrifying news.

Jessie's leg bounces as he says, "Yeah, sure, if you wanted to be stuck in Geneva for eight hours. This flight gets us there at the same time without the side tour."

Steven clenches his jaw as he glances at the television. "I don't relish the idea of sitting on a plane that long."

Declan peers up from his phone. "Being tall has its disadvantages on a plane. Also, I like this view much better than Geneva." Four girls in string bikinis parade by, seemingly unaffected by what is happening in the US.

It amazes Steven that so many holidaymakers can go about their day while so much destruction has taken place in the USA. Then again, to them, it's a problem on the other side of the pond, well away from their slice of paradise. But the vast majority are concerned and have crowded around every available screen inside the restaurant, mirroring the same apprehension as Steven's group. He doesn't understand why the US hasn't retaliated against the countries that launched missiles at it. Then again, maybe they did? The news coming out of home is so broken and scrambled, it's hard to make sense of any of it. There are reports that his country did launch missiles, but if they did, their targets haven't been identified. Of course, if the US *has* hit distant enemy targets, its enemies are hardly going to advertise it. The iron grip of the Russian and Korean regimes will keep those reports hidden from the public if they can. Still, a review of the latest satellite data indicates that none of those countries shows signs of attack. Why?

"Hate commercial flying," Charlie adds. "Gives me leg cramps."

Heads dip back down to phones. The rhythmic tapping of fingers fills the silence. They all know they are wasting their time texting home, but they keep trying. Only Steven has given up. If the electrical grid is down in the US like the news is saying, no calls or messages will get through. If they had a satphone, they'd be okay, but no one he knew had one of those.

Charlie looks up from his phone again. "Holy guac, Steven! The White House?"

"What about it?"

"It's just gone."

The jaws of the men around Steven fall open, their faces turning a pale gray. Steven expects they are all pondering the same question he is: *Was the president in the White House at the time? Explains the lack of missile retaliation. Things are dire indeed.*

Horror contorts Sean's features as he emerges from the restaurant, moving like a zombie. "Declan, you're from Minneapolis, right?"

Declan's gaze shoots upward. "Yeah. Why?"

Sean swallows, fighting back tears, and grabs Declan's shoulder. "Auntie took out the airport, the 133rd National Guard, and the VA hospital."

Declan had told the guys more than once that his mom's house is just a few blocks from that depot. He chokes back a mournful cry. "Mom!" Jessie leans across and puts a comforting arm over his shoulder.

"My city, too," Sean says with surprising restraint. "My mom..." He breaks. The nearest guy yanks Sean in for a bear hug and slaps him on the back.

Phil's head snaps up. "Billings?"

Sean nods, then his eyes search out Steven. "And Spokane. The reports from Washington state are detailing widespread casualties."

Steven watches as the news worms its way through Jessie, who removes his arm from Declan and leans forward. He looks like he's going to be sick. "They're taking out major cities, but why the smaller ones? Makes no sense."

"There's an air force base in Spokane," Steven reminds him.

"Are they taking out cities or bases?" Sean asks.

Phil shakes his head. "Billings doesn't have one."

Silent through it all, Neil has been scrolling on the other side of the table, his face etched with concern. His shoulders slump, and he lets out an audible sigh that grabs everyone's attention.

"More news, Neil?" Steven asks.

"National Guard is mobilizing on the Eastern Seaboard. It's futile. By the looks of those craters, they used the Aunties there, too. My family didn't make it."

"How do you know?"

Neil holds up the phone to Steven. The aerial view is from miles above New York City: Manhattan's tip is non-existent beneath a fiery maelstrom of several dark circles. "My home is in one of those craters. Casualties are in the tens of millions along the Eastern Coast already."

Steven closes his eyes to take this in, noticing how the awful news contrasts with the warmth of the morning sunshine, the sound of the palms rustling gently in the warm breeze coming off the lapping water. The gravity of the loss is settling in, but surrounded by such beauty, it still feels like a dream.

"I want to get back to base to kick some major ass now," Phil fumes, his voice thick with anger.

Hank pushes off the cushion he's been lounging on. Sliding his hands in his pockets, he strolls out to the edge of the deck and looks out. "Who're they blaming?"

Sean says, "Russia and China. They're denying it, of course."

Neil looks up from his phone again. "More missiles."

All eyes swing to the TV screen. Some men rise to their feet, and everyone holds their breath. *The US is a smoldering crater. Where is there left to hit?* Between the closed captions and the scrolling words at the bottom, it's hard to keep up with the news anchor, but the panic in his face and voice is evident. Steven concentrates on the ticker tape at the bottom. It reads, *NATO countries are being wiped out one by one.* Familiar country names follow: *Canada, Portugal, the United Kingdom...* The television screen goes blank.

Steven blurts out, "Spain's a NATO country." He gazes back at the stark blackness of the TV. A flash of light reflects off the screen so fast. Did he imagine—?

An invisible force of wind slams hard into his body, and the world goes dark.

It takes a moment for him to realize he's moaning out loud. A surge of pain is pushing its way through his body. Steven tests himself and his surroundings by extending his arm out and pushing against wood beams and woven materials. *The roof must have caved in.* Metal creaks. From under a pile of debris, Steven lifts one of the corrugated roof panels and shakes his head. Emerging back into the sunshine, he looks around to see that the restaurant is nothing but rubble, a flat expanse of debris where it once stood. He registers the bodies next.

He rises slowly, feeling lightheaded. Then he's surprised to see the shape of a nuclear cloud hovering over the far-off mountain range to the northeast, its distinct mushroom head curling and climbing and growing. *Oh, shit!*

Before he can wrap his head around what that cloud means, more debris shifts and groans around him as people emerge in disarray. *The guys!* Hearing a moan from under a closer lump, Steven crawls over in desperation to uncover who's underneath. Jessie materializes, scraped and dusty, as blood trickles down his forehead. "Are you alright? You're bleeding." Steven holds his hand out and hauls Jessie up.

Jessie steadies himself. "My head hurts." He probes his wound.

Declan pops up in the same chalky condition as Jessie, coughing and checking himself for damage. One by one, the group emerges. Other sections of the roof move. Declan reaches for Hank's hand and pulls him from the wreckage.

Steven does a head count, then turns to Jessie. "We have to find the others!"

"Sean!" Jessie calls out and searches through the rubble as the rest join in a frantic search. Steven jumps into the sand and walks away from the rubble that used to be a restaurant to get a feel for the damage in the area. He scans the hotels, finding minimal damage to the windows, but the vegetation didn't fare as well. Twisted and broken branches dangle.

The men follow his lead onto the beach. Paul and Dhillon walk slowly to the edge of the deck. *Two injured.* The guys assist them onto the sand. Up and down the beach, people cry and gasp and scream.

"Holy guac!" Hank exclaims, jabbing his finger at the sky from the deck, his eyes wide. "Is that what I think it is?!" Everyone on the beach who hears him turns to where he's pointing.

Phil comes to stand next to Steven. "Mallorca?"

"It's about what, sixty miles, you think?" Steven asks, shielding his eyes from the sun. "Nuke?"

"Don't know, but there were none detonated in the US."

"Guys, ah, is that a plane?" Hank asks with a clear tremor in his voice.

He's right. Two large planes are drifting toward them. They dance with each other, side by side, racing to land at the airport. One veers left and tries to bank right. It grows bigger and bigger as it approaches from the ocean side. The other plane stays on its course, its wings tilting up and down as the pilots struggle to keep it on an even keel.

"What's wrong with them?" Hank asks.

"Listen!" Steven shouts, then a moment later, he says, "There's no engine noise. Whatever hit Mallorca, it had EMP capabilities."

With the first plane bearing down, a frantic scramble ensues all around them. Some people run off the beach, while others climb out of the water, all fearing the aircraft is about to come down on top of them. Only Steven and the other men stand their ground, not out of fear, but knowing they can't outrun a plane at any speed. With the way the pilot is struggling, the plane moving left and right, it is just as likely to hit them if they run as if they stay still. Steven prays for protection as his heart rate elevates. Will it reach the airport or crash into the ocean? Which is best for the pilot's chances of survival, water or land? The runway is behind them, but the plane isn't in line with it anymore.

The plane continues its silent descent and, in doing so, expands in size. All of a sudden, Steven isn't so sure staying still was the right thing to do. The realization of what is about to happen dawns on him, and he accepts it. *I love you, Lisa.*

The plane banks, its one wing dipping. The pilot's trying to line up with the runway, but the landing gear isn't all the way down.

With an eerie silence, the plane drifts by them. Steven lets out the breath he was withholding and closes his eyes in relief as his skin tingles all over his body. He will live another day. God, help them.

So absorbed in the first plane's approach, no one remembers the second one until the sound of an explosion tears their attention away. The plane has sliced through the Hard Rock Hotel, causing a mass exodus from the beach as people scramble to escape the danger zone. Fiery metal debris is propelled in every direction.

One chunk comes spinning straight at Steven and his men.

Screams rend the air. A frenzied rush for cover ensues. Men and women dive out of harm's way, searching for a haven from the unavoidable fallout of the blast.

TRIGGER WARNINGS

Flee and the Haven series are intended for adult readers and include scenes with the following content that may distress some readers. Please consider your well-being before choosing to read.

Body horror

Consensual sex

Dead bodies & body parts

Death

Hostage situations

Incest

Kidnapping

Murder

Physical assault

Rape (not on page)

Scars

Sexual assault

Stalking

Strong language

Violence, including gun & knife

About the Author

Tracy is the award-winning author of Escape, a fast-paced post-apocalyptic romantic thriller that hit #1 Top New Release within hours of launching. She's spent most of her life writing and most of her childhood buried in books at the local library—basically, she's been preparing for this gig forever.

The first book in her Haven series features a cast of complex, relatable characters, high-stakes survival, and just enough romance to make you blush. Expect found family, sassy/timid heroines, heroic heartthrobs, and spice levels that vary depending on who's telling the story. (Some characters are more into slow burns. Others? Not so much.)

Before diving into full-time author life, Tracy worked in the tourism industry. Now she writes in yoga pants, cruises when she can, and has an obsession with strawberries. She shares her life with her husband and two sons.

Her future writing plans include tackling romance, space opera, romantasy, and westerns—assuming she doesn't run out of time before she runs out of ideas (or lives... She's pretty sure she's part cat). Yes, she's a cat and dog person. Please don't make her choose.

Visit Tracy's website at www.tracymyhre.com.

Leave a review for *Flee* here:
https://www.amazon.com/gp/product/B0FQ1H1WRH

Follow Tracy on social media:

- Instagram: https://www.instagram.com/tmyhrewriter/

- Facebook: https://fb.me/tmyhrewriter

- Pinterest: https://www.pinterest.ca/tracymyhreauthor/

- Tiktok: https://www.tiktok.com/@tmyhrewriter?lang=en

ALSO BY TRACY MYHRE

The Haven Series
Escape
Flee

Manufactured by Amazon.ca
Bolton, ON

54448658R00203